THE
IMMORTALS

In ancient days, she would've already known the perpetrator's identity. As Artemis guided the moon across the sky, she heard the pleas of women and witnessed the crimes of men. No one could hide from her swift vengeance. But she'd lost such supernatural abilities more than a thousand years before. Selene raised a finger to the swollen bruise on her chin, feeling the silky texture of the powder, a tangible reminder of how far she'd fallen.

In recent decades, she'd preferred to work in the shadows, defending only women who asked directly for her help—those like Jackie Ortiz, whom the cops usually ignored. Now, if even a bully like Mario Velasquez could overpower her, what use would she be tracking a murderer? Then again, how could she not try?

She looked down at the woman. *You were killed steps from my home,* she realized. *Sacrificed as a sick invocation, a perversion of rituals I once held sacred. And I did nothing to stop it.* Disgusted, she thrust aside her self-pity, her hopelessness, her despair. *I may be only a shadow of what I once was, but that doesn't mean I'm powerless. Not yet.* "I promise," she said aloud, "this will not go unpunished."

She would let the cops do most of the legwork, but she didn't intend to let them arrest the murderer. This heretic would die. Not in some cell, after a drawn-out trial and years of appeals, but at the swift and deadly point of a goddess's arrow.

THE IMMORTALS

OLYMPUS BOUND: BOOK 1

JORDANNA MAX BRODSKY

www.orbitbooks.net

ORBIT

First published in Great Britain in 2016 by Orbit

3 5 7 9 10 8 6 4

Copyright © 2016 by Jordanna Max Brodsky

Helen is reproduced with permission of Curtis Brown Group
Ltd, London, on behalf of the Beneficiaries of the Estate of
Rex Warner. Copyright © Rex Warner 1951

Excerpt from *Wake of Vultures* by Lila Bowen
Copyright © 2015 by D. S. Dawson

The moral right of the author has been asserted.

Title page illustration by Rob Wilson
Designed by Leah Carlson-Stanisic

A CIP catalogue record for this book
is available from the British Library.

ISBN 978-0-356-50726-2

Printed and bound by CPI Group (UK) Ltd,
Croydon, CR0 4YY

Papers used by Orbit are from well-managed forests
and other responsible sources.

MIX
Paper from
responsible sources
FSC® C104740

Orbit
An imprint of
Little, Brown Book Group
Carmelite House
50 Victoria Embankment
London EC4Y 0DZ

An Hachette UK Company
www.hachette.co.uk

www.orbitbooks.net

For Jason, who believed

CONTENTS

THE GODS' FAMILY TREE

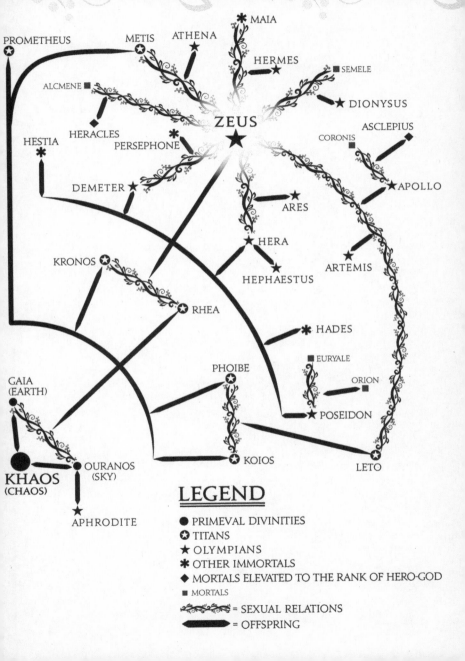

LEGEND

● PRIMEVAL DIVINITIES

✪ TITANS

★ OLYMPIANS

✴ OTHER IMMORTALS

◆ MORTALS ELEVATED TO THE RANK OF HERO-GOD

■ MORTALS

= SEXUAL RELATIONS

= OFFSPRING

I sing of Artemis, whose shafts are of gold, who cheers on the hounds, the pure maiden, shooter of stags, who delights in archery, own sister to Apollo. Over the shadowy hills and windy peaks she draws her golden bow, rejoicing in the chase, and sends out grievous shafts. And when she is satisfied and has cheered her heart, this huntress hangs up her curved bow and leads the Muses in dance while they sing how neat-ankled Leto bare children supreme among the immortals.

Hail to you, children of Zeus and rich-haired Leto!

The Homeric Hymn to Artemis,
CIRCA SIXTH CENTURY BC

Chapter 1

PUNISHER

Selene DiSilva crouched in a narrow alley between two run-down apartment buildings, watching the street. When she'd begun her vigil hours before, the smells of roasting chicken and frying plantains had wafted from the surrounding apartments. Families laughed and bickered, doors slammed, cars honked. But in the small hours of the morning, the only scents were those from the trashcans overflowing nearby, and the street before her lay nearly deserted. Even in the city that never slept, there were quiet corners like this: a forgotten neighborhood perched at Manhattan's northernmost tip. Here, most people obeyed the ancient human instinct to seek refuge from the dark. But not Selene—and not the man she'd been sent to hunt.

A single dark SUV rolled by, a wave of Caribbean hip-hop pouring through the open window to briefly shatter the silence. From her hiding place, Selene peered at the driver, but let him pass unmolested.

Later, a group of swaggering young men strolled along the street, laughing and shoving as they claimed the sidewalk for themselves. Selene watched them carefully but didn't move. Then two women passed her alley, speaking in slurred Spanish, their eyes purple with fatigue. She felt no empathy—as usual, she'd slept all day and only awoken with the moonrise.

Finally, a solitary figure appeared at the far end of the block. Long before she could see his face, Selene knew him by his stride. *Chin forward and shoulders high like he's looking for a fight,* she thought, *but only with someone he's sure he can beat.*

She glanced at the apartment building across the street—a wide 1920s façade, its art deco grandeur long since gone. A window on the third floor flickered blue behind thin curtains. Jackie Ortiz was awake and watching TV, just as Selene had instructed.

She stood up slowly as the man approached the building. Mario Velasquez. Medium height—shorter than her own six feet—but broad across the shoulders, his muscles bulkier than hers. He wore a rhinestone-studded cross on a thick gold chain around his neck and kept his hands shoved into the front pocket of his sweatshirt. She couldn't be sure if he was armed or not, but she'd find out soon enough.

She could see his face now, the same one she'd been stalking for a week: high cheekbones and a neat goatee, dark skin that made his light blue stare all the more alluring. *Once again,* she thought, *a woman falls for a pair of pretty eyes and never bothers to find out what's behind them.*

Mario stopped opposite Jackie's building. Looking up at her window, he pulled a cell phone from his pocket. Selene couldn't make out his murmured conversation, but she recognized the aggravation in the rising pitch of his voice. It wouldn't be long before he started throwing punches.

She let the tiniest of smiles cross her lips. She was, after all, going to enjoy this.

Mario stepped into the building's small vestibule. Through the cloudy glass of the front door, Selene watched him jab repeatedly at the buzzer for Jackie's apartment. Next to him stood a doorman's podium. *Just for show,* Selene knew. No lobby guard would appear to protect Jackie from her boyfriend. Her only defense was a weak lock on the building's inner door and the woman she'd hired to strike Mario down.

Selene crossed the street and waited just out of Mario's sight. *Come on, Jackie,* she urged silently. *Be brave.* The young woman appeared in the vestibule, closing the inner door behind her so that Mario couldn't get upstairs. Selene tensed, ready to spring forward. *But not yet, not yet.*

Jackie, short and skinny, looked even younger than her twenty-two years. She'd made a vain attempt to cover her swollen black eye with a smear of turquoise shadow. One hand nervously twirled a lock of dyed blond hair. She held her other arm across her body like a shield. Mario flashed her a smile and sneaked a quick kiss on her neck. Jackie shuddered—whether with delight or fear, Selene couldn't tell. Then he took a step closer, and the woman put a hand on his chest, pushing him away. He kept coming, backing her into a corner, still smiling despite Jackie's protests. He rested one hand possessively on her neck and hooked the other around the white leather belt at her waist, pulling her against him. Jackie struggled in his grip, her eyes darting back and forth, searching for Selene.

Just a moment more, Selene thought, *so the police have evidence.* Then it happened, quick as a snake bite: Mario slapped Jackie across the face.

Selene yanked open the outer door and put a light hand on Mario's shoulder. Still holding on to Jackie's belt, he turned to the intruder.

"Hey, Mario," Selene said with her best attempt at casual courtesy. She didn't want to antagonize him until Jackie was safe.

"Who the fuck are you?"

"You don't recognize me?" Selene gave him what she hoped was an alluring smile.

His defensiveness dissolved as quickly as it had appeared. He made a low sound of pleasure, like a man savoring some succulent morsel. Jackie slipped from his loosened grip as he turned all of his attention toward Selene. His eyes traveled appreciatively over her body, seeing past her loose cargo pants to the long, lean legs underneath. "If I'd nailed you, I think I'd remember." Unnoticed, Jackie scurried back through the inner door and pulled it shut behind her.

"Perhaps." Selene nodded with exaggerated thoughtfulness. "But considering the number of women you're currently sleeping with, perhaps not."

"What do you know about—"

"Lyla? Miriam? Fatima?" She ticked them off one by one on her fingers. "Raquel? Yolanda? And, of course, Jackie. Although you don't sleep with Jackie so much as beat her up, so I'm not sure I should count her."

Mario put his hand in his sweatshirt pocket and didn't draw it back out. *A knife,* Selene decided. *Hopefully not a gun.*

"You a cop?" he asked.

"Not at the moment."

"Then back away, lady. Mind your own business."

"It's my business to keep you away from her."

He smirked. "And how you going to do that?"

Selene drilled a right hook into his face, spinning him away, then a left into his kidney. With great satisfaction, she watched a line of bloody spittle drip from his mouth onto the floor as he doubled over. But Mario recovered quickly, coming upright with a long, serrated hunting knife in his hand. He barreled toward her. She sidestepped him easily, thrusting out a foot to send him stumbling forward into the opposite wall. Before he could regain his balance, she jabbed an elbow into his spine, bringing all her superior height to bear. Mario grunted and dropped the knife but stayed on his feet. Faster than she'd anticipated, he spun toward her and kicked her hard in the knee.

Biting back a yelp of pain, she fell, slamming the injured

knee into the ground. He kicked again, striking her in the jaw. Her teeth sliced the inside of her cheek; she tasted blood. Cold panic rushed through her veins as a third kick smashed into her ribs, knocking the breath from her body. Vision wavering, she reached across the floor toward the fallen knife—Mario beat her to it, bringing the blade down in a slicing arc toward her face. She moved her head just in time to prevent losing her nose; the knife whistled through the air beside her ear and struck the tiled wall with a sharp ping.

"You're going to wish you hadn't gotten in my way, *puta*." He kicked her backward and kneeled over her body, pinning her in place. For decades, she'd been dreading this moment—the fight she couldn't win, the woman she couldn't protect. *Have I finally grown so weak that a mere man can defeat me?*

"Who do you think you are?" he demanded, raising the knife once more.

Selene grabbed his upraised wrist. "You wouldn't believe me if I told you," she gasped, her arm shaking with the effort of holding him off.

"Try me."

A hundred names came to mind, whispered in long-forgotten tongues, but she couldn't lay claim to a single one. Not any longer.

Mario laughed at her silence and waved the knife just out of her reach. "Don't even know your own name, huh? Guess it's true—the hot ones *are* dumb."

One look at his grinning face burned away Selene's self-pity. As he leaned forward, ready to strike, his rhinestone cross swayed above her. The symbol of everything she'd lost, everything she despised. She allowed herself a quick second to imagine grabbing it and punching it through his pretty blue eye. Then she hooked the base of the doorman's podium with her foot and brought it crashing down on Mario's head instead.

He collapsed, unconscious, on top of her.

Jackie rushed back into the vestibule. She stopped a few feet away from Mario, her hand to her mouth. "Did you kill him?"

"Unfortunately, no," Selene wheezed from beneath his bulk. To her dismay, it took Jackie's help to free her from the dead weight.

She slipped a length of wire from her pocket and tied Mario's wrists together.

Jackie stared at Selene's face, wincing. "Damn, you okay?"

Selene raised a hand to her throbbing jaw, wondering just how bad it looked.

"I already called the cops," Jackie went on, as if that would make Selene feel better.

"I told you to wait until I was gone," she said, more angrily than she'd intended.

"I saw him kicking you. Then I saw him holding that knife over you like he was going to slice off your eyebrows." Jackie put her hands on her hips. "Was I supposed to just let him carve you up?"

"Yes, that's exactly what you're supposed to do. I make myself the target so you don't have to." She looked at the red handprint on Jackie's cheek. "At least...not anymore."

"The cops will be here in five minutes. They're bringing an ambulance. You sure you shouldn't get your face looked at?"

"Don't worry about me. Just make sure to tell the cops that this time you're pressing charges. And tell Mario that if he ever threatens you again, the police are going to be the least of his worries."

Jackie looked down at her boyfriend. "He's not going to be a vegetable when he wakes up, is he?"

Selene just shrugged.

"I mean, I didn't think about that before, but the podium made this sound when it hit his head...like a *thunk*, like a wet *thunk*."

Selene stared at the young woman for a moment, a scowl creasing her forehead. "What're you doing?"

Jackie looked up. "I just—"

"You're worried about him."

"He's not just a—"

"Have you already forgotten our agreement?" Selene couldn't keep the acid from her voice. "I protect you, just like I protect all the women who come to me. And all I ask in return is two promises: You won't tell the cops about me, and you won't hook up with assholes again." Jackie opened her mouth to protest but Selene cut her off. "You want to get down on your knees and tell him you're sorry. I can see it in your face."

Jackie huffed indignantly. "I asked you to get him away from me, not to tell me what to feel."

Selene tried to summon the fury that had once defined her life. Instead, she just felt tired. She'd heard it all before—thousands of times over thousands of years. "If you go near Mario again, you're on your own," she said wearily, opening the door.

Limping down the sidewalk with her head down and shoulders hunched, she listened to the approaching sirens. She ran her fingers along the swollen bruise on her jaw and the tender spot on her ribs where she'd been kicked. The pain in her knee flared with every step she took. In the moment before she knocked the podium into Mario's head, she'd been in real danger, as vulnerable and helpless as the women it was her duty to protect. If he'd had a gun instead of a knife, Selene would be the one waiting for an ambulance.

And what would happen then? she wondered. *If a man put a bullet through my skull, would my tenuous hold on immortality finally rip free?*

She looked up at the moon, a hazy crescent just discernable between the buildings, heading toward its daily oblivion beneath the horizon. *And if I die—so what? The goddess Artemis vanished a long time ago. What's left of her is nothing but shadows and memories. Both disappear with time.*

Maybe I should, too.

Then, despite the balmy air, a sudden shiver crawled along her arms, as if from a distant shriek more felt than heard.

In another age, she might have recognized the sensation as a summons. She might have listened more closely to the prayer upon the wind. She might have heard the anguished cry of a woman in mortal danger, far away on the other side of the city, calling out for the goddess who might save her.

Now, Selene merely grimaced and zipped her leather jacket a little higher beneath her chin.

Chapter 2

THE HUNTRESS

Hippolyta, her tail wagging noisily against the walls, met Selene at the door of her brownstone on West Eighty-eighth Street. The four-story building was half as wide as the usual Manhattan townhouse but still far too large for a single woman and a dog—even a dog as large as Hippo. The exterior walls were chipped and crumbling, the wrought iron detailing rusted through, and the interior didn't look much better. Unlike many of her relatives, Selene had never bothered to accumulate vast sums of wealth over the centuries. But using her meager earnings from her time on the police force, she'd acquired the building in the 1970s, when few dared buy in the crime-ridden neighborhood. Now it was worth millions, and rather than hunting down drug dealers on her corner, she had to fight her way past torrents of young mothers blocking the sidewalk with their double-wide strollers. Sometimes, she missed the drug dealers. At least there'd been more work for her to do.

She paused in front of the age-speckled mirror in her front hall. The welt on her face remained red and swollen. A few centuries earlier, such injuries would've healed immediately. Now, even the uninjured parts of her face betrayed evidence of her decline: Faint lines fanned from her eyes and nostrils, the skin above her eyelids sagged. She leaned closer to the mirror, stared at her forehead, and cursed. The deep crease between her brows, which she'd first noticed a few months before, was still there. *Too much scowling,* she thought, scowling once more. Angrily, she riffled through a drawer in the credenza until she found a compact of pale face powder. She hated the stuff, but she hated answering questions even more. She didn't want anyone thinking she was the victim of domestic violence or barroom brawls. She patted the powder across the welts on her jaw and temple. The wrinkles she'd have to live with.

She lifted the hem of her sweatshirt and felt tentatively along her ribs. Bruised, but not broken. Her stomach remained lean and etched with muscle, a testament more to her all-protein diet and her demanding running regimen than to any supernatural hold on strength. She flexed her knee. Thankfully, the long walk home seemed to have helped rather than exacerbated the injury, and she could put her full weight on her leg.

"Nothing I won't recover from," she assured Hippo. "Eventually." She leashed her dog, who scrambled eagerly toward the door. "Wait a sec," she said, opening the hall closet. She stared down at the dusty backpack in the corner. She hadn't opened it in years. "I don't even deserve to use it," she muttered to herself, "especially after tonight." Yet something urged her forward, and she found herself reaching for the bag.

They trotted down the block, following a sloping pathway into Riverside Park. The waterfront always reminded her that she lived on an island. She'd been born on one—Delos, a dry drop in the turquoise Mediterranean, the only land brave enough to provide sanctuary to her exiled mother, Leto. Nearly three thousand years later, the Huntress had arrived with a boatload of Dutch merchants in what the Lenni Lenape called Mana-hatta— the Island of Many Hills—and she hadn't left since. Back then, there were forests and meadows, streams and swamps—sacred spaces for the spirits of the wild. Now, the slim stretches of green parkland tucked along the city's margins and hiding between skyscrapers were the only places where she could escape from the world of men.

She often wondered why she stayed. What place was there for the Goddess of the Wilderness in a city of grids? Streets reached to the horizon. Towers stretched to the sky. *But beneath the glass and steel, the city's heart still beats wild,* Selene thought, looking southward to the skyline rising along the riverfront. New York was untamed, a city of dissidents and immigrants, a multihued patchwork of humans refusing to conform, where even the strangest residents—like a six-foot-tall woman with eyes like the moon—rarely garnered more than a curious glance. In a small town, she would've been under constant scrutiny, forced to move every twenty years when her neighbors began to wonder why she aged barely one year for their fifty. Here, no one noticed. The city's denizens ignored her, and she, for the most part, ignored them right back.

Usually, Selene found the park a welcome relief from the travails of her half-mortal life. But today it failed to cheer her. She couldn't shake the memory of Mario's knife above her face. She'd grown so weak that a mere mortal could threaten her. What sort of existence was that?

Hippo, oblivious to her mistress's distress, pulled against her collar, her tongue lolling with exertion. Selene gave up telling her to heel and unclipped the leash. After all, they had the park to themselves. It was officially closed before dawn, but that had never stopped them.

The dog bounded ahead with unrestrained joy, chasing an errant squirrel. She'd been a shelter rescue puppy, starved and brindled, sporting huge paws and elephantine ears, growling and snapping at everything in sight. *A kindred spirit,* Selene had known from the first time she saw her. The fierce Amazonian queen Hippolyta made a fitting namesake; although, after over-indulging in Selene's carnivorous diet for the past five years, the nickname "Hippo" seemed far more appropriate.

With a shift in the wind, some of the warm humidity dropped away, leaving only the bracing chill of approaching autumn. "Hello, Boreas," she greeted the god of the North Wind, know-ing full well he'd never hear her—if he even still existed. Selene pulled off her leather jacket and sweatshirt, letting the cold air rush against her bare arms and through her tank top, and jogged down the stairs leading to the boardwalk.

Having lost the squirrel to an arboreal escape, Hippo waited for her mistress at the river's edge, her tail pounding the asphalt. Together, they headed north along the shoreline. A single barge floated far out in the Hudson, but Selene had no interest in the boat. She scanned the water closer in, squinting in the dark, until a low *woof* from Hippo drew her attention farther upriver. She hadn't bothered hunting any prey besides men in a very long time, but her dog sensed her desire.

"Good girl." Selene scratched briefly beneath Hippo's chin. The dog stood, tail high and quivering—when she wanted to, she could be an exemplary hunting companion. Selene opened her backpack and pulled out two graceful lengths of curving gold—pieces of a bow almost as old as she. Quickly, she screwed the upper limb into the handgrip, then braced the bow between her legs so she could slip the string on more easily. She plucked the string once; it gave a satisfying thrum. Even after so long, it still felt like an extension of her arm.

Before she and the other gods had left Greece during the Olympian Diaspora, Hephaestus the Smith had made the bow detachable. "So you can hide it more easily," her stepbrother had said. "You carry around a bow and arrows in plain sight and the mortals are liable to think you're a witch, or something worse."

He'd been right. Even with her bow hidden away, she'd never fit easily into the patriarchal constraints of the Middle Ages. Or of the Renaissance, or really of any time in the last fifteen hundred years. She'd been accused of witchcraft on three different occasions, burned at the stake one and a half times, and exiled from more towns and villages than she cared to remember. Even in the live-and-let-live tumult of twenty-first-century Manhattan, flaunting her status as the erstwhile Bearer of the Bow would be ill-advised. Accusations of witchcraft would pale in comparison to suspicions of terrorism.

Selene nocked an arrow to her bowstring and aimed at the large Canada goose blithely paddling by. Without a second's hesitation, she loosed the arrow toward the bird.

The shaft flew right past, two feet off target, and disappeared beneath the river water.

"Styx," Selene cursed under her breath. She tried again. This time, as the arrow passed harmlessly by, the goose squawked and flapped into the air for a few moments before settling down once more.

She lowered her bow, suddenly very weary. "What?" she demanded of her panting dog. "I know I shouldn't be wasting the arrows. I'm just still not used to missing." The arrows were only wood, after all. She'd used up her gold ones centuries before. Not that it mattered. Only divine prey required divine weapons—and this goose was anything but godly.

With a loud splash and a spray of dirty water, Hippo jumped into the river. The goose took to the air, honking angrily, and flew off toward Jersey. Hippo, the tips of her long ears floating on the water, paddled happily, a look of pure innocence on her face.

"There goes dinner. Thanks," Selene grumbled. She whistled for the dog to get out of the water, but Hippo didn't respond.

Despite Selene's increasingly frustrated commands, the dog

started paddling away. A hundred yards upriver, where the boardwalk ended, she clambered out onto the rocks with a whimper. The dog looked back toward her mistress and gave a sharp bark of alarm, then began to sniff the ground.

Slinging her bow over her shoulder, Selene jogged toward her dog. "If you're sniffing someone's picnic leftovers, I'm going to shoot *you* next. And this time, I promise not to miss." But she stopped scolding when a sudden gust of wind carried the scent to her. Death. Human flesh in the first stages of decomposition.

Hippo disappeared for a moment behind the rocks, only to reappear dragging a corpse by its long, pale blue leg.

Instincts honed by a long-ago career on the police force took over as Selene rushed forward. She ran along the asphalt path, avoiding the soft ground. In her youth, they'd called her She Who Leaves No Trace; her powers of stealth might be sadly diminished, but she still knew better than to add her footprints to a crime scene. As she sprinted, she scanned both sides of the walkway, the surrounding trees, the boulders crowding the river's edge—it wasn't unusual for criminals to remain near the murder scene to watch the police. But the only observers this morning were a red-tailed hawk circling above and a cloud of flies already swarming over Hippo's head.

The wake of the passing barge sloshed rhythmically upon the shore as Selene leaped across the grass and landed next to her dog on the boulders.

With a curt gesture, she commanded Hippo to drop the leg. The dog looked up quizzically, wagging her tail. "I said drop it," Selene insisted, staring her straight in the eye and pitching her body forward. For once, Hippo obeyed. The dog took a few steps backward to shake a fine mist of water across the body. It lay half out of the river, with its legs and pelvis on land and its torso floating in the shallows. With each wave, the dead woman's head thudded against the rocks with the hollow clunk of a rotten pumpkin. She lay facedown, her torso wrapped in a sodden yellow bed sheet, her outstretched arms the delicate blue of a robin's egg, not yet marbled green and black.

Long blond hair floated around the woman's head in a nest of matted braids, catching between the rocks as another swell of water washed the body farther ashore. As Hippo lunged forward to retrieve the corpse, Selene grabbed the dog's collar to stop her.

Looking at the dead woman, Selene forced herself to set aside her rising anger and to summon the detachment of a detective instead. Never her strong suit. Pulling on the black leather gloves stowed in her backpack, she crouched beside the body. The woman couldn't have been dead long. Less than twelve hours judging by the tautness and color of her skin and by the limberness of her leg. Four or five days later, her waterlogged skin would tear or slough off at the merest touch. Lucky for Selene, the body was still in good enough shape to withstand a little rough handling. Carefully, she lifted the corpse's shoulder, checking for the purple-red stain of pooled blood in the woman's breasts or face. An old policeman's trick. If she turned the corpse and the lividity moved with it, then she'd been dead for less than eight hours. But the woman had no lividity at all; the flesh on her chest was as perfectly blue as that on her back. Impossible— unless all the blood had been drained from her body before she'd been tossed into the river.

Gingerly, Selene pulled the body out of the water. It was lighter than she'd expected—the woman's lungs must still be largely full of air. No wonder she'd floated so quickly. Drowning victims inhaled so much water that they wouldn't float until their own digestive acids began to decompose the body, filling it with buoyant gas. *Someone killed this woman before putting her in the river,* Selene decided, turning the body over for a better look. She raised a hand instinctively to her mouth.

Sea lice had already eaten away the woman's eyelids. The bare orbs stared upward at the starless sky. Hazel once. Now filmy. Perfect, straight teeth winked through the swarm of tiny crustaceans devouring her lips. She must have been quite pretty once.

Other insects appeared. Already, the flies smelled the feast. Selene wanted desperately to swat them away, but she needed them to guide her. The flies landed on the woman's pelvis, a dark, pulsating girdle.

Selene moved the sheet aside, knowing what she might find. A woman's flesh was delicate, and a man's instrument blunt. But she hadn't seen anything like this since the sacked city of Troy. This was a mutilation. Where the woman's genitals should be, only a gaping hole remained. The sea lice had done their work and were doing it still, feasting on her womb. But no crustacean could've formed such perfect slices in her flesh. Someone had cut her apart with a blade. Four incisions, a perfect diamond of meat.

She faltered. For a long moment, she stayed crouched, catching her breath, before she found the strength to continue searching the body.

No blood smeared the sheet. Either the woman had been wrapped after the mutilation, or her attacker had protected the sheet from staining. A scrupulous killer. The kind seeking not just bloodlust but ritual. No defensive wounds marked the woman's palms, but thin red welts snaked across her wrists and ankles, perhaps from a narrow rope. On the ring finger of her left hand, a narrow indentation, as if from a too-tight band. Selene bent close. The ring's shadow still remained, pale against tanned flesh, wrapping the finger in the familiar geometric pattern of the *meandros*—the Greek key. She sucked in a breath. Such rings weren't unusual. Still, Selene couldn't help looking at the ravaged corpse with new eyes.

That nest of leaves in her matted blond hair might be more than just river detritus. Laurel sprigs—she recognized the leaves that had so often graced her twin brother's brow—twined together in a crude crown. She examined the sheet more carefully. A safety pin still held it closed at one shoulder, and a tiny hole showed where a second pin had secured the other side. She sat back on her heels, struck by a realization: The sheet was no makeshift shroud. It was a chiton. A draped garment not unlike those worn by ancient Greek women. This woman had been wreathed and draped like a priestess. *Or,* Selene realized with a shock, *like a sacrifice.*

She looked again at the braids in her hair. She turned the head gently from side to side, counting. Six braids. A *sex crines.* The hairstyle worn by Roman virgins.

"You're one of mine," she murmured. Instinctively, she pulled the leather glove off her right hand and laid a fingertip upon the woman's brow. In that moment, a vision swam before her.

River water sloshes lazily against the shore while my heart drums with terror. His footsteps, swift on the pavement, draw closer and closer no matter how fast I run. I glance behind—but shadows cloak his face even as he passes beneath the lampposts. Then a knife glints red in the darkness.

He catches me, binds me. "I wish there were another way," he says, slipping the ring from my finger and holding it to his lips. "But you know there isn't." He puts aside the knife, and for a moment I clutch at hope. Then he pulls forth something else—small and silver and curved like a fishhook. He pushes aside the folds of my yellow robe; my bare thighs tremble on the cold ground. There is pain beyond imagining. I look toward the heavens, searching for help. Searching in vain.

Feeling as if she'd awoken from someone else's dream, Selene grasped at the swiftly receding images. *A needle,* she saw in the final flash. *He had a suture needle and black thread.* She reeled, sitting down hard on the rock, clutching her hand to her chest with a gasped curse.

Selene hadn't received a vision of a woman's last moments

since the Diaspora. *Why now? Why this?* Her heart still raced with the woman's fear. Selene could picture her, braids streaming as she ran from her attacker, a modern simulacrum of the innocents who'd once prayed at the altar of Artemis.

The image brought swift rage to blot away her terror. She rose to her feet, frantically scanning the riverside once more. The names she'd rejected only hours before now sprang to her lips. "I am the Goddess of Virgins," she seethed under her breath. "I am the Protector of the Innocent." For millennia, she'd guarded her own virginity, the most sacred of her divine attributes. Much of the time, such abstinence felt like an anachronism: Few of the women she helped were virgins anymore. Yet she had never forgotten the duty she owed her ancient worshipers.

She reached for her bow.

Then she froze, uncertain.

In ancient days, she would've already known the perpetrator's identity. As Artemis guided the moon across the sky, she heard the pleas of women and witnessed the crimes of men. No one could hide from her swift vengeance. But she'd lost such supernatural abilities more than a thousand years before. Selene raised a finger to the swollen bruise on her chin, feeling the silky texture of the powder, a tangible reminder of how far she'd fallen.

In recent decades, she'd preferred to work in the shadows, defending only women who asked directly for her help—those like Jackie Ortiz, whom the cops usually ignored. Now, if even a bully like Mario Velasquez could overpower her, what use would she be tracking a murderer? Then again, how could she not try?

She looked down at the woman. *You were killed steps from my home,* she realized. *Sacrificed as a sick invocation, a perversion of rituals I once held sacred. And I did nothing to stop it.* Disgusted, she thrust aside her self-pity, her hopelessness, her despair. *I may be only a shadow of what I once was, but that doesn't mean I'm powerless. Not yet.* "I promise," she said aloud, "this will not go unpunished."

She would let the cops do most of the legwork, but she didn't intend to let them arrest the murderer. This heretic would die. Not in some cell, after a drawn-out trial and years of appeals, but at the swift and deadly point of a goddess's arrow.

Chapter 3

THE CLASSICIST

Seventy eager young students stared at Professor Theodore Schultz, their hands poised above laptops or clutching pens, ready to absorb his wisdom. *Make that sixty-nine,* Theo amended, noticing Anant Paravastu's eyes slowing rolling back into his head.

"We have to ask ourselves, what are the myths that shape our own lives, our own society?" Theo paused, as if waiting for an answer. No hands rose, unsurprisingly. Students these days preferred to be told what to think. But he didn't believe in letting them off that easy.

"Mr. Paravastu, what about you? What are the myths that shape you?" he asked cheerfully. All eyes swung toward the dozing boy in the back row. Theo's unusual insistence on learning all of his students' names, even in large lecture classes, had made him the object of both their adoration and their greatest fear.

Anant sprung upright in his chair and chuckled weakly. "Umm...that you can get two hours of sleep and still be functional for your nine a.m. class. Turns out to be a complete myth. No truth to it at all."

As the students laughed, Theo threw Anant a formal salute.

"Nice save. I won't ask why you only got two hours of sleep. Wouldn't want you to tell another myth." The laughter built to a crescendo as Anant turned beet red beneath his sheepish smile.

"I've got my own myth," Theo went on. "I often tell the story of how, when I was eleven years old, my mother handed me *D'Aulaires' Book of Greek Myths*. I read it cover to cover in one day, memorized the Twelve Olympians, and constructed my own papier-mâché replica of Athena's helmet and spear, which I proceeded to wear to school all week. And how did that go over in my very bland suburban middle school, you ask? About as well as can be expected. I got my ass kicked all over the playground, called all sorts of names we would now deem hopelessly homophobic, and was eventually asked by the principal to stop acting like such a, I believe his term was 'anomalous child.' But did I back down? Did I hang up my helmet?" He raised his fist defiantly and shouted, "Of course not! Because I knew the Goddess of Just War was on my side. I was the epitome of self-righteous heroism—at least until the rain turned my helm into a yeastily odiferous paste, and I was forced to relinquish my warrior's raiment." More laughter.

"Or at least, that's the story I tell everyone. Why? Because it follows an archetype. I'm given a magical talisman—the book of myths—by an older mentor, I follow my heart into danger, I'm given a powerful weapon that only I can wield, and I come out a hero on the other end. Just like in so many Greek epics. But is my story *true*?" He paused for dramatic effect.

"Trick question. I'll never tell." A few groans, rueful smiles. "Because it *doesn't matter*." He waited a moment for that to sink in, then launched into the conclusion of his lecture.

"Our definition of 'myth' in common parlance: a widely believed, but *false* story. That's the definition Anant so helpfully illustrated. But that's not how the Greeks defined it." Theo turned to the whiteboard behind him and scrawled "μῦθος: *muthos*" in large blue letters.

"*Muthos* just means 'story.' No connotation of fictitiousness. The Greeks didn't question whether Persephone had actually been abducted by Hades, or whether Artemis truly turned the hunter Acteon into a stag. On one level, they understood that these stories certainly weren't meant to be taken literally, but on another level they believed that the stories held ultimate *truth*. Ways to understand their society, their own behavior, their relationship and duties to the gods. That's something that fundamentalists in our own day have trouble grasping. That the words in the Bible could be both true and false at the same time. It's natural to be literal-minded with holy texts, because written words are essentially static. But the Greeks had *oral* traditions, constantly adapted by different storytellers, coming from the mouths of men—no one ever conceived of them as the direct, immutable, literal word of the gods. So. Here's the hypothesis I propose. Drumroll, please." He pointed to Anant, who obliged with a quick thrumming on his desk. "The very nature of their myths, even more than their politics, their economics, or their geography, advanced the Greeks to unparalleled heights. Perhaps, I submit, creating a society even more adaptable, more flexible, more *creative* than the monotheistic, literal-minded Judeo-Christian civilization that followed."

May Chin in the front row raised her hand. "Are you saying the Greeks were more advanced than we are? Even though they lived in, like, 400 BC?"

"Did we invent democracy, theater, and philosophy in less than a century?"

May grinned at him and scribbled in her notebook while a serious boy with a worried frown raised his hand.

"Yes, Mr. Freemantle."

"Are you suggesting we'd be better off as pagans?"

"I certainly don't intend to be reading my future in the entrails of dead birds anytime soon, and I don't recommend you do either. Might get me into all sorts of trouble with the authorities. What I am saying is that as we enter the second month of this course together, I want you to shake up your perspectives. Open your minds. That's your assignment for next week. Five pages on how the complex, contradictory, ever-changing nature of Greek mythology may have influenced the progress of Greek civilization as a whole *and* how our own myths influence our lives today—one copy to me and one to Professor Halloran. Sky's the limit. Go crazy and have fun with it. Now get out of here—and get some sleep tonight, Anant!"

The students rumbled to their feet. Belatedly, Theo shouted over the hubbub, "Professor Halloran will be taking over next week to discuss gender relations in Greek drama, so don't forget to read *Lysistrata*! You won't regret it, I promise. Dick jokes and snarky heroines—it's like the latest Amy Poehler comedy. Enjoy!"

As the students streamed out of the hall, his co-teacher, Everett Halloran, rose from the front row and clapped Theo on the back warmly. Everett was six-three, his wavy dark hair nearly sculptural in its perfection. Although only an inch or two shorter, Theo, with his narrow frame and floppy fair hair, always felt like some pale mole creature standing next to him.

"I could listen to you all day," Everett said, squeezing Theo's shoulder one more time for good measure. "Your connection with the students is just mesmerizing."

"Thanks," Theo said, a little uncomfortable with what felt too sycophantic to be genuine. But that's who Everett was, making everyone else feel like they were the center of the universe, while simultaneously pulling them into his own orbit.

"I hate that I missed the first half of the lecture," Everett went on.

"Busy morning?"

"Up all night working in the office on some research for my latest article."

"Helen must've been thrilled with that." *Stupid—I shouldn't even mention her,* Theo thought. *It only makes things awkward.*

But Everett just laughed good-naturedly. "She's been so busy with her own preparation for the conference that I'm sure she had no idea. She's going to present an abstract of her book."

"Really? It's about time. I feel like this book is her Holy Grail, and she's decided none of us are virtuous enough to see it."

"Well, soon enough. Meanwhile, she's been holed up in the library or at her apartment or God knows where, and I haven't seen her in days. I've been teasing her that she's the worst fiancée ever!"

Theo laughed weakly. Everett and Helen had gotten engaged only six months after they started dating. He'd found their haste disconcerting, but not all that surprising. Sitting near them at conferences lately felt like sitting beside a furnace—all heat and flame and glow. If Theo felt it was all a little stifling, well, who could blame him?

"You coming to the faculty meeting later today?" Everett asked as Theo shoved his lecture notes into his satchel.

"Only if they threaten me with corporal punishment. Even then I might beg off."

"The privileges of tenure."

"Damn straight. God knows they would've already fired me if they could."

"Come on. It can't be that bad."

Theo snorted. "You're refreshingly naïve. Wait until you've been here a little longer. Trust me, the best way to get your colleagues to resent you is to be their students' favorite teacher. Second-best way is to thwart their dreams of bigger, cushier office space."

"You think they're still sore about the eminent domain dispute?"

"Word gets round, I see."

"Rumblings. It was before my time."

"Let's just say the protest group I formed with the students pissed off the administration to no end. We managed to stop just enough of the university's expansion so that a few low-income families got to keep their homes, but the Columbia Classics Department will still be stuck here in musty old Hamilton Hall in perpetuity."

"And let me guess, our esteemed department chair never forgave you."

"That sort of brilliant supposition is why you're on the tenure track, Professor Halloran. Eventually you, too, will be able to infuriate your boss and still hold on to your job."

Everett's phone buzzed in his pocket. "Ah, speak of the devil." He held it up so Theo could see Bill Webb's name on the screen.

"What can I do for you, Bill?" Everett asked, his voice perfectly smooth and ingratiating as he spoke to the department chair. Theo cringed a little, but he couldn't help a twinge of jealousy as well. He'd never had Everett's skill at managing his superiors. "I'm just finishing up our *Intro to Myth* class. I'm still downstairs in 516." His eyebrows flew upward as he listened. "Uh-huh. A policeman?"

Just then, the door to the lecture hall swung open, revealing a bantamweight man in a neat blue suit. He made his way toward the podium, a serious frown just visible beneath his grizzled mustache. "Everett Halloran?" he asked, pulling a badge from his pocket. "I'm Detective Brandman." With his gravelly voice and stiff brush cut, the cop reminded Theo of an ex-Marine, maybe the veteran of some covert '80s Latin American operation gone wrong.

Everett said a hurried good-bye to Webb and stepped forward to greet the detective. "What can I do for you?" he asked, clasping the Brandman's hand with what Theo knew would be an impressively manly grip. Helen—and everyone else—loved the passionate sincerity Everett's strong grasp implied. Theo always found it mildly suffocating.

"Would you like to sit down?" the detective asked.

Everett obeyed, folding his large frame into a narrow seat in the front row.

Theo was getting a bad feeling. "What is this about?" he asked.

The detective ignored him and spoke to Everett. "Your chairman said Helen Emerson listed you as her emergency contact. You're her fiancé?"

"Yes..." His polite smile dissolved. "Is she okay?"

The detective cleared his throat. Then he ripped apart Theo's world. "I'm sorry to inform you that Helen Emerson's body was found early this morning in Riverside Park. She'd washed up out of the Hudson wearing only a sheet."

Everett stared dumbly ahead as the color drained from his face.

Theo felt the room around him begin to spin. He sat down heavily beside Everett.

"How?" he whispered, his mouth gone dry.

"We don't know yet," the detective replied calmly. "But this was no suicide. And certainly not an accident."

"Are... are you sure?" Everett stammered. His hands trembled like an old man's despite his white-knuckled grip on the chair's arm.

For the first time, Brandman's impassive façade slipped a fraction. "We don't usually reveal the details of the investigation at this point, but we're having trouble tracking down Miss Emerson's next of kin. There's no delicate way to say this." His lower lip tugged at his mustache as if he would swallow the words. Then, while looking at Theo and Everett as if to gauge their reaction, he said, "Her genitalia had been removed."

Theo felt a mantle of ice settle around his shoulders. "Removed?"

"With a sharp instrument."

As if felled by a giant's fist, Everett slumped forward in the chair and buried his hands in his hair. The detective was still talking, but Theo heard nothing except Everett's choked sobs and his own racing heart.

He squeezed his eyes shut, but images of Helen streamed through his mind in an unstoppable torrent. Her fair head bent over a thick stack of books in the library. Her hazel eyes shining up at him as they argued over the meaning of some ancient text. Her laughter as she discussed her favorite Egyptian pyramids with a group of undergrads.

Her body, so frail, so delicate, sprawled across cold rocks, covered in blood.

Her gentle smile as she lay, flushed and tousled, in his bed.

Chapter 4

SINGER OF STITCHED WORDS

Perched on the limb of a maple near the river's edge, Selene stood vigil. Hippo lay silently beneath a cluster of rhododendrons nearby. Together, they'd watched the official from the medical examiner's office zip the body into a black shroud and carry it to the waiting ambulance. Then a short, gray-haired detective and his team had scoured the area, photographing the rocks, picking among the boulders with tweezers.

All morning, she'd sat forward on the branch, straining to hear the policemen's conversations from twenty yards away. Another private investigator might've brought a parabolic microphone to eavesdrop more effectively, but Selene had a senior citizen's view of advanced electronics. Computers and touchscreens and the Internet all seemed like very recent inventions that she couldn't possibly be expected to understand. Not all gods avoided such innovations, but as the Goddess of the Wild, Selene found it especially hard to adjust to a digital world. Her ten-year-old cell phone, essential for keeping in touch with clients, was her only concession to modern technology. She'd recently learned to text—that was plenty of progress for now.

Soon, a light rain began to fall, forcing the cops to speed up their investigation before the evidence washed away. Not long after, a uniformed officer reported that a researcher at Columbia had called in a missing person report on her roommate—a woman matching the victim's description.

She listened carefully, hoping to catch a name, an address, something to provide a lead, but learned nothing of use. As far as she could tell, the police never noticed the evidence of Greek ritual at the crime scene. Their lack of insight didn't surprise her, but did disappoint; she had no doubt the chiton and the wreath held the key to understanding the crime. She couldn't tell the cops herself: The anonymous phone tip she'd left about the body carried enough risk. She had a long, fraught history with the police force she'd once belonged to. Drawing their notice would be incredibly dangerous.

The rain fell harder; the cops bustled around the riverside, their expressions dour, packing up their equipment before the rain could damage it. They left a few straggling pieces of yellow police tape around the scene and a row of wooden barriers blocking the area from curious passersby and nosy reporters. Selene found her maple tree secluded in a rare midday quiet.

She moved closer to the tree trunk, resting her cheek upon the bark, trying to shield herself from the worst of the storm. The tree was old, its roots reaching past hunks of granite bedrock, twisting around water mains and steam pipes to reach into the ancient loam beneath the city. Selene tried to hear the pulse of the tree's veins. Now, it was only sap. She kept telling herself that. But she couldn't forget the days when it had been a heartbeat—a last reminder of the dryad within.

One by one, the nymphs had grown wan and weary, their glossy hair dulled, their long limbs attenuated. The changing world saved no room for the creatures of glade and spring. Selene still felt drawn to the trees, those hardy denizens of the city, eking out a life among cement and steel. Yet she found little comfort in them—only heartache, a remembrance of the companions she'd lost. One more reason she chose not to live in the forests and mountains that were her birthright. Too often, the woods only reminded her just how alone she really was.

The squall passed as suddenly as it had arrived. Broad sunbeams pierced the scudding clouds and filtered through the maple leaves, drying Selene's skin and clothes. Hippo rolled into the sun's warmth with a contented sigh and fell instantly asleep. Selene gave a sympathetic yawn: She Who Roams the Night wasn't used to being awake in the middle of the day.

Selene would've liked to lie back in the crook of the tree limb and join her dog for a brief nap. But there was work to be done. If she couldn't trust the cops to investigate the crime thoroughly, she'd have to do it herself. By the height of the sun, she knew it was nearly noon. Time for the regular dog walkers to enter the park for their lunchtime foray. The most dedicated came late at night as well. If anyone had seen something suspicious in the park last night, it'd be them.

Selene woke Hippo and walked back down the waterside path. She hopped over the blue police barricade while the dog crawled underneath, nearly lifting it off the ground with her wide back. After the quiet of the secluded crime scene, Selene winced at the crowds. To her, Riverside Park meant darkness and dusk—a slash of rock and tree and wild animals suspended between river and city. But at lunchtime, the park buzzed with people snatching a few gulps of fresh air. They stretched across benches, faces turned to the sun, or strode lazily along the boardwalk at the river's edge, squinting at the light bouncing off the water.

The narrow, fenced dog run roiled with yapping, fetching, peeing canines, all seizing their fifteen minutes of freedom before their owners (or more likely, their hired walkers) confined them inside an apartment for the rest of the day. Before long, a barrel-chested woman appeared, a water bottle in one hand and seven leashes in another. Her army of retrievers, German shepherds, and cockapoos walked just ahead of her down the stone stairs toward the dog run. Selene didn't know the woman's name, but she saw her often in the park late at night.

"Excuse me," she said, approaching the woman before she could enter the enclosure. The pack of dogs immediately strained at their leashes, lunging toward Selene with unbridled glee.

The dog walker grunted and leaned back on her heels, sweat popping from her brow as she restrained her charges. "Whoa, they're usually better behaved than this. Your dog's not in heat, is she?"

Selene shook her head, equally bewildered. As the Lady of Hounds, she'd once been irresistibly attractive to dogs, but she'd lost the power of that epithet along with all the others.

The dogs continued to strain toward Selene. The cockapoo began yapping, and the others followed suit. Then the dogs in the nearby enclosure bounded to the fence, adding to the commotion. The tallest ones stood on their hind legs, paws resting on the chain-link, and howled. The little ones ran in crazed circles. Hippo began to whimper, backing up with her tail between her legs.

Selene turned toward the dog run and growled. The dogs instantly calmed. Next, she took half a step forward toward the dog walker's charges and snapped her teeth at them. They froze, silent. Then the largest shepherd rolled over on his back like a submissive puppy. Hippo sniffed his belly disdainfully. Selene was pleasantly surprised she'd managed to control them. More often, dogs just got more riled up when she tried to use her old powers of command.

The dog walker's eyes widened. "You've got to teach me how to do that."

"Only if you answer a question first."

"Thirty dollars an hour. But I'm not sure I could handle that monster of yours. What is she, part Newfoundland?"

"I don't need you to walk my dog. I just want to know if you saw anyone suspicious in the park last night."

"Like a murderer?" she asked with a grimace. "I saw the news this morning."

"And?"

"I never went that far up. There was a sign from the Park Service saying the area was closed for repairs."

After striking out with the first dog walker, Selene approached a few others. But all had been similarly dissuaded from the northern end of the park. On her predawn hunt, Selene hadn't noticed any closure sign, meaning the killer had removed it after he completed the murder. He *wanted* the body to be found. A thoughtful, organized killer, who believed he could play with the police and not get caught. *But he wasn't counting on me,* Selene thought as she walked back toward the river.

A few passersby peered past the barricades in idle curiosity, but none stopped to investigate. From here, a slight hill obscured the murder site, and unless they saw blood on the ground, jaded New Yorkers showed little interest in crime scenes.

So she was surprised to glimpse a flutter of movement at the crest of the hill. Probably just another cop, come back for further investigation. But still...

She and Hippo slipped past the barriers and moved up into the woods so they could approach unseen.

A man crouched on the rocks beside the shreds of police tape, staring out at the river. He'd clearly jumped right over the barricades, but he didn't look like a cop: too narrow across the shoulders, too slumped in his posture. She felt a tremor of excitement. *This could be the killer, returned to gloat over the scene of his crime.*

He looked downriver for a moment, revealing a sharp nose and a gentle mouth. Sunlight winked off his wire-rimmed glasses, obscuring his eyes. *I know the type,* she thought, disappointed. *A man happier in an office than a forest, who wouldn't know how to wield a weapon if his life depended on it.*

When he stood, his lanky height surprised her—he'd seemed small and defeated huddled by the water's edge, but now she could see the corded strength of his movements. *Maybe he is strong enough*, she relented. *The woman wasn't very big, after all.*

Suddenly, he spoke. "*Se tan enaulois hypo dendrokomois,*" he began.

At first, Selene could barely process the words. Then she couldn't help smiling triumphantly. *Ancient Greek. What better evidence that he's involved in a ritual killing?* She forced herself to remain hidden, listening.

"*Mouseia kai thakous enizousan.*"

It had been centuries since she'd heard a mortal speak the ancient tongue so fluently, but she had no problem understanding his words.

> "*O you who settle in the leafy coverts,*
> *Singing melodious bird, sorrowful nightingale.*
> *Come to my help in the dirges I make,*
> *As I sing of Helen's pitiful pains.*"

Selene recognized the elegy. A summons to the wild birds of the forest to join in a requiem for Helen of Troy.

> "*Who among men, though he search to the uttermost end,*
> *Can claim to have found what is meant*
> *By god or the absence of god or of something between?*
> *For he sees the works of the gods*
> *Turning now here and now there,*
> *Now backwards again through a fate*
> *Beyond calculation or forethought.*"

Selene felt his words like a wound. Nearly two thousand years ago, the Olympians' capriciousness—protecting then punishing, manifesting then vanishing, healing then destroying—had pushed men toward a new god, one both understandable and understanding, who cemented his will in commandments and wrote his words in books. Mankind abandoned Artemis and the other Athanatoi—Those Who Do Not Die—and the Diaspora began. They fled their heavenly perch, condemned to wander the mortal realm below, remembered only as figments of ancient imagination, insubstantial as dreams.

> *"You, O Helen, carry to the sorrowful sorrows*
> *And pain upon pain."*

The man's voice drifted to a murmur. He stood for a moment in silence, the wind whipping his fair hair across his high forehead. Finally, he turned to face the boulders where the woman had lain in her yellow shroud.

With Hippo beside her, Selene left the shadows of the woods. She stood for a moment, watching the grieving man at the waterside. Normally, she avoided talking to men—female clients like Jackie Oritz were hard enough to deal with. She preferred hurting first and asking questions later.

But in truth, Selene had little choice. His dirge had not just summoned the birds of the wild—it had summoned the deities of the wild as well. It would seem that the gods were not forgotten after all.

Chapter 5

MOON GODDESS

Only after Theo had finished the poem did he look down at the rocks where Helen's corpse had lain.

"Katharsis," he said aloud with a bitter laugh. "All these years explaining it to my students, and I guess I finally understand what it means." He took a last shaky breath and lifted his glasses to rub his eyes, glad no one was around to see the tears that had finally come.

He kept imagining Helen's terrified screams as she realized what was about to happen to her. He could do nothing to help her now, but at least he'd marked her passing in a way that might return some of her stolen dignity. The right words had eluded him: He'd used Euripides' instead.

The boulders revealed no sign of tragedy—at least none that Theo could see—but hopefully the police had found plenty of evidence that would bring Helen's killer to justice. For him, there were other responsibilities to attend to—making sure Everett hadn't thrown himself off a bridge, providing a shoulder for Helen's roommate to cry on, dealing with the inevitably tone-deaf press release no doubt already drafted by Bill Webb. He turned to go.

A woman and a large shaggy mutt stood a few yards away, staring at him.

"Holy Roman Empire!" he yelped, stepping backward and nearly tripping over his own feet.

She lifted one perfectly sculpted black brow and looked at him with eyes so light they seemed almost silver. "Don't worry. I'm just walking my dog. I'll pretend I didn't see you jumping the police barricade."

"Good. And I'll pretend I didn't just exclaim something utterly pretentious." He started walking away. As he passed, he glanced again at the woman and almost stopped in his tracks. Flawless pale skin, aquiline nose, chin-length black hair peeking out from beneath a ratty New York Liberty cap. At first he assumed she was young, but something about her stern gaze made him suspect she was closer to his own age. Perhaps thirty. She was extremely tall—almost as tall as he—and though she wore a leather jacket over baggy pants, nothing could hide the sleek lines of her long limbs. A gust of wind blew across Theo's face, carrying the scent of a summer cypress forest that only added to her allure. *I must be delusional,* he thought, looking at the maples and oaks in their September foliage. *Wishing I were back in Greece.*

"Did you know the woman who was murdered?" the stranger asked suddenly, stopping him when he was a few yards past her.

He wanted to shake his head and keep walking. The standard New Yorker's response to nosy tourists or needy panhandlers. But Theo had never been the standard New Yorker. And he couldn't bear to deny Helen's existence. *Soon enough, no one will ask after her again.*

"We taught together up at Columbia," he said. "Her name was Helen Emerson."

"So you're here looking for evidence?"

"Me? The closest I've ever gotten to detective work is piecing together potsherds from ancient urns."

"Then what're you doing in a crime scene?" the woman asked. "My dog refuses to pee in any other part of the park. I've got an excuse."

"Maybe I refuse to pee anywhere else, too."

She didn't smile. Instead, she closed the distance between them. Now she stood only a few feet away, her face cloaked in the shadow of a nearby tree. Again the scent of cypress washed over him.

"You're sure you aren't involved in the investigation?" she asked.

"Police work's beyond my pay grade. I'm a classicist."

"You were close to her?"

"You've got a lot of questions, you know."

She shrugged. "Just curious." She stroked her huge dog absently as she spoke, as if only vaguely interested in what Theo was saying.

"You're not a reporter, are you?" Theo asked, suddenly suspicious.

"Do reporters usually bring their dogs to crime scenes?"

"Maybe they should. Might provide some much-needed cheer." The woman just stared at him. Theo gamely placed a hand on the dog's wide head. It snarled and snapped at his fingers; he took a quick step back.

The woman didn't even try to restrain the dog. "She doesn't like men."

"Oh. Well, honestly, right now I don't either."

She finally laughed. Brief, dry, bitter. "I don't hear that every day."

"Well, it's not every day a man kills a friend of mine and dumps her body in the river," he retorted, suddenly angry.

The woman's levity vanished as quickly as it had appeared. The set of her jaw, the narrowing of her eyes, made him think she understood exactly what he meant.

"Theodore Schultz," he said impulsively, offering his hand.

The woman just stood, staring at him, *through* him with her silver eyes. Judging. He noticed her fingers twitching and thought for a moment she might refuse to touch him. But finally, she stretched out her hand. Her flesh was as cold and smooth as shadowed marble. She didn't offer her name.

When she spoke again, all hint of idle curiosity had vanished. "Tell me exactly what Helen taught," she demanded.

Theo nearly walked away right then, shaken by her sudden, startling ferocity, but he found himself answering. "Unless you're a classicist, it won't mean much to you. We spend most of our time trying to convince our students that the ancient world is still relevant, but they're all too busy trying to get jobs as hedge fund managers to really believe us."

"Tell me anyway."

"She was a professor with the Archeology and Art History Department, with a specialty in images of femininity across ancient cultures. Priestesses of Isis, the Panathenaic Festival, Vestal Virgins, a whole range of things."

"And was she one?"

"One what?"

"A virgin."

"No."

"You're sure?"

"Yes," he said, struck by a sudden image of Helen, lying naked in a sunbeam on his rug, flipping through the latest *Bulletin of the American Society of Papyrologists*. "Why does it matter?"

"Don't you see what happened to her?" Her lip curled in a snarl. "You really think this is some random homicide? She was *mutilated*. Ravaged. This was a ritual."

"How do you—"

"Did you care about this woman or not?"

"Of course I did."

"Then start using your head, Professor. A criminal this heinous doesn't usually stop with one woman. He'll strike again. Trust me. So I need you to tell me everything you know about this case."

"I don't know anything," he said, angry now. "If I did, don't you think I'd be doing something about it? Who *are* you anyway?"

"I'm a private investigator of crimes against women. I found her."

"Oh, Christ."

"I found her lying on the rocks with her eyes open and her womb cut out. A bloodless piece of meat. Torn apart by some man who wrapped her up in a chiton, bound a laurel wreath around her brows, and dressed her hair in six braids. Did they tell you that part?" She narrowed her eyes, as if waiting for his reaction. "Your friend Helen was dressed up like a virgin sacrifice. You've read your Homer, right, Professor? The gods don't like human sacrifices—and neither do I."

Theo doubled over, his stomach heaving, body convulsing. He'd eaten little that day, but still he retched until bitter bile dripped from his lips.

He took a final rasping breath, then straightened, wiping his mouth with the last scrap of dirty tissue in his pocket. She watched him coldly, unsurprised. "*That's* catharsis," she said.

Had she given him a clean tissue, offered to call for help, or expressed her sympathy in any way, Theo would've gone home that day, mourned his former lover, and eventually gotten on with his life: immersing himself in intellectual challenges, taking on the occasional social justice cause, basking in his students' adoration. But the complete lack of pity in those steely eyes was like a slap in the face, challenging him to be a bigger man.

"Have you told the police what you know?" he asked.

"That's your job. I don't work with the police. I don't work with anyone. But you can give them all the facts so they've got a chance to solve this thing." She grimaced. "But I'm warning you, they may not believe you. Policemen don't always accept the extraordinary."

"Why not? Sure it's a bit bizarre...but if you're right about the chiton and the wreath, a ritual sacrifice makes some sense to me."

"Yes, but you're an expert in the field. A learned man."

Is that what I am? His academic knowledge had never felt less relevant. "But I've got no expertise in life and death circumstances. No one gets hurt, or even particularly disappointed, if you translate Virgil poorly."

"The cops need you. You'll see things they can't, or won't." One brow lowered skeptically, she looked him over. Judgment. Again. But she must have seen something she thought worthy, because after a moment, she reached into the bulky black pack on her shoulder, pulled out a pen and a scrap of take-out menu, and scrawled a few lines. "Here's my number. Tell the police everything, but leave me out of it. And if they let you down, call me." She took a single step closer to him. The sharp scent of pine tickled his nostrils. "I have no intention of letting Helen's murder go unavenged."

"Neither do I."

"Good."

He looked down at the piece of paper. *Selene DiSilva. Private Investigator.*

He thought immediately of the Homeric Hymn to the Moon Goddess. *Hail, white-armed goddess, bright Selene, mild, bright-tressed queen.* He'd never understood the "mild" part. The Moon had always seemed fierce and lonely to him, like Artemis, the celibate Huntress who shared Selene's mastery over the night sky.

"Good luck, Professor."

"And to you, Moon Goddess."

She laughed. A bitter, harsh sound. Her huge dog pranced and barked along.

Then she left, her every motion a lesson in grace, melting back into the woods as mysteriously as she'd emerged.

In the myths, he thought, watching her go, *you can tell by her blazing eyes and her proud bearing that a goddess has visited you in mortal form.* Then, for the first time since he'd learned about Helen, he laughed.

Chapter 6

A LEARNED MAN

Theo dreamed of making love in a moonbeam. The light was a palpable thing, a bright, cold cradle that cast the woman's features in bold relief. Yet when the phone rang and dragged him from sleep, he couldn't remember her face. Only that he was surprised it wasn't Helen's.

He sat up, drenched in sweat, fumbling for his glasses and then his phone. When he saw that it was six in the morning, he was sure another woman had been murdered. Why else would someone call at such an hour?

He checked the caller ID and swallowed hard. "Jesus, Gabriela, are you okay?"

"No, I'm not okay!" came the shrill reply.

"Where are you?" Theo was already out of bed and trying to pull on yesterday's pants while balancing his phone between his ear and shoulder. Still half asleep, he decided the killer had struck again. *Selene DiSilva warned me—why didn't I do something sooner?* "I'm on my way."

"You don't need to come, for Christ's sake. What're *you* going to do? The stuff's already been stolen."

"Stolen?" Theo sat down hard on his bed, one foot half out of a shoe. "What?"

"There was a break-in at the museum—can you believe it?"

"Ah. So despite hysterically calling me at the ass-crack of dawn, you *haven't* been ritually mutilated by a psychopath."

"What? Oh, because of Helen—no, no, sorry, *querido*. It's nothing like that."

Groaning, Theo lay back on his bed and retreated under the covers, his pants still around his calves. It was like Gabriela to scare him half to death for no reason.

"I didn't think," she went on. "You sound awful. You holding up?"

"Barely. I was up all night poring over Helen's published journal articles, trying to find some clue to explain what happened. Then when I couldn't see straight anymore, I gave up and regressed to my fifteen-year-old self, watching *Saturday Night Live* reruns."

"You see the one with the new girl, Jenny Thomason? You know she's only nineteen?" As usual, Gabriela could switch gears on a dime.

"Yeah. She did this amazing Beyoncé bit—part coy striptease, part feminist manifesto. I remember thinking Helen would've loved all the subversive symbolism, then that just depressed me further. I must've finally passed out sometime before dawn. But I'm definitely awake now, and if I keep thinking about Helen, I'm going to completely break down, so just tell me what's up."

Theo and Gabriela had become fast friends while teaching at Kansas University after their postgrad stints at archeological digs. Theo left Kansas's Classics Department after only a year, when the siren call of the Big Apple lured him to Columbia. Gabriela left the Anthropology Department a year later; she'd never been much of a teacher. She spent the next three years doing fieldwork throughout the Southwest on the Pueblo and Anasazi reservations until New York's American Museum of Natural History recruited her to help them update their moribund Native American exhibits.

"I came in super early to work this morning to get started on that cursed Navajo diorama," she began, "and I was cutting through the Division of Vertebrate Zoology on my way to the fabrics storeroom when I nearly sliced my foot open on broken glass. Someone broke in through a skylight. I swear it's just like *Mission Impossible* in here."

Everything seemed more dramatic to Gabriela Jimenez than it did to the rest of the world, which was part of why she and Theo had become friends: Each had a rather overactive imagination.

"What'd they take?" Theo asked with a sigh. Normally, the theft of a museum artifact would've been the most shocking news in his week, but after yesterday, he had much more important mysteries to solve. "Was it from your collection?"

"No, otherwise I'd be going after the guy myself, police be damned."

"Then why are you so upset? I thought you didn't even like the museum." He yawned and felt his eyes drift closed. They'd spoken a thousand times about Gabriela's love-hate relationship with her career. He could do it half-asleep.

"That doesn't mean I don't *respect* it. I do *work* here, you know. I just think—"

"That it's racist that they put brown people in dioramas down the hall from the dinosaurs as if they were some other form of extinct wildlife, while the white people wind up in art museums and historical societies? I couldn't agree more."

"Right. But it *is* the most famous natural history museum in the world, and it's not okay for people to break in and steal stuff!"

"I never said it was," he soothed.

"And you know this isn't the only museum robbery this week?"

"Really?" Theo sat up a little in bed.

"Monday night someone broke into the Met. Stole two pieces of pottery."

"That's outrageous. Who's running museum security in this town?"

"I know. But honestly, they're such prissy bitches over there that I'm glad they got robbed, too."

"Very collegial." He could imagine her sticking out her tongue at him. "Now tell me what was stolen from Natural History." He was used to steering her back on track; she did the same for him.

"I called the guy who runs the herpetology collection because the lock on his storeroom had been busted open. He got here half an hour ago and is still searching through the inventory, but he said that at least one specimen is missing. A *Zamenis longissimus*, or something like that."

Translating scientific Latin out of context was never easy, but he hazarded a guess. "The Longest Angry One?"

"It's just a European rat snake, Mr. Show-off. The herp guy said it's pretty rare, but not that valuable or anything."

"Rat snake... Why does that sound familiar?"

"I have no idea. I'd never heard of it before today."

"You'd think they would've stolen some one-of-a-kind prehistoric serpent with ten legs or something." He stifled another yawn. "Who cares about a rat snake except—" He sat bolt upright.

"What?"

"Except *classicists*. I know why I've heard of the rat snake. A lecture that Martin Andersen gave a few years ago on animal species in Greek and Roman myth." Throwing off the blanket and hiking up his pants, he moved to one of the tall bookshelves lining the walls of his apartment.

"Andersen? Is that the preternaturally boring old guy in your department? The one who keeps trying to ask you out?"

"Be nice, Gabi. It's not his fault he has the personality of a black hole. And he's not gay, just lonely."

"Sure."

"His wife died a few years ago."

"Okay, fine, sorry I'm so insensitive. Now get back to what you know about rat snakes."

"It was actually pretty fascinating." Theo started pawing through the old notebooks on his shelf, checking dates and titles. "He talked about the real species that correspond to the animals mentioned in classic myth. For example, he theorized that the Nemean Lion defeated in the first labor of Hercules may be a reference to the ice age cave lions found in prehistoric cave paintings."

"Fascinating to you maybe. This is the problem with your life's work, *chico*. You keep searching for the meaning behind myth. Why not just skip the fiction part entirely and go straight to the facts?"

"Because the ancients didn't differentiate as easily as you do between fact and fiction. Myths illuminate a society's behavior and beliefs on multiple levels all at the same time. So you can learn more 'truth' from a fictional epic than you can from a bunch of bone shards. No offense."

"Some taken."

"Besides, you know how bored of digging I get after about a week at a site."

"You get bored of everything after about a week."

"Ouch." He riffled through a legal pad of notes.

"I didn't mean Helen." Theo wished she'd stop there, but Gabriela rarely felt constrained by tact. "Although that is sort of what happened, isn't it?"

"I didn't get bored of Helen," he retorted.

"You just decided that you were too scared to commit to her, so you went off to Greece and sabotaged your own relationship by forgetting about her, and then she dumped your ass and ran into the arms of hottie Everett Halloran instead? Is that how it happened?"

"Well, I'm never going to forget about her now, am I?" he snapped.

"Whoops. Too soon?"

"You think?"

"Sorry. I just wish you'd find some relationship that wasn't so...I don't know...*fraught*."

He didn't bother replying. She didn't know the half of it.

He pulled a spiral-bound pad labeled "Conference Notes, 2013" off the shelf. He flipped through the scribbled pages. "European rat snake! Also known colloquially as the 'Aesculapian snake,'" he read aloud, "and widely believed to be the serpent traditionally identified with Asclepius."

"Who?"

"He's a Greek god of medicine and healing. The Romans called him Aesculapius," he said absently, his mind beginning to turn. "Carries around a staff with a snake twirled around it."

"You mean like the FTD guy in the florist windows?"

"The FTD guy—Hermes? That's a caduceus. With *two* snakes. You're breaking my heart. Have you listened to anything I've said in the last ten years?"

"Please. Like you know the difference between the Cheyenne and the—"

Indeed, Theo wasn't listening anymore. When he'd returned home the night before, he'd found nothing in Helen's published research that related to human sacrifice. He'd begun to believe the woman in the park might have been leading him astray. But the theft of classically related artifacts at two museums couldn't be mere coincidence.

"I've gotta go, Gabi."

"Don't hang up!"

"You're just using me for my exemplary moral support skills."

"But I'm still seething—"

"You don't understand." He barely understood himself. But the kernel of an idea had begun to form. Asclepius had inspired one of the most dedicated and active cults in the ancient world. His acolytes presented the god with a clay model of their injured body part and asked for healing in return. The ruins of Aesculapian temples contained dozens of terracotta legs, arms, heads... and genitals. Theo thought of Helen's mutilation. Could her killer have wanted her womb for a similar purpose? "Your Aesculapian snake," he said, "I think it's related to Helen's murder."

"When did you become the next Sherlock Holmes? I don't see how—" she began.

"Trust me." He looked up at his bookshelf, eager to start the research. Enough knowledge, Theo had always believed, could solve any problem, whether it be translating a choral paean or piecing together a shattered amphora. "I may need to call the cops."

"Hold on there, cowboy. You really think you know better than they do about how to investigate a murder?"

"No, but I'm...a learned man," he said, realizing belatedly how ridiculous Selene DiSilva's words sounded coming out of his mouth.

"A *learn-ed* man," Gabriela mocked, drawing out the two syllables. "Okay, Mr. Fancypants. You sure this isn't just another case of you being self-righteous and impulsive?" One thing about Gabriela, she never pulled her punches. "Or trying to distract yourself from grief? I'm worried about you. How are you doing? Really?"

"I'm like a numb limb," Theo said after a long pause. "Unfeeling one moment, then I move wrong and there's searing pain, but I sort of want to keep beating on myself, hoping I'll wake up and this'll all be over." Helen's face swam before him unbidden: not as he'd known it, but as Selene DiSilva must have seen it in the park. Hair braided like a Roman virgin's. Yellow chiton pinned across her breast. A bloody hole between her legs. "But it's not a nightmare, is it? It's real. Helen's dead, and her murderer is still out there. How can I refuse to help find him?"

He'd told Selene DiSilva he had no intention of letting Helen's murder go unavenged. And though he had his faults—distractible, stubborn, and sanctimonious being just the first three of an undoubtedly interminable list—he'd never been a liar.

"All right," Gabriela said, a little more gently. "Go be a hero."

Chapter 7

SHE WHO LEAVES
NO TRACE

Selene stood across the street from Theodore Schultz's apartment building for nearly two hours before he appeared at the doorway just after ten in the morning, a large satchel slung over his shoulder. With his rumpled overcoat, tousled hair, and feverish eyes, he looked like he'd either just rolled out of bed or been up working for hours. A scowl of concentration made him seem sterner than she remembered. Selene stayed away until he'd barreled down the sidewalk and out of sight.

She'd almost held an arrow to his jugular yesterday in the park and insisted he confess to killing Helen Emerson. And if he admitted to the crime, she could've pushed that same arrow through his windpipe with no compunction. But as they spoke, something about his grief, clearly deep despite his attempts at humor, had stopped her. She'd told him the details of Helen's death to see his reaction, and he seemed genuinely horrified. She never shied from punishing men if the victim identified them, or if she herself saw the crime committed, but a long-ago tragedy had taught her not to rely solely on hearsay or circumstantial evidence. And with Schultz, that's all she had: friend of the victim, expert in Ancient Greek, loiterer at the crime scene. She needed to be patient if she wanted to find proof of his involvement. To stalk her prey a little longer before moving in for the kill.

It took only a few minutes before another tenant left Schultz's building; Selene held the door for her with the warmest smile she could muster, then slipped nonchalantly inside. She wished she could get into Helen Emerson's building with such ease. When she'd swung by earlier that morning, cop cars lined the block and officers trooped in and out the front door. Selene had no choice but to let the police investigate the victim while she pursued the suspect.

In her backpack, she'd stowed all the tools she might need for this little adventure. It felt good, using her old skills again. In her time in exile, she'd been a cop, a bodyguard, a naturalist, and briefly, an assassin. And that was just the beginning of the list.

She donned a pair of gloves and used her picks to jimmy his door open. Schultz hadn't bothered with high-security locks; maybe he was naïve enough to think he'd never get robbed. Selene had three different locks on her own door. It wouldn't do to have a burglar discover the god-forged golden bow in her closet.

The door swung open with a creak, revealing a large studio apartment with a living and dining area separated from the bedroom by a folding screen. The room was clean, but far from neat. Books and papers littered every surface, like an ancient library pillaged by Visigoths.

Selene moved to a small dining table completely covered by tall stacks of papers. She picked up the first, a student's essay on the *Odyssey*, and thumbed through. The professor's red ink emendations lay between the printed lines, streamed down the bottom of the page, curled into the side margins, and continued onto the back. Finally, a scrawled C+, accompanied by yet another comment: *Impressively meta: You've taken a tortuous journey of Odyssean proportions before arriving at your point. But next time, don't bury your thesis statement on page ten.* Selene checked the other papers. All similar palimpsests of black text and red ink. It must have taken the professor an hour to grade each one.

Next to the papers lay a stack of lecture notes. She skimmed the first few pages with a raised eyebrow. *Someone who actually thinks the gods have something to contribute to the modern world,* she thought, impressed. But as she kept reading, she grew disheartened. *I see. Myths are manmade creations, not to be taken literally, but to be torn apart and dissected and put back together. They're all about* human *civilization, because of course humans are the center of everything. Such arrogance.* She looked at the anthologies of myths lining the bookshelves. Within their pages lay the history, the loves and losses, the deepest secrets of beings far removed from mere mortals, if only the professor knew to look.

But, she had to admit, Schultz was right about one thing: The line between fiction and reality was never clear—not even for her. Like all the gods, she had little control over her pre-Diaspora memories. Artemis had existed more as a metaphor than as a maiden, her very reality shaped by the tales poets told of her. Thus, her recollections of the first two thousand years of her life were like scenes viewed through a forest pool—twisted and warped, sometimes so cloudy she could remember nothing, sometimes so bright that she was equally blind. How could the mind of an omnipresent being—a goddess presiding over her temple at Delos, hunting through the forests outside Rome, riding the moon across the sky—be contained within a mind that grew more mortal with every passing day? Only certain memories remained sharp—mostly those described by the poets and retold over the centuries. She knew that those stories—the transformation of Acteon, her father's bestowal of her divine attributes, the punishment of Calisto, and many others—had actually happened, but her memories were like sand dunes in the wind, carved by poets who both augmented and eroded the past in equal measure. Most maddening of all, Selene could never be sure how much her memories had changed; she could only trust that some kernel of truth remained within them.

The books and notes in Schultz's apartment spilled off the shelves, then lay like a trail of breadcrumbs across the living area before joining another pile of research lying on, around, and under a large desk. She scanned the titles briefly—cult practice, mainly.

She hadn't considered the murder could be the work of multiple people in an organized group. She flipped through one of the professor's books, her heart sinking. *I might have more than one Greek-inspired killer to deal with,* she thought. *Just what I need.* For the last thousand years, she'd barely thought about Greek cults. Holy Roman Emperor Theodosius had banned cult worship in the fourth century, and it had died off quickly after that, taking most of the Athanatoi's supernatural powers along with it. As their godhood waned, her father Zeus summoned his divine family to a Great Gathering on Mount Olympus. The golden roofs of their palaces had grown dull, the marble colonnades cracked and listing. There, Zeus declared that the Diaspora was at hand. Since the people of Greece and Rome had abandoned the Olympians, the Olympians would abandon them in return. No longer would they provide protection in return for homage. In fact, Zeus swore a great oath upon the River Styx that the Olympians would not step foot in their ancient homeland again. Instead, each Athanatos gathered what sacred objects he still possessed and walked forth into the world to make his way among the thanatoi. Some traveled to Africa, others to the farther reaches of Europe, and eventually, many made their way to the New World, lured by the promise of a land not yet dominated by Christianity. Never, in all that time, had the gods believed that mankind would revive the old cult practices.

But maybe the books strewn across Schultz's apartment proved that the professor himself had decided to do just that. Or perhaps he was just following her advice to look into sacrificial rites. She couldn't be sure.

Selene scanned the rest of the room, looking for the sort of mementos that ritual mutilators kept of their kills. If you looked hard enough, especially if they lived alone, you were bound to find some proof of their hobby. But so far, Schultz seemed more eccentric than truly crazed. Photos hung on most of the walls and stood propped on the mantle of his small fireplace. She recognized the professor's teenage self in many—gangly, acne plagued, but grinning hugely—always surrounded by people. The same faces showed up in later photos, when Schultz's skin had cleared and his frame filled out—even once his temples had gone gray. This was a man with strong personal bonds: not exactly the profile of a serial killer. Women featured prominently in many of the photos. *A player?* wondered Selene. But something about the laughter in their faces made her think not. The backgrounds—the Coliseum, the Louvre, the Palace at Knossos, and a series of archeological digs on dusty hillsides— indicated they might be fellow academics.

She picked up a beach photo of Schultz and a short, curly-haired Latina woman who appeared in multiple photos. The woman filled out her red bikini in a way Selene's boyish figure never would, all breasts and hips, with a slightly rounded stomach. Schultz, wearing shorts and a T-shirt reading *Vivant Linguae Mortuae!* ("Long Live Dead Languages!"), stood with his arm around her, his lean frame bent nearly horizontal so he could rest his fair head against her dark one.

Selene put down the photo and walked to the coffee table in front of the couch, curious about the mess of cardboard scraps littering its surface. Only when she got close did she realize they were jigsaw pieces, all turned upside down. The puzzle was half-done, a beige expanse fitted together with a watchmaker's skill.

Behind the folded screen stood a rumpled queen-sized bed.

Beside it teetered three piles of well-thumbed books—everything from *Star Trek* novels to presidential biographies to the works of Cicero and Ovid. She crouched to peer beneath the metal bed-frame. If you really wanted to find a man's secret vices, this was the place to look. Sure enough, she spotted a battered shoebox. As she lifted the lid, she winced in preparation for the inevitable trove of porn. Instead, she found a pile of letters and a few photographs.

She wasn't just your colleague after all, Professor Schultz, she thought, pulling out a picture of a short, pretty woman with a fall of long blond hair and a guileless grin—a woman who had appeared nowhere in the other photos littering the room. Helen Emerson wore a strapless blue sundress and held a plastic cup of wine, toasting the camera. The Hudson River glinted in the background, with New Jersey apartment complexes visible beyond its shores. *The Boat Basin Café in Riverside Park,* Selene realized. Less than a mile downriver from the scene of Helen's death.

One other photo from the same day. The light golden as the sun set, flaming orange and violet over the water. Helen and Schultz. His arm outstretched as if taking the photo with one hand while his other arm lay protectively around her shoulders. His lips pressed against her cheek. Her face scrunched with delight.

Selene put the photo back where she found it and pulled out the stack of letters. An envelope addressed to the professor, care of the University of Athens in Greece. Beneath the torn flap lay a letter on thick stationery, a Greek key embossed in gold around its border. The handwriting was barely legible: a miniature garden of curlicues, some words too small to read, others obscured by long, trailing flourishes. It took Selene, who'd never been much of a reader in the first place, nearly a minute to decipher each sentence.

Dearest Theo, Helen had written. *You've been gone for two weeks, and it feels like an eternity.*

Selene checked the date at the top of the page. September. Almost exactly a year ago.

This last year with you has been the happiest of my life, and now I feel it's all slipping away. I know you're coming back, but January feels so far away. How can I bear it?

Every time I pass the Met, I think of our first kiss. Every time I walk by your apartment, I think of our first night together.

Selene shifted uncomfortably, but forced herself to keep reading. In her job as a private investigator, she was used to watching people exhibit their lustful perversions—love, on the other hand, always discomfited her.

I love your letters. Love to think of you visiting the digs in the hills of Crete and spending your evenings watching Aeschylus and Sophocles in the place they were meant to be performed. But it's not the same as being with you.

The letter went on in a similar vein for three excruciating pages, closing with *Mainolai thymoi*, "With a raving heart." Selene rolled her eyes. The next letter was more of the same. And the next. But by December, Helen's missives changed.

I write every day, sometimes twice. And all I get from you are e-mails full of academic details and superficial jokes. You say you miss me, you care for me, but where's the passion, Theodore? I keep waiting for the part where you say how you've bought a plane ticket on a whim and flown home to surprise me, if only for a day, because you can't bear to be away from me. Instead, you sound like you're enjoying yourself, while I feel increasingly insecure.

She signed it *Syn philoteti*, "With friendship." Finally, the last letter to Greece. Dated just before Christmas.

I've fallen in love. I met him and it was a flood tide. Like all my thoughts of anyone else were just wiped away and I was left newborn, clean, with my eyes finally opened to another world. He makes me feel confident, strong, complete, and at the same time, I can't help feeling you never really loved me enough. I'm sorry if this hurts you, but I know something you don't—sometimes Aphrodite just can't be stopped.

Selene let out a dismayed whistle. *Ouch.* Was wounded pride enough to push the mild professor over the edge? One final note lay in the box, a single folded sheet with no envelope. It was dated only three months ago.

I can't stop thinking about last night. One moment keeps replaying in my mind. After you fell asleep, I ran my fingers along your ribcage—as if I were a blind woman and you the map. I followed the line of your sternum, my hands rested along your collarbone, I traced your jaw until I found your lips. I didn't know what I sought at the end of the trail—you? Everett?

I miss you, Theo. I love you. I always have. But I'm with Everett now, and I love him, too. My engagement ring seems more appropriate than ever. A Greek meandros . . . maybe because love isn't always a straight line? It twists and turns back on itself. But, I hope, it continues to move forward. And that's what I have to do.

You said we shouldn't have let last night happen. Now, in the light of day, I know you're right.

The letter ended there, but the image still lingered in Selene's mind—for an instant, she recalled how it felt to run her palms over the hard muscles of a man's chest. She'd had a lover of her own once. Schultz's books told their own versions of the tale, but this was the one memory from her pre-Diaspora godhood that she'd managed to preserve in its true, unaltered form. It had taken a great act of will, but from the moment she'd realized her memories had begun to shift and fade, she'd started reciting the story of her love, in all its passion and heartbreak, over and over to herself through the millennia, so the poets' versions might not eclipse her own. So, while the rest of her history had slipped away, this story remained clear.

Hesitantly, she traced the sharp contour of her collarbones, the square lines of her own jaw, trying to imagine her lover's caress.

"*Orion.*" She whispered his name aloud, the shape of it like a kiss upon her lips. She closed her eyes, falling into the memory of the only man she had ever loved—*would* ever love.

Stag and boar flee before us, but we chase them down. All through the night we hunt, my silver moon lighting our path. Even my hounds cannot keep pace, and dryads and naiads fall panting behind us. Only Orion and I remain, leaping over rivers and across hills, then crouching down to hide behind the sheltering trees, ready to spring forth once more when prey crosses our path, I with my golden bow and the Hunter with his bronze sword.

I marvel at my own unfettered joy, so unlike the wrathful vengeance of my hunts with Apollo. My twin and I chase those who insult us, those who do not pay proper homage. But with Orion, I am only the Huntress of Beasts, the Goddess of Wild Places, Mistress of the Moon. To be with him is freedom. It is ecstasy.

I kneel with my Hunter behind a fallen tree, watching a stag and its doe pace silently into a moonbeam's path. I start to raise my bow, but Orion takes my hand in his instead. I might protest, but for the look in his eyes, both gentle and hungry. "I would do anything to be with you," he whispers. His words are a flame, heating my skin. There, in the shadow of the trees where even my father the Sky God might not see, he takes my face in his hands and kisses me.

I taste a man's lips for the first time. I run my hands through his dark curls. I feel his heart beat strong against my breast, and I suffer both heat and chill when his hand slips beneath my tunic to rest against the small of my back.

Heart pounding, Selene pulled herself from the memory. She replaced the love letters in their box. As Helen's ex-boyfriend and sometimes secret lover, Schultz looked even more suspicious. But no visible fingerprints marked the dust covering the lid. The professor hadn't opened it in months. If Helen had indeed been his prey, he likely would've sought the photos and letters often, reliving his humiliation and heartache, stoking the fires of vengeance. Shaking her head resignedly, she stowed the box back under the bed. She'd had thousands of years of experience with hunts like these, and she prided herself on knowing when a man was guilty. But now she just wasn't sure.

As she stood up, her skin prickled as if sensing something just beneath the range of human hearing. She stayed still for a moment, listening closely. Her hearing hadn't been supernatural in centuries, and yet—yes, a quick step on the stairs, the jingling of keys. She snatched up her backpack and dashed toward the window, hoping for a fire escape. No such luck. Still, there was a narrow stone ledge overlooking the alley. Once she would've hopped onto the ledge without a thought, but that was before she'd lost her uncanny balance and agility—not to mention her ability to quickly heal from a fifth-story fall. Still, hiding in the closet seemed even stupider.

She opened the sash and swung onto the sill. Balancing on the six inches of granite with one booted foot, she slid shut the window with the other, then sidled out of view along the ledge, her back pressed against the brick wall of the building. Gingerly, she pulled off her left glove with her teeth: Her bare fingers could better grip the masonry. When she took the glove out of her mouth to shove it into her pocket, it slipped from her grip. Instinctively, she reached after it, bending down as it fluttered past her fingertips.

Then she froze. With a gasp, she realized she hung suspended fifty feet in the air, her feet on the narrow ledge and all her weight hanging over the abyss, with only the fingers of one hand to hold her steady. Yet somehow, she didn't fall. Slowly, she stood upright, willing her heart to stop its panicked gallop.

From the apartment behind her, she heard the sound of an opening door. Curious, she glanced down at the window. Double-paned, as she thought. She shouldn't be able to hear through it so easily. *So I can hear through walls again,* she mused. *If only I could see through them, too.* She'd give anything to see what Schultz was up to. *Don't do it, don't even think about it,* she chided herself. *Just because you're feeling particularly agile doesn't mean you're suddenly Artemis again.* But she couldn't help it—she raised herself onto the toes of her boots, then bent into a precarious squat so she could lean toward the window. She twisted her head over her shoulder and peeked inside.

Schultz was on his hands and knees beneath his desk, shuffling through more papers. He finally emerged, dusty-haired, with a thick book. Selene could just make out the title: *Asclepius* by Trismegistus. An ancient Arabic text translated first into Greek, then from Greek to Latin, then Dutch, and finally into English in the seventeenth century. She doubted such an oft-translated text would hold any reliable clues. Reading it would be like playing an ancient game of telephone, with words, stories, entire chapters corrupted by time.

The professor moved toward the door, knocking a mug of tea off a shelf as he went. The mug didn't break, but the tea spilled all over his chest. With a huff, he dropped his satchel and tore off his overcoat and T-shirt. A sunbeam from the window illuminated a blond tracery of hair across the taut planes of his chest. It seemed scholarship was better exercise than she imagined. His body was slimmer, less heavily muscled than Orion's had been—surely it was only her recent reminiscing that brought a flush of heat to her cheeks. Her eyes traveled the path of Helen's fingers: across the curve of his lower rib, up the shallow declivity of his sternum, resting for a moment in the hollow between his collarbones before skimming the sharp point of his chin and coming to rest on the thin line of his lower lip.

When Selene's phone rang, she nearly fell off the window ledge.

She cursed and stuck her hand in her pocket, silencing the ringer as she pulled it out. She glanced back through the window, but Schultz was busy yanking a new T-shirt over his head. He hadn't heard. She waited until he left the apartment again, then answered the call.

"Moonshine?" asked a familiar voice. "Hello... are you there? Moonshine, it's me."

"I know who it is." Only one man ever used that nickname.

The cold shiver down her spine had nothing to do with her hazardous perch.

"Mother gave me your number—"

"I asked her not to do that. Look, this isn't a good time." She bent back toward the window, but realized she wouldn't have enough leverage to open it again from the outside.

"I don't care. This is an emergency."

"Oh, yeah?" Awkwardly, Selene swung her backpack around her body and fished inside with her free hand until she found the length of rope she'd packed—just in case. "Another girl get out of your grasp? Now that they don't turn into trees anymore, I thought you'd have an easier time of it." Selene balanced the phone against her shoulder and made a quick loop in the rope. Above her, an exhaust pipe stuck through the brick. She slung the rope over and tightened the knot, praying the pipe would hold. "Why are you calling?"

"It's Mother. She's at New York-Presbyterian."

"The hospital?" Selene swayed a little, and only reflexes she'd thought she'd lost centuries before kept her from toppling off the ledge. She gripped the rope harder to steady herself.

"Yes. I'm here with her. You need to come soon. She's...she's fading."

Numbly, Selene pushed off from the wall and slid down the rope. At the bottom, she stood frozen, clutching the rope in one hand and her phone in the other.

When her twin brother spoke again, his voice, usually smooth and velvety, shook and cracked. "It has begun."

Chapter 8

THE SCHOLAR

Researching the cult ritual that might have inspired Helen's murder—and could provide the key to preventing others—was the best proof yet that myth and story mattered. Despite the sadness still shadowing him, Theo felt reborn. He was always searching for battles to fight, causes to champion. Now, for the first time, his knowledge could actually save lives. With a feeling of growing urgency, he jogged up the stairwell and into the Classics offices in Hamilton Hall.

"Theo!" He came to a resigned halt when an all-too-familiar voice called his name.

Nathan Balinski, short and broad, with a smattering of red freckles that kept him looking younger than his forty-odd years, called to him from down the hall. "Heard you were with Everett when he got the news. Rough, man. I guess I should call him or something, but you know I'm not the best shoulder to cry on." He took a swig of something from a tumbler. It looked suspiciously like scotch.

Theo suppressed a disgusted grimace. *That's an understatement— how could Nate, a man without morals, provide moral support to anyone?* Theo and Nate had known—and disliked—each other since grad school, where Nate, although nearly a decade older than his classmates, had spent most of his time stoned and drunk at Theo's roommate's orgiastic parties. When Theo inevitably slipped away from the revels, Nate had coined the nickname "Theo-bore," which he still let slip whenever he was feeling particularly dickish.

Theo felt the nearly unbearable urge to slug Nate in the face. Thankfully, Violet Macon, the office administrator, saved him from himself by waddling toward them, waving a copy of the *New York Post.*

"This is so horrible," she choked, passing the newspaper to Theo.

MURDER MOST FOUL! it blared, in an atypically literary headline over a front-page photo of Helen. Theo knew the shot— he'd taken it. She stood on the steps of the Metropolitan Museum of Art, her blond hair streaming, her smile so bright it outshone the sunlit marble around her. They'd gone together to the Greek and Roman galleries and laughed over the erotic vases like two undergrads. That afternoon, they'd made love for the first time.

"Yes," Theo said. "It's terrible." How many other ways were there to describe it? Dreadful. Shocking. *Nefarius. Horribilis.* No words of dismay would bring her back.

"You must be so upset." Violet's penciled brows drew together as she patted him on the shoulder. "I know how you felt about her."

"We *all* liked Helen," interjected Nate, unwilling to let Theo best him even in grief.

"Yes, but Theo *loved* her." Violet ignored Theo's wince. "Don't you remember, they dated for a year before Everett showed up? Now Theo, have you spoken to Bill yet? He's been calling everyone to see if they're all right."

"That's uncharacteristically sensitive of him." In Theo's eyes, Bill Webb never cared for anything except his own reputation. When the chairman was diagnosed with throat cancer a few years back, Theo had instantly regretted all the horrible things he'd said—or at least thought—about his boss. But Webb's illness had made him, if anything, even more of an asshole than ususal. "I haven't heard from him, no." *Unsurprising, since of everyone in the department, he likes me the least.*

Nate started to say something, but Theo wasn't in the mood to listen. He turned to go.

"I'll see you at the vigil tonight, all right, hon?" Violet called after him. "And the university's planning a memorial service for Sunday. Details are in the memo."

"Memo?"

"In your in-box. You know, the one you never check," she chided. Theo's determined resistance to all memos, meetings, and functions he considered purely administrative was the bane of Violet's existence.

He dutifully collected the unruly mountain of envelopes from his in-box, resting the *Post* on top of the pile. As he walked back to his office, Helen stared up at him from the newspaper. Memories of those first days with her came flooding back.

"Moments like this make me want to live forever," she'd purred, curled in his arms. Theo felt cold and hot all at once, sweaty where she pressed against him, chilled where the air conditioner panted against his back, fighting off the humid July heat.

"If life is so extraordinary, how can we bear to die?" she asked, suddenly serious.

"I don't think we have much of a choice," he'd murmured, tracing the perfect shell of her ear.

"But if we did, I'd stretch this moment, here with you, until the end of time," she went on.

"I'm not sure I'd want to live forever."

"Then I'd be like the Dawn. I'd tell Zeus to make my lover immortal, whether he wanted to be or not."

"So, like Tithonus, I'll grow older and older, and never die, until eventually I shrivel into a grasshopper? Then you can put me in a box and carry me around in your pocket." Theo made a convincing cricket chirp in her ear.

Helen sat up, flipped her hair out of her face, and frowned at him.

"I'm serious. I never want this to end."

"Okay."

"Okay? I say I want you to be with me for eternity and that's the best you can do?"

He laughed. "As a grasshopper? I doubt I'd live for eternity. If the lawnmower didn't get me, some Japanese food cart would."

"Okay, fine, what if I'm Selene instead, and I look down from the moon, and I see you lying here, my beautiful Endymion." She traced the valley of his chest with a finger. "And I grant you eternal sleep so you'll never age and never die."

"Better. You know how I hate waking up in the morning."

"You're always joking," she pouted. "You know it's part of why I love you, but it's a defense mechanism. You're too scared to say how you really feel."

"That's not true."

"Okay, then promise me we'll always be brutally honest with each other. Starting tonight. Tell me what you're thinking. Right now."

He couldn't stop himself from kissing the gentle curve of her breast. She pulled away.

"Don't *show* me. *Tell* me. I know you don't have a problem talking." True, he'd spent much of their lovemaking quoting Catullus.

I'm thinking that you scare me, he'd thought about saying. *You cling so tightly I feel sometimes like I'm a fig tree, and you're the strangler vine, using me to reach ever higher toward the sun.* But at the moment, her embrace felt pretty damn good. So instead, he said, "I'm thinking that maybe talking's overrated." He'd kissed away the rest of her protests.

Theo closed the door to his office and summarily tossed the contents of his in-box onto the floor. *I'd be your grasshopper now,* he thought, *if only it would bring you back.* He tore the front page off the *Post* and threw the rest of the newspaper into the recycling bin. Then he push-pinned Helen's picture above his desk, where it stared down at him like an icon at a shrine.

When she'd started dating Everett, Helen had been brutally honest, as promised. Theo had let her down, made her feel small, and she wanted someone else. Theo felt guilty about all of it—he should've just broken things off cleanly with Helen once he realized the relationship was doomed. Instead, he'd been too chicken to confront her. How could he tell her that she loved him *too* much? He hated sounding like a typical male—turned off by a "clingy" woman and afraid to commit. It was more than that—Helen's single-minded devotion to their relationship made him wonder if she was incapable of standing on her own two feet. He'd interpreted her intelligence and determination as strength, but the more tightly she clung to him, the weaker she appeared. So he'd pulled away gradually, unwilling to hurt her feelings, until she got fed up and left on her own. He'd been unsurprised that she'd found Everett so soon—it only confirmed his suspicions about her dependencies. Still, he couldn't help being a little hurt. It didn't feel good to be so easily replaced. Perhaps that's why he'd gone home with her that night. After barely seeing Helen for months, he'd run into her at Book Culture, one of the last independent bookstores left in a neighborhood once replete with them. She'd been picking up a fresh copy of the *Pocket Oxford Classical Greek Dictionary* (her copious annotations had made her original copy illegible), and he'd been browsing the science fiction section, looking for a new escapist adventure. A quick hug and a few self-deprecating jokes later, Theo found himself staring at her naked body while studiously avoiding looking at the ring on her finger. It'd been dumb and dishonorable—and they'd done it anyway. His stupid male ego.

couldn't help preening at the thought that she'd come back to his apartment because she wasn't satisfied with Everett. And for all her faults, Helen was a brilliant scholar and a beautiful woman. She was hard to resist.

Groaning, Theo pulled the photo back off the wall. For the first time in nearly a year, he allowed himself to feel angry with her. Not for leaving him, not for tempting him back again, but for abandoning him now. Barely aware of his actions, he tore the picture in half. Then he ripped it again, and again, until Helen's image lay in mangled fragments in his palm. Ashamed, he thrust the shreds into his desk drawer.

Theo turned his attention back to his research. Helen had focused much of her energy on deciphering and translating fragments of papyrus from the Oxyrhynchus horde. It was as good a place to start as any. There was no obvious correlation between the papyri and Greek cults, but with the Oxyrhynchus Project, anything was possible.

In 1896, two British Egyptologists had discovered a massive trove of over four hundred thousand papyri fragments buried in a rubbish heap at the site of the ancient Hellenistic city. Egypt's dry climate had allowed for the preservation of documents that would have moldered away two thousand years earlier in Greece or Italy. At first, elated archeologists were sure they'd uncovered the lost plays of Sophocles or the final works of Pythagoras. But before long, it became clear that most of the fragments, some no bigger than an inch across, were unreadable, blackened by exposure to minerals or damp. In a century of work, archeologists had succeeded in translating a mere four percent of the total horde.

But in 2005, new multispectral imaging technology revolutionized the field of papyrology, allowing for the decipherment of previously illegible texts. The researchers at Oxford had put the entire trove online so scholars all over the world could participate. Theo'd joined the project for a year, gaining instant acclaim for his uncanny ability to piece together the fragments with the same speed he'd shown reconstructing vases. For a while, at least, he'd enjoyed the mind-boggling game of ancient Tetris. But depressingly, most of the documents he translated were household accounts, tax receipts, and marriage contracts. The most interesting thing he'd ever translated: a deed for the purchase of a parcel of uncultivated land for twelve drachmae. A far cry from the earth-shattering discoveries he'd hoped for. The scholars at Oxford were loath to let his talents go, but Theo, who preferred to study myth and epic, had moved on. Helen, however, had never lost the conviction that the papyri held secrets worth learning. When she joined the faculty at Columbia, she'd already been working with the Oxyrhynchus Project for years. Theo had happily shared his own techniques with her and wished her luck on her search.

Theo pored over the project's recent publications. Perhaps the last year had uncovered new information on Aesculapian worship—the city of Oxyrhynchus had been a Greco-Roman society, and even as Christianity spread through Egypt in the fourth century AD, the inhabitants would have known about pagan cult ritual. But after reading for hours, Theo concluded that no such discovery had been made—at least not by the official project at Oxford. *That doesn't mean Helen didn't find something,* he reminded himself. She'd always been very secretive about her research, but she hinted often enough that she was keeping some revolutionary discoveries for inclusion in her first book.

Still, his reading wasn't a total waste. One thing caught his eye: a newly discovered version of the myth of Narcissus. In the familiar Roman tale as told by Ovid, the beautiful young man fell in love with his own reflection while resting beside a pool. Unable to tear his gaze from his own beauty, Narcissus eventually wasted away, disappearing mysteriously and leaving in his place only the bright narcissus flower that bore his name. Theo had never been able to walk by a daffodil without remembering the story. As he told his students, it symbolized the numbing death that occurs when an individual or a society embraces materialism rather than altruism. But in the recently discovered Greek version found in the papyri, Narcissus wailed and wept, violently stabbing himself; his blood seeped into the ground, where it transformed into the eponymous flower. *Violence hides behind the gentlest of myths, and there are always untold stories within stories, hidden meanings, and lost symbolism,* Theo reflected. *The early Greeks were far more bloodthirsty than their later Roman translators admitted.* The thought made his stomach twist. *What sinister findings did Helen uncover?*

Unfortunately, without access to her closely guarded research, he might never know. She'd always seen the ancient world a little differently than other archeologists. In her disregard for academic orthodoxy, Theo found a kindred spirit—he'd known they had a connection from the very first time they met, at a Classics faculty meeting two years earlier. As an archeologist specializing in the ancient world, Helen had attended, even though she wasn't technically a member of the department. Theo and Helen sat across the conference table from each other, listening as Martin Andersen launched into a typically soporific diatribe against the department's tolerance for substandard Latin grammar.

"To those who say our scholarship is slipping, well, there's a grain of truth there," Andersen intoned. "*Exempli gratia:* the use of *Salve* as the greeting on our web page. Even our freshmen know to use *Salvete* when addressing plural readers." He placed his hand over his heart, repeating somberly, "A grain of truth, I tell you"—and Helen's eyes met Theo's for the first time.

He'd smiled impulsively, and something in the quirk of her mouth made him glance toward Andersen and roll his eyes. A mean gesture perhaps—Martin was a harmless old coot—but Helen's ensuing grin made the sin worthwhile.

He doodled through the rest of the meeting, and when it finally ended, he handed her the product of his labors. A detailed cartoon of the professors in the conference room, each dressed as an Olympian. His best caricatures: Chairman Bill Webb as a stooped, peevish Zeus and Andersen in drag as a dour, bespectacled Demeter, Goddess of Agriculture, holding aloft a sheaf of wheat and saying "A *grain* of truth!" while the other gods snoozed around her. He'd cast himself as a caduceus-wielding Hermes: floppy fair hair, wire-rimmed glasses, pointed chin, and a mischievous smile. Not a bad representation. Helen, of course, was Aphrodite, perched on an overlarge scallop shell, sea foam spattering her long blond hair. As she took the paper, he was surprised to notice that her head barely reached his shoulders—something about her confidence had made her seem taller when she was sitting across the table. She took a long look at the drawing, then stood on her tiptoes to whisper in his ear, "Not bad. But I'm a better Persephone. Because I'm going to bring this department back to life." She walked away with a wink. He watched her go, noting the way her hair swayed in time to her light step.

Helen's prophecy proved true, at least for a time. She certainly gave Theo a whole new reason to attend faculty functions. But eventually, after she and Theo broke up, she grew so consumed by her research that she nearly disappeared. She'd stopped teaching undergrad classes entirely, confining her professorial duties to a single graduate seminar meeting once a week and spending most of her time either with Everett or in the library. She'd become something of a recluse, all the passionate intensity she'd once showered on Theo now transferred to her fiancé and to her pursuit of knowledge.

But what, exactly, had she discovered? Theo plowed back into his research, searching for information on human sacrifice within Aesculapian cult practices, but growing more disheartened by the minute. The connection with Helen's murder just didn't make sense. Most other gods in the Greek pantheon contained both benign and maleficent aspects. Asclepius's father, Apollo, for example, was known as both the Plague-Bringer and the Savior. His twin Artemis was the Stormy One and the Good Maiden. Even Athena—Goddess of Wisdom, Civilization, and Crafts—was also a Goddess of War. Asclepius, however, was an entirely benevolent deity. He was the Healer. Associating him with the murder of an innocent woman was simply nonsensical. On top of everything, no Greek cults were known to even involve human sacrifice in the first place. Bulls, goats, birds, sure. But people?

Theo's adrenaline leaked away. He found himself staring, glassy-eyed, at his computer screen, wondering if Gabriela was right and his research was merely an obsession to be used up and thrown away after a week or two, a distraction to stave off the grief that crouched just out of sight, ready to strike. How likely was it that the theft of a snake from the Natural History Museum correlated with a murder in Riverside Park? Had Helen really worn a chiton and a wreath? Maybe Selene DiSilva was just some delusional voyeur.

Theo rose from his battered desk chair and stretched. *Tea,* he thought. *I need very strong, very sweet tea if I'm going to keep this up.* As he moved toward the door, he knocked over the pile of papers from his in-box, sending them into a long fan across the floor. There, buried amid the memos, lay a small envelope addressed to "*Theodore*" in a minuscule, flowery script that only his long months of practice allowed him to easily decipher.

Theo picked up the envelope and sat back in his chair, his hands gone cold. How long ago had Helen left it? For half a second, he considered that he might be tampering with police evidence. Then he tore the envelope open.

Her usual stationery, with its gilt Greek *meandros* along the border.

> *Grasshopper—*
>
> *I've been working up an abstract of my book to present at the conference next month and I'd love to hear your thoughts on it. I'll send over the manuscript, but in the meantime I've enclosed a little preview. Enjoy the challenge.*
>
> *Syn philoteti,*
> *H*

In the bottom of the envelope lay four irregularly shaped paper scraps, each no more than two centimeters across. He dumped them on his desk. Ancient Greek covered each shred. *Xeroxes of papyri fragments from the Oxyrhynchus horde.*

There was no date on the letter, but from the memos surrounding it in the pile, he interpolated that Helen had probably left it for him five or six days ago. It was just like her not to send an e-mail or leave him a voice mail. For someone who'd made her reputation using new technology to piece together papyri, she had a surprisingly old-fashioned affinity for handwritten notes and fine stationery. "A thousand years from now, it only seems fair that some fool will have to piece together *my* thoughts from charred fragments of paper," she'd said once.

Theo spread the four paper fragments out so that the letters on each faced upward. *She hasn't called me Grasshopper since we broke up,* he thought, pushing together two fragments with matching shapes. *Why now?* Theo pushed away such questions—it was too easy to get pulled back into futile hypotheticals.

With only four small fragments to work with, it didn't take him long to string them together into the semblance of a sentence. Small holes scattered across the papyri made translation more challenging, and many of the letters were blurred beyond recognition. But that had never stopped him before. A few minutes later, he'd written down his best approximation:

ΟΡΩΤ_ΕΛΕΥΣ_ΚΑΙΤΩΝΙΕΡΩ___ΟΝΑΜΥΣ_ΗΣ

He stared at the second group of letters for a moment. "Eleus..." he said aloud. Then he glanced at the end. "Mus—es." After a moment, a slow smile spread across his face.

If he was right about the cultic connection with her murder, the words could only be *Eleusina mustes*. From there, he easily determined the full sentence:

Horō tēn Eleusina kai tōn hierōn gegona mustēs.

I see Eleusis. I have become a mystes *of the sacred things.*

He spun to his bookshelves, pulling down his copy of Burkert's *The Anthropology of Ancient Greek Sacrificial Ritual and Myth* and flipped to the chapter on the Eleusinian Mysteries. Like any classicist, Theo knew about the famous ritual, but he remembered it as a cult dedicated to Demeter, the Goddess of Grain, and her daughter Persephone, the Goddess of Spring—not to Asclepius. Still, it wasn't unusual for the larger cults to incorporate the worship of other, tangentially related deities. The gods were syncretic, after all; their numerous epithets and titles were reminders of the foreign deities they'd absorbed and the many, often contradictory, aspects they embodied. He skimmed ahead. Sure enough, one day of the rite had been devoted to Asclepius. And that wasn't the only correlation. The book said that the Mysteries at Eleusis had taken place in the early autumn: The timing matched up perfectly with Helen's murder. And Helen did have a thing about Persephone...

Theo flipped back to the beginning of the chapter. It explained that on the first day of the ritual, Demeter's priests processed to Athens, carrying with them two holy vessels—a *kiste* and a *kalathos*. Theo couldn't help a muttered, "Holy shitbuckets." The two stolen pots from the Met.

He called the front desk from his office phone. "Violet?"

"Just leaving, Professor."

"Hold up a sec. Did Helen leave a manuscript for me some-time this week?"

"Nope."

He cursed himself for his disorganization. "You sure?"

"Sure as sugar, hon."

"Do you know if she gave anyone a preview of the abstract she was working up for the conference?"

"I didn't hear anything about it. You know how she was about her research."

"I know. Like a miserly dragon defending her horde. You don't have keys to her office, do you?" Last year, as her work on Hellenistic sources grew more intense, she'd moved her office out of the Art History and Archeology Department and into Hamilton Hall to be closer to the classicists.

"Wouldn't do you any good if I did. The police were here, took a few boxes of stuff, and sealed it up already."

Theo dove back into his research, searching the Oxyrhyn-chus site for anything on Eleusis and coming up empty. Next, he tried to reconstruct the structure of the Eleusinian ritual from the available primary and secondary sources, many of which were overlapping and contradictory. Thankfully, piecing things together was one of Theo's many specialties. By four in the afternoon, scribbled outlines shrouded his desk and index cards plastered his walls.

Reaching into his pocket, he fingered the scrap of take-out menu with Selene DiSilva's number on it. He imagined her voice, calm and cold, then warming as he told her what he'd discov-ered. She'd been right about the Greek connection. Maybe they could work together to figure out who killed Helen, track him across the city, and bring him to justice. He felt a slight, anticipa-tory flutter. *Her with her silver eyes and fearsome hound, me with my glasses and teetering piles of books.* The image was ridiculous.

Who am I kidding? This whole situation is horrible enough without getting mixed up with some disturbed private investigator. The last time he'd felt such instant attraction to a woman had been with Helen. And now he knew how that had turned out.

He reached for a fresh index card and penned:

Selene DiSilva. Moon Goddess.

Probably deranged. Definitely dangerous.

Contact only if desperate.

DO NOT BE AN IDIOT.

He push-pinned it to the wall with a single angry jab, then sat there staring at it, still unable to banish the image of her glowing eyes.

Chapter 9

DEER HEART

In all her millennia of existence, Selene had never been to a hospital. She found the mortal struggle against death unbearable—the lingering, fruitless agony of medicines and surgeries and prayers. Even if they escaped this time, they would still die. Why bother fighting so hard? Selene had never been known as merciful, but she usually granted her victims a quick death. She'd never understood why mortals so often chose a slow, painful end. Yet now, here she was, walking into the lobby of New York-Presbyterian Hospital and asking the woman behind the reception desk, "Where can I find a patient named Leticia Delos?"

The receptionist glanced up briefly before returning her attention to her computer screen. "Are you a relation?"

Selene swallowed hard. "I'm her daughter."

The remark elicited no pity. The receptionist gestured curtly toward the correct elevator bank. "Room E 304."

The Huntress hadn't seen her mother in nearly two decades, even though she lived only a few hours away on Shelter Island, a small dollop of land floating between the two forks of Long

Island. Time passes strangely when you're immortal. What's twenty years among thousands? Like most children, Selene always meant to be better about visiting and somehow never got around to it as often as she'd have liked. And now it was too late.

"Mother," Selene whispered at the doorway of the hospital room. The woman now known as Leticia turned her head; Selene had to hold her breath to keep from crying. The smile that had stolen the heart of Zeus himself remained the same. But everything else had changed. Without her customary veil or scarf, her hair was visible—brittle and gray, cut short around her face in a fashion last stylish in about 1984. Her eyes, once as turquoise as the Aegean, were cloudy, her figure so shrunken and frail that it nearly disappeared within the hospital bed.

"Deer Heart," murmured the Mother of Twins. She held out a shaking hand.

Selene's legs felt like ice. She walked forward slowly and took her mother's hand in her own, aware of each fragile bone beneath the papery flesh.

"Hey, Moonshine," her twin brother said softly from the other side of the bed, where he sat limply in a plastic chair.

Selene flicked her eyes toward him. She hadn't seen Paul Solson—that was what Apollo called himself these days—in years, not since they'd inadvertently run into each other on the subway one evening. He'd been as radiant as usual—she'd watched the eyes of every woman, and many of the men, turn toward him. Even standing silently, the Bright One was powerfully charismatic. If he'd actually opened his guitar case and begun to play, he would've had to fend off the adoring masses with his silver bow. Instead, the Delian Twins had merely stared at each other across the subway car. They had never needed words. Silently, he asked for forgiveness. Silently, she refused. Their old rift remained unhealed. She got off at the next stop and had avoided the Lexington Avenue line ever since.

But today, no one would've looked twice at the God of Light and Music. His golden hair, usually so bright, fell in dim, defeated curls across his forehead. Without his usual air of cavalier arrogance, he looked vulnerable, small. His shoulders slumped beneath his designer blazer and tastefully shabby T-shirt.

"What are you doing here, Mother?" Selene asked. There was no point in bringing a deity to a hospital. No mortal medicine would have any effect on her ailment.

The Gentle Goddess squeezed her hand—the touch as light as that of a bird's wing. "My neighbor got worried when he hadn't seen me in a few days, so he called the police." She spoke as if every word were an effort. "You will make sure my patients are taken care of, won't you? I hate to abandon them like this."

"I already did it, Mother," Paul interjected. "I called another midwife and made sure she'd take your clients. You need to worry about yourself now." He turned to his sister. "The idiots in that hospital out on Long Island couldn't figure out what was wrong with her. They were getting all these crazy readings on the lab results so they had her transferred here. The morons are totally stymied."

"Mother, why didn't you call before now? I would've come and stayed with you so you wouldn't have to come to this horrible place."

"I couldn't bear the thought of my children sitting by my deathbed and waiting for something which could happen in a matter of days, or years, or centuries. Then this morning..."

She left the rest unsaid. Selene realized that Leticia wouldn't have called her children to her side if she weren't sure that the end was very near. They had little time left together in this world. But what does one say to the mother who has loved you for over three thousand years? Paul was the poet, the musician. Perhaps he knew the right words. Selene felt only anger.

"I don't like you being here—these doctors treating you like a lab rat," she said sternly, her eyes on her mother's wan face. Leticia merely smiled gently as if to say she didn't mind. Selene turned to her twin. "Didn't you try to get her out of here?"

"Don't give me that look. I'm not some nymph who cowers under your glare. I tried, okay? The hospital won't release her without a whole lot more testing and paperwork."

Selene sat gingerly on the edge of the bed, careful not to tug on any of the IV tubes and electric wires running from her mother's flesh to a bank of computers. "I want to pull these out," she said, her voice low and dangerous as she watched the oscillating green line of her mother's heartbeat—too slow and too weak—on a nearby monitor. "They're not doing you any good."

"I already tried it," Paul said. "The doctors will come running, put them all back in, and then threaten to call the cops."

"I'll put an arrow through them before they can stop me."

"Do us all a favor and don't go crazy, okay? All this time and you still don't know how to act around mortals. You can't just kill anyone you want to. It doesn't work that way anymore."

"Well, then, I miss the good old days," Selene shot back. "When we could kill with impunity."

"You killed. I healed," Paul sniffed.

"And how's that going?" she snarled. "Do something, Apollo!"

Her twin flinched at the use of his real name. It was a terrible breach of etiquette—it not only put him in danger of exposure, but also still carried some power of compulsion. An immortal did not use it lightly.

"Medicine now is nothing like the craft I practiced." He gestured angrily to the monitors and tubes. "I can no more heal a person by laying hands on them than you can control the phases of the moon. We've all lost our powers, *Artemis*."

Selene would've struck him but for the sudden tightening of Leticia's hand on her own. Her mother gave her a pleading look. "Please, it brings me such comfort to have you both here." She didn't say that it also brought her great pain to see them still at odds, but Selene knew it did.

Leticia slowly raised her bony arm and laid her hand upon her daughter's smooth black hair, tucking a stray strand behind her ear. "Your hair..." she said. "You haven't had to cut it again, have you?"

Selene shook her head. In one of the strange side effects of immortality, her cells died so rarely that her hair hardly grew. She'd cut the long tresses into a bob in the 1920s, and it had remained short ever since.

"Good," Leticia said. "It may be my time, but not you, not yet."

"Don't say that. I know you'll get better."

"Don't wish for the past. I've lived as a mortal for many years now. It's fitting that I should die as one."

"What do you mean?" Selene asked.

"The fading started centuries ago. First a gray hair. Then a few wrinkles." She paused to catch her breath. "Then sometimes years would go by and I would feel no change."

"I, too, have aged over the years."

"Not like I have. I'm no Olympian. Merely a Titan. A minor deity. For a while now, life has sped up. I live it now at the pace of a thanatos, growing older each time I look in the mirror. My time is over."

"No, Mother," Selene said, her voice thick. "I won't accept that."

Leticia chuckled faintly. "I don't think you have the power to stop time anymore. I doubt you ever did. There's nothing you can do."

Selene wanted to tell her mother about her experience at Schultz's apartment. Her balance, her hearing—if those powers were back, why not her other attributes? Yet she couldn't give her mother false hope. The morning's adventure must have been a fluke. The fading might progress at a different pace for each deity, but Selene had never heard of it actually *reversing*. Once a goddess lost her abilities, they were gone for good.

A nurse came into the room carrying a paper cup of pills. Selene started to protest, but Leticia dutifully swallowed the medicine with a small smile for her daughter.

"Your mother has very restricted visiting hours," the nurse said, not unkindly, as Leticia's eyes fluttered closed. "She needs her rest. You can come back tomorrow."

Selene met her brother's eyes. She felt his frustration mirroring her own. Who was this mortal to tell them to leave Leticia's bedside? And yet, who were they any longer to protest? As one, they kissed their mother on each cheek and left the room.

In the hallway, Paul walked ahead of her for a few steps, his shoulders thrown back and chin high. Then he teetered to a stop and slumped against the wall, his face buried in his arm. When he turned to her, his golden-brown eyes were full of tears. "She's dying. Just like Pan and Eos and Asclepius. And the nymphs. No one left to worship them. All their power gone. Back into the Khaos from which we all sprang."

Selene turned away from him, refusing to break beneath the emotions buffeting her, even as her own eyes welled. She would not show pity or weakness in front of her twin. So she clung to her ancient anger against him, letting it burn off some of her grief. "No one to worship her! How dare you say that! She has you and me, doesn't she? Have we not always paid homage to the mother who bore us?"

"You never even visit her." The Bright One's anger leaped to meet her own, their flames feeding each other, as they always had. "She came all the way to America to be close to you, and you've spent the last four hundred years protecting mortal women who don't even know your name, instead of looking out for Mother."

"That's my *job*."

"If she dies, it will be your fault."

Selene punched him, hard, on the corner of his jaw. A nurse at a nearby desk gaped and leaped to her feet. "You need to leave this hospital *immediately*, or I'm calling security!"

Selene ignored the nurse long enough to watch the red welt along Paul's chin swiftly fade away, leaving his golden skin flawless once more. "I see you're still healing just fine," she sneered, thinking of the bruise on her jaw from her fight with Mario Velasquez. Without makeup, it would be a bright red reminder of her own continued vulnerability.

"What's that supposed to mean?"

"It means our mother's dying and you've somehow got the key to eternal youth. We're twins and I look ten years older than you. Explain that."

The nurse moved toward them. "I'm going to have to insist!"

Selene spun on her heel and headed toward the elevators, Paul hissing behind her, "The worship of sun and music are still strong, you know that. But death is coming for all of us. Even for me."

"Don't be absurd. They may not call me the Unwithering One anymore, but none of the *Twelve* has ever actually died." *Wanted to, maybe,* she thought, remembering yesterday's feeling of hopelessness by the river, *but never done it.* She jabbed the elevator call button.

"No? Look." He pulled a piece of paper from the tight pocket of his jeans, unfolded it, and thrust it toward her. Selene grudgingly stepped closer. A single white hair, many yards long, lay on the paper in a tight loop.

She drew a deep breath. "Who?" she asked finally.

"The Eldest," he said, using the ancient epithet for Zeus's oldest sibling—Hestia, Goddess of the Hearth.

"No one's seen her since the final Gathering. How did you get this?"

"The Smith. Kronos knows, I never had anything to say to the Eldest—she was always such a boring prude of a woman, but I guess the Smith bonded with her over their love of fire. I happened to be in Casablanca last week—"

"You were?"

"I was on tour to promote my new album," Paul said, as if she should've known.

"I don't read your *blog*, okay?"

"Do you even have a computer?"

"No. Get to the point, Paul."

"I don't like to travel abroad without arrows. Unlike you, I refuse to use those cheap wood pieces of crap, so I needed to find the Smith. You'd think a cripple would be easy to catch up with, but he's a tricksy little gimp."

"You know, for the God of Poetry, sometimes you're remarkably crass."

"Poetry died a slow death a long time ago."

"But rock and roll is here to stay, right?"

"No, that's what I'm trying to say," he said, deadly serious. "*Nothing* is here to stay. Not even us."

"If we fulfill our traditional roles and protect the realms assigned us, we should retain at least some measure of immortality—that's how it's always been, at least for the Twelve. You play music, I hunt predators. We live on."

"You're not listening. It may not be enough anymore. When I finally caught up with the Smith, he told me he was worried about our aunt, so he took me to the Eldest's little hideaway. I think we were in Tunisia, who knows. Terrible place. The whole thing's like a furnace, maybe that's why she likes it there."

"And?"

"There she was in this hut, sitting by the fire—of course—and just staring at it, like she always did. It was burning up outside. Over a hundred. The hut was sweltering, but she just kept stirring the damn coals. Trying to be the Goddess of the Hearth, as always. But her hair. It was so long."

"It's always been long," Selene interrupted.

"Not like this. It hung down her back, to the ground, and it never stopped. It coiled. Around the walls. Around her stool, around the fire. Yards and yards and yards of it, like it'd been growing for a century. And all of it was white. Every strand."

The elevator finally arrived. They got in beside a nurse and her charge. Selene was grateful for their presence—it meant she didn't have to respond to Paul's revelation—but she couldn't bear to look at the patient, a wizened infant in a large wheelchair. Her flesh looked like paper that had been crumpled and smoothed out again, over and over until the slightest breeze would tear it to shreds.

"I won't do it. I won't become that," Paul said, trembling, as they moved through the lobby.

"The Eldest wasn't really one of the Twelve, you know," Selene insisted. "She gave up her seat to the Wine Giver, remember?"

"Of *course* I remember. But still, she was an Olympian once and now she's *dying*. Man stopped worshipping her long ago, but at least they revered the hearth for another fifteen hundred years. Not anymore. Now it's all central heating and LEDs. She might try to play out her old role, but it's not enough anymore."

Selene kept walking. "Don't worry, Brother."

"Don't tell me what to feel. I *am* worried."

The door to a large black Suburban parked in front of the hospital swung open. A pretty young woman launched herself out of the car and into Paul's arms. "Oh, honey, is everything okay?" she cooed, kissing his cheek.

Paul kissed the girl back. "Sophie, this is my sister. Selene, this is my muse."

Selene took in the girl's outfit—a torn crepe skirt that barely brushed the top of her thighs, tall motorcycle boots, an expensive cardigan—and rolled her eyes. Little rich girl trying to look edgy for the indie-rock musician. *His muse, indeed.* Had Paul so easily forgotten the real Muses? Their nine half sisters, goddesses of inspiration and art? They were probably long dead by now, but calling pallid Sophie by their name was the height of disrespect.

Three young men emerged from the SUV, hipsters with unfortunate facial hair and conspicuously large glasses. Paul introduced them in turn: his bassist, drummer, and keyboardist. Each patted Paul on the arm or shoulder, as if unable to keep their hands off him, demonstrating an unmistakably slavish devotion to their frontman. Paul's manager unfolded himself from the front seat, significantly better dressed in slim trousers and a button-down. He took a headset out of his ear and nodded dismissively to Selene. "Paul, we're running late, buddy. You've got a sound check in twenty."

Selene shook her head at her brother. "I told you not to worry about a lack of worship anytime soon."

Paul gestured for his entourage to get back into the car. "It's not the same thing, and you know it," he said, turning his back on their adoring faces. "And it's certainly not going to help Mother. But I'm not going to let her die. I'll do whatever it takes."

"You're saying I won't?"

"I'm just saying you may not have the strength. The worship of sun and music continues, but hunting…"

"Leave it." She turned to go.

"You may despise me for what I did two and half *thousand* years ago, but you're still my other half."

"Do you even remember?" she hissed, spinning toward him. "Or has the memory of your treachery faded, along with so much else? I *wish* it would fade for me. But it's still here." She jabbed a finger into her temple. "And here." She struck her chest. "A bright, sharp blade honed by centuries of retelling. Every time I see you, it's like I've been stabbed all over again. I came across an ocean to be rid of you, and you followed me here. I know if I moved again, you'd just keep tracking me. You and all your damn *groupies*. So *please*. It's the one thing I ask of you—leave me the fuck alone."

Chapter 10

THE DETECTIVE

"I know when and where Helen's murderer will strike next," Theo began after an officer had shown him to Detective Brandman's desk in the precinct house.

The cop turned away from his computer monitor and raised his eyebrows in a gesture halfway between curiosity and skepticism. He folded his hands on his desk beside the orderly stacks of files. "Whoa there. Who are you again?"

"Theo Schultz. I was with Everett Halloran yesterday."

"Right. The other professor. And what's your relationship to the victim exactly?"

I should tell him, Theo thought. But it was none of the cops' business, was it? His relationship with Helen was long over. And as for that one illicit night in her bed...better no one knew about that. The last thing Everett needed was more grief.

"We were colleagues. Good friends."

"Um-hum. And you think you know about our killer? Interesting. I'm listening."

Theo placed his own bursting folder of notes on the desk and announced, "There's a cult attempting to reenact the Eleusinian

Mysteries, and their next ritual takes place *tonight*, so we better get moving."

The detective ran a hand across the gray stubble shadowing his chin and blinked his bloodshot eyes. Theo felt no pity: He, too, had spent the whole day researching the case. "You're going to need to start from the beginning, Professor," Brandman said wearily. "A *cult*? Like Hare Krishna or something?"

"Neither so amusing nor so innocuous, I'm afraid. The Greeks took their cults extremely seriously. Nearly everyone belonged to at least one. There were cults devoted to each different god, each with its own rites that only initiates were allowed to know. That's why we call them 'Mystery Cults,' from *mysterion*, meaning 'secret ritual.' The one in the Greek city of Eleusis was the most popular Mystery Cult in the ancient world, and I believe Helen got mixed up in a group trying to bring it back."

He could tell from the way Brandman kept glancing back at his computer that he'd already determined the theory was a waste of time. Theo wasn't used to having his ideas so summarily dismissed. On the way to the precinct house, he'd imagined the cops' gratitude when they realized Theo had solved the case. A call from the commissioner maybe. A thank-you note from the mayor. Instead, Brandman merely demanded, with thinly disguised impatience, "Where are you getting this from?"

"From Helen. I found a note she left for me." Theo flipped open one of his files and handed Brandman the letter. "She was writing a book on the Eleusinian Mysteries."

The detective scanned the note. "And this manuscript she talks about—"

"I never got it. Maybe you found it in her office?"

Brandman ignored the question. "So what do you know about this supposed cult?"

"A lot. Also—nothing."

The cop grimaced, but Theo kept going before he could interrupt. "Some of the rites were public, but most were reserved for initiates only. If you dared to reveal the climax"—he drew a finger across his throat—"*snnnnnnnk*. So no one blabbed. Hundreds of thousands of initiates participated over almost *two thousand* years, even after Christianity took hold. Yet all that time, not a peep."

The cop dropped the letter into a file folder of his own. "I see." A young black woman in a suit vest and shoulder holster approached the desk, but Brandman waved her off with a "this will only take a second" gesture. He frowned at Theo. "I've got work to do, Mr. Schultz, so I hope you're about to explain how a ritual you know nothing about is relevant to the Emerson case."

Despite Brandman's clear disdain, Theo smiled. He'd made a whole career out of explaining the modern pertinence of long-dead civilizations. "Never underestimate a classicist. Scholars have pieced together an impressive amount from the various sources that allude to the Mysteries." He pulled a calendar from his files, each day crowded with notes, and pointed to Monday. "Here's where the cult ritual begins. Day One. Traditionally, this is when the priests carry the cult's Sacred Objects from Eleusis to Athens."

"Sacred objects?"

"Yup, the *hiera*. Can't have a cult without them. Try to think of them like the saintly relics Catholics keep in cathedrals: holy objects only revealed on special occasions and believed to have supernatural properties. We don't know what the Eleusinian *hiera* were exactly, but they might have included a clay model of a vulva."

"And you think they cut out Helen Emerson's—"

"Yes, exactly."

Theo knew the cop was hooked when he deigned to pick up a pen and make a few notes of his own.

"That's not all," Theo went on. "The priests need special containers to transport the *hiera*. On Monday night, I believe the cult members robbed the Met Museum and stole two pieces of ancient pottery for that purpose." He paused, waiting for Brandman to make the connection.

Instead, the cop just beetled his brows. "We have absolutely no evidence tying the Met robberies to Helen Emerson."

"Tell me exactly which artifacts were stolen and I'll prove it to you. I bet anything they were a *kiste* and a *kalathos*, but the press reports didn't specify."

"A what and a what?"

"A chest and a basket, like the special containers used in the original Mystery."

"You'd have to speak to the Nineteenth Precinct. It's not my case."

"Not your case!" Theo said too loudly. "You think the burglaries of ancient Greek specimens from two major New York museums and the murder of an archeologist in the same week are unrelated?"

Above his mustache, Brandman's cheeks flushed red. "*Two* museums? If you're referring to the Natural History—"

"Day Three," Theo interrupted, jabbing at his calendar and ignoring the detective's sour scowl. "They called it 'Seawards Initiates.' The Eleusinian initiates bathe in the ocean—like a baptism. That's when Helen was killed. The cult members didn't just *dump* the body in the river, they put it there as part of a ritual seawater purification. The Hudson's really a tidal estuary. It's partly salt water."

Brandman tossed down the pen, rolled his chair back a few inches, and crossed his arms. "A tidal estuary. Huh."

Theo pressed on. "And here's the Natural History connection. Last night, someone broke in, and did they steal the Star of India sapphire or a priceless fossil of a feathered dinosaur? Nope. Just an Aesculapian rat snake. That's preparation for tonight, Day Five of the ritual: the *Asklepia*, a celebration in honor of the medicine god, Asclepius."

The young female detective approached once more, this time handing Brandman a piece of paper. While he read the note, she looked pityingly down at Theo, as if she'd sat on that side of the desk before and understood how frustrating it could be.

Brandman read the note, nodding. "Thank you, Detective Freeman. We're almost done here." He checked his watch before returning his attention to Theo. "Your friend Everett Halloran's alibi checked out. He was at the office that night, seen by a few other professors. Where were *you* two nights ago?"

"In my apartment. Grading papers."

"Anyone to corroborate that?"

"I live alone."

The detective raised an eyebrow. "The forensic report comes back tomorrow. Detective Freeman just made contact with one of Miss Emerson's other colleagues. I need to leave in a few minutes, Professor. But before I do, let me get this right. Has this cult of yours ever been associated with murder?"

"Well, no, not originally," Theo admitted. "All surviving Greek texts describe severe societal proscriptions against human sacrifice."

"And how long has it been since this cult's even existed?"

Theo shifted a little in his seat. "About sixteen hundred years."

Brandman rolled forward and rested his elbows on the desk so he could lean closer to Theo. "So *why* would they want to kill a nice girl like Helen Emerson?"

"Because the Mysteries weren't just a random religious festival. They were *life-changing*. The great philosopher Cicero wrote that among all the divine institutions that Athens contributed to human life, the Eleusinian Mysteries were the best. Considering the accomplishments of the Athenian Golden Age, that's saying a lot. Supposedly, the secret climax of the ritual answered mankind's greatest questions: how life began, how to live happily, and how to die well. Those are the same questions we're still asking today. They're the fundamental basis of our religion, philosophy, poetry—*everything*. So if Helen had somehow uncovered what those answers were..."

"Killed over a secret that hasn't mattered for thousands of years?" Brandman gave him an incredulous look. "Or are you saying some classicist murdered her over academic jealousy?"

"It's not that simple. They might have thought—"

"You keep saying *they*." Brandman said with an angry wave of his hand. "We have no evidence that there's more than one killer at this time."

"It's *got* to be a 'they.' These cults usually have a priest—a hierophant—leading the ritual, but they're all about group-think. Otherwise it's like an *American Idol* where Ryan Seacrest is the only guy in the audience. Cults don't work if it's just one initiate."

"This sounds like a conspiracy theory." From his tone, Theo could tell the cop suspected he was one more crackpot in a city full of them. "When you walked in here, you told me you knew where to find the killer. So get to the point, Professor."

"My pleasure." He smothered his growing frustration and gave Brandman an earnest smile. "Tonight is the feast of Asclepius, when the initiates ask for magical healing dreams. They sleep in a cave with a sacred well, not far from Asclepius's Temple. *That's* where we'll find them."

"Mm-hmm." Brandman gave him a cold smile. "I see. You're saying we need to find a cave. Near a well. Near a temple."

"Exactly."

"Fine. Come back when you find one within a fifty-mile radius of New York."

"But Detective—"

With a grunt of frustration, Brandman pulled a photo from a folder and tossed it onto the desk. Theo's words died in his mouth. Helen—splayed across a slab of gray rock. A yellow sheet covered her breasts, but the rest of her body lay revealed. He saw only a glimpse of the bloody desecration between her legs before he looked away.

Brandman said nothing for a long moment, but Theo could feel the cop's small eyes boring into him. "This isn't some academic exercise, Professor," he said finally. "It isn't about philosophical pondering about life and death in another era—it's about *real* life. And *real* death. *Today*."

Theo swallowed hard and looked back at the photo. The sheet was pinned on one of Helen's shoulders. "Was there another pin in the sheet?" he asked. Traditional chitons were secured on both sides of the body.

Brandman guffawed, then shook his head incredulously. "You're staring at the mutilated body of young woman and *that's* your first question?"

"Well?"

"No. There was no other pin."

Strange, but that didn't prove anything. "What kind of plants are those?" Theo pointed at the foliage in Helen's matted hair. Selene DiSilva was right—it did look like a wreath. "Bay leaves?"

"Yes. So?"

"So?" Theo snapped. "Don't you see?"

"I see that botany is another one of your areas of supposed expertise. What of it?"

"We call them bay leaves, but Greeks call them laurel. The laurel wreath is specifically associated with Apollo. Since Asclepius was Apollo's son, this only corroborates my Eleusis theory."

"My turn to teach you something, Professor. Cops call it 'confirmation bias.' Once you've got a theory in mind, everything you see backs it up. It's a delusion. So as amusing as I'm finding all this—"

"Late-night comedy is *amusing*. Cat videos are *amusing*." Theo wasn't sure when he'd stood up, but he found himself leaning over the desk, close enough for the detective's cologne to assault his nose. "Bumbling cops who don't know a good lead when they see one—that, too, might be considered *amusing*. But the fact that bay laurels only grow in the Mediterranean, so those leaves didn't just drift into Helen's hair, they were *put* there by her killer—that's deadly serious."

Brandman stood. His jacket fell open, revealing the leather corner of a shoulder holster. Theo took a step back, instantly regretting his belligerence. The cop's mustache twitched with a hint of a sneer. "On behalf of the NYPD, I thank you for your academic insight. We'll pursue every lead, I assure you. We'll be working on this case to the utmost of our ability and hope to have it resolved shortly."

Theo wondered what sensitivity training course that line had come out of. He handed Brandman his annotated calendar. "At least take this. You're going to need it."

The detective put the calendar in a folder without looking at it further. "I can assure you that if, in the course of the investigation, we happen to find a bunch of guys meditating in some cave with your stolen snake, I'll let you know." He started shutting down his computer.

"You're still missing the point," Theo said between clenched teeth. He knew it was useless to keep arguing, but what choice did he have? "In the *original* Mysteries, they would've just dreamed and feasted. But if this new cult killed someone for a ritual as innocuous as the seawater purification, think what they might try next. The ritual goes on for *ten* days, and we're only on Day Five. Every day the ceremony becomes more intense, until the final climax. We need to catch them *now*."

"Agreed. He might kill again. Which is why you need to leave."

"Maybe I could look through the stuff you took from Helen's office? See if her manuscript is—"

"Time to go, Mr. Schultz. If we need an expert in dead languages and dead snakes, we'll know where to find you."

Selene DiSilva warned me the cops might not be up to the task, Theo thought as he watched Brandman and Detective Freeman get into a black sedan and pull away. Now he realized the extent of her understatement. But if he had to find Helen's killer on his own, he would.

Across the street from the precinct house, the banner of a public library flapped in the wind. Mothers toting young children, old men with canes, and teenagers with suspiciously thin backpacks all made their way up the concrete steps and into the nondescript beige building, seeking knowledge...or at least Internet access.

Libraries... Theo mused. Nothing in that building would help his quest, but he knew a librarian whose assistance might be invaluable. As he started toward the subway that would take him back to Columbia, he called the Metropolitan Museum of Art's Greek and Roman Collection.

"Come on, you're saying you can't tell me what happened over there?" he begged Steve Atwood, a staff researcher who worked in the museum's Onassis Library for Hellenic and Roman Art. Over the years, Steve and Theo had worked together many times, building a friendship based as much on their shared fondness for eighties science fiction as on Theo's invaluable assistance translating the collection's manuscripts. "Was there any weird evidence of cult ritual during the robbery? Laurel leaves left behind maybe?"

"Sorry, Theo. We're all under a strict code of silence about the details of the burglary. They're afraid of copycats."

"At least tell me what kind of pottery they took."

"Can't do it."

"Wait a sec. You're the one who once 'borrowed' a third-century Greek terracotta of a satyr head to use as a prop in your latest webisode, and you're telling me you can't bend a few rules?"

"It was only a Roman *copy* of a Greek terracotta. But I see your point." Steve lowered his voice. "The stolen items weren't on display, I'll tell you that. Whoever broke into the storerooms knew how to get through some pretty tight security—or they had a connection on the inside. The whole thing's a huge embarrassment, that's really why they're being so hush-hush. Afraid to stain our 'institutional reputation.'"

"And?"

"And what? I'm not supposed to tell you *anything*, remember?"

"I'll make you a deal. Give me the details and I'll help on your next film."

"Really? I'm doing an homage to *Land of the Lost* next and I need a *Tyrannosaurus rex*."

"I'm your man."

"Let me hear it."

"What?"

"Your dinosaur, of course."

"You are such an asshole," Theo grumbled. He attempted his best screeching roar.

"More like a dying housecat, but you'll get better once you've got the costume on."

"No doubt. So the artifacts..."

Steve's voice dropped to a whisper. "One was a bell-krater, pretty valuable." Theo felt a twinge of disappointment. A large, two-handled vase shaped like an upside-down bell was nothing like a *kiste* or a *kalathos*.

Steve went on. "I'm not sure about the other one, but I get the impression it wasn't very interesting. I swear I don't know anything else."

"Then who does?"

Steve gave an exasperated groan. "Okay, fine. I'll talk to the curator and see if I can get you photos. Since you've helped us out before, they might make an exception. I'll have to do some major sucking up on your behalf first, so you're just going to have to be patient. It might take until tomorrow. If they relent, I'll messenger the pictures over to your office."

"Messenger? Talk about *Land of the Lost*. What sort of prehistoric operation are you all running over there? Can't you just e-mail me a scan?"

"Don't look at me. They don't want any traceable Internet chatter about the details because they're worried about hackers selling the information to the black market. And I'm putting my ass on the line for you here, so your *T. rex* better be good."

"I'm working on waving my midget forearms right now."

Chapter 11

THE OLYMPIAN

At the 168th Street subway station, a few blocks from the hospital, Selene leaned back against a steel girder and closed her eyes, trying to steady herself after the encounter with her family. Seeking to wipe away the memory of her mother's frailty, she willed herself to remember her sacred grove instead: the forest at Ephesus. The tops of the tall cypress trees whispered in the wind, creating a natural wall around the spring-fed pool, their scent banishing the odor of hospital antiseptic that clung to her clothes. The soft swish of willow fronds dabbling their leaves in the water replaced the memory of beeping heart monitors. The image of her sleek hounds rolling in the grass brought a smile to her face where before there had been only sadness.

But she couldn't keep the sacred grove before her eyes. One memory supplanted another. The waving cypresses gave way to the marble halls of her home on Olympus, where she'd spent her childhood in her mother Leto's loving embrace. It was there that mother and daughter had fought for the first and final time.

I push open the high wooden doors of our home with a strength that belies my childish frame. Skipping with joy, I rush to find my mother where she sits in the courtyard, a sunbeam illuminating the distaff in her hands. As she turns to greet me, her dark veil slides askew. Her hair, a thick river of burnished chestnut, catches the sun's glow before she tugs the veil back into place.

"I have been with Father," I announce proudly. A shadow crosses my mother's face, but her smile never falters.

"He has granted me six wishes. His love for me knows no bounds."

"Indeed?" she asks calmly, turning her attention to the golden thread wound around her spindle. "And what has mighty Zeus promised you?"

"A bow like Apollo's, but gold instead of silver." I raise my arms into an archer's stance, already feeling the weight of the bow in my hands. "To roam the wild and hunt all my days." I glance around the marble courtyard with its careful mosaics and I yearn for escape.

"Won't you be lonely?" my mother asks gently.

I scowl at her. "Of course not! I have wished for more epithets than any other Olympian. And when my own names cannot keep me company, Father has given me maiden nymphs to hunt at my side. And animals, too—a pack of lop-eared hounds to join in the chase and wide-antlered stags to pull my chariot."

My mother chuckles. "And what was your final wish, my little Huntress?"

I do not hesitate.

"To remain eternally chaste."

The distaff clatters to the ground. My mother's soft turquoise eyes flash with unaccustomed anger. "You have chosen a hard life for yourself, child."

I cross my arms across my chest. "Harder than being forced into a loveless marriage, like Aphrodite's to crippled Hephaestus? Harder than being chased across the world by a jealous wife, as you were?"

"Aye, child." My mother stands and looks down upon me. I try to stand up taller so I might look her in the eye, but her anger cows me. "I was chased," she says. "Hounded mercilessly by Hera's fury. But in the end, was not my struggle worth it? I knew the love of Zeus, King of the Gods, Lord of the Sky. I have you. And your brother. The greatest happiness a woman can ever experience. Will you give that up?"

"I know what I'm doing, Mother. I give it up in return for a far greater joy."

"You're only a child! What do you know of life's pleasures?"

"I am a goddess! An Olympian!"

Mother bites her lip and sinks once more onto her stool. "Yes, an Olympian." She picks up her distaff and slowly rewinds the unraveled thread. "And so, like your father, you'll never question the rightness of your actions. You act for your own pleasure, your own whims, like the rest of them." All the anger is gone from her voice. "I thought perhaps—as my daughter—you would be different."

I kneel at her feet and lean my head upon her knee. I will not ask for forgiveness and I do not regret what I have done—not for an instant. But her sadness strikes like an arrow in my breast. After a moment, her gentle hands brush the hair from my forehead, and she presses a kiss against my temple. "I see now you are your father's child. I only hope you might remember that you are mine as well."

Now, so many years later, Selene couldn't get the conversation out of her head. Leto had never alluded to it again, and her devotion to her daughter had never wavered. But deep in her heart, Selene always knew that she'd disappointed her mother in some fundamental way—not by remaining childless (her brother Apollo had provided plenty of grandchildren), but by denying herself love. Her mother had been right—when the nymphs and forests had been destroyed by an age of plastic and wavelengths, Selene was left to pass the centuries in solitude. But about one thing at least, Leto had been wrong. Selene did feel guilt. Sometimes it seemed it was all she *could* feel. And now, with Leto dying, that guilt only grew heavier. She had not made her mother proud. And now she never would.

In the subway station, a stifled shriek ripped her from her memories. She spun toward the sound like a lioness catching the scent of prey. Nearly sixty feet away, on the far end of the opposite train platform, stood a thickset man in a Yankees sweatshirt. His bulk blocked her view, but she glimpsed a pair of delicate high heels just beyond him. Standing in the lee of a steel column, the man no doubt thought he was safe. They always did. Even an alert cop might not have noticed anything amiss.

It was one in the afternoon. The station should have been packed with workers on break, rushing to lunch dates or doctor's appointments or snatched moments at the gym. Instead, due to a lucky chance, the platform stood nearly empty. Even so, under normal circumstances, Selene would never hunt her prey in the light of day. Back alleys and darkened parks were her usual stomping grounds. But with her mother near death, the normal rules of Selene's existence no longer applied. Her heart began to pound, banishing the cold fear that had settled in her gut back at the hospital. *Maybe this morning wasn't a fluke. Maybe I'm really the Punisher again, not just a counterfeit pretending to epithets I no longer deserve.*

The faint vibrations in her feet told her that a downtown train was still at least a stop away, and she could hear an uptown train on the opposite track, even farther. Fifty yards down the platform, a security camera's eye shone knowingly. She ducked behind a column and assembled her bow. She nocked a shaft to the string and stood so only the arrowhead peeked out from behind the column. She couldn't see to aim. But unlike Selene DiSilva, the Far Shooter had never missed. *Here goes,* she thought, visualizing the camera. She breathed in, then out, to steady her hands, and let the arrow fly. A faint tinkling of glass was her reward. She jogged down the platform to retrieve the fallen arrow, unable to wipe the grin from her face, and stuffed the shaft and bow into her bag.

A murmur of protest from across the track drew her attention. The thickset man stepped closer to his companion, who cringed before him. Selene leaped down onto the track. Deftly avoiding the electrified third rail, she crossed all four tracks in a few graceful leaps. Bracing one hand on the far platform, she swung onto it effortlessly, landing just out of the station agent's sight.

She sprinted silently toward the couple; she could already see the big man's arm drawn back, ready to strike.

In an instant, Selene was beside him, grabbing his fist with her own.

He gave a grunt of surprise. His muscles bulged as he fought to free himself, but her grip held firm, her weakness in the face of Mario Velasquez a dim memory.

Selene could see the woman clearly now, her mascara smeared under tired eyes, limp orange hair falling in choppy bangs across her forehead, tight tank top barely concealing her breasts. "Get out of here," Selene commanded her. The woman hesitated for an instant, her eyes darting to the man. "Don't worry about him. Just *go*." High heels clicking on the concrete, she ran toward the exit.

The Punisher turned back to the man in her grasp. Suddenly, a gust of warm wind from the tunnel. Then, the unmistakable clatter of the approaching uptown train.

"I'm giving you two options: Swear to leave her alone, or refuse and I break your arm." Reveling in her restored strength, Selene bent his arm backward until his eyes grew wide with pain. "I need an answer. Now."

"Fuck you, lady."

"Not one of the options." She bent his arm a little more. His tendons strained beneath her grip, about to snap.

"Okay, okay, option one! Option one!" he gasped. His eyes streamed as she released him. He stepped away, rubbing his arm. "You crazy cunt." He spat at her feet. "You know she's gonna come back to me anyway."

"Huh. Then I guess I'm going with option three." The rest was a blur of motion. Selene lunged forward, the fat man scuttled backward, the roar of the oncoming subway drowned out any further conversation, and then he was tripping, falling, mouth wide open in silent astonishment as he tumbled off the platform edge—directly into the path of the uptown train.

Chapter 12

THE HIEROPHANT
PART I

The name written on the whiteboard beside the bed was "Sammi Mehra." The girl was already on tranquilizers. The hierophant had only needed to adjust the IV drip to make sure she didn't struggle when he lifted her into the wheelchair and rolled her to the elevator. When they'd strung her up, she'd woken long enough to begin sobbing in a language he didn't know. From the chestnut color of her skin and the wave of her patchy black hair, he assumed she was from South Asia somewhere. India, maybe, or Bangladesh. It didn't make any difference.

She wasn't an ideal choice. He'd have preferred someone healthier. This girl had been on chemo for a while. Still, she was pure. Young. Fourteen at most. She looked even younger, tiny and frail in her hospital gown.

As she hung there, limp and silent, her blood dripping into the container below and her chest moving almost imperceptibly, the hierophant considered the perfect symmetry of it all. One dies so another can be reborn. Balance. Harmony. These forces had always ruled the universe, and would again.

He ordered his acolyte to lift the dead snake and wrap it

around the girl's throat, squeezing away her last few breaths. For the snake is a creature of the earth. It knows the dark secrets of the Underworld. It hisses them in the ears of those willing to hear.

Tonight, sleeping beneath the gently swaying body of his sacrifice, the hierophant would pray for dreams of prophecy and healing. *I will listen to the whispers of snakes,* he thought with a shiver of excitement. *And tomorrow, I will go forth once more into the city. The bringer of destruction. The father of creation.*

Chapter 13

UNWITHERING

Selene sat on the floor of her tub, her arms curled around her knees, sucking at the steamy air as water dripped off the end of her nose in a thin stream. The joy she'd taken in her sudden return to strength had drained away the moment she'd fled the station. Killing that bastard on the subway hadn't helped Leto.

She could've just talked to the guy. Broken his arm, like she'd threatened. Maybe called the police or taken the woman somewhere safe. But *killing him*? Since the Diaspora, Selene had developed her own code of justice. The days when she killed any man who looked at her wrong were long over—even she couldn't cover up *that* many bodies. Instead, Selene usually settled for commensurate punishment, plus a little extra to drive home the point. So a man who slapped his girlfriend got beaten unconscious. One who raped a woman—well, he'd be lucky to get past her with his penis intact, much less his testicles. But a murderer could have no punishment but death. Of course, murders were a tricky thing. They usually drew police attention. Thankfully, since Selene usually only concerned herself with women who asked directly for her protection, she rarely dealt with killings—her clients didn't die on her watch.

But tonight she'd murdered a man just for *looking* like he was going to hit his girlfriend. What would her mother think? Is this what it meant to get her powers back? Vengeance killing like in days of old? Paul had reminded her that the Huntress's swift arrows had brought down mortals, not stags. They'd called her Stormy, Untamed, Relentless. Was she ready to embrace those names once more?

Was I always so reckless? she wondered, remembering her stunt with the security camera. If her abilities had miraculously returned, all the more reason not to draw attention to herself. Hopefully, the police would think the big man only slipped, but if they tracked down his girlfriend, she'd undoubtedly mention the strange, tall woman to the cops. That was the last thing Selene needed. If they found her, they'd ask an awful lot of unanswerable questions (including why her fingerprints identified her as a former police officer discharged in 1975 and currently wanted for murder) that would probably land her in jail for a very long time. With a groan, Selene buried her face in her hands and concentrated on the hot water pouring over her back.

Then, a sudden wave of adrenaline rushed through her, and she bolted upright. The energy felt as tangible as heat, nearly sexual, and completely unexpected. She stood and, dizzy with the sensation, leaned her hands against the wall. She had no idea what could cause such a feeling.

Flexing first one foot against the bottom of the tub and then the other, she stretched her long toes, cracking the joints. She shifted her weight, noticing the coolness of the tile on her palms. Her heart drummed in her ears. Every inch of her body, every sensation, felt more precious than it had for a very long time. She felt her flesh, usually so cold, grow hot as the blood rushed to the surface.

Selene opened her eyes to stare at her skin, as bright pink as a newborn babe's. She made a fist, watching the play of muscle along her arm, then ran her hands along the sides of her body, enjoying the taut flesh. *Other gods may be fading, but I'm stronger than I've been in years. Why chastise myself for enjoying it a little?* Tentatively, she moved her hand between her legs, surprised by the sudden tightening pull. She hadn't bothered with her own sexuality in centuries—she'd almost forgotten it existed. But chastity hadn't always been so easy. Memory pulled at her like a coaxing lover, and she let herself fall into its embrace.

The boar we chase leaps ahead of us, its tusks glinting in the moonlight. Orion keeps pace beside me, his footsteps pounding in counterpoint to my own in a hunt as graceful as music, as dance. I pull forth an arrow without slowing my speed, and my shot sends the boar tumbling headfirst into the ground. My companion severs its throat with his sword. We stand beside our kill. Orion pants. I do not. He looks up from the carcass and our eyes meet. His are dark, deep, and I fight the urge to look away. Suddenly, the only prey I want to hunt is him.

I dip my fingers into the boar's blood and reach for him. I draw a line down the strong bone of his nose and another across his brow. Finally, I dot his lips with red. "You are my acolyte now," I tell him.

"I worship only you." He sucks the blood from my finger and the moment is sanctified. I can feel the heat rising from his body—I can hear the blood thrumming in his veins. He grabs my arms and pulls me close. I taste the blood on his lips. The boar lies forgotten at our feet.

When we return to my nymphs with no carcass across our shoulders, they laugh and wink. Merope, my beloved friend, silences the others with a frown. "Artemis," she whispers to me as the sun rises over our grotto and Orion sleeps at my side. "You court danger, my dearest. To be free of men is a gift. Would you throw that away? Would you bind yourself to a man?"

"I do not bind myself," I demur. "Orion is the companion of my freedom."

"You have vowed to be chaste."

I rise and drag Merope away from our sleeping companions. "You dare to remind me of my most sacred oath? I have no intention of breaking it. You should not think it of me."

"You may not think of it," she protests, forging ahead despite my rage. Such is her love for me that she will risk my wrath to speak the truth. "But he will. He is a man."

"Orion is no man. He is the son of my uncle, Poseidon."

Merope nods solemnly. "But he is half-mortal as well. He is a than-atos and will die someday. He must seize life while he can. And no male, whether god or mortal, or something in between, is free from a man's desires. Your own father, your brothers and cousins—you've seen the way they chase our kind, and all the mortal women, too. We are never free of them."

"Do not speak ill of my friend," I hiss. "You shame him. You shame yourself."

But as I lie down once more beside Orion, I cannot find sleep. He rolls over and stretches a heavy arm across my shoulders, resting his head against my breast and his leg upon mine. I have slept thus entwined with my nymphs many times. But this is different. I don't know what scares me more—the hardness I feel pressing against my thigh, or the answering quickening in my own body.

It was a long time before Hippo's scratching on the bathroom door finally dragged Selene from the shower. She let the dog in while she toweled off, trying not to resent the interruption. Hippo took up most of the tiny bathroom, her thwacking tail threatening to knock Selene back over the lip of the tub.

She glanced in the mirror to check the bruises on her jaw and temple from her fight with Mario. To her astonishment, they were gone. No swelling, no discolored flesh. Just flawless skin.

Am I dreaming this? she wondered, realizing how little sleep she'd gotten in the last two days. Somehow, the rush of power she'd felt in the shower had healed her injuries at a pace she hadn't experienced for a very long time.

She pulled on a T-shirt and moved to the bedroom, although she knew her racing mind would preclude sleep. There were too many questions to be answered. She opened the window wide and knelt before the sill, looking up at the sky above the rooftops. Even now, at the darkest hour before dawn, it shone with an unearthly glow.

Selene knew it was just light pollution bouncing off the clouds above, but sometimes she imagined the city possessed the sort of divine radiance once reserved for the gods. Just as in ancient times the Olympians had chosen to walk among mortals in disguise rather than reveal themselves in all their terrible glory, so New York clothed itself in dirt and noise and stench. Its true power would be too much for mortal eyes to bear.

"Imagine, Hippo," she said as the dog rested her chin on the windowsill. "Once I was the Lady of the Starry Host." She'd placed her victims in the heavens as eternal reminders of her rage and mercy. First Ursa Major—a nymph who broke her vows of chastity and was metamorphosed into a bear by Artemis's uncompromising justice. Then Ursa Minor—the son of that illicit union who met the same fate. "But now, even the strongest Athanatoi no longer possess the ability to make men into stars. Especially not here, where the stars themselves are hidden from view. New York's radiance outshines my own."

Over the centuries she'd watched the city's lights quench heaven's fire. With the constellations' disappearance, the history written in their outlines—her own history—dimmed alongside. She'd always imagined herself fading as well. Slowly, imperceptibly, disappearing into myth. But now, for the first time in an age, she felt hope.

She knew the most obvious explanation for her strengthening, and she didn't want to face it. She could barely admit it to herself. It was possible that her mother's decline was adding to her own strength. With one fewer god to siphon away the limited worship man still provided, the remaining Athanatoi might benefit.

Father, she prayed silently. *Mighty Zeus, who once granted me six wishes, grant me one more. Help me find the answers I seek. Let my rebirth not come from my mother's death. And if you ever loved gentle*

Leto, help me save her. She closed her eyes and imagined her words reaching up to the vault of heaven, then soaring past the city, over the vast ocean, all the way to Zeus's lair on the island of Crete. And there the prayer died. Because her father could no longer hear.

Since the Diaspora, Zeus had lost his strength and his wits, eventually breaking his own vow of exile and returning to the Cave of Psychro, where he'd spent his infancy. In the nineteenth century, her half brother Hermes had finally dared visit the Father of the Gods.

"By day, he looks up at the sky through the cave's mouth and watches the clouds pass," he told the Huntress afterward. "He waves his hands about as if he would bend the wind to his whim, and pouts when the sky doesn't obey. He's gone mad, Sister. There's moss in his hair and mold on his skin. By night, he crawls from the cave and raids the flocks of nearby farmers, eating sheep and goats raw. Mostly, though, he lives on bats and worms."

"Maybe that's all this is," Selene said to Hippo, rising to her feet and reaching for the bow leaning against the windowsill. "My own inevitable descent into madness." She twirled a shaft between her fingers before settling it against the arrow rest. "Maybe this is all a dream." She sighted between the swaying branches of an oak over a hundred yards away on the border of the park, noting the skittering movement of a squirrel. It dashed down one branch then up another, hidden in the shadows of night. "Maybe I'm not going to make this shot," Selene said quietly. Then she loosed the arrow. A heartbeat later, the wind carried the faintest of squeals to the Huntress's ear. She lowered her bow. "For tonight, at least, I'm the Far Shooter. The Huntress. The Swiftly Bounding One. Go ahead," she said, looking down at Hippo. "Pick an epithet. I've got dozens." The dog just cocked her head, oblivious.

For the first time in a long time, Selene wished she had a real friend. *Can you see me, Orion?* she wondered. *Do you revel in my return to power—or dread it?*

She looked up to where the scudding clouds left bare a patch of night sky and felt her triumph slip away. In a painful irony, the only stars bright enough to outshine the city lights were those that most tormented her. A star for each broad shoulder, a star for each strong leg, three stars slung in a glittering belt and a last for his sword. Cold, remote, a bare suggestion of a man, light-years away from the one she'd known. Yet in the dark gaps of night, she saw strong limbs and fierce eyes, curling hair and a flashing smile. Orion, at once infinitely distant and just beyond reach, stared down like a reproachful judge upon the woman who'd loved him. The woman who'd killed him. The woman who'd placed him in the heavens as an eternal reminder of her guilt, her shame, her heartbreak.

Selene rose and moved to her narrow bed. She thought suddenly of Theodore Schultz. He, too, had lost someone he loved. But in every photo, friends surrounded him, smiling, laughing, touching. He would grieve, but—unlike Selene—he would not be alone.

She fell asleep with the wind streaming across her face from the open window. For the first time in centuries, she dreamed Orion was with her. He smelled like the dry hills of Attica. Like oregano crushed underfoot. Like sweat and heat and the thrill of the chase. His warm flesh pressed against her back. His fingertips traced a line of fire up her arm, to her neck, where his lips, rough and wind burnt, pressed a kiss into the hollow of her ear.

With the frenzy of a drowning woman, Selene pulled herself from the dream and sat up, sure Orion was there. She imagined she could still smell him on the wind. But dawn reddened the sky, the stars had been put to flight, and she was alone.

Chapter 14

PROTECTOR OF THE INNOCENT

Selene's cell phone vibrated angrily on her bedside table, wrenching her from a fitful sleep. She hesitated. If it was Paul, then he could be calling for only one reason: The rush of power she'd felt last night had indeed come from their mother's death.

"Ms. DiSilva? It's Theodore Schultz. From the park." The professor sounded angry.

"Schultz. I didn't think I'd hear from you." She could breathe again.

"I didn't think I'd be calling." In the background, she heard the unmistakable hiss and beep of police radios. "But I told them this would happen and they didn't listen to me."

"What's going on? Another murder? Already?" It made no sense. Killers who practiced ritual mutilation—especially the precise kind shown on Helen Emerson's body—were usually organized murderers. Like Jack the Ripper, Jeffrey Dahmer, or the Hillside Strangler, they struck repeatedly over the course of weeks, months, or years. Not twice in three days.

"Yes, a teenage girl. A *hospital patient*, for fuck's sake..."

"Where are you?" she asked tightly. *Another innocent killed.*

Again, she couldn't help thinking. *I've failed* again. *I spent the night dreaming of the past, while the present keeps moving forward.*

"I'm outside Mount Sinai Hospital right now. I went to the lead detective yesterday and warned him about the *Asklepia,* and—"

"Hold it—*Asklepia?*"

"That's what I said," Schultz snapped, as if she were the fiftieth person he'd explained this to. "It's part of the Eleusinian Mysteries."

Cold sweat beaded Selene's forehead. *If a mortal is messing with a revival of Demeter and Persephone's rites, he must be either very foolish or very brave.* The rites in Eleusis had always been the most secret, the most envied, and the most feared among the gods—although they never involved human sacrifice. Still, if someone was tying murders to the ritual, it might explain the pace of the killings. The Mystery Cult's rites had taken place over the course of only a few days. Which meant more victims. And soon.

"That's what we're up against—Greek ritual, just like you said," Schultz continued. "But the detective didn't believe me. I couldn't sleep all night, then I turn on the TV at five in the morning and see there's been a murder in a basement storage room in the children's wing. The perfect place to pay homage to Asclepius. So I'm here now, but I might as well be a prepubescent D&D player left out of the cool kids' party. They won't tell me anything and they won't let me inside. I'm about to throw my dodecahedral dice at someone."

By the time Selene hung up, Hippolyta was already pacing eager circles in front of her, tail swinging wildly. "Looks like Professor Schultz isn't our culprit," Selene said as she latched the dog's leash. "But he might just be the lead we need after all. The hunt's back on."

◄◦►

Officer Nguyen had been patient with Theo for the last thirty minutes, but he could tell she was about to snap. "Thank God," she said, looking across the curious crowd to where an unmarked black sedan had pulled up to the curb on Fifth Avenue. "Detective Brandman is here, sir, just like you asked."

"It's about time." Theo drummed his fingers impatiently on the blue police barricade between him and the hospital.

"You need to step back, sir," she reminded him for the fifth time. "This is an active crime scene."

"Sorry." She was only about five feet tall and wore her black hair pulled back in a demure bun, but she did have a gun strapped to her waist. Theo hadn't completely lost his mind.

Brandman shoved his way through the gathered crowd. Even from across the street, Theo could see the stormy look on his face. "Professor Schultz. Of course."

Officer Nguyen shook her head wearily. "Sorry, Detective, I know the last thing you want is to get involved here. We've already got half of the Twenty-third out, not to mention"—she lowered her voice and gestured discreetly to a wiry woman with close-cropped gray hair standing nearby—"Captain Hansen from Counterterrorism. But Mr. Schultz here insisted—"

"They used the room in the hospital for the *Asklepia* ritual," Theo interrupted. "Just like I said they would."

"Really? Just like you said?"

"I said a cave near a well sacred to the God of Medicine. A basement storage area near a pump room in a hospital amounts to basically the same thing once you transpose it into the twenty-first century. You've got to let me inside to take a look."

"Absolutely not." Brandman moved aside the heavy barrier with one hand so he could walk past, then firmly replaced it in front of Theo.

"You won't know what you're looking at. Do you have the first idea how to identify cultic elements?"

Brandman pulled at his mustache and replied with careful sarcasm, "I didn't realize you were a forensic expert, too. They really do make 'em smart up there in the Ivy League. Interesting, though, that you left out the most crucial piece of information yesterday."

"What do you mean?"

"I spoke to a few of your colleagues at the university. Turns out you *dated* Miss Emerson. Wildly in love with her, according to some, and then she threw you over. It was the talk of the department. Didn't you think that was something you should've told me?"

"It was almost a year ago. Water under the bridge."

"Huh. Well, let's just say it casts your 'cult' argument into a whole new light. As does the rest of your record. Let's see." He raised his hand to tick off Theo's misdemeanors, mocking the professor's didactic manner at the police station the day before. "One: arrested for drunk and disorderly conduct at Harvard."

"That was my lunatic roommate Dennis's fault—"

"Two: a warning for trespassing in the New York Public Library after hours."

"I fell asleep and—"

"Three: taken into custody while leading a sit-in against your own university's eminent domain policy."

This time Theo didn't protest.

Brandman showed his teeth. He was enjoying this. "The department chair seems to consider you some kind of self-serving traitor, more concerned with your reputation among your bleeding-heart liberal students than with the good of the university. He really doesn't like you."

"Well, for once, you've got your facts straight."

"Glad you agree." Brandman turned to walk into the hospital. "I'll be in touch, Professor, you can be sure of that. We've got plenty to talk about. And ancient Greeks are just the beginning."

"Wait. What about the snake at the crime scene?"

"How did you know about the—" interjected Officer Nguyen before Brandman silenced her with a curt wave.

Theo pounced, glad his bluff had paid off. "It was the *Zamenis longissimus* specimen from the Natural History Museum. Right? Guess you needed an expert in dead languages and dead snakes after all."

"What I need is the crime scene investigation team that's waiting inside. They're the ones finding the clues."

"Are you sure?" Theo retorted, voice raised. "Because so far all you've found is rumor, lies, and conjecture." From the corner of his eye, he saw the gray-haired female police captain from Counterterrorism turn to watch the altercation. Brandman glanced at the captain and then turned narrowed eyes back to Theo.

"Are you done, sir?" he asked tightly.

"You're guilty of negligence, Detective, and if you won't let me in there to examine the scene, I may have to call your superior." As soon as the words were out of his mouth, he knew he'd gone too far. Gabriela was right. Since when was he Sherlock Holmes? But it was too late now to pull his punches. "Or maybe I should just talk to *her*." He gestured up the street to the captain. Brandman stood silently for a moment, his barrel chest heaving, rocking onto the toes of his small feet as if he would try to match Theo's height.

"That woman deals with Islamic extremists. She has as little to do with your crazy conspiracy as I do," he finally said, his voice careful, as if every word were an effort. "I suggest that you climb back up your Ivory Tower. Make yourself useful doing some more library work and wait for my call." He turned to walk into the hospital.

Theo reached across the barricade to grab the detective's shoulder. "You have to listen—" Brandman spun around and threw off Theo's hand.

"*You* need to not touch me, sir," Brandman said, his voice soft and dangerous, sarcasm gone. "Not unless you want to add another charge to your record."

Nguyen put her hand on her billy club and stepped forward. Other cops were watching now, too, ready to spring into action.

"If you won't help me, I'll go to people who will," Theo warned. "I've hired a private investigator."

"Are you threatening me, Professor?"

"I just—"

"'Cause if you're threatening me, I'm going to need to take you into custody."

"If you don't listen to me now, I can guarantee that something even worse will happen next."

"That sounds like a threat to me," Nguyen piped up.

"Agreed. You're coming with me, Professor." Brandman moved forward to put a hand on Theo's elbow.

Theo instinctively jerked backward.

"That's it. Resisting arrest and assaulting an officer."

"What! That's not—" Before Theo could protest further, Brandman had jumped the barricade with surprising agility, pinned Theo's arms behind his back, and secured plastic handcuffs around his wrists. "Makes your drunk and disorderly charge look like nothing."

In the backseat of Brandman's sedan, Theo kicked the back of the seat in front of him, accomplishing nothing but bruising his toe. He cursed loudly. No one could hear him anyway behind the bulletproof glass.

In a moment, his righteous anger dissolved into anxiety. Should he be calling a lawyer? He couldn't reach his cell phone anyway. *Shit shit shit. Do I never learn?* He threw his head back, staring at the roof of the car as if it could tell him how he got into this mess. *I blame Selene DiSilva,* he decided. *She's the one who got me started.*

As if she'd heard him, the woman's perfect pale face suddenly appeared in the window. Theo nearly yelped as she pressed her nose against the glass, staring at him quizzically.

"How did you get here so fast?" he exclaimed, forgetting for a moment that the thick window was nearly soundproof. It didn't seem to matter, though. She apparently heard him.

What are you doing in there? she mouthed.

"Contemplating the depths of my own stupidity!" he shouted back. She raised an eyebrow, but he plowed on. "I was just trying to get inside and they arrested me on trumped-up charges. You should try to get a look at the—" He wanted to say more, but Selene DiSilva's eye had been caught by something he couldn't see. Once again, she vanished like a ghost, leaving Theo alone, angry, and thoroughly miserable.

Chapter 15

THE GODDESSES OF ELEUSIS

Selene didn't take well to being ordered about by mortals. Nonetheless, the professor was right—she needed to get inside the hospital. In fact, the sooner she could get more evidence, the sooner she could stop relying on Schultz to pass her information. Even though he wasn't the killer, she'd rather not be involved with him: too unpredictable, too excitable, too *human*. Then again, he'd been dedicated enough to get himself arrested. Stupid, but impressive.

She left Theo in the police car and walked calmly along the block, examining the scene while trying to dredge up what she knew of the Eleusinian Mysteries. The first days of the ceremony, she remembered, involved a series of processions in homage to Demeter and Persephone. The rite's climax, however, had been performed behind the closed doors of the Telesterion. Over the years, a few other gods joined the Mystery—including Dionysus, who was usually so drunk he would tell anyone anything—yet the rite remained secret. The other gods envied the Eleusinian deities their continued worship. Some, such as Apollo, begged in vain to know the secret so he might form a cult of his own. "They're doing something that they don't want us to know about," he'd complained once. "Even my own son Asclepius won't tell me what it is."

Artemis had scowled at her twin. "Why would you want to be worshiped by those fools? All that fuss over the goddesses of farming and flowers. Do you really want to spend more time with a girl as insipid as Persephone the Discreet?"

She'd always wondered why the story of Hades's abduction of Persephone into the Underworld had endured as one of mankind's favorite myths. *Probably,* Selene surmised, *because men find the idea of kidnapping and raping a virgin irresistibly titillating. No wonder no man ever wants to revive an Artemis cult. In my stories, it's the man who winds up underground.*

Selene moved to stand behind the knot of reporters crowding the police barricade. Over their heads, she watched various uniformed cops coming and going from the hospital. She had no chance of getting into the crime scene while their investigation was under way. She'd have to wait for the press conference like everybody else. The thought galled her. *At least I have a lead to pursue while I wait—one no reporter or detective could ever imagine.*

She dialed one of the few numbers in her phone.

"Selene!" crowed a voice on the other end.

"Hi, Dash." Hermes had recently incarnated himself as a movie producer. She could picture him, his curly black hair in a wild halo, his sharp eyes hidden behind completely unnecessary thick-rimmed glasses to make him look older. Once, he'd sported a thick beard, but he'd shaved it off in the first century to look more Roman. Now, he looked about fifteen years old—but he was a master of disguise. Most mortals probably thought him a well-preserved forty-three.

"Why aren't you asleep?" she asked her half brother. "It's four in the morning in California."

"Still at work. What can I do for you? Looking to leave town finally? Realized Hollywood is infinitely superior to that humid gray cave you live in?"

"The New York weather has been perfect recently," she sniffed. "It's autumn. Remember autumn? Remember seasons?"

"Don't miss 'em," he laughed. A high-pitched chatter distracted Dash's attention for a moment. His muffled reply: "Just tell him that chickens are *funnier* than ducks."

"So what's up, Selene?" he said, clearly now. "I'm in the middle of a shit-storm of a script crisis." He was always like that. *Mercurial,* for lack of a better word. Thrilled to hear from you one moment, rushing you off the phone the next.

"This man and I—"

"Whoa! What!" Suddenly she had his attention. "Selene has a *man*? Cut! Bobby, get out of here, dear boy. Hold my calls." More muted babbling, rustling of papers, closing of doors. Then—"Are you telling me that the *Untamed One* is shacking up with a mortal *man*?" His delight was clear.

Selene blushed furiously, grateful he couldn't see. "How dare you," she seethed. "I barely know the man. He's just been arrested and he told—"

"Arrested! A bad boy! You always did know how to pick 'em. Orion was certainly no puffball. So this man of yours," he continued. "Madly in love with you?"

"I told you, I don't even—"

"I'll take that as a 'yes.' Or an 'I hope so.' Hah! I can *feel* you blushing over the phone. By Kronos's gullet, Selene, you're not still a virgin are you?" Selene could only splutter. "Why? I mean, what's stopping you now?"

"I'm a *virgin* goddess," she managed. "If I lose that, I lose everything."

"Feh."

"What do you mean, 'feh'? That's the fundamental rule of godhood. You've got to hold on to your most essential attributes if you want to hold on to any semblance of immortality. If

Ares were to become a pacifist or Aphrodite swore off men, they wouldn't be Athanatoi anymore."

"Maybe. Or maybe we just can't imagine anything else for ourselves."

That's where Dash was wrong. She could imagine. She could still feel Orion's heat against her cheek. And for an unsettling instant, a vision of Schultz, shirtless in his apartment, flashed before her eyes. "There are more important things going on than my sex life."

Dash shifted topics as effortlessly as always, becoming suddenly serious. "You're talking about the fading. It's speeding up. And not because Aphrodite's become some lesbian. I mean she's been traipsing across Paris—"

"Is everyone fading?" she interrupted.

"The Goddess of the Hearth. The Smith. Your mother. Not everyone."

"You?" She was afraid of the answer. Hermes, the eternal child. How could he grow old?

"I'm the Messenger, remember?" he said with a laugh. "God of Communication and Travel and about a dozen other extremely lucrative domains. Between cell phones, the Internet, and jumbo jets, I'm doing just fine. Sure, machines do more than I ever could, but they're like magic to most people. They're still in awe of the mysterious force that beams their voices across space, because they can't possibly understand how the technology really works. I harvest power from their ignorance. And you?"

She wasn't sure how to answer that. Her powers were still too new, too uncertain.

"Are some of the Athanatoi actually getting stronger?" she asked instead.

"Stronger? Wouldn't that be nice! There's always been a theory that eventually the decreasing number of gods would mean more power for the rest of us, but I haven't heard of it actually happening. Then again, now that some of the Twelve are threatened...well, maybe. Wait—is that why you're calling? Selene, you little minx, are you holding out on me?"

"No," she said quickly. "I'm calling about the murders in New York."

"Aren't there always murders in New York?"

"Not like this. Some killer has revived the Eleusinian Mysteries and is sacrificing women along the way."

"No shit. I didn't hear that on the news."

"I just figured it out."

"Always the cop, huh? I never should've convinced you to join the force back in the twenties—you've never gotten it out of your system."

"You remember anything about Eleusis?"

"Wouldn't be caught dead there. Too many pigs."

"Then I need to talk to the Athanatoi who ran the cult," she said, exasperated. "Where are"—she realized she didn't know Demeter's, Hades's, or Persephone's current aliases—"the Goddess of Grain, the Receiver of Many, and the Goddess of Spring?"

"Gwenith, Aiden, and Cora."

Selene shook her head. Just as the gods needed to keep their old roles, so they held on to some semblance of their old names and titles. But they were obviously running out of ideas. Gwenith was Welsh for "grain"—Demeter had been going by some variation of the name for centuries. Aiden sounded more like an Irish poet than a nickname for "Aides," the Hidden One, one of Hades' many titles. And Cora? *From Persephone's alternate name "Kore," I suppose, but not particularly dignified. It's only slightly better than "Paul" for Apollo.*

"Gwenith's not doing well, I'm afraid. Very weak. All those genetically modified crops and chemical pesticides have really taken their toll on the Goddess of Grain. She was living somewhere in Peru last I heard, with no phone. No way to get in touch with her unless you want to fly to the Southern Hemisphere. You'll have more luck with Aiden and Cora. Most of the time they live in an old oil well in Houston. He's working his Lord of the Dead and God of Wealth epithets like a pro. Got it all decked out with plasma screens and a lap pool—the works. But he still keeps a little pied-à-terre in New York."

"And you know how to find it?"

"That's my job, isn't it? Leading people to the *Underworld*." Dash chuckled when he said the word, as if it were a haunted house in a cheesy theme park.

"I don't suppose you could tell me how to get there and I could just go myself?"

"I don't give out addresses. But as the Conductor of Souls, Aiden's lair is one place I can take you personally. That's how it works."

"Okay, but I need to get this done fast. This cult will strike again, probably tonight. You don't still have those winged sandals, do you?"

"Sure I've got 'em. But they don't work. Haven't in a thousand years."

"Damn."

"But who needs magic sandals when I can get to you tonight by private jet?"

"Your production company's doing that well, huh?"

"Sure, but I'd have the jet either way. I'm not the God of Thieves for nothing, darling."

In front of the hospital, the knot of reporters started shoving one another for position as a young detective in a trench coat emerged from the crime scene. Selene hung up with Dash and moved closer to watch.

As the detective pulled off a pair of latex gloves, a sixty-ish woman in a boxy pantsuit joined him. A badge hung around her neck, but even with her newly keen vision, Selene couldn't read the precinct designation from so far away. Something about the woman's blade of a nose and grimly set mouth looked familiar. Uneasy, Selene hid herself in the crowd of journalists who pressed close to the barricades, trying in vain to decipher the cops' hushed conversation.

Selene concentrated on their moving lips, willing herself to hear the distant whispers. Suddenly, as if popping from a return to pressure, her ears opened and their words were clear.

"How much do you want me to tell them about Sammi Mehra, Captain? Do we say she had cancer?" asked the young man.

"Just the basics. I don't want to get the entire city in a panic. I'll check with the commissioner before we reveal anything else." The woman's voice was rough with cigarettes and age.

"Do I mention the snakes?"

The captain shook her head. "Not yet. Any ID on them?"

"No, ma'am. But I'll tell you, I never seen anything like it. One of the guys started screaming like a little girl when we walked in. Uh...no offense, ma'am."

"None taken. I never screamed like a little girl, even when I was one."

"You don't seem too shaken by this. You seen something like it before?"

"Not in forty years on the force. But you cease being surprised after a while. Any other evidence, Detective? Anything that might point to organized extremists?"

"Plenty of hair and fingerprints, but there were dozens of custodians going in and out of that storeroom all the time. It'll take a while before the lab sorts through it all, but we'll send the results over to Counterterrorism as soon as we get them back. Our perps left all kinds of stuff behind. Must've run off in a hurry. Maybe heard someone coming. Everything's labeled, but we've sealed the room until the animal guy gets here."

"When's he expected?"

"'Bout twenty minutes."

The detective finally approached the reporters to give his statement. He introduced himself then turned to the older woman. "This is Captain Geraldine Hansen with the Counterterrorism Division." As the reporters clamored to know why Counterterrorism had been summoned to a murder investigation, Selene slipped away.

She'd thought all the cops who'd known her when she was last on the force were surely long dead or retired by now, but Geraldine had been barely out of her teens when she joined the NYPD in the early seventies.

The last thing Selene needed was her old protégée asking why "Officer Cynthia Forrester" had barely aged a day in forty years.

Chapter 16

MISTRESS OF BEASTS

Selene checked the position of the sun. She had about ten minutes left before the cops reentered the basement storage room. They'd have a guard outside the door, but she knew from experience there was usually more than one way into a crime scene.

Behind a tall wrought-iron fence, a trench stretched the length of the building. Most likely, this was a service area that allowed light to penetrate the basement windows. Leaving Hippo tied to a parking meter with strict instructions not to growl at the passersby, Selene slipped behind the fence and crouched down to peer through the metal grate covering the trench. Sure enough, she saw a basement window, clouded with dirt and only two feet square. Too small for a fully grown man to crawl through, but perfect for a slender woman. To get to it, of course, she'd have to get through the grating. The access hatch wasn't locked, just incredibly heavy. The bigger problem was that someone—especially the two police officers standing guard outside the hospital entrance—might see her jumping down through the grate.

Selene whistled sharply to attract Hippo's attention. The dog stood immediately, tail wagging, eager to be of use. With a quick hand gesture, Selene gave Hippo a command to bark. Miraculously, the dog obeyed perfectly. She sat on her haunches and commenced an ear-splitting concert of whimpers, howls, and growls. As the cops turned toward the sound, Selene seized the opportunity to pry up the hatch and drop feetfirst into the passage below.

She landed in a puddle of rainwater and oil, muffling a curse as the cold liquid seeped through her boots. Heating and ventilation units whirred and clicked around her, masking any sound she made. She donned her gloves, then pushed open the small window. After unlacing her boots, she grabbed the window ledge, levered herself out of her shoes and through the opening, and landed lightly on her stocking feet in a small storage room.

Something cold and slick struck Selene in the face. She batted it away before she realized what it was. Like streamers at a prom, dozens of live snakes dangled head-down from the ceiling in four concentric circles, their whiplike tails wriggling grotesquely as they swayed from thin cords looped around the rafters. The snake Selene had struck spun crazily, knocking into the others and setting them waving like a perpetual motion machine.

In the center of the writhing mass hung a child. Someone had slit open the veins above her bony wrists; blood coated her hands. Her feet, overlarge for her withered shins, dangled toe-down, arched and graceful like those of a ballerina about to pirouette.

From her nearly bald scalp, a few remaining hanks of black hair fell to her waist in six skinny braids. Again, the Roman sign of virginity. But why such an obsession? And how did Helen—surely no virgin—fit in? Then she remembered her vision of the night Helen was killed. *A needle, curved like a fishhook.* The suture needle had never made sense, until now. Whoever led this cult needed each sacrifice to be pure—and if she wasn't a virgin, he would make her one.

By the Styx, I pledge, Selene swore silently, *that I will stop this before another innocent dies. It ends tonight.*

Carefully ducking beneath the writhing snakes, she stepped toward the dangling corpse. The thin hospital gown hung untied, crusted red from the girl's blood. Selene forced herself to resist the desire to rip the girl from her noose and wash her clean. *Find the killer first,* she told herself. *Then you can have your revenge.*

She pulled off a glove and brushed a finger across the girl's forehead but received no vision of her last moments. She still couldn't fathom how she'd experienced Helen Emerson's dying thoughts, but she was used to making do without supernatural visions to provide answers. She would focus on the evidence instead.

She squatted to peer more closely at the evidence tags on the floor beneath the corpse. A pool of Sammi Mehra's blood, sticky and thick as congealed pudding, covered the ground. Scattered nearby were three large scales, too big to belong to any of the common snakes writhing around her. Another label marked a small patch of oily ash. A burnt offering. Selene shuddered, remembering the mysterious surge of power she'd felt the night before. Could it be that her return to strength had nothing to do with Leto's fading? Could she be responding to the revival of cult worship instead? *No,* she decided. *The offering was not for me. No worshiper of mine would use snakes in my rites, much less kill a virgin.*

She stood up, accidentally knocking a snake, which twisted violently in its noose, vibrating its tail. Its long tongue lashed out to brush against her cheek. With a start, she recognized the wide brown bands across its back—a venomous copperhead. Selene hissed at it to calm down. The snake ignored her. Once, at the height of her power, she could do more than command dogs—she could speak to wild animals of all kinds in their own tongue. But even then, snakes had refused to tell her their secrets. They were creatures of prophecy and rebirth, sacred to Asclepius and Apollo, never ruled by the Huntress. The copperhead snapped its jaws at her, long fangs bright in the fluorescent overhead light. Selene reached to snap its neck, then stopped herself. Tampering with the crime scene would be deeply unwise.

Keeping low to the ground, she searched the rest of the room in a careful spiral pattern. Metal shelves filled with supplies lined the walls. She sniffed cautiously at the folded blankets and sheets, wondering how much her sense of smell had heightened along with her other powers. *Bleach. Detergent. More bleach.* She passed to the last row of linens, still sniffing. There. The bottom five blankets, folded a bit less neatly than the others. *Fear. Male lust. Sweat. Euphoria. More sweat.* The emotion in each scent was as distinctive as an animal's print. She cursed inwardly. *Looks like the professor's cult theory's correct—I've got more than one man to hunt.*

She unfolded the blankets carefully, looking for stray hairs. Nothing. If only Hippo were a little more svelte, Selene might have brought her through the window to let her have a sniff. With her renewed hunter's nose, Selene could tell that there had been a number of different men sweating on the blankets, but unlike Hippo, she probably wouldn't recognize the individuals' scents if she smelled them again.

After snipping off tiny samples of each blanket, then refolding them neatly, she crouched to peer beneath each shelving unit. There, under the last corner, lay a large, dark object, shiny enough to catch the light amid the shadows. Maybe just an old vacuum hose or plastic bedpan, but if the men had left in a hurry, they could've lost something beneath the shelves, something the cops might've missed. Her arm barely fit underneath, but she managed to brush the object with her fingertips, sending it spinning into her grasp. She pulled it out, blew off the dust and dirt, then sat back on her heels, unable to believe what she was looking at.

A tusklike tooth, black and cracked with extreme age. Nearly eight inches long, wider at the base then narrowing to a sharp canine point. Animal sacrifices appeared in most rituals, as the snakes attested. What confused her, though, was the origin of this particular tooth. It was far too large for a lion or a grizzly. Perhaps a tusk from a young elephant or rhinoceros? She thought not. In fact, she was fairly certain that it belonged to an animal with a special meaning for the Olympians.

But where would anyone get ahold of a tooth from the Caledonian Boar?

Well, probably not *the* Caledonian Boar, she acknowledged. Thousands of years earlier, Artemis had searched far and wide for the perfect beast to ravage the lands of Calydon after its king had refused to pay her proper homage. The wild boars of classical Greece weren't nearly terrifying enough to serve as divinely inspired monsters. So, with some help from Great-grandmother Gaia, known to most as Mother Earth, Artemis resurrected a piglike monster from a primeval epoch. Six feet at the shoulder, with a face uglier than a warthog's, the animal sported a mouthful of enormous, widely spaced teeth, all pointing in different directions. Heroes came from far and wide to hunt the Caledonian Boar. Eventually, Artemis guided the spear of Atalanta, the only woman to join the chase, into the heaving side of the monster, bringing glory to the young huntress and her divine mentor alike.

Perhaps this specimen came from the same ancient species. But why would anyone bother to procure a prehistoric boar tooth for a ceremony honoring Demeter? The *pig* was sacred to the Goddess of Grain and Agriculture, not the boar. And of all the porcine animals to chose from, why select the one that held special significance to Artemis? Maybe she'd been wrong— maybe the offerings *were* meant for her.

She gazed once more around the room with its ceiling of snakes, filled with the sudden suspicion that larger forces than just psychopathic mortals might be at work. She wouldn't know until she made a positive identification of the tooth. Maybe it was just a specimen from some hospital experiment gone wrong. She could always hope.

"Brace yourself," said a voice just outside the door. Probably the guard talking to the animal control guy. "You're not going to believe this one." Selene's ten minutes were up.

With a last silent promise to Sammi Mehra, she left the way she'd come, out the narrow window and back into her boots. As the animal control specialist entered the room, Selene swiftly closed the window and knelt out of sight beneath the sill. Pain shot through her right knee. She hissed and glanced down. A shard of green glass had sliced through her pants and embedded itself in her flesh. *That'll teach me to not look where I'm going.* She sat back on the dirty concrete and yanked the glass from her knee. Blood poured down her leg.

Whatever extraordinary healing had occurred last night in the shower seemed to have been an isolated incident. She tied a makeshift tourniquet tightly around her knee, removed her gloves, and pulled her baseball cap low over her face.

Wincing with the pain, she jumped up to grab the grate overhead. When the sidewalk stood momentarily empty, she held on with one hand and used the other to raise the hatch. She pulled herself through and walked, as nonchalantly as possible, across the sidewalk to where Hippo waited. Kneeling beside the dog, she retrieved the blanket snippets, letting Hippo smell each in turn. "These are our killers, girl. So promise to keep a nose out, okay?"

Selene limped away from the hospital and into Central Park, heading toward the North Woods, a patch of dense forest at the park's far northern end. After a few minutes, she came to the small, gurgling spring once known as Montayne's Fonteyn. It spurted forth between two rocks, feeding into the nearby stream. A small iron ring protruded from an overhanging boul-

der: In the nineteenth century, long before water fountains, a
ladle had hung from the ring so passersby could drink from the
spring. But even before the ladle, before the park was a park,
before a white man called Montayne gave the spring his name,
a Lenni Lenape girl had shown it to Phoebe Hautman, a silver-
eyed white woman who tracked and hunted better than the
cleverest warrior.

Beside the spring, a small waterfall rushed over a cliff of boulders and into a larger, fast-moving stream. Checking first to see
she had the secluded area to herself, Selene sat beside the water,
removed her boots, and rolled up her pants. Motioning Hippo to
stay on the rocks, she waded into the water.

As she suspected, the fresh, rushing water had a healing effect,
just as it had when she'd been the Goddess of the Wild. The
wound did not disappear entirely, but she watched as it scabbed
over before her eyes. "I'm getting stronger. It's really happening, Mother," she murmured. "I just wish it were happening to
you."

She felt the dappled sunlight kiss her cheeks and looked up
through the leaves at the sky—as blue and clear as her father's
eyes. *Was Apollo right? Will it be my fault if my mother dies?* she
wondered. *Am I wasting my time searching for a killer of thanatoi,
when an Athanatos stands poised on the shores of the River Styx, ready
to cross over to the land of the dead?*

———◇———

A fly settled on the nearest Danish. Little black mandibles nibbled at a crumb of jellied apricot. Theo didn't bother shooing it
away. At least it was something to look at.

The walls of the small interview room (Theo couldn't help
thinking of it as an interrogation chamber) were completely
bare. At this point, he almost wished Brandman would come
back. At least his bulldog face would relieve the monotony.

The detective had grilled Theo for an hour, asking again

about his whereabouts the night of Helen's murder (*in my apartment watching* Battlestar Galactica *reruns while grading papers*), his relationship to Helen (*yes, she was my girlfriend for a while, and yes she left me, but no, I didn't want her dead, for God's sake*), and his status within the department (*sometimes university politics are more soap opera than symposium, you know how that is*). For most of the questioning, the young black detective he'd seen during his first foray to the precinct house had also been present: Maggie Freeman, plump, fresh-faced, and a good deal more pleasant. But if Freeman and Brandman were playing "good cop, bad cop," it wasn't working. From Theo's perspective, it had been more "silent cop, asshole cop" than anything else. Finally, Brandman got around to asking Theo to outline his Mysteries hypothesis one more time. While the two detectives took diligent notes, Theo ran through the first five days of the ritual until he reached the present.

"Tonight's the start of Day Six, the *Pompe*," he explained, "meaning 'procession.' It starts off on a morbid note, at a cemetery outside Athens. Then it gets a little rowdy during the journey down the Sacred Way. And finally it ends all hush-hush at the secret Telesterion, or 'Hall of Completion,' in Eleusis. So, if we want to catch them before the procession gets started, we should hit the city's graveyards. Otherwise, it'll be hard to predict where they'll show up." He went on to explain the last days of the ritual, trying his best to keep things simple and engaging, just like he would for a classroom of economics majors.

When the little lecture was over, Brandman placed his notes carefully in a manila folder, then sat back and stared at his captive for a long, painful moment. "There's one thing...or one major thing in a whole slew of things...I don't understand, Professor."

"Ask. I *want* you to understand so you can catch these guys."

"Why. Why would anyone bother?"

"Because it's a powerful Mystery."

Brandman's brow wrinkled. "It *was* powerful, three thousand years ago—"

"About sixteen hundred years ago would be more—"

"—but not now, Professor." He sighed, a bit dramatically. Theo noticed Freeman stifling a grin. *They're playing with me,* he thought. Brandman tapped his papers more exactly into place. "You're an Ivy League man, right?"

Theo bridled. He knew that tone. It meant that someone was about to accuse him of being stupid just because he'd been smart enough to attend the best schools. The detective leaned an inch forward in his chair. Theo found himself staring at a single gray hair protruding from Brandman's otherwise impeccably trimmed nostrils.

"You know about Occam's razor?"

Theo nodded. "*Lex parsimoniae,* 'the law of parsimony.' All things being equal, the simplest explanation is usually the right one."

Brandman looked to Freeman, who joined him in a brief golf clap. The older detective then spun the folder to face Theo, so the professor could see the densely written page of notes and calendars created from his testimony. "Does this look simple to you?"

Theo bit the inside of his lip to stop himself from retorting.

"You know what I think is a *much* simpler explanation, Detective Freeman?" Brandman asked.

"What's that?"

"That our professor here had something to do with the gruesome murder of the woman who broke his little heart in two. He's trying to distract us with a wild-goose chase across the city based on some ancient mumbo jumbo. And I think that if there really is some 'Mystery Cult' involved, then Schultz is probably the one heading it up."

Theo choked a little. Brandman pushed a paper cup of water toward him with a solicitous smile.

Now, hours later, staring at the Danish, Theo realized, *That's probably when I should have asked for a lawyer.* But the two detectives had left the room after the accusation, and no one had ever read him his Miranda rights.

Eventually, a technician had arrived and asked to take blood and hair samples. Fingerprints, too, although he assured Theo he wasn't being arrested. Theo complied without question. At some point, Freeman had returned to escort Theo to the men's room and bring him cold coffee and a box of Danish. Normally, he abstained from junk food—he'd read too many terrifying articles in the *Times* about killer preservatives and carcinogenic chemicals—but if they kept him much longer, he might have to relent. He was eyeing the least offensive of the bunch—a round pastry with a sweet cream cheese center—when he heard a raised voice in the hallway. The nearly soundproof door prevented him from catching the words, but he recognized Brandman's gravelly voice.

Moments later, the door swung open and Brandman, red-faced, strode into the room.

"Well, Professor, you're free to go. We're not bringing any charges at this time." He adjusted the cuffs of his suit as he spoke, as if to distract himself from whatever rancorous thoughts raced through his head.

"Really?"

"Do you want to stay?"

"Not unless you change the menu."

"Oh, I'm sorry. The taxpayers can't afford 'arugula,' or whatever it is you usually eat for your afternoon tea."

You walked into that one, Theo thought. Antagonizing Brandman further was, he decided, counterproductive. "Sorry if I sounded like a prick. Thank you. For the Danish. And for letting me go."

"Don't thank me. Thank the criminal justice system. We

can't hold you indefinitely. And—so far at least—we don't have enough evidence to secure a warrant for your arrest."

"Because I didn't do anything."

"You lied about your relationship with the victim. You threatened a policeman. And tonight, we'll be searching every cemetery in Manhattan because of you, even though it's probably a colossal waste of time. You've done plenty, Professor, trust me. Stay close. We'll have more questions for you. I guarantee it."

Chapter 17

HUNTRESS OF THE WILD BOAR

Selene and Hippo left Central Park at 100th Street. A block and a half later, they reached the Twenty-fourth Precinct. Selene didn't need to come down this particular street to get home. But she knew this precinct had jurisdiction over the section of Riverside Park where Helen Emerson's body had been found.

"Theodore Schultz is inside," she said to Hippo. "Probably talking his way into even more trouble." The dog looked up at her, tongue flapping.

"You think that's funny, huh? Might be good for him to be in a bit of danger, right? Get him out of the library. What do you think, should we stay and talk to him? Or leave this one to the cops and go worry about my own family for once?" Hippo wagged her tail. "That's an awfully noncommittal gesture," Selene complained.

She moved to sit on the steps of the library across the street, staring at the entrance to the police station, still unsure if she should wait or not. She certainly wouldn't go inside. She hadn't been inside a police station since 1975, when she last wore the uniform. She'd hated that outfit—the miniature fedora perched on her head, liable to fall off at any moment, wide-heeled pumps made for walking, not climbing or sprinting, and worst of all, the stiff blue knee-length skirt. She and Geraldine Hansen had often laughed about that skirt. Every time they detained a suspect by kneeling on his back, they had to choose between splitting the seams or hiking it up and displaying their pantyhose-encased buttocks to the world.

Back in the 1920s, when the Huntress joined the force the first time, she hadn't worn a uniform at all. The original "patrol-women" were meant to be motherly figures—they didn't even carry guns. She'd never been able to tell Geraldine about that experience, of course, but she'd often thought the young woman would've enjoyed hearing about the NYPD in the Jazz Age.

Silver-eyed Melissa DuBois had applied to join the newly established Policewomen's Bureau using a stack of references painstakingly forged by Swifty O'May, the fastest officer on the force, known for chasing down criminals for dozens of city blocks without breaking a sweat. They might have called him Superman, if the character had been invented yet. To the Huntress, he was just Hermes.

Her tenure at the all-female Bureau was a heady time for the Relentless One. For the first time in centuries, she found herself among a group of women who shared her passion for protecting the innocent and bringing the men who harmed them to justice. Against her better judgment, she'd made real friends. She clung to the job like a lifeline, careful never to kill the men she arrested or reveal any of her more suspiciously preternatural attributes. She wanted to remain Melissa DuBois for as long as possible.

Yet after twenty years on the force, when her companions had grown stout and gray and she remained as young as ever, she'd had no choice. One day, Melissa DuBois fell ill. A week later, she was dead. The Huntress moved to a new neighborhood, took a new name, and forgot the friends she'd abandoned.

But with or without a badge, she'd never forgotten the women she'd sworn to protect.

And I'm not about to now, Selene thought, staring at the precinct house. *He won't escape. Not this time.*

"We'll wait for the professor, Hippo," she said, scratching the dog behind her ears. "Mother will understand." As if in response, the dog bounded up, tearing the leash from Selene's grasp, and loped across the street. "Come back here, you ridiculous—" She stopped her scolding when she saw Hippo's target. Theodore Schultz had finally emerged.

The professor stood a few careful paces shy of Hippolyta, his shoulders hunched. The dog didn't look happy to see him, but she also wasn't growling. More confirmation of his innocence: Hippo didn't recognize his scent from the blankets.

"Schultz," Selene called.

He started as if from a dream. "Ms. DiSilva?"

As she approached, he stood up a little straighter, his look of surprise dissolving into one of relief. "I didn't think I'd see you here," he said with a small, crooked smile. *He's handsome,* Selene decided. *In a scholarly sort of way.*

"Well, I'd almost given up on you, but I see they finally let you go."

"Yeah, they never formally arrested me," he sighed, rubbing at his chin as if he expected to have a full growth of beard—as if he'd been in the slammer for three months rather than in a station for three hours. "Just took me in for questioning. The lead detective thinks I'm involved."

"You're no killer, Schultz."

"I wish you'd tell that to the cops. They can't decide if I'm a bookish crackpot, eccentric but harmless, or a malevolent mastermind about to slaughter another victim."

She cocked her head. "Neither, I don't think."

"I was thinking more Indiana Jones, myself. Saving the world while rakishly handsome and incredibly erudite." His sudden grin coaxed a dimple to his left cheek, matching the one on the tip of his pointed chin.

Hippo woofed at him, and Selene gave him a cold stare. She had no intention of encouraging his flirtation. "Sounds like Hippolyta disagrees with your assessment."

"Hippolyta!" Schultz's eyes lit up. Selene cursed inwardly, realizing she'd opened up a whole can of worms (*a whole Pandora's Jar,* she thought ruefully) by mentioning a Greek name.

"You named her after the Amazonian queen," Schultz went on. "And you recognized the chiton and the wreath. Even the *sex crines* braids. Since when is a PI also a myth geek?"

"Hippolyta wasn't a myth," Selene couldn't help herself from replying, rather tersely.

He adjusted his wire-rimmed glasses and frowned skeptically. "Well, that depends on how you define 'myth.' If you mean she was a historical person, as far as I'm aware, the literature on the subject is inconclusive. Most likely, the Amazonian legends are reflections of the ancient Greek patriarchy's fear of matriarchal societies. After all—"

Selene was saved from the lecture by his cell phone.

"I'm sorry, I need to answer this," he said. "Gabriela? You'll never believe where I just spent the last three and half hours. What—how did you? It's *online*?" He was pacing the sidewalk now, his face pale as he listened intently. The woman on the other end spoke loudly enough for Selene to hear her screeching through the earpiece. Something about the "Pervy Professor" and a "person of interest" in Helen's murder.

"No, thanks for telling me. I was bound to find out soon enough. I'm okay, hon—" Selene wrinkled her nose at the endearment. "Not about to drink my poison hemlock quite yet. I'll be fine. But I have to go. I love you, too." He hung up and leaned against a nearby lamppost for a moment. Before Selene could ask him what was wrong, he straightened and started walking back toward the precinct house.

"Where're you going?"

"To tell Detective Brandman where to shove his unwarranted assumptions. Might just get myself arrested for real."

"Wait!" Impulsively, she placed a hand on his forearm. His tendons jumped beneath her fingers as if he'd been hit with an electric shock. She pulled her hand back quickly. "What happened?" she asked, trying to cover her discomfort.

He turned toward her, his face a mask of anger, and she couldn't help feeling a tug of empathy. "Somehow the press got wind of the fact that the cops hauled me in," Schultz said. "It doesn't even matter that I've been released. According to the always reliable Twittersphere, I'm a person of interest." The hand clutching his cell phone shook. Selene wasn't sure if it was from rage or fear.

"They don't have a choice. Since you're Helen's ex-boyfriend, they have to investigate you."

He nearly jumped. "How did you—"

She shrugged. "Men don't usually stand by rivers mourning their dead professional colleagues."

"It was a long time ago," he said tightly. "I don't see why it's anyone's business."

"It's everyone's business actually. Although her current boyfriend is the more obvious suspect."

"Fiancé actually."

"That was fast."

"He's pretty hard to resist. And he loved her, that was clear just by looking at them together. Besides, he's got an alibi. I, on the other hand, was dumb enough to be all alone. Like most nights. Now if you'll excuse me, I have to go commit professional suicide." He turned back toward the precinct house.

"You may want to rethink," Selene said, gesturing toward a news van rumbling down the street toward them. "Seems news has spread."

"Shit-balls."

"Just turn back around and walk calmly. Follow me." This man had information she needed—she couldn't afford to have him back in jail or terrorized by reporters.

Theo walked beside her, glancing nervously over his shoulder every few steps. Under his breath, he kept up a nearly incomprehensible stream of vituperation. "Gonna shove my Ivory Tower so far up his...Twitter my ass...Teach him to mess with a classicist..."

"I understand your anger," Selene said, a little alarmed by his rambling. She needed him lucid. "I've wanted to strangle more than a few cops myself over the years, but it only ever gets you deeper in trouble. How long has it been since you've eaten?" she asked. That sounded like the sort of thing mortals asked when trying to calm each other.

He stopped cursing. "I think I had some toast at like six last night."

"Well, I know it's still early, but I'm getting hungry for lunch." That was an understatement. For the last hour, she'd been positively famished. The aching hunger reminded her of the first few centuries after the Diaspora when, deprived of the gods' usual nectar, ambrosia, and burnt offerings, she'd needed ten thousand calories a day to sustain her. "We're out of sight of the reporters, and I know a good place around here. Why don't you come?"

"Really?" He looked suspicious. With the day he'd been having, she couldn't blame him.

"Why not?" she asked, trying to sound nonchalant. She could actually think of a million reasons why not. In most of her interactions with men, they ended up dead.

"You're not afraid to be seen with the notorious Pervy Professor? Seems the hashtag's going viral."

Selene, as usual, wasn't exactly sure what he meant, but she got the gist. "Hippolyta will bite the testicles off any man who looks at me wrong, so I think I'm good."

A moment later, Schultz gave her a grateful, dimpled grin, obviously deciding she'd been joking. He was wrong.

——◆——

Theo spent the first part of the meal eyeing the tower of pork dumplings, moo shu pork, pork fried rice, and Chinese spareribs on their table with something akin to awe.

Selene caught his eye. "Do you have a problem with women with big appetites?" she asked as she tore the last strip of meat off the bone with her perfect white teeth.

"Big? I think this qualifies as more like Colossus of Rhodes meets Coney Island hotdog champ." He looked down at his modest portion of beef with broccoli. "I'm feeling inadequate."

She shrugged as if to say he was probably right—and it wasn't her problem. Then she pulled off her baseball cap. She ran a long-fingered hand through her hair, then let it fall back against her pale cheek in a wave as smooth as a raven's wing.

Theo had never seen her without her hat shadowing her face. Only the waitress's arrival could drag his attention from the perfect symmetry of Selene's features. The young Chinese woman balanced another plateful of steamed roast pork buns on the overcrowded table. "Does she always order this much?" he asked with a smile.

The waitress shook her head emphatically. "She comes in once a week. Always pork. But never like this." She looked at Selene. "You pregnant?"

Selene dropped the bone to her plate with a clatter, spots of red flaring on each pale cheek. "How dare you," she hissed. She grabbed the edge of the table as if she might rise.

"Ha! She's just training for an Iron Woman triathlon," Theo said quickly. He was surprised by his instinctive need to smooth Selene's way in the world. Social skills were clearly not her strong suit. "Needs all the calories she can get." Besides, a triathlon seemed perfectly reasonable: When Selene had removed her leather jacket and rolled up the sleeves of her flannel, he'd had to tear his gaze away from the lean muscles in her arms.

"Okay." The waitress laughed and winked at Theo. "But if this happens next week, we'll need to order more pork just to keep up."

"Does she always give you such a hard time?" Theo asked Selene when the waitress left.

"I've never spoken to her before—except to order."

"She seemed to know you."

Selene's brows lowered. "You think because someone teases you and you laugh and she winks...you think they know you?"

"Well—"

"They don't. No one really knows anyone." Before Theo could respond, she continued, "Now tell me what else you know about Helen's murder."

He started a little at the abrupt transition, but then found himself smiling, glad someone finally wanted to listen. "Well, first off, if we're right about this whole cult thing, we're not just looking for one killer. But I don't know if the cops found any concrete evidence to back me up."

Selene paused with a dumpling halfway to her mouth. "They may not have. But I did. There're multiple men involved."

"Really? How did you—"

"I snuck inside the hospital after the police left." A tiny, self-satisfied smile pulled at the corner of her lips.

"I know I wanted you to look at the crime scene, but isn't that illegal?"

"So's assaulting a police officer," she said dryly, dunking the dumpling in soy sauce.

Despite his penchant for pissing off authority figures, Theo had never been the type to engage in deliberate criminality. Until this morning, his brushes with the law had either been misunderstandings or, like the eminent domain sit-in, done in the service of a higher purpose. Once, when he'd absent-mindedly walked out of a grocery store without paying for his six-pack of beer, he'd run six blocks back to the store when he realized his mistake, arriving so flushed and sweaty and full of mortified contrition that the cashier wound up apologizing to him rather than the other way around. Yet here he was, aiding and abetting a woman who clearly made a habit of subverting the police. The idea shivered uneasily down his spine. Then he thought of Brandman's sarcastic grimace and decided that maybe a little more of Selene DiSilva was exactly what he needed.

He took a ruminative bite of broccoli, then asked, "So you're *sure* there were signs of Asclepius at the crime scene?"

"There were probably thirty or forty snakes hanging from the ceiling and scales from some larger serpent on the floor. That evidence enough for you?"

Theo nearly coughed up his food. He'd predicted the snakes, but never so many.

"And I saw the body. A girl. A virgin this time, not just a woman dressed up as one."

Theo put down his chopsticks, his appetite gone. "We have to get these guys."

Selene's silver eyes burned into him. "That's why I'm here, Professor. You tell me what you know, and I'll find them."

"What else was in the room?"

"The remains of a fire. And a tooth. A tusk maybe."

He smacked the table, rattling the teapot. "Burnt offering of a piglet to Demeter, the Goddess of Grain. I was right."

"Piglets don't have tusks, Professor."

"Technicalities," he replied, unfazed. "This is definitely a re-creation of the Eleusinian Mysteries. Let me start from the beginning, so you understand. The ritual is based on the story of Demeter and her daughter Persephone—"

"I know that part," she interrupted.

"You sure?" He crooked a skeptical eyebrow in her direction. "It's essential that you—"

With an angry scowl, she cut him off. "It begins when the Goddess of Spring and Flowers—and other mild and useless realms—was wandering in a meadow, making wreaths with her equally vapid maidens."

He laughed at the image of Persephone as an idiot teenager with her clique of best-friend mean girls. "That's not how it's usually told."

"Then listen closely. The Lord of the Dead, not known for his taste in women, looked up from the Underworld and found his dewy niece irresistible," Selene continued. "A wide chasm opened in the earth and four black stallions bore the Hidden One's chariot into the light of day." Her voice had lost its brisk cockiness. She spoke slowly, almost formally, and her gaze turned inward as if watching an old memory unspool before her eyes. "He seized the girl by her hair, dragging her to his side. The earth closed above their heads, but her screams could still be heard, very faint and growing ever fainter as he took her deeper into his realm. The Goddess of Grain searched in vain for her daughter, nine long days of bewildered grief, until Helios the Sun, who sees all, took pity and told her what had happened."

Her cadences reminded Theo of the Homeric *Ode to Demeter*. He stared in awe as Selene continued. *Who was this woman?*

"The goddess refused to enter Olympus until her daughter returned. She wandered the earth until she came to rest in Eleusis. There she stayed, and mourned, and withheld her bounty from the land. Famine spread and mankind starved. Finally, even the gods suffered when men lacked the food to make burnt offerings. Only then did the mighty King of the Gods send his son, the Conductor of Souls, to fetch the girl back. But it was too late." Selene's voice grew quiet and anger furrowed her face. "The girl sat on her throne of black marble, her golden skin ashen, her face turned to the ground. All those long months, while mankind starved beneath her mother's wrath, she'd suffered in her uncle's bed. Every night, he took her, and every night she felt as if the great chasm had opened beneath her once more. No one ever heard her screams." Selene paused in the telling, as if listening for Persephone's echoing cries.

Theo took a long swallow of tea to fill the silence. "I've always told my students these myths are malleable," he ventured finally, "but I've never quite heard it like that."

Her gaze snapped to him, her eyes narrowed. "What do you imagine happens when a man abducts a virgin for his own pleasure? That they sit and chat about puppies?"

He felt himself backpedaling. "I just mean this went from ABC Family to HBO really fast. Pretty dark."

"How else should it be? The Hidden One forced the food of the dead—three pomegranate seeds—down her throat so that even once she left the Underworld with the Conductor of Souls, the Goddess of Spring would still be forced to return to her husband for a portion of every year. Three months of torture, repeated for eternity, because of three lousy seeds. If that's not dark, what is?"

Theo wasn't sure what to say. He couldn't help being impressed with her knowledge—and a little unnerved by her passion.

She speared a dumpling with a chopstick. "Now tell me what you know about the Mysteries."

"You seem to know plenty on your own."

"I know the story. That doesn't mean I know what men did with it when they turned it into a ritual. That's where you come in."

"Ah. Glad I can be of some use." He took a pen from his coat pocket and spread a paper napkin across the table. He regretted handing Brandman his careful calendar, but decided to make do. Drawing a rough outline as he spoke, he explained the first five days of the Eleusis ritual. First, the procession of the sacred objects from Eleusis to Athens. Day Two: the *Agyrmos* gathering, complete with singing and dancing to announce the beginning of the ritual. Next, the purification in seawater. On the fourth day, the sacrifice of grain or piglets to Demeter. Then, the *Asklepia*. As a healing god known for bringing the dead back to life, Asclepius fit in with the Mysteries' overall theme of rebirth.

Unlike the detective, Selene listened with rapt attention. "So far it seems pretty mild," she said when Theo finished explaining how the hospital basement room had served as a stand-in for the traditional cave used in Aesculapian rites.

"It gets rowdier," he assured her. "Day Six is the *Pompe*. It begins, again, with sacrifices to the goddesses. Then, a procession from the Kerameikos cemetery in Athens back to the temple in Eleusis. Now I know this sounds like a lot of walking in circles: Take the *hiera* from Eleusis to Athens on Day One, then back again during the *Pompe*. But you have to remember that every part of the ritual is symbolic, every myth contains many truths. The procession likely represents approaching death by walking through the graveyard and then returning to life by reentering Eleusis. While the initiates walk across the Bridge of Jests, the head priest—the hierophant—yells obscene jokes. Supposedly, he's honoring the memory of the foul-mouthed crone who was the only one to make Demeter laugh during her long search for her daughter.

"At this point, the hierophant also invokes Dionysus, the God of Wine. He probably wasn't connected to the Eleusinian Mysteries originally, but later incarnations of the ritual definitely involved him. Not surprising, since he's also a fertility and harvest god. Besides, every good party needs a little social lubrication, right?" He flashed Selene a grin, which she ignored.

He took another fortifying drink of tea, then returned his attention to the napkin. "The initiates—*mystai*, that's the correct term—gather in a field for nightlong revels called the *Pannychis* on Day Seven. Dancing, sacrifices, the works. But it's the

next two days," he continued, fiercely underlining *"Days 8 &
9"* on the napkin, "that get really interesting. The *mystai* go to
the Telesterion—the Hall of Completion—for the two Nights
of the Mysteries, the *Nychtes Mysteriotides.* That's where the ritual
reaches its climax with the 'Unspeakables.' "

"Which are..."

He raised his hands in futility. "Who knows. Unspeakable
meant unspeakable, so the Greeks kept the secret tighter than
pants on a hipster. *But,*" he went on before Selene could protest,
"that hasn't stopped classicists from speculating for centuries.
Supposedly, there were three stages. First, the *Legomena*: 'Things
Said.' Possibly, this involved the retelling of Demeter and Persephone's story. Next, *Dromena*: 'Things Done.' Maybe they actually
reenact the story here—the abduction, the rape, the return. Last,
Deiknumena: 'Things Shown.' This is the important part, the real
climax. The initiates learn the answers to life's greatest questions, communicated through epiphanic visions given to them
by the gods." He laughed shortly. "Not really, of course, that's
just what they claimed. Probably they were just reacting to
drinking *kykeon*, the 'specialty cocktail' of the Mysteries." He
scrawled *"kykeon"* on the paper napkin. "We don't know the
exact ingredients, but it probably incorporated barley water, so it
may have contained a grain fungus that mimics the chemicals in
LSD. I suspect the whole 'communing with the gods' thing was
just one big acid trip.

"Then, on Day Ten, they wrap things up with the *Plemochoai*,
the offering of libations to the ancestors. Sort of anticlimactic,
if you ask me, but a chance to slowly acclimate back to the real
world." He passed her the napkin, crowded and wet with bleeding ink.

"This is all about grain, fertility, wine," she said, scanning
the paper. "Approaching death, yes, but coming back to life.
Why would someone use it as a basis for a murder cult? No one
worships agriculture in New York City anymore or cares about

the rape of a virgin. Why not bring back the worship of some more interesting deities?" she asked with a hint of ferocity. Theo wondered whom Selene would consider worthy of homage—probably Ares and Athena, the war gods.

"Maybe because what they were doing in Eleusis was somehow more powerful and more meaningful than any other religious cult in ancient Greece. If you're going to bring back a cult, you might as well bring back the best."

"Maybe." Selene didn't look convinced. "And you told all this to the police?"

"I tried, but it seems my relationship with Helen compromises my theories. I don't think they'll be consulting with me any longer. Also, I may have accused the lead detective of criminal negligence in not following up my lead sooner."

"Not the best move."

Theo cleared his throat. "Well, no. It seems Brandman's now deliberately devastating my professional and personal life." He laughed shortly.

"You think he leaked your name to the press? That's not standard procedure. Did you tell anyone about getting arrested?"

"I wasn't really *arrested*. And the only person I called was the chair of the department—I had to warn him I was going to miss my translation seminar today." Theo had been relieved to just leave a message on Bill Webb's voice mail. He couldn't have borne hearing the sanctimonious chair's reaction. *Once again, you've brought scrutiny and shame on this department, Schultz. The only option for you is honor killing.*

"Maybe the police are playing politics," said Selene. "Trying to convince the public that they're making progress on the case before the commissioner winds up with his head on a platter for not keeping the women of New York safe."

"Great. I'm just a pawn, huh? Sounds a lot like university politics."

"Look, Schultz—"

"Theo—please."

"I think I've got enough to go on." Selene put the lecture-soaked napkin in her pocket and stood up. "You can stop worrying about all this."

Theo stared at her. "I don't *want* to stop worrying about this." She hadn't understood at all. "I'm going to catch whoever killed Helen."

Selene sighed, the way Theo did when his crosstown bus was stuck in motionless traffic. Like there could be nothing more frustrating. She reached behind her chair for her black leather jacket. "I know you cared about her, but—"

"I owe her this."

"Things are going to get very hairy. I can take it from here."

"Not without me. You wouldn't have known about the Eleusinian connection without me, and I'm the one with access to photos of the Met robberies."

"*What* Met robberies?" She dropped back down into the seat.

Theo mustered a smile, glad to see her calm façade crack. "On Monday night, two ancient containers were stolen from the Greek and Roman Collection. A colleague from the museum is sending me the photos—they should be waiting at my office up at Columbia by now." At least, Theo *hoped* they were waiting for him.

"Anything else you haven't told me?" She leaned forward across the table.

She might have been trying to intimidate him, but all Theo could think was, *I wouldn't mind telling you how beautiful you are. The sort of strong nose and square jaw that most women couldn't pull off. But you look like you were fashioned from white marble by Pygmalion himself.* Her skin didn't even have pores.

"Well?" she pressed, her flashing eyes drawing his attention back to the situation at hand.

"There was actually a rash of robberies," he admitted, refilling his teacup and dumping in another packet of sugar. "A snake was stolen from the Natural History Museum two nights ago. That's how I knew to expect the *Asklepia*."

Selene sat back, looking grim. "Well, if that's the case, now I know where they got this." She pulled an enormous blackened tooth from her backpack. Theo felt his jaw drop. It could have been a dinosaur fang—if dinosaurs had fangs. Selene flipped the tooth casually in her hand.

"*Now* who's withholding information? I thought you *saw* a tusk in the hospital, not *stole* it." Breaking into the crime scene was one thing...but theft? What was he getting himself into?

"It was under a shelf in the storeroom. Did you really want me to just leave it there? The cops missed it in their search and I couldn't very well tell them I'd broken in and done a better investigation than they had."

"That's too big to be some random sacrificial offering. It must be one of the *hiera*. You've got to give it to the police."

"Right. Because they've done such a good job so far?"

"Then give it back to the museum," he insisted.

"Not until I figure out exactly what it is," she shot back.

Theo found himself transfixed, watching her nostrils flare with every seething breath.

Then he started to laugh, suddenly elated. All the pieces of the puzzle were coming together. He'd found the perfect partner. Sure, he could do the research himself, but he didn't have a lot of practice with the more illegal aspects of their quest. For Selene DiSilva, on the other hand, it seemed all in a day's work.

"Now you're stuck with me—I've got a friend at Natural History. We can return the tooth, get it identified, *and* check out the crime scene from Thursday night." He downed the last of his tea, grabbed his coat, and waved at the waitress for the check. "But first, we should look at the photos from the Met before I get fired and locked out of my office. We'll zip up to Columbia, then head back down to the museum before it closes."

Selene stood up, reaching into her back pocket for her wallet.

"I'll get it," Theo began, but she glowered him into silence and carefully counted out her share of the check. Then they stood without speaking, staring across the table at each other. He still didn't know what to make of her. Despite her attempts to hide herself behind her baseball cap and loose clothes, only a eunuch or a blind man wouldn't find her attractive. *No, scratch that,* he amended, *a blind man would still smell the cypress forest she seems to carry around in that huge backpack of hers.* Theo stayed still, sure she'd disappear if he moved, just as she had that morning by the hospital. So he waited for her to make the first move.

Finally, she picked up her backpack and slung it over one shoulder, then took a step toward him. "Before these assholes kill another woman, I'm going to find them—with or without you. Nobody hired me. Nobody's paying me. I don't talk to the press or the cops. I'm just going to track them down and catch them and—" Theo could have sworn she was about to say "kill." "If your museum contacts can help me do that, then I'll come with you." She put on her baseball cap and pulled it low, so he could barely see her eyes glaring at him from beneath the brim. "But don't think we're partners, because we're not."

Theo grinned and snagged the sole leftover pork dumpling off her plate, chewing with relish. "Good. I think I'm going to like working with you."

Chapter 18

DAUGHTER OF LETO

On the walk north, Selene tried hard to ignore her self-appointed sidekick. He didn't seem to mind, rattling on about the details of Mystery Cults through the ages. She found his enthusiasm unnerving. Solving crimes had usually been serious, solitary work for Selene. Occasionally over the years she'd had a female partner. But never a man. For the Virgin Goddess, mortal men had always fallen into two categories: those to be punished and those to be ignored. Slowly, she was coming to realize that Theodore Schultz didn't fall neatly into either camp. In fact, she had to admit that working with him might even be useful. Mankind had invented writing and painting to compensate for their inability to perceive multiple realities at once. As a result, Theo's books taught him more about the Mysteries than Selene's own hazy memories of godhood could offer. The Eleusinian goddesses themselves, Persephone and Demeter, might not even remember their own rites in as much detail as the books provided. Their memories would be as cloudy and confused as Selene's.

The one thing Theo's books could never teach him, of course, was the true purpose of the cult. He could spend years trying to justify each ritual in its broader social context, but he'd never understand the fundamental truth—the ancients worshiped the gods because the gods were real. The gods demanded it. And the gods would torture you for eternity in the pit of Tartarus if you refused, just as they'd sentenced Sisyphus, who stole their sacred food, to push a boulder up a hill in the Underworld, only to have it eternally roll back down. When Theo had grabbed her last dumpling, he didn't know how lucky he was that Selene was Artemis no longer.

As for Theo's theories about the supposedly hallucinogenic properties of *kykeon*, however, he might have a point. In their prime, the Olympians could send dreams and prophecies to anyone at any time—no assistance necessary. But as their power had faded, and their threats of punishment grew empty, the gods had turned desperate. Selene wouldn't put it past her kin to consider drugging their followers.

Still thinking wistfully of Sisyphean torture, she followed the professor through the tall gates of Columbia's main quad. For every student who noticed him and looked askance, whispering in a friend's ear, another trotted up to Theo and offered to help.

"What the hell, Dr. Schultz?" asked one young Indian man with a surfer's accent. "It's bullshit, what they're saying. The cops have their heads up their asses. We'll have another sit-in. Like we did to protest the expansion. We won't move until they clear your name."

"Slow down, Anant. There's no need to go all *Lysistrata*," Theo assured him.

Selene gave a little snort of amusement, grateful for a reference she could finally understand, but the student just looked at him blankly.

Theo looked at the kid over his glasses. "The Aristophanes play where the women of Greece withhold sex from their husbands until they agree to end the Peloponnesian War? I reminded you to read it at our last class?" Nothing. Theo sighed. "I appreciate the effort, Anant, but let's hold off on the sit-in until you finish the homework. I'll be fine, I promise."

When they reached Hamilton Hall, Selene and Hippo followed Theo up the steps of the stately Greek Revival building. A bronze statue of the building's namesake stood guard on a pedestal at the top of the stairs. "Asshole," Selene couldn't help muttering as they passed. Theo shot her a startled glance.

"Not you. Him." She jerked her thumb at the statue, then immediately regretted it. She forgot sometimes how strange she seemed to mortals.

"Alexander Hamilton? What do you have against *him*?"

"Long story," she mumbled, following Theo through the massive wooden door. She couldn't very well explain that on a particularly humid July Fourth in 1804, Hamilton had run into Dianne Delia, a strikingly tall, black-haired beauty, on the streets of Greenwich Village as he stumbled toward his carriage, drunk and reeling from a night of celebrating the republic he'd helped create. He tried to lure the young woman to a nearby inn and wouldn't take no for an answer. Dianne finally resorted to kicking Hamilton soundly in the groin and pushing him into the horseshit-strewn street. He'd had her arrested for disorderly conduct. She spent a week in a fetid jail cell next to a mildly insane Irishwoman who sang rude Gaelic ditties from dawn to dusk. History remembers that Hamilton was fatally shot in a duel with Aaron Burr on the shores of New Jersey soon after Dianne was released. Those who knew Burr were surprised—he was supposed to fire into the ground. Those who knew the Huntress were not—she'd been hiding in the woods with a pistol beyond the dueling ground, and when Burr fired, so did she.

Theo led the way to an empty lobby area on the top floor of the building. He walked behind the reception desk to his in-box. "Ah-hah!" He waved a slim envelope with the Met's logo in the corner. "Got it."

He led her down a long, musty corridor lined with offices. One bore a conspicuous red sticker pressed between the door and its frame, reading "EVIDENCE" in large block print.

"I see the cops have already been here," said Selene.

"Yeah. Took the good stuff from Helen's office and sealed it up."

Selene blew out a frustrated breath.

"I know," he concurred. "I'm desperate to get my hands on the manuscript she was working on, and no one knows where it is. I'm sure she must have kept some research notes in her office—she always preferred to handwrite things anyway. It's possible the cops may have left something useful behind, since I doubt they even knew what they were looking for."

"You think her notes would be helpful?"

"Definitely. They'd tell us her sources, which might lead us to whoever got her mixed up in this cult in the first place. And we might find more of the papyri fragments she translated. Then we'd know what she uncovered about the Mystery itself. My own predictions about the cult's next move are guesswork. But Helen must have spent at least two years on this. I bet she had all the answers."

Theo led her down a long, musty corridor to his office and gave a relieved sigh when the door clicked open. "At least they haven't changed the locks on me yet."

He ushered Selene inside the cramped room. Floor-to-ceiling bookcases jammed the walls, stuffed two rows deep with volumes in Ancient Greek, Latin, English, and Acadian. Masks, vases, and miniature plinths competed for space on the shelves, many of which looked ready to give way with the addition of one more pamphlet. Above his desk—a desk piled a foot high with notes—hung maps of ancient Greece alongside a photo of the Parthenon, a reproduction of the Minoan *Phaistos* Disc, and dozens of scribbled index cards tacked to the wall. Memos and lecture outlines littered the floor. With a frustrated huff,

Hippo wedged herself into the only space big enough for her—underneath the desk. Papers crunched under her weight as she curled into a surprisingly small ball.

"Who's that?" Selene asked, pointing to a color photograph of a man with shaggy blond hair and a draped white tunic, who could've been a younger version of Theo. "He looks familiar."

"Because he's Luke Skywalker," he said, looking at her as if she were mentally disabled.

"Oh. Right."

"You've never heard of *Star Wars*?"

"Of course I've heard of it," she said brusquely. Even the Huntress couldn't avoid imbibing a certain amount of pop culture. "I've just never...you know...seen it."

"Wow. It doesn't get much more like a Greek hero archetype than *Star Wars*. The ancient myths tell about classical civilization; our own myths do the same for us. And some stories are so good that they're as relevant today as they were three thousand years ago, and they'll be just as relevant in a galaxy far, far away. Young man from the sticks—not unlike Perseus or Achilles—goes off to battle evil, finding an inner strength he didn't know he had, wielding a magical weapon, overcoming some challenging father-son issues, and finally fulfilling his destiny to save the world." Seeing the utter delight on his face, Selene felt the stirrings of a smile. But only the stirrings. "I'll show you sometime," he said. Then his smile faded, and he looked away. Selene wasn't sure what expression he'd seen on her face, but she assumed it hadn't been encouraging.

"Let's just look at the photos from the Met," she said.

"Right, right." He turned to his desk. Then he paused. He moved a few stacks of papers. "Wait. I put it down right here... I can't have possibly..."

"Is this a joke? We don't have time for this." She didn't want to smile anymore. She wanted to growl.

"Did you see where the envelope went?" He was on his knees

now, sifting through the drifts of documents on the floor. "Maybe it slid off one of the piles."

"You may be the most—"

"Amazing classicist you've ever met? That's what I thought you were going to say. The good news is, I have a background in archeology and my office is always a midden, so I'm an expert at this sort of dig."

Sometime between when he donned a floppy safari hat from his desk drawer and when he started referring to Hippo as "Cerberus the Hell Hound, guarding the entrance to the UnderDesk," Selene found herself more entertained than annoyed.

"Or are you a Sphinx?" he asked the dog, who cocked a baleful brow at him. "Must I answer a riddle before you will allow me access to the treasures on which you sit? What's that?" He squatted down, his face hovering close to Hippo's. "What tastes better than it smells, you ask? Hmm . . . good one . . ." He rubbed his chin thoughtfully.

The dog lifted her head and licked his face.

"That's it!" he spluttered though the cascading drool. "A tongue!" Theo looked up and met Selene's eyes from beneath the brim of his ridiculous hat.

Only then did she realize she was actually grinning.

"Ah!" He shook a victorious fist in the air. "I've done it! You're laughing, I dare you not to." She spluttered a bit, failing to control the chuckle burbling inside. Theo looked at the ceiling, raising both hands as if to an unseen deity. "You see, she *is* human after all!"

With that, Selene threw back her head and let loose. Not her usual dry snort, but her true laugh—a very silly, very loud, honking guffaw. She'd once complained to her father that if he was going to give her such a preposterous laugh, he should've at least spared her the ability to feel shame. Zeus had only smiled and winked. *Your mother sometimes says I can't feel shame, but she's wrong. And good thing, too. Because if she thinks I'm incorrigible now, only think how I'd be if I didn't feel at least a little guilt!*

Theo was laughing, too, a convulsive, breathless hoot. "Don't cover it up," he insisted as Selene's hand flew to her mouth in embarrassment. "That's a fantastic laugh. Completely contagious." Hippo finally scuttled out into the room, woofing her agreement. Theo grabbed the missing envelope from under the desk, rumpled and covered with dog hair, and held aloft his hard-won trophy, as triumphant as Jason with his Golden Fleece.

Selene felt a door inside her crack open despite herself. She couldn't quite wipe the smile from her face. *It's going to be okay*, she thought suddenly. *No one else needs to die.*

Still chuckling, Theo ripped open the envelope and held a paper out toward Selene. "Check it out. Courtesy of my friend Steve over at the Met."

She examined the first grainy photo. A terracotta vase with a wide, flaring lip. The faintest suggestion of wheat sheaves painted in darker brown around its base. Theo leaned forward.

"Damn, I love it when I'm right," he said, beaming. "That's a clay replica of a *kalathos*. Exactly like the basket they used at Eleusis to carry their sacred objects." He did a quick search of the Met's online database. "Accession number 74.51.1137 probably," he mused. "No photo on the website, but the description matches up. It's old. Really old—1200 BC, they think. Our cult's reaching way back before the Athenian Golden Age—all the way to the beginning of Greek religion as we know it. To be perfectly authentic, they should've used a woven *kalathos* rather than a terracotta one, but the real wool-gathering baskets didn't survive the way pottery did."

Selene flipped to the next page.

"Hmm. Terracotta red-figure bell-krater," Theo announced. "Those were usually used for mixing wine and water. Not a chest, like the *kiste* should be, but maybe all they could get their hands on. That means they've got their two sacred containers. Thank God they lost their tusk in the hospital. If they're missing one of the *hiera*, that may slow them down. Give us time to catch up."

He leaned closer to the paper, his head bent. Selene found herself staring at the threads of silver that curled out from his sideburns. Oblivious to her scrutiny, Theo went on. "Interesting red figure. Three stags. Doesn't seem relevant to the cult, does it? Strange. If they couldn't find a real *kiste*, they should at least choose something with a meaningful design—wheat sheaves or pigs or something to do with the Underworld."

"Don't tell me you're rethinking your Eleusinian theory."

"Absolutely not." He looked up at her, and for a moment, his face was only inches away. "I'm way too stubborn for that." He swung to his computer, and Selene felt oddly relieved. "Besides," he continued, "don't you know the key to understanding Greek pottery is looking at the back? Two sides to every myth. Two sides to every vase." He gave her a cocky grin as he checked the online database. "Fifth century BC bell-krater with three stags on the obverse. Voilà. And on the reverse...drumroll please... four unidentified figures." Selene applauded sarcastically. "Okay, not helpful, I admit. But let's just take a look, shall we?" He clicked open a photo of the vase's reverse. "A young man and two women, one with a veil and a lotus staff, the other holding a child's hand..."

But Selene wasn't listening.

She had no photographs of her mother. Mortals amassed pictures and keepsakes as a dress rehearsal for the inevitably permanent parting of death. The Athanatoi, on the other hand, never feared forgetting each other's faces—never needed to seize and remember some special moment. There would be countless such events in the future, and there had been countless such events in the past. But staring at the painting of her brother, her mother, and herself on the face of the pottery, Selene began, for the first time, to understand why humans had been making representations of their loved ones for so long. The painting was an unusual one, since none of her family carried their traditional attributes—no bow for her, no lyre or wreath for Apollo—but she recognized the figures immediately by the telltale shiver that coursed over her arms. Her mother would've loved it. In it, Leto held the lotus staff, a symbol of royalty usually reserved for more important goddesses like Hera. Artemis stood with a child. Not her own, of course, but one that represented all the world's youth. The Goddess of Girls had always been Leto's favorite epithet for Artemis—the only aspect of her daughter that the Goddess of Motherhood truly understood.

Selene sensed Theo staring at her. "Selene? Are you okay?"

She felt his hand on her shoulder and jerked backward. She hadn't let a man touch her without her consent in a very long time. "Don't." Hippo growled, suddenly alert. Selene put a hand on the dog to quiet her.

Theo's brows flew upward. "I'm sorry...I just..."

A swift knock on the door saved her from having to explain herself.

The hunched man in the doorway with bug eyes and pockmarked skin reminded Selene of a goose caught mid-swallow. Selene could feel Hippo's fur bristle as the man stepped into the room. The dog barked once, and Selene shushed her. "Theo. Ah. I didn't know you had company."

"Bill Webb, meet Hippolyta and Selene. Ladies, this is the chairman of the Classics Department."

"Since when are dogs allowed in the university offices?" the man asked, staring at Hippo, who raised her lips in a snarl.

"She's a certified emotional support animal," Theo said before Selene could respond.

"I see. I'm sorry to hear you need such measures, but I suppose we're all dealing with Helen's death in different ways." He eyed Theo's safari hat.

"Exactly."

"May I speak to you in my office?"

"Of course." Theo pulled off the hat and flashed Selene an unconvincing smile. "I'll be right back."

A paragon of grace, Selene leaned back as far as the protesting desk chair would allow. "I'll try to make myself comfortable."

When they were gone, Hippo instantly quieted. Soon, she was snoring loudly. Selene picked impatiently at the stuffing creeping through the chair cushion, noting the position of the sun outside the window. She didn't have time to waste on either Theo's laughter or his office politics. And she certainly didn't like the way his smile made her feel a little better about the world.

Selene moved to the window, resting her forehead on the pane. Beneath her, students walked across the quad in the afternoon light, their cheeks rosy with the flush of youth. A pair of young women in short skirts and tall boots giggled as they straggled behind a larger group of students. *Women like them aren't safe anymore on the streets of New York,* Selene thought, remembering Sammi Mehra's dangling feet. *And here I am laughing with a mortal instead of protecting them.* As she backed away from the window, her jacket caught on one of the many pushpins stuck into the wall, yanking it free.

An index card fluttered onto the desk. She picked it up, glancing only briefly at its contents—something about the Dionysian connection to the Mysteries—and stuck it back on the wall. Then she saw her name on the next card over: *Selene DiSilva. Moon Goddess. Probably deranged. Definitely dangerous. Contact only if desperate.*

So that's what he thinks of me. A desperate lunatic to be avoided at all costs. Surprisingly, the revelation stung. Angry, she flung her backpack over her shoulder and turned to go. If the professor didn't want anything to do with her, then she'd be more than happy to oblige.

Chapter 19

SHE WHO HELPS ONE CLIMB OUT

"Are you aware your name is all over the Internet?" Webb seethed as they walked toward his office.

"As a suspected psychopathic killer," Theo replied calmly. "Actually, I'd managed to forget for a moment, but thanks so much for reminding me."

Webb opened the door to his office and gestured Theo through.

Oh, good. Witnesses to my torment. Fritz Mossburg lounged in one of the leather armchairs, a glass of dark liquor held loosely in one hand, his piercing blue eyes moist. Theo could smell the alcohol from across the room. Too sweet, almost rotten. Mossburg jumped from his chair and embraced Theo, muttering horror-stricken platitudes all the while. He specialized in Greek theater and was known around campus for his Anderson Cooper good looks. When the other professors had begun to snub Theo after the eminent domain dispute, Mossburg had remained cordial. "God, Theo, what a disaster. And now you've been hauled in by the cops. What a day."

"The police station left a bit to be desired as a Saturday brunch destination," Theo concurred.

In the other armchair, Martin Andersen frowned over his own glass. "I don't know how you can joke about this," he chided. The older man's grief for his dead wife lent an air of melancholy to everything he did, and yesterday's tragedy had left him more dour than usual. Over the years, Theo had taken Martin out to dinner a few times, but his altruism quickly dissolved in the face of the older man's nearly pathological lack of personality. Martin had continued to pursue the friendship with the doggedness of an antibiotic-resistant infection, offering to loan Theo esoteric volumes of Latin oratory, borrowing his dress shoes for a faculty club event, inviting him to dinners and plays, cornering him in the hallways to lecture him about the latest trends in Latin grammar. Theo tried to avoid him as politely as possible, and Martin had finally gotten the hint. He hadn't called Theo in months. Now, Theo wished he'd been nicer. He had a feeling he was going to need an ally.

Bill Webb cleared his throat. "Gentlemen, give me a moment with Dr. Schultz."

Andersen downed the last of his drink and left the room without saying more. Mossburg offered Theo a condolatory smile then followed him out.

Webb settled into the leather chair behind his wide desk. *He looks pretty good,* Theo noted. Maybe Webb had finished his chemotherapy treatments.

"Look, Schultz, I asked the senior faculty here, even though it's a weekend, to try to sort out the best way to help the department deal with Helen's passing." Theo wasn't sure when he'd been suddenly excluded from the "senior faculty," but he held his tongue. "Obviously, you've been having an especially difficult time. But I'm afraid it's become equally clear that your actions since Helen's devastating loss have been less than professional."

"I'm not sure what you're referring to," Theo said with careful nonchalance.

"Understandable, since there are so many possibilities. Where to begin? You've obstructed the murder investigation, gotten taken into police custody, and—let me see if I remember what the detective said—proposed an absurd theory about Helen's participation in a latter-day Mystery Cult."

"It's not absurd."

"It casts this university, and *Helen*, in a very poor light. What would her parents say?"

"You spoke to Brandman?" said Theo, ignoring Webb's last comment. Helen's parents had died when she was in college, although clearly the chair never cared enough about her to learn that. "Are you the one who told him about my relationship with Helen?"

Webb thrust out his chin. "What I did or did not say to the police is no concern of yours."

"And the sordid details of my love life aren't yours."

"Anything to do with this department is my concern. I have a responsibility to uphold our reputation. Your actions have cast serious doubt on your judgment. We think it would be best if you take a leave of absence until this all blows over."

The words stung less than he'd expected. The humiliation paled in comparison to the murder case at hand. Still, he wasn't going to go down without a protest. "What kind of scholar jumps to such shoddy conclusions? Even my students know better than to be swayed by scurrilous online rumors."

A smile floated across Webb's lips, so brief Theo thought he'd imagined it. *That bastard,* he realized, *he's been looking for an excuse to fire me and I just played right into his hands. He's enjoying this.*

"Oh yes, we all know about your 'special relationship' with the students and the community." Webb made it sound as if Theo'd been sleeping with them rather than engaging in civil disobedience. "But it's the parents, not the students, I'm worried about. We've been fielding angry calls all afternoon." As if on cue, a phone rang down the hall at the reception desk. Theo could hear Violet answering the call, then speaking in soothing tones. He could only imagine the voice on the other end—*How dare you let an accused murderer teach my son! What kind of institution are you running?* "They're the ones whose checks keep this institution afloat," Webb went on. "And unlike you, some of us care about the future of the university. I might have let your misjudgments slide, but now half the city thinks you were involved in Helen's murder."

"Do you think I killed that little girl in the hospital, too?" Theo snapped.

"Of course not. But we can't help the Internet rumors, can we?" This time, Webb's smile was hard to misinterpret.

"What about my classes?"

"Nate Balinski already took over this morning's seminar on translating ancient textual fragments. And once Everett is back on his feet, he's perfectly capable of teaching *Intro to Myth* by himself." Webb picked up a piece of paper from his desk. Theo recognized it as the syllabus for his course. "I see you're spending the next unit comparing mythic heroes to comic book characters." He gave Theo a pursed, condescending smirk. "I'm sure Everett will be up to the challenge."

I shouldn't have eaten that pork dumpling, Theo realized. *Because I might just puke it right up again.* "Thank you, Bill," he said lightly. "You've been surprisingly helpful—now I'll have plenty of time to focus on the investigation." He stood up. "I'll let you get back to deciding how to destroy my career. It's an unusual way to honor Helen's memory, but I know everyone grieves differently."

As he headed back down the hall, Theo met Everett standing by the water cooler, a sheaf of papers under his arm.

"Everett, what're you doing here? I thought I told you to stay home as long as you needed."

"I was going crazy in my apartment. I just needed to be doing something, anything. And Bill asked the senior faculty..." he began, then dropped his gaze. As an assistant professor, Everett had never been considered "senior" anything. But it seemed that with Theo's fall from grace, Everett had received an unofficial promotion.

"Don't worry about it," said Theo.

"I *am* worried," Everett insisted. "I've been hearing all sorts of crazy things."

"I had nothing to do with Helen's murder." Theo felt ridiculous even needing to say it.

"Of course not." Everett blanched. "But this Mystery Cult theory Bill said you're floating... it's just nuts, Theo."

"Speaking of which, do you know where Helen would have kept the draft of her book?"

"She kept it on her laptop, but the cops said it's missing from her apartment. Look, I know how much you cared about Helen. But—"

Everett's knowing tone made Theo's cheeks grow hot. "She was a friend, that's all." He fought down a rising wave of guilt that threatened to have him blurting out the truth. *Don't be an asshole. Everett can never know about that night with Helen.*

"Of course. I just think your emotions are clouding your judgment. God knows they've been clouding mine. But I know we've got the best police force in the country. I think we should let them do their job."

Theo didn't want to fight with Everett. But nor did he have any intention of giving up his search. "What's that?" he asked, eyeing the pile of papers in Everett's arms.

"I was just picking up Helen's mail. I thought maybe there was something I could give to her siblings. The cops took everything out of her apartment yesterday." Theo immediately regretted not going through Helen's in-box himself. Who knew what clues he could find?

"It's all just memos and junk mail, though," Everett went on. He shrugged helplessly. "Already, there's so little of her left." He slid the papers into the recycling bin, his eyes gleaming wetly.

"I'm sorry." Theo said. *For your loss. For my betrayal.*

"Me, too. And I'm sorry you've gotten all mixed up with this."

The genuine sympathy on Everett's face suddenly made Theo want to enlist his help. Everett was a fine scholar with as much reason as Theo—more, even—to bring Helen's killer to justice. And it wouldn't hurt if Webb's new favorite put in a good word for him at the next faculty meeting. *Don't be ridiculous,* he chided himself sternly. *Everett doesn't make decisions for Webb or anyone else. He's got enough to deal with without shouldering my problems, too. And you don't deserve his help. Not after what you did.*

Together, they walked down the hall toward Theo's office. His door was closed. As they approached, Everett turned to Theo in surprise, as if he'd heard something. "You have a visitor?"

"I did." He patted Everett on the back, aware once more of how the younger man's well-muscled shoulders compared to his own narrow frame. "Let's hope I still do." Theo hesitated outside the door. Somehow, he didn't feel up to introducing Everett to Selene. Everett took the hint and left by the back stairs.

I bet she's not even in there, Theo thought as he stood outside his office. *Probably already left, unwilling to wait for a disgraced former professor.*

Theo steeled himself for disappointment and opened the door.

———◦———

Selene winced when she heard the door open behind her. She'd hoped to disappear before Theo got back. Instead, she was balancing precariously on his rolling chair beneath a gaping hole in the ceiling, a ventilation grate in one hand and a Swiss Army knife in the other. Theo closed the door quickly.

"Something tells me you're not just fixing my air-conditioning."

She stepped down off the chair and laid the grate on the floor, taking a moment to decide what to say. She was half tempted to retort, *I'm bad news, remember? Listen to your own advice and just leave me alone.* Instead, she asked, "What did your boss say?"

"Just that he wants me to take a leave. Probably lose my tenure position, not to mention all chance of ever being hired by another university. Not in so many words, of course, but that was the gist. But you never answered my question. Why are you taking apart my office? And," he continued with a small smile, "if it's going to help us find our killer cult, can I help?"

Selene stared at him for a second. She couldn't help admiring his fortitude. After losing their jobs, most mortals she'd met would be completely incapacitated by humiliation. Shouldn't he be weeping somewhere? Or getting drunk? Instead, he seemed determined to press on. So either he was surprisingly stalwart or naively optimistic. *Or despite the notecard*, she considered reluctantly, *he just wants to spend time with me*. She wasn't sure if she found the thought terrifying or encouraging.

"Well, if you must know, I'm breaking into Helen's office."

"We're going to crawl through the air ducts? We can actually do that?"

"There's no *we* here. *I'm* going to crawl through. Her office is just down the hall, so all the vents should connect. The police put a tamper-proof seal on the door. If I break it, they'll know. But there's no way I'm leaving this building without checking for her research notes."

He frowned for a second, as if considering the step he was about to take. Then he nodded. "I'm in."

"No, you're not. You should stay here with Hippo."

"You know an awful lot about mythology for a PI, but you won't be able to decipher Helen's notes. Unless you're going to tell me you happen to read Ancient Greek?" He flashed her a smile.

Selene bit back a retort. No way she could answer that question. "You're going to leave prints all over the place," she said instead.

He dug into the pocket of his overcoat and pulled out a pair of knit gloves with a flourish. "Fine," she said with a resigned sigh. "But you have to do *exactly* what I tell you."

"Of course." He nodded somberly, but she couldn't help noticing the glint in his eye. For a man who didn't get out of the library much, he was clearly enjoying the adventure.

She raised a skeptical brow, then dug in her backpack for a moment and pulled out a flashlight. She'd be able to see in the dark, but Theo wouldn't.

"You certainly come prepared," he said. "What else do you have in there?"

"You don't want to know," she said, zipping it closed before he could catch the glimmer of her disassembled bow. She hopped lightly back up onto the rolling chair. "Who's in the offices between here and Helen's?"

"It's all associates and adjuncts, but none on of them are here on a Saturday."

"Good." She handed him the flashlight. "But you'll still have to be quiet. Any sound will carry into every office with a vent on the same shaft."

Selene grabbed hold of the vent's edge, flipped upside down, then launched herself, feet first, into the airshaft. A moment later, Theo's head appeared. She wriggled backward out of the way as he attempted to lever himself inside with his elbows. He managed to get his torso in, then turned to look at her with a mixture of humiliation and hilarity. "I'm stuck," he mouthed. Selene rolled her eyes, but grabbed his elbow and hauled. An unfortunate clanking ensued, but eventually the professor lay securely inside the duct.

Theo's face was too close again, his pupils huge in the dim light. For a moment, she studied him with her newly improved night vision, knowing that he couldn't return the scrutiny. His narrow lips were parted slightly. A lock of fair hair stuck behind his glasses, poking at his eyes. He brushed it aside, looking surprisingly vulnerable. Then he turned on the flashlight, blinding her. She winced and spun around, more comfortable with her feet in his face. With a whispered "Follow me," she began shimmying down the shaft.

Astoundingly, they made it to Helen's office without mishap. Selene's multi-tool easily opened the vent cover. She lowered herself through the hole and dropped the few feet to the ground, landing soundlessly. The professor followed, his legs swaying as his feet searched for purchase. She rolled a chair underneath him, but his shoe caught on the back, wrenching the chair from her hands, then spinning it toward her and knocking her backward. Before she could rise, the professor tumbled on top of her, his flashlight rolling free.

They lay tangled together for a moment in the dark, his chest smothering her face, his knee between her legs. Selene bit her lip to keep from loudly demanding that he immediately remove his hand from her ribs. Her shirt had ridden up in the fall, and his gloved fingertips were warm against her skin.

With her nose pressed to his sternum, the smell of his sweat overwhelmed her. A mix of exertion and excitement, with just a hint of fear. She expected to be repulsed. Strangely, she wasn't. Then he was rolling off her with a whispered apology.

"Next time I'm trying to help you, just let me," she hissed.

"Only if you let me do the same." He held out a hand to help her up. She ignored the gesture and got to her feet unaided.

Theo retrieved the flashlight and panned it across the shelves lining the walls of the small office. "Looks like the cops already took a lot," he whispered, opening the drawers of Helen's desk. Selene nodded absently, standing in the middle of the room. Turning in a slow circle, she scanned the photos adorning the walls in tastefully asymmetrical arrangements. A fresco painting of the Minoan snake goddess. The Egyptian temple of Isis at Philae. Another of the ruined temples of the Vestal Virgins in the Roman Forum.

"Interesting collection." She pointed at the walls.

He glanced up and frowned. "Those are new. Last time I was in here—months ago, probably—she had the usual archeologist's collection of maps and museum prints." He opened a file cabinet. "No sign of her laptop." He gestured to the empty drawer. "And I don't see any of her research related to the Mysteries either."

Selene turned to another tall file cabinet near the door, sure it, too, would be empty. To her surprise, it was sealed with a combination padlock. The cops probably planned on coming back with a bolt cutter. But in the meantime...

Selene tugged at the lock, feeling the metal cabinet bend a little in her hands, but even with her increased strength, the lock itself didn't give. Theo moved to stand beside her.

"Helen liked to do everything the hard way. Handwritten notes, hidden compartments, secret ciphers—I sometimes think maybe she was a CIA agent posing as an archeologist. But, you know, that would imply the government gave a crap about Greco-Roman society, so unlikely." He shone his flashlight onto the padlock.

"The combination's only three digits," Selene said. "We should be able to figure it out."

Theo shook his head. "Three digits means a thousand possibilities."

"Well, try *something*."

He attempted Helen's birthday. Then the first three digits of her phone number. Then the last three. Then he stepped back from the cabinet and folded his arms, staring at it.

"Are you trying to glare it into submission?" Selene asked.

Theo pushed his glasses a little farther up his nose. "That's more your style. I'm thinking."

"Try doing it a little faster. We need to get the tusk identified at Natural History before it—"

"I've got it." He grinned and gestured to the calendar on Helen's wall. The dates were written not in Arabic numerals, but in Greek characters. "Helen hated math. She once told me that one of her favorite things about studying Ancient Greek was spending a day without seeing modern numerals. She liked that the Greeks used letters for their numbers. Alpha is one, beta is two, and so on. Her lucky number was 98, the sum of the number values of the letters in the Greek translation of her name. So if we take her favorite Greek three-letter words, then turn the letters into their number equivalents, we'll have a possible combination."

"Sounds just absurd enough to work."

"Worth a shot." He grabbed the padlock. Then he just stood there.

"What are you waiting for?"

Theo cleared his throat. "There are actually very few Greek words with only three letters."

"What about 'Theo'?" Selene suggested impatiently. "That's Greek, right? The 't-h' is one letter, so that's three letters total."

"I know, awfully fitting for a classicist, right? 'Theodoros,' meaning 'gift of the gods.' I try not to let it go to my head. But I don't think it's our combination. The 'o' in Theo is an omicron, which corresponds to seventy. Too many digits, but if we add them together..." He did some quick mental math. "No good. It's nine, five, seventy, so that's only eighty-four. Not enough digits. It would be a little weird of her to use my name anyway. Maybe not Theo, but 'theos,' meaning 'God.' Add it up, you get...two hundred and seventy-nine." He spun the combination lock. "Nope. Damn. We probably need a word that uses only alpha through theta, so it corresponds to our nine modern digits."

Selene stared at the lock for a moment, then around the room, searching for inspiration. Theo just stared blankly at the ceiling, his lips moving silently. Then, at the same moment, they both turned to the photos of the temples.

"Are you thinking what I'm thinking?" he asked. "Not 'Theos.' *Thea.*"

Selene nodded. "What better password than *Goddess*?"

"Theta, epsilon, alpha. Nine-five-one." The lock sprang open in Theo's hands. He gave a quiet whoop. "I'm not saying we *are* geniuses, but I am saying it's damn possible."

He opened the drawer and shone his flashlight inside. Selene peered over his shoulder.

"A *lararium*. A Roman shrine to the *lares*—their household gods," he murmured, awestruck. Beneath a cardboard roof stood four small clay figurines, a shallow dish of wine, and a pile of burnt incense sticks. "Usually, the *lares* were unnamed protective spirits—local gods of the hearth or the crossroads—or sometimes personal ancestors. But that's definitely Persephone," he said, focusing the light on the statue holding a clay pomegranate. "Or I guess, since this a Roman shrine, I should say Proserpina." He swung to the next figurine, this one bearing a wooden arrow made from a toothpick.

"Artemis. Diana," Selene said, the names heavy on her tongue.

The third idol had no symbolic accoutrements and barely the suggestion of a face, just full, pendulous breasts and a round belly. "That one doesn't look Greek or Roman at all," Theo whispered. "More like a primitive Earth Mother goddess." The last figure, clearly male, carried only an unadorned toothpick. "And that one could be anything. But probably Asclepius with his staff. Then again, it could be a sword."

Selene glanced up at the photos on the wall once more. "This whole place is a shrine," she said. "Your friend Helen didn't just study the gods, she worshiped them."

The night of her death, Helen must have invoked Artemis in her moment of need. The magnitude of her faith had awakened senses long dormant, allowing Selene to receive the vision of the woman's last moments. That explained why touching Sammi Mehra's corpse had no effect—whatever god or gods the girl had worshiped, they weren't Greek. *But Helen prayed to* me, Selene realized with a heavy heart. *I felt a tingling, a summons, as I left*

Jackie Ortiz's apartment the night Helen was killed—and I didn't even realize what it was. Now, when it was too late, she could almost hear the woman's prayer, offered up as she lay bound and gagged at the river's edge, a man poised above her with a needle glinting in the light of a single lamppost:

Artemis, Protector of Women, aim your arrow true.
Find him, Huntress, show no mercy.
Pierce him through the heart like a stag on the run.

Selene shuddered, thinking of how Helen's last breath must have reached for Olympus and found it empty. The unanswered prayer would fall from heaven to earth. There, it would slide past the city's spires, sigh along the canyon streets, and rush down the back alleys into dark and hidden places, to finally whisper in the ear of a goddess who could no longer hear. *The one supplicant I have left, and I came too late to save her,* she admitted. *Maybe it's Helen's faith, not my mother's decline, that has brought back my powers.*

As he looked from the figures in the *lararium* to the photos on the wall, Theo's face paled. "I always talk about how we've lost something by embracing literal-minded monotheism, but I never dreamed she'd go this far. What did she get herself into? And who—"

The distant sound of Hippo's urgent barking interrupted him.

"What's she—" he began, but Selene cut him off by laying a finger on his lips. They were dry and soft to the touch. He looked astonished, but a second or two later, his eyes darted to the door as footsteps entered his hearing range. They stood, frozen, as the footsteps stopped. Hippo's muffled barking continued from down the hall in Theo's office. Selene could almost feel the presence of a man on the other side of the door. She sniffed the air, but smelled only Theo, scared and excited, beside her. Removing her finger from his lips, she padded silently to the door, leaning her cheek against the wood.

Is it the cops? Theo mouthed.

She shook her head. Too quiet. Too still. Someone staring

at the tamper-proof seal on the door, wishing he could get in. Someone whose scent Hippo recognized.

The instant the footsteps moved away, she took a flying leap onto the desk chair, then launched herself into the ductwork with barely a clatter. Moments later, she'd come out the other end into Theo's office and thrown open his door so Hippo could bound through. Selene followed the sprinting dog to one end of the hallway, where the hound stood, pacing uncertainly, her nose lifted. She sniffed the ground for a few seconds, then took off in the opposite direction. Selene ran back down the hallway after her dog, past Theo's office, then Helen's. Hippo took a sharp turn into another room, then started barking maniacally. Selene halted, made sure she could easily reach the bow in her pack, then treaded cautiously into the room. A skinny old man in a three-piece suit huddled in the corner of the office kitchen, clutching a ham sandwich to his chest.

"Stay back!" he shouted at the drooling dog crouching a foot away.

Selene groaned. "Sorry," she said, pulling Hippo away. "She has a thing for pork." She scolded the dog as she dragged her back down the hallway to Theo's office and slammed the door behind them.

"What? What is it?" Theo panted as his head appeared above her in the vent.

"I thought Hippo'd caught our suspect's scent, but she was more interested in some professor's lunch. If it was the killer outside the door, he's already gone. I was too slow."

"Too slow? Are you kidding? I blinked and you were gone." He swung his feet through the hole in the ceiling. "Are you some sort of gymnast?"

"I'm a lot of things." She pushed the chair under Theo. This time, he dropped onto it without sending her sprawling.

"The way you ran, I was convinced something was about to attack us."

"If something had been about to attack us," she said dryly, "I wouldn't have run."

"That makes one of us." He began gathering books and papers from his desk.

"Are you a coward?"

"Wow. Personal question. Only when facing a pile of mid-terms to grade. You should see the grammar these kids use. But if you're talking about *violence*? I've never actually hit anyone. Wanted to, sure. But I don't believe in putting myself or others in needless physical danger. I'll leave that to stuntwomen like you."

"We need to get going before Natural History closes. You have two minutes." She hefted herself back into the airshaft and shimmied down the duct to Helen's office to replace the grate in her ceiling. A minute later, she was back doing the same to Theo's. He was still packing.

"I just need to grab a few things to take with me while I'm on...vacation," he explained.

Selene maintained her patience for nearly a minute, then found herself clenching and unclenching her fists, trying not to snap at him as he attempted to shove an entire library's worth of material into a satchel.

"I'm just going to go," she said finally, grabbing Hippo's leash and turning toward the door.

"You can't go without me."

Selene spun back to the professor and took a step toward him. She was surprised to notice he was actually an inch or so taller than she. "We are *not* partners, remember?" She narrowed her eyes, but unlike most people she encountered, he neither backed down nor grew defensive, but only looked at her calmly.

"You're going to just walk up to the museum and ask to speak to their paleodontist on a Saturday afternoon?" he asked. "Okay, I'm sure that'll work."

Selene frowned. "I'll *make* them let me in."

"Threats? Sure. Curators usually respond to threats."

Selene snarled, grabbed the teetering pile of books off Theo's desk, and stuffed them into her own large backpack.

"You don't have to—that's going to be really heavy!"

But she was already out the door, angry at Theo for slowing her down—but even angrier at herself for her unwillingness to leave him behind.

Chapter 20

STORMY ONE

"So you're not a fan of Alexander Hamilton. What about Roosevelt?" Theo couldn't resist asking as they pounded up the steps of the American Museum of Natural History under the watchful gaze of the former president's equestrian statue. Selene maintained the same grim expression she'd had since they left Columbia, but Theo reasoned that if he was going to lose his job, he might as well have some fun.

"Teddy? Him I liked."

They'd taken a cab to the museum to save time. He'd spent the trip with Hippolyta's drool cascading down his neck and her paws digging into his crotch. When they'd arrived, Selene tied the dog to a lamppost in front of the museum. Most of Hippolyta's hair, on the other hand, came with them, embedded in his corduroy blazer.

"You a fan of progressive politics?" Theo asked hopefully. "He's just about the only Republican since Lincoln that I admire."

"Politics?" She shrugged. "He liked National Parks. So do I."

Theo'd never been one for outdoorsy vacations (unless they

involved ancient ruins, of course), but he caught himself imagining hiking past Old Faithful with someone like Selene at his side. Not a bad way to spend summer vacation.

"Mostly, though, I liked him because he was a great hunter," Selene added over her shoulder. "Like me."

Smile banished, Theo followed her mutely into the grand marble rotunda, hoping she was referring to hunting down criminals, not animals, but fairly certain she wasn't. He had no problem picturing the tall, graceful woman traipsing through some upstate forest and bringing down deer. It made him a little uneasy just thinking about it. He'd never been friends with someone who hunted before. Although he wasn't sure if he could quite consider Selene DiSilva a *friend*. Mostly, she seemed to want to get rid of him.

Theo approached a bored-looking security guard.

"I'm here to see Dr. Gabriela Jimenez. She works in the Anthropology Department."

The woman shifted ponderously in her chair, as if reaching for the phone were immensely difficult.

"And you are?"

"Theodore Schultz."

Her eyes grew round. Sure enough, the woman had read about him already.

"Just tell her we're here," Selene said, staring down the guard.

"Humph." The woman covered her mouth with her hand as she spoke into the telephone. "It's the guy they keep talking about... *Schultz*," she hissed audibly. "For Dr. Jimenez."

"I'm a colleague of hers," Theo added lamely.

"She'll meet you on the west side of the rotunda," the guard said finally, putting down the phone and handing them a pair of security passes. "Near North American Mammals." Theo heard her mutter something to a co-worker as he turned away. Selene spun back, planted both hands on the desk, and leaned forward as if she might leap right over it.

"Don't go gossiping about something you know nothing about."

"Lord have mercy, I—"

"If you do, I'll shoot you, skin you, and stuff you. You'll fit right into the Hall of Human Origins, somewhere between Turkana Boy and the Cro-Magnons."

Theo waved his hands in a placating gesture. "Hey, Bruce Banner! No need to Hulk out. You're going to get us kicked out." After a last scowl at the security guard, Selene backed off. "You don't need to defend me, you know," he added as they hurried toward the exhibit halls.

"Because you're doing such a fine job of it yourself?"

Theo found himself grinning, flattered by her defensiveness on his behalf.

Gabriela emerged from the elevator bank. He gave her a quick hug. "I know it's a Saturday and all, so thanks, Gabi."

"For you, Theodear, anything." She flashed him a ready smile. "Besides, half the staff is here, still freaking out about the theft. It's been a hellish two days, but nothing compared to your week." She grabbed Theo's hand and squeezed.

Theo stepped aside to introduce his "friend" Selene and watched Gabriela's eyes widen as they traveled up her six-foot frame. Next to the pale, slender woman, Gabriela looked like a miniature Mayan fertility goddess.

She tapped the elevator call button and leaned her backside against the wall, folding her arms across her chest. "A lot's happened since you got yourself arrested this morning." She ushered them into the car, slipped her access key into a slot, and pressed the button for the staff-only sixth floor.

"Oh yeah? Find anything else missing from the collection?"

Her jaw fell open. "How did you know?"

"Well, we have something that might belong to the museum." He could feel Selene stiffen beside him. "But, Gabriela, you *have* to promise not to ask where we got it, okay? None of your usual relentless pestering."

She frowned. "Since when are *you* all secretive?" She glanced at Selene and then back at Theo, her eyebrows raised. As usual, her expression lacked all subtlety.

"Since I found myself the hapless victim of the criminal justice system." The doors slid open and they exited into a long, cramped hallway of research offices. "Selene?"

Stony faced, Selene pulled the huge tooth from her bag.

"Whoa! How did you—right, right. No questions. Very cloak and dagger. Fine. Well, I have no idea if that's the right tooth or not, but it sure looks promising. They've been flipping out all day."

"Why didn't you tell me that something besides the snake had been taken?"

"We didn't know until they started the complete inventory this morning. I was going to tell you, but then I heard about your little run-in with the cops. I figured you had enough on your mind. Besides, I was waiting for the security guards to scan through all the surveillance footage from Thursday night to see if they came up with anything."

"And did they?"

"*Oh* yeah. Crazy stuff. But first, speaking of crazy, let's return that specimen to the tusk guy before he goes any more *loco*. You know there's a whole Tusk Vault in the attic? Freaky, right?" She leaned in conspiratorially. "No one ever sees the guy who runs it except at mandatory staff meetings. He hangs out up there with the teeth all day." She wiggled her fingers in spooky delight. "Be forewarned, he might bite."

"Wait—I finally get to enter the Holy of Holies? I thought I was only allowed into your offices in the Anthropology Department. Otherwise I need a whole application and special permission."

"I think returning stolen property to the museum entitles you to a little leeway, right?" Rules had never meant a whole lot to

Gabriela when justice was at stake. That was something else she and Theo had in common.

As they sauntered through the corridors, Gabriela looped her arm around Theo's waist and tucked her head beneath his shoulder. Theo could hear Selene's impatient breathing behind them, but there was no use trying to hurry Gabriela. They would get there when they got there.

"You going to be okay, *chico*?"

Theo pressed a brief kiss into the mass of curls piled high on her head. "I'll be fine. The whole 'hunting down bad guys' thing is actually sort of thrilling. And thanks for sticking with me, Gabi. I'm glad you don't believe everything you read online."

Gabriela gave him a quick peck on the part of his chest closest to her face. "What's up with Ms. DiSilva?" she whispered. "She's not your type."

"I have a type?"

"Brainy, short, and overly emotional. Why else would we have become friends?"

Theo laughed, keenly aware of Selene walking behind them. He could feel her eyes on the back of his head. Gabriela was always—erroneously—convinced of her complete discretion. He had little doubt Selene could hear every word.

"I was right about the Met robberies, by the way," he said, trying to distract his friend from discussions of his love life. "They're related. We think the guys who robbed both museums are the same ones who killed Helen. And now they're gathering sacred objects for a Mystery Cult ritual." Gabriela pulled a face. "Okay, I admit it seems a bit extreme. You'd think they'd just use a vase or a tooth that wasn't under lock and key at one of the world's most secure institutions."

"Well, no. *If* what you're saying about a cult is true," she considered, "and I assume it probably is, since you're the most brilliant man I know—even though you sound totally nuts—the rest of it makes perfect sense." Theo gave her a quick grateful squeeze. It didn't hurt to be reminded that, despite Bill Webb's disdain, he was damn good at his job. "Native Americans come to the museum all the time. We give them access to tribal artifacts and they actually perform rituals right here on site. They say the artifacts are more powerful than anything still belonging to the tribe. So, if your cult is serious, then it stands to reason they'd go to whatever lengths necessary to procure the authentic sacred objects."

Theo turned around to give Selene a thumbs-up. It felt good to be vindicated. Her lips twisted a little in what he assumed was acknowledgment.

"How did Helen get mixed up in all this?" Gabriela asked.

"We don't know yet, but we did find out that she actually *believed* in the Greco-Roman gods."

"You mean not just like a 'wouldn't it be cool if...' kind of thing?"

"More like an 'I should give them offerings in the secret shrine in my office' kind of thing."

"Whoa! Took your theories one step too far, huh? I always knew she was a nutjob."

"You were berating me just yesterday for messing things up with her!"

"That's just 'cause I like ragging on you. You always said Helen was a little... *intense*. Guess you were right."

"Are we there yet?" Selene interrupted.

Blithely, Gabriela started the tour. "Here's the Mammals Department." She waved her hand at the closed doors as they passed. "They call that room the 'alcoholics' because it's filled with huge vats of animal specimens preserved in 150-proof grain alcohol. And I don't mean just weasels and mice. I mean *gorillas* and *giraffes*. Like whole ones. Skinned. The skins, they keep in that room," she said as they passed another door. "I mean, I think it's all revolting, but I guess we do have a collection of

Maori shrunken heads in the anthro vaults, so who's to say?"
Theo had to smile. He knew she was trying to gross out Selene,
but Gabriela had no idea who she was dealing with. After hearing her description of the snake-bedecked hospital room, Theo
knew Selene had nerves of steel. "Supposedly," Gabriela went
on, "they've got a blanket made from the skins of forty platypuses. Or would that be *platypi*? No idea, not my thing."

"Platypuses is correct," said Theo. "If it were Latin, we'd say
platypi, but it's actually a third declension in Greek. The plural
should really be *platypodes*, if you want to get technical—"

"We don't, *querido*." She led them up a narrow, steep staircase
to the attic floor. "Here we go, up to the really fun stuff." The
ceiling was low, the lighting dim, and the hallway exceptionally
narrow and twisted. Labels on the doors read, "Hippo Room,"
"Elephant Room," "Pig Room." Finally, they came to a small,
unmarked door. "The Tusk Vault," she whispered.

Gabriela knocked loudly.

No answer.

Selene gave a frustrated snort. "He's probably gone home. It
took us long enough to get here."

"Patience, *chica*. The guy basically lives here." Again, the loud
whisper: "He's probably just extracting himself from some elephant jaw. Goes in there to get his kicks."

"Sorry," said Theo to Selene. "Gabriela gets *her* kicks from
studying human cultures—she doesn't get why anyone would
study animals instead. She's a bit dismissive of the natural sciences."

Gabriela shot him a hurt look. "I like animals. Live ones. Cute
fluffy kittens. Polar bear cubs. It's all the stuffed ones around
here that give me the creeps."

"And the Pueblo dioramas don't? All those topless manne-
quins pounding maize?"

"At least they didn't stuff actual *corpses*. Although honestly,
knowing the nineteenth-century naturalists' complete disdain for
indigenous peoples, I'm surprised they didn't. They certainly—"

Gabriela's diatribe was cut off by the slowly opening door.

"*Hola*, Gregory."

The small Asian man before them blinked through his glasses. From the state of his dusty suit, he'd been crawling through closets and under cabinets all day. A lint ball clung to the scanty stubble of his chin.

"I've brought you visitors. Guys, this is Dr. Gregory Kim."

Not budging, the researcher frowned angrily, his gaze skipping over them as it would over anything still wearing flesh. *Gabriela was right,* thought Theo. *This guy reminds me of that kid in third grade who gave the class an hour-long lecture on whale behavior, without even asking for extra credit. Even the teacher thought he was weird.* He deliberately ignored the memory of a similar lecture he himself had given in middle school on the correlation between Achilles and Han Solo. That time, the teacher had been thrilled—but his friends mocked him for the next year and a half.

"I'm very busy, Dr. Jimenez," Kim said tightly. "I need to double-check each specimen shelf to make sure nothing else has been illegally procured from the collection. This is the worst possible time to allow visitors anywhere near the vault."

"You're taking this very hard, Greg," Gabriela said with a hint of wickedness in her condolatory smile. "Every tooth is like a baby to you, huh?"

Theo was about to step in before Gabriela could torture the poor man any further, but Selene beat him to it. "We're with law enforcement." She pulled a faded leather wallet from her back pocket and flipped it open, flashing a tarnished badge briefly before Kim's face.

Gabriela leaned toward Theo, her question clear in her narrowed eyes. He silenced her with an emphatic shake of his head, trying to look unfazed. Surely impersonating a police officer was a felony. *Then again, this is why I teamed up with Selene in the first place,* he reminded himself. *Because she'll do the things I wouldn't dream of.*

"Oh!" Kim's face lit up. "Please!" He stepped aside so they could enter the small office. Theo assumed the green metal door in the far wall was the entrance to the vault itself. "Have you found them?" Kim begged.

"Is this what you're looking for?" Selene asked, holding out the blackened tooth to the researcher.

"Where did you——" he began, his gloved hands reaching for it.

"That isn't important," she said sternly. "You need to tell me exactly what this is."

Kim took the tooth reverently and brought it close to his face as if to identify it through smell alone. "Oh yes, this is either the authentic specimen or a very convincing copy." He scurried to his desk and placed the tusk under a large magnifying glass.

Selene crossed her arms as the researcher gently poked and prodded at the specimen. Theo wanted to tell her to be patient, but he already knew she wouldn't listen.

"Obviously, the catalog label has been removed. Without carbon dating, I can't be a hundred percent certain, but preliminarily, I believe this is one of the paleodontal specimens stolen yesterday."

"*One?* You mean they took more than one tooth?" Selene snapped.

"I told the policemen this morning—there was a pair of teeth taken from the same animal."

Selene cast a significant glance at Theo, who felt his heart drop. If the initiates still possessed one tooth, they'd probably have enough to complete their collection of sacred objects.

"If you recovered this one, surely you can——" Kim began.

"Just tell me what animal it came from," Selene said, stepping closer to the researcher, who shrank like a small rodent at her approach.

"Selene—" Theo began.

She growled. Actually growled.

Theo looked to Gabriela, who clapped a hand over her mouth, her face red with suppressed hysteria. She moved her hand enough to silently mouth, *Who the hell is she? You're not into her, are you?*

Dating Selene would be like watching a glacier: waiting for the ice to crack so you could witness the beauty and roar, but knowing it might mean an avalanche that could pummel you to death in a heartbeat. Still...

Gabriela poked him hard in the ribs, her eyebrows rising to meet her hairline. *Are you?*

If Helen had been intense, then Selene was a veritable extremist. Yet the two women embodied entirely different types of passion. While Helen clung to her lovers—both Theo and Everett—as if she couldn't live without them, Selene clearly needed no one and nothing but a cause to fight for. Weakness just wasn't part of her vocabulary. In fact, he suspected she might be the strongest woman he'd ever met—both in terms of her obvious physical prowess and her unshakable determination to see justice done. Yet beneath that adamantine exterior he sensed a secret emotional sensitivity. The combination was undeniably attractive. So—was he into her? He gave Gabi what he knew was an enigmatic smile, then turned back to the paleodontist.

Kim rose to grab a thick book off a nearby shelf. "Entelodont. Known colloquially as the Extinct Giant Pig, Hell Pig, or Terminator Pig, although it's actually more closely related to whales and hippos. Endemic to the woodlands of the northern hemisphere in the Eocene and Miocene epochs for approximately twenty million years." He flipped to a page without consulting the index and passed the book to Theo. "But extinct for the past sixteen million or so."

A vicious, six-foot-tall saber-toothed hog stared from the

pages, a slavering primordial monster painted in full-color detail by someone with a very vivid imagination. Gabriela peered over his shoulder. "That's why I don't like animals, Theodear."

Selene only glanced at the picture, her brow furrowed. As if she'd already known about the Hell Pig. As if she found the illustration laughably inaccurate. *Stranger and stranger*, Theo thought. *She shows up in places she shouldn't. Knows things no one should know. As if she's listening to the world on a frequency a few kilohertz off from everyone else.*

"Dr. Jimenez said you have surveillance footage of the theft. Show me," Selene said.

"Haven't you already seen—" Kim began.

"Just do it."

Gabriela bent to Kim's computer and brought up her e-mail, no more immune to Selene's demands than anyone else. "Security sent it out to everyone this morning so we could see if the perp looked familiar. You ready for this?" she asked over her shoulder. "It's going to be all over the news tonight, I bet you. YouTube's gonna have a field day."

The beginning of the video looked promising. A portion of the museum's pink granite and brown sandstone exterior. Nighttime. A man in a hooded black jacket, wearing a small backpack, appeared in the lower corner of the screen with his back to the camera, illuminated by one of the many high-powered spotlights shining on the museum's neo-Romanesque façade. "That's the Central Park West side of the museum," Gabriela explained. "He already jumped the fence in order to get that close." The shadowy figure was about six feet tall and broad in the shoulders. The man was careful not to turn his head as he knelt down beside the nearest spotlight and, as far as Theo could tell, punched it with his bare fist. The light went dark.

"You've got to be kidding me," Theo groaned. Now they could see very little. Only a grainy silhouette slightly darker than its surroundings. The figure sprinted to the base of a large tree, jumped up, and grabbed the lowest limb. "How high is the branch of that oak?" he asked.

"Linden tree, not oak," Selene said immediately, with more than a hint of irritation. "I'd say at least eleven feet up."

Theo whistled. Gabriela shook her head smugly. "You ain't seen nothing yet, keep watching."

The man began to climb the tree. Theo lost sight of him for a few moments as he moved in and out of focus among the branches. "Wait, is that...no way..." The figure had emerged on one of the topmost limbs, walking along it more swiftly and surely than a circus performer. The branch narrowed as it reached out toward the museum's fifth floor. It sagged beneath his weight, forcing him to stop at least ten feet from the façade. "How's he going to..."

Gabriela shushed him angrily. The thief began to bounce up and down as if the branch were a trampoline. Just when Theo was sure it would break, the thief launched himself into the air, then landed gracefully on the wall, his hands secure in a crevice between the stones, his feet resting on a decorative ledge that couldn't have been more than a foot wide.

"No one noticed? No amateur video already going viral?" Theo asked.

"First of all, it was about four in the morning. And it happened in the span of about twenty seconds. You're watching the tape on slow mo." Gabriela grinned at Theo's obvious astonishment. "And you're missing the good part," she said with a wink.

The thief craned his head backward, as if judging where to head next, then began to climb up the wall as easily as if it were a ladder. Except it wasn't a ladder. It was tightly packed granite blocks with no handhold in sight. Seconds later—*or milliseconds*, Theo realized—he'd grabbed hold of a gutter pipe and pulled himself onto the steep tiled roof. Then it was only a quick run across the rooftop to a skylight. He disappeared for a few moments.

"Let me guess," Selene spoke up. "That's the Snake Room." Gabriela nodded. Then the thief emerged once more and sprinted across the roof and out of the frame. Theo cursed.

"No worries. It switches to another camera here." Gabriela gave Theo's arm a reassuring pat. "Seems we've got the whole building under surveillance. What we *don't* have is an alarm system on the attic skylights."

The thief crossed the roof to a large stone dormer with a small window in one end. Gabriela jabbed the screen. "This is where we are right now. The Tusk Vault." He walked swiftly across the dormer's roofline, grabbed a large, egg-shaped finial with both hands, and swung, feetfirst, onto the deep windowsill. Theo swore, sure he would plummet to his death, but Gabriela merely smiled. "We've got our own resident Spider-Man." The man opened the window and disappeared inside the gable. A moment later, he reappeared.

Theo whistled in admiration. "It didn't take him long to find what he was looking for."

"I keep the collection perfectly catalogued," Kim said with a catch in his voice.

"Shh, you're missing the best part." Gabriela waved her hands for silence.

The hooded figure jumped off the sill, landing lightly on the sloped roof of a turret at least twenty feet away. He sidled along a ledge until he reached the corner of the main building, braced himself between the two walls, then proceeded to shimmy down until he was only two stories above the ground. Then he let go. Theo gasped, Gabriela clapped, and Selene muttered an angry "Show-off" as the man fell to the ground, did a quick somersault, backpack be damned, and leaped lightly to his feet. He dashed offscreen and the video snapped to black.

Selene strode to the vault entrance. "Let me in."

Kim shook his head vigorously, inserting himself between

her and the door. "The collection is in a state of extreme vulnerability at the moment. I cannot allow it to be disturbed."

"I'm not going to steal any of your precious teeth, okay?"

"Let me see that badge again," he demanded, clearly beginning to doubt Selene's credentials.

Theo wondered what gave her away. Her complete lack of professionalism? The way her fist curled like she was about to punch the scientist in the face?

Kim pursed his lips suspiciously. "Why was the entelodont tusk in your possession?"

"I'm trying to help you," Selene said, her glare belying her words. "I *am* in law enforcement, I just do the enforcing a little differently. I'm going to catch whoever's been stealing your stuff. Unless you get in my way. Then I may come back here and mix up all the specimens just for kicks. Put the dinosaur horns in with the walrus tusks."

"You can't threaten me," he said, his small chin thrust forward.

In a blur of movement, Selene seized the keys from Kim's pocket. "I don't have to." She smiled as she pushed him aside and unlocked the vault.

Chapter 21

THE FAR SHOOTER

Selene didn't pause to admire the floor-to-ceiling shelves of carefully labeled tusks. She yanked open the window, then levered herself onto the narrow sill, her torso dangling precariously into the ether. She could hear Kim on the telephone, calling museum security despite Gabriela's pleas for him to be patient.

"Selene, is this really necessary?" Theo asked from behind her. "I can see the headline now: PALEODONTIST PETRIFIED BY PERVY PROFESSOR."

She didn't respond. She had to see the crime scene for herself, even if she didn't want to explain to Theo exactly why. She inched out a little farther and peered down. Six stories of large, rough stone blocks with deep seams. Enough for her to get a handhold, especially with her heightened strength, but not a mortal—unless he was some sort of champion mountain climber. She craned her head upward toward the egg-shaped sculpture that had provided the thief's handhold when he swung onto the ledge. She looked for signs of grappling hooks, rope marks—anything that might have been invisible on the poor-quality video and could explain how he could enter so easily.

Somehow, she knew she wouldn't find anything. Her hunt for the killer had just gotten infinitely more complicated.

Someone grabbed hold of her foot.

"Careful!" Theo warned.

She slid back inside, too surprised to protest, and turned toward him. She wasn't used to the look of concern on his face; no man had ever worried about her before.

"I'm okay," she managed, trying not to sound defensive.

"Look, I appreciate your dedication to figuring out what happened, but I'd rather not have to deal with *another* dead friend quite yet, okay? There's no need to risk your life hanging out sixth-floor windows."

She was already his "friend"? When had that happened? She felt a shiver of something halfway between discomfort and pleasure. "We need to get out of here before the security guards show," she said. "It's going to look awfully suspicious if they find us up here."

"That's what I just said. But now that Kim told them we're here, won't it look suspicious if we leave?"

"Oh? Your girlfriend will rat us out?"

"My girlfr—Gabriela? She's not my girlfriend."

"Uh-huh." Selene had recognized her from the photo in Theo's apartment. She remembered the way they'd stood together, half-naked, on the beach.

"First off, she's gay."

"Oh."

"Secondly, that's just her way. If you knew her for a few hours and she liked you, she'd be all over you, too."

"She wouldn't like me."

"You don't know that. You're really very—"

"Schultz."

"Yeah?"

"We have to leave."

Kim was still fuming in the other room, despite Gabriela's

efforts to soothe him. Selene stood behind him and dropped the keys on his desk. She placed her hands on his shoulders in what she hoped would seem a calming gesture. "We didn't touch anything. It's going to be just fine." She tried to look penitent as she slowly moved her hands up his neck and used her preternatural strength to pinch his carotid artery. While Theo and Gabriela argued over what to do about the security guards' imminent arrival, Kim collapsed with a *thud* onto the open book of ancient mammals, his cheek pressed against the drawing of the Caledonian Boar. Hopefully, he wouldn't remember the details of the last few minutes when he awoke.

"Fainted," she deadpanned. "Probably in shock. Poor guy." She turned to Gabriela, who stared openmouthed at her unconscious co-worker. "You want to show us a quick way out of here?"

"The guards—" Theo explained quickly. "I'm a person of interest with the police, remember? This doesn't help."

"You're going to run from the cops?" Gabriela asked, jaw falling farther agape. "What happened to my sweet Theodorable?"

"Come on, Gabi."

"I'd help if I could, but all the exits have security guards."

"Air shaft?" Theo suggested to Selene, looking surprisingly sanguine.

"And spend all night trapped in the museum's ductwork while our killer strikes again?" Selene turned back to the Tusk Vault. "I've got a better idea."

As he followed her inside, she told him to shut the door behind them. From her pack, she withdrew a steel-tipped arrow, a length of rope, and her disassembled bow. She knew she was taking a risk showing it to Theo, but she couldn't afford to be caught by the cops. Not now, when she finally knew something about the killer.

Surprisingly, Theo had yet to comment on her stash of weaponry.

"Are you going to shoot the guards?" he finally asked as she finished screwing her bow together.

"Of course not," she snapped, tying the rope to the arrow. "I don't kill innocent people."

"Just checking." Another thoughtful pause. "Are you going to shoot *me?*"

"Only if you don't shut up and help me," she said, tossing him one end of the rope. "Tie that to something high. And sturdy." She squatted on the edge of the open window and nocked the arrow. Over her shoulder, she watched Theo tie the rope to the top of a steam pipe. "You know you just made an overhand knot, don't you?"

"A what?"

"You're going to hold our weight with the same knot you use to tie your shoes."

"We're not really going to—"

She cut him off by marching over and retying the rope in a perfect boom hitch. "Tell your friend to release the knot as soon as we're safe." Theo nodded and shouted instructions through the door to Gabriela, who retorted with a muffled, bewildered assent.

Selene returned to the window, took aim, and let fly. With a satisfying *thunk*, the arrow pierced deep into the trunk of an ash tree just beyond the museum's fence. The rope hung taught above their heads, stretching between the vault and the tree—a perfect escape route. She withdrew a small curved handle from her pack and hooked it over the rope. "Let's go."

Theo paused for a moment. She saw his chest heave in a deep breath. Then he smiled. "I thought you'd never ask."

She sat on the sill, her legs dangling out the window. "Grab on to me." She couldn't quite believe her own suggestion, but she wasn't sure what other option she had.

"Are you sure you can hold my weight?"

She glanced disdainfully at his lanky frame. "I'm sure I'll manage."

He started toward her, then hesitated.

"Won't someone see us? I thought we were trying not to attract attention."

She rolled her eyes. "First of all, we're mostly screened by trees. Second, you'd be amazed how few people ever look up above the fourth floor or so of a building. And if they do, we'll be moving so fast they won't believe what they've seen. If I keep sitting here on the windowsill, on the other hand, someone's bound to notice."

He clambered into the window and sat behind her, his legs straddling her and his arms wrapped lightly around her hips. "Like this?" he asked.

Selene grabbed his clenched hands and slid them higher, just below her breasts. His heart pounded against her spine. "Tighter," she said, wondering why, this time, his touch didn't disturb her the way it had in Helen's office. He obeyed, the muscles of his forearms taut across her ribs. Without preamble, she jumped.

As they flew down the impromptu zip line, Theo nearly squeezed the air from her chest. She felt his mouth open against her neck in a silent shout. In less than a second, they'd slammed into the tree. Well, *Theo* slammed into the tree. Selene braced her landing with her legs, but they twisted on impact and Theo's right hip smacked into the trunk.

She swung a leg over a thick branch and hoisted herself securely into the crook of the limb, hauling the groaning professor up beside her. She looked back toward the museum's attic window, where Gabriela stood watching with both hands covering her mouth as if to repress a scream. Selene tugged at the rope, and the other woman gave her a weak wave before disappearing into the vault. A moment later, the rope tumbled out the window. Selene reeled it in, then reached up to yank the arrow from the trunk. Throughout, Theo watched, speechless, his knuckles white on the tree limb.

"Nothing to say?" she couldn't help asking.

"I've got a million questions, but they all sound so crazy I'm afraid to ask." Of course, as they climbed down the tree, he asked anyway. "Are you special ops? A Navy SEAL? Or just a superhero?"

"None of the above." She arrived at the lowest branch, ten feet above the ground, and vaulted off without hesitation.

"Too bad. I was hoping you were Catwoman or something. Between you and our acrobatic tusk robber, it's like I've entered my own private comic book." From his perch on the low branch, his feet dangled above the sidewalk. He grabbed hold of the branch and dropped heavily to the ground, only tripping twice before he came to a halt.

"Wow!" came a high-pitched squeal from nearby.

Selene spun toward the young boy who stood clutching his nanny's hand, staring up at Selene and Theo in wonder. "How'd you do that?"

Selene froze. She'd been hoping no one saw them.

"Science experiment. For the museum," Theo said easily. "Velocity versus acceleration and their effects on the heart rates of normally sedentary men. Cool, right? Don't tell anyone though, because we're still working out the kinks." The kid nodded eagerly. His nanny gave them a suspicious frown and pulled her charge away.

The sound of a siren wiped the grin from Theo's face. "Shit. Security must have called the cops."

They retrieved Hippo and hurried west along the sidewalk, hoping to put some distance between themselves and the museum. But for once, Selene had more pressing worries than the police.

She was far more concerned about the immortal who had broken into the American Museum of Natural History.

Chapter 22

GODDESS OF GIRLS

As Selene walked swiftly away from Natural History, her mind wouldn't stop reeling. *No mortal could have infiltrated the museum like that,* she decided. *And only Olympians knew the truth behind the Caledonian Boar. The cult's hierophant must be one of the Athanatoi. But why? There's only one reason an immortal would bother with a long-forgotten ritual...*

"I see another cop car," Theo said, interrupting Selene's musing. He led the way north up Broadway, where the crowds of Saturday fun-seekers were thicker. "Come on, in here." He gestured toward the AMC movie theater.

"What about Hippo?" she hissed after him.

He just waved her inside and dashed up to the teenage ticket taker. "Excuse me," she heard him ask. "My friend here is epileptic. That's her seizure dog. And I just wanted to know if there're any flashing lights or quick edits in *Last Woman Standing*."

"Uh...yeah..."

"Okay, so then we'll definitely bring the dog in with us. That way we'll have some warning."

"You're not allowed to bring—"

"No, no, she's a *seizure dog*. For the disabled."

"Shouldn't it be wearing a sign or something?"

"We don't believe in *labeling* people with disabilities, okay?" Theo said, with a glare that Selene could've sworn he'd learned from her. Before the teenager could ask any more questions, he was walking back toward Selene, grinning.

"What're we doing here?" she whispered.

"Isn't this what people always do in movies to avoid arrest? Hide out in movie theaters?" He flashed his dimples at her. "I've always thought it was just another way for Hollywood to plug itself, but it's better than nothing."

Selene had to admit, it wasn't a terrible idea. Theo walked to a kiosk, tapped the screen with practiced ease, swiped a credit card, and retrieved two tickets from the slot. She watched warily. She didn't own a credit card because it made her too easy to trace, touchscreens mystified her, and she hadn't been to the movies since the 1980s classic *Clash of the Titans* came out. She'd taken her mother, and the two of them sat howling with laughter as the actors playing their family stalked around in glowing white togas and teased hair, maneuvering the mortals below by playing with poorly sculpted clay figurines. "Why didn't we think of that?" she'd asked her mother. "Making voodoo models would have been *so* much easier than giving them cryptic prophecies and hoping they'd do the right thing!" Finally, an usher had asked them to leave.

She and Hippo followed Theo up the escalator and into a dark, nearly empty theater full of large red leather seats. Movie trivia and advertisements flashed silently across the screen. They took seats near the front, close to the emergency exit, just in case they were being followed. Selene eased herself into the wide armchair, a far cry from the cramped, moldering seats she remembered from her last cinematic foray. Next to her, Theo pressed a button on the side of his chair. The back began to recline while the front rose into a footrest. Soon, he lay nearly horizontal, a Roman aristocrat on his chaise. Cautiously, Selene followed suit.

Hippo growled a complaint or two but finally wedged herself beneath the footrests with a sigh. Selene shifted restlessly, unused to such decadent comfort. Theo, on the other hand, sat with his head thrown back and eyes closed, more relaxed than she'd ever seen him. "That was close," he murmured. "I have to admit, this whole running from the law thing is exhausting."

Selene had barely broken a sweat, but she, too, felt the weight of the hunt on her shoulders. *This isn't what I wanted,* she thought. *I never meant to chase one of my own.*

Theo's eyes opened a crack. "Henry Thomas."

"What?"

He pointed at the screen and read aloud. "Who played Elliott in 1982's *E.T. the Extra-Terrestrial*?"

"Why do you know that?"

"More importantly, why don't *you*? You might be damn handy with a bow, but we're going to have to work on your cinematic education."

"I've heard of it, just never seen it. It's good?"

"One of the best. A little boy meets an alien from another world and they become friends. Then the cops are chasing them, but they escape." He slid a glance toward her. She knew what he was thinking. It sounded a bit like a story about them.

"The little boy is one of the great heroes of film. Would brave anything, go anywhere, to save his friend. Sort of like the dedication you see in Odysseus, who risks his life a hundred times to make it back home to Penelope. My kind of hero."

Selene couldn't help comparing the man sitting beside her to the legendary adventurer she'd once watched fight his way across the seas. Odysseus had been a short, burly king inclined toward flatulence, and he'd never met a sorceress he wouldn't sleep with. But he also possessed tenacity unmatched by any other Greek hero. He used every tool he possessed—brawn, brain, and bluster—to accomplish his goals. Theo might not know it yet, but she suspected he and Odysseus had that in common.

"You know why else I love movies?" Theo was saying. "Because, except for the very bad ones, you always understand the plot, at least by the time the credits roll. Unlike real life." He sat up a little straighter and turned to her. "You're going to have to explain the bow."

"No. I'm not."

He frowned, and she thought he'd protest, but he just sighed. "Fine. Then answer another question. Why's someone bothering with all this? Breaking into two museums? Creating a cultic retreat in a hospital basement?" He pulled his coat tighter, despite the theater's warmth.

The answer, which Selene had been formulating since she saw the entelodont picture, finally made sense: *Because there's someone out there who used to be a god and is trying to become one again.* Cult worship and burnt offerings had sustained the Athanatoi for millennia, but once mankind had stopped such worship, the Olympians' power began to wane. Selene and the others had long ago given up hope that men would turn away from Christianity and return to the worship of the Greek deities. They'd resigned themselves to living as neither mortal nor fully immortal, but stuck somewhere in between. Yet if someone could actually re-create a cult ritual—not just going through the motions but finding true believers to offer sacrifices to the Olympians—the gods' power might be restored.

But how could she tell Theo any of this? Even if she did, he wouldn't believe it. How would it sound? *I know our killer's an immortal because he's probably one of my brothers. Oh yeah, I guess I forgot to mention that your friend Helen had the right idea—the Greek gods are real and I'm one of them. Or at least . . . I used to be.*

"Let's just focus on the fact that, whatever their motivations," she said instead, "we know what the *mystai* are doing next. If they've collected all the *hiera*, including one of the Hell Pig's tusks, they're going to be ready for the next step in the ritual."

Theo glanced around the nearly empty theater and lowered his voice, "And the next murder."

"We're up to the *Pompe*, right?"

"You remember." He looked pleased. The lights in the theater dimmed to black. Selene looked over her shoulder. No sign of police bursting through the doors. Only a few other people sat scattered in rows behind them. It must be a particularly terrible film.

A swell of music accompanied the first preview. Theo leaned over and whispered loudly in her ear: "So far, every ritual's been amplified. Besides the murders, we have massive porcine entelodont teeth instead of Demeter's traditional suckling pigs. They use *dozens* of snakes for the *Asklepia* instead of just one. Tonight's *Pompe* involved a procession to the temple in Eleusis. How will our hierophant amplify a parade?"

"It's already an intensified ritual," she whispered back, "because they processed in front of the whole city, while the previous rites were held in secret."

"You think they're going to do something tonight in public?" Theo clutched at the armrest, his elbow brushing hers. "You think they'll kill someone where everyone can see? That'll throw the city into a complete panic."

She could see the crease of concern behind the bridge of his glasses. "We need to stop them," she said, aware of her breath fanning the fair hair on his forehead. She turned away, back toward the movie preview, where a superhero ran through the streets of New York, dispatching three masked thugs with a magic whip, then flew through the air, chased by fighter jets. If only being a real hero were so easy.

"Then Trinity churchyard it is," Theo said. "I bet we'll catch the bastards there."

"Why Trinity?"

"It's the most famous cemetery in Manhattan, and the *Pompe* always started at Kerameikos, the most important burial ground in Athens. Leaving the graveyard symbolized a progression from death to life, remember? They're not going to change that part."

Selene knew Trinity churchyard: She'd stood there feeling smug the day they laid Alexander Hamilton in his grave. But she'd also lived in Manhattan long enough to know that many other cemeteries lay scattered throughout the city. "You're forgetting about the two nineteenth-century Marble Cemeteries off Second Avenue and the Jewish graveyards near Sixth Avenue— one of those is from the late 1600s. And Trinity Church has an overflow graveyard way uptown, too."

Theo whistled appreciatively. "You're certainly a font of morbid knowledge. Hopefully, after my conversation with the cops, they'll stake out all the cemeteries, but I'd like to have eyes on them. You have any discreet friends who might help?"

Selene laughed abruptly. "I don't have a whole lot of friends, in case you couldn't guess." She couldn't call the city's other immortals her friends—she hadn't spoken to most of them in years. Besides, one of them was likely the very killer they were seeking. "And don't go dragging your friend Gabriela or any of your adoring students along. You don't want them getting into trouble with the cops, too, do you?"

Theo turned back to the screen, chewing his lip. He was clearly devising some plan, but she, on the other hand, found it increasingly difficult to concentrate. The main attraction had begun, and for just a few minutes, she longed to escape into a fantasy world where the enemies and heroes were clear. To stop worrying about the ancient stories that defined her existence and to start enjoying the new ones mankind created instead.

A spaceship roared across the screen, spurting laser fire. Ahead of it, a blue-white nebula surrounded a red-orange planet. A burst of fire struck the spaceship, exploding the vessel into a thousand fragments of molten metal. The deafening sound thrummed through Selene's bones. She reached a hand down to pet her whimpering dog. Was the pilot dead? No, a figure in a spacesuit ejected from the blast, falling toward the planet. After shooting down a passing enemy ship with a handheld laser gun, the pilot finally landed on the planet's surface. When the space helmet's visor flipped up, the face underneath was that of a young woman. She pulled off the helmet and shook out long orange hair that contrasted strikingly with her ebony skin. Then she stalked off into the orange jungle, her gun at the ready.

Half an hour later, as the heroine met up with her long-lost, half-alien love interest and was about to engage in some inter-species eroticism, Theo tapped Selene lightly on the wrist. She turned to him sharply, as if awoken from a dream, her cheeks flushed.

He bent toward her, "Earth to Selene. Come in, Major DiSilva. We should get going."

As they walked into the theater lobby, Theo chuckled. "You were totally transfixed."

"Please. It was terrible," she said defensively.

"Terribly *awesome*, you mean," he said. "Don't worry, it'll be online in a month and we can watch the whole thing."

Selene snorted, but in truth, the idea was oddly appealing. She stopped at a water fountain to hide the smile she could feel creeping over her features. When she straightened up, a little girl, no more than three years old, toddled over to her. In that moment, she felt a pull so sharp she nearly stumbled forward, as if the child had tugged on an invisible rope attached to her rib cage. Selene planted her feet and stared at the girl in wonder. This time, she recognized the sensation immediately—the pull of the worshiper on the worshiped. Artemis reigned over many groups: virgin women, hunters, wild animals, hounds—and children. Of them all, it was the children she'd never really liked, never understood. Maybe because she would never have any of her own.

"Come back here, Lydia!" A harried mother scurried over to retrieve her child. "Sorry, is she bothering you?"

"No, it's okay," Selene managed, unable to move. Hippo sniffed curiously at the girl, who completely ignored the enormous dog.

"You glow," said the child, raising a hand to pat the air around Selene's body. "Sparkles." She grinned, showing a gap between her pearly baby teeth.

The mother laughed. "She's been watching too many cartoons."

Theo started up a conversation with the woman about the animated movie she'd just left, but the girl's eyes never left Selene's. And in that moment, the Huntress knew the truth about why she was getting stronger. The answer lay in the trusting gaze of this little girl.

The cult was actually *working*. Her strength, speed, aim, hearing—all were gifts from the Eleusinian Mysteries. Now, miraculously, even a hint of her divine radiance had returned, visible only to those whose extreme youth made them able to sense the secret worlds around them.

The boar tusk, the painting of her family, the obsession with virginity. Everything fell into place. She wasn't just reaping residual benefits from the revived cult: The cult had chosen her specifically as one of the deities it invoked. But could the murders themselves, not just the ritual, be giving her power? *No,* she decided. The Athanatoi had long made clear their stance on human sacrifice, reserving their most heinous Underworld punishments for those who dared make an offering of human flesh to the gods.

But why invoke me? Who would care enough to help me? And perhaps most important, Selene thought, *can I convince them to save my mother as well?* In half an hour, Hermes would lead her to the Underworld, and she might find some answers. Persephone and Hades, as central figures in the original Eleusis cult, topped the list of possible suspects to be leading this new one. If they were involved, she'd know soon enough.

"You look so familiar," the mother was saying to Theo. "Have I seen you on TV?"

Theo shook his head, all innocence, but Selene could see the sweat beading his brow.

"I have to go," Selene said abruptly.

Theo shot her a grateful glance and followed her and Hippo back onto the street.

Selene looked up and down the block. "No cops in sight."

"Great. Good thing we're going to the cemeteries next. At least dead people won't recognize me."

"I'm not going to the cemeteries, not yet. The sun won't be down for another half hour. Nothing's going to happen before then. Probably not until the dead of night, like the other crimes." She couldn't bear to look him in the eye. What would he say if he knew she was *benefiting* from the cult? Would he trust her to punish the killer? Did she trust herself? She headed toward the nearest subway. "Right now, I've got another lead to pursue."

"Where to?"

"I have to go alone."

"You keep saying that, but I—"

"Not this time." Her tone brooked no argument. This was about Athanatoi now. No mortals allowed. While Theo continued pondering Helen's research into the Eleusinian Mysteries, Selene would talk to the Goddess of Eleusis herself. Theo couldn't know that. Now or ever. "I'll call you later and we'll make a plan for tonight," she said, forestalling any further protest.

Selene left Theo at the uptown subway entrance, acutely conscious of her lie. Returning from the Underworld was rarely easy. She might never see Theodore Schultz again.

Chapter 23

CONDUCTOR OF SOULS

In Union Square, Selene's half brother Hermes waved exuberantly as he spotted her across the plaza.

Before she could stop him, the man currently known as Dash Mercer threw his arms around her and pressed a kiss on each cheek.

"Selene, darling. You look spectacular." The platitudes sprang forth as easily as always. "No one pulls off bulky and baggy quite like you."

"I don't like to attract attention."

Dash had no such compunction. Linen suit, open-necked pink shirt, suede loafers. Large black eyeglasses, of course.

"Nice touch," she said, pointing at the delicately patterned silk handkerchief peeking from a breast pocket.

He winked. "*Hermès*. Cost a fortune. But worth every penny."

"You've stooped to branding?"

"Every little bit of name recognition counts, you know," he said reproachfully. "Our little cousin Victory looks great for her age, even though she's not one of the Twelve, because a track coach decided to name his sneaker line 'Nike' back in the seventies. You look stupendous at the moment, but you know the fading comes for everyone eventually. You should think about it." He pressed a finger to his lips as he led the way through the square. "Artemis Athletics. A chain of workout clothes 'for the goddess in every woman.' Hah! I should go back into advertising."

Rolling her eyes, Selene followed Dash down into the subway station. At the entrance, she turned to offer him a MetroCard, but he passed effortlessly through the turnstile. She raised an eyebrow. "I haven't lost *all* my powers," he grinned.

Inside the station, Dash led the way to the end of the downtown Number 6 platform. He leaned against a pillar, his cheerful nonchalance contrasting sharply with the heaviness permeating the station. The two recent grisly murders had worried even the most jaded New Yorkers. Lone women stood with their backs to columns, their headphones hanging from only one ear so they could hear their surroundings, their eyes scanning the crowd for suspicious young men.

A train clattered and squealed into the station, blowing Selene's hair against her cheeks. Dash airily waved her aboard the last car. Crowds jammed the train as if it were rush hour—a time she always avoided. Dash maneuvered his way through with the ease and grace only Olympian gods or seasoned New Yorkers could muster. He leaned against the back wall, and Selene wedged in beside him, his curly hair in her nostrils. Two stops later, a short Latina woman jammed in beneath her arm, and a businessman's briefcase slammed against her bruised kidney. Selene found the smell of so many bodies, pungent to any human, noxiously fetid. She looked out the window, trying not to breathe. An uptown train flashed by on the adjacent track, and windows passed like frames of film: a dreadlocked white guy with enormous headphones, grooving in his seat; a little girl swinging on a metal pole while her father looked on warily; a woman in pearls, her palm pressed to the glass, as if in entreaty.

This was *her* city. *Her* people. They might not kneel at her statue as her acolytes had of old, but they worshiped at the same altar she did. *We're all* mystai *in the same cult,* she realized. *Bowing to a city that can be as harsh and as compassionate, as fickle and as stalwart, as any Olympian.*

"Brooklyn Bridge. End of the line!" blared the announcement as the train squealed to a stop. *"Last stop on this train! Everybody please exit the train!"* The doors opened and the crowd poured forth like air released from a balloon. Selene could finally exhale. She started toward the exit, but Dash put a hand on her arm and shook his head.

The motorman's door swung open and a short black woman in an MTA vest and goggles emerged, shouting, "Clear the train! This train is going out of service then heading back uptown!" In a moment, she'd realize Dash and Selene weren't moving.

"Oh my God!" Dash suddenly cried, pointing to the front end of the car, where a crowd made its way out the door. "What's that guy doing? Is that a *live monkey*?" Like marionettes, every head in the car, including the motorwoman's, turned toward a perfectly innocent Sikh in a yellow turban standing in the doorway, looking as bewildered as everyone else.

As swiftly as only a god once known as Hermes could manage, he'd opened the rear emergency exit, jumped up to grab the top of the doorframe, and swung himself out of the car, his feet disappearing over Selene's head. She sighed, but hitched her backpack more firmly onto her shoulders, and, before the motorwoman could turn around, seized the lintel in both hands. Using the rubber safety ropes as a ladder, she clambered to the train roof and kicked the door shut behind her.

Dash lay flat, his head pointing toward the front of the train, his curls a mere foot from the tunnel ceiling. Selene pulled off her backpack so it wouldn't get ripped from her body when the train began to move and settled herself beside him, one hand holding her bag and the other gripping the side of the car. "This is a terrible idea," she whispered to him. "Train hopping gets people killed."

He just grinned. "What's the fun of being immortal if you can't cheat death every now and again?"

"I try not to push the limits," she grumbled as the train headed toward the turnaround loop farther downtown. "You know we're not completely invulnerable anymore." Dash just giggled. Stony-faced, Selene shifted her weight to hug the train's roof more securely. *I may be getting stronger,* she thought, *but this is just foolhardy.*

"Ready?" Dash shouted above the rattle a minute later.

"For what?"

"Jump!" He let go. His body flew backward, sliding off the top of the car and disappearing into the darkened tunnel behind them. *Dash has grown as mad as the rest of us,* she thought with a groan.

Zip lining out of the museum was one thing. This was entirely more stupid. She swung her body around carefully to face the back of the train. Glancing at the electrified tracks rushing beneath her nose, she shook her head and then rolled off the end of the car.

It would've been history's most graceful exit from a moving subway—if it hadn't been for the rat.

As she flew off the roof, Selene turned a midair somersault, almost floating to the gravel rail bed and hitting the ground feet-first—landing on a scurrying, squealing, subterranean rodent. Then falling on her ass. Dash spluttered from somewhere nearby.

"I can see you laughing, you know," she snarled. "My night vision's pretty good."

"You have to learn to laugh at yourself."

"And you have to learn to take some things more seriously," she returned, trying to regain some dignity as she rose to her feet. "You're telling me this is the only way to get to the Under-world? We couldn't just get off at the last stop like everyone else?"

"Our stop's *beyond* the last stop."

"And we couldn't walk down the tunnel from the last station like the MTA employees do?"

"But this was *so* much more fun! You were always the best sister for adventures, you know, and I haven't had an adventure like this in decades!"

"You're ridicu—" She stopped mid-word as another rat ran over her feet. Swift as the wind, she pulled an arrow from her bag and thrust the shaft through the rodent's pulsing side. "—lous."

Dash whistled in appreciation. "Not bad. But where're your gold arrows?"

"Used up."

"I could get in touch with the Smith for you."

Selene wasn't used to offers of help. She was even less used to accepting them. But since divine enemies required divine weapons, Dash's suggestion couldn't have come at a better time. "Thanks. That might be a good idea. I haven't talked to the Smith in a long time."

Selene remembered Hephaestus as a child, a strapping boy with a wide grin that softened the coarseness of his features, always investigating and inventing. Puttering around in his forge, playing with fire and iron the way a mortal child might with blocks and string. Hera, Queen of the Gods, who'd defied Zeus himself to birth Hephaestus without the aid of a man's seed, watched her son with pride. But when the Smith took his mother's side in one of her many arguments with her husband, Zeus flung him from the heights of Mount Olympus. His body careered from boulder to boulder, landing in a broken heap on the island of Lemnos. The Smith could fashion a gold bow for Artemis, a feast hall for his family, or winged sandals for Hermes, but he could not rebuild his own legs. That day, the Huntress had learned her first lesson about the limitations of the gods: No mortal could defeat them, but the Olympians could damage one another irreparably.

Dash's smile flashed white in the darkened tunnel as he walked beside her. "I'm sure he'll be glad to hear from you. The Smith always liked you best, you know."

"Did he?"

"You sound surprised!" A dim light from up ahead glinted off his glasses as he turned to her. "For someone with such keen senses, you can be pretty oblivious."

"When you're hunting, it only matters if you can find the animal and track it down, not whether it laughs at your jokes or wants to go out for dinner."

Dash let out a burbling laugh. "Take note. *I* think you're funny. That means I *like* you. As a sister, as a friend. Of course, our Smith actually *liked you* liked you. Hah! You're blushing again."

"You can't possibly see that in this light," she snapped.

"But I don't have to. God of Communication, remember? I'm *great* at sensing people's emotions."

"Oh? Then why can't you tell you're pissing me off?"

Dash skipped a few steps down the tunnel then turned and gave her an elaborate bow, pulling his handkerchief from his pocket to wave a final flourish. "That's exactly my goal, sweetheart. I want to crack some of that icy shell. You're not the Moon anymore, you know. You don't need to be so cold and stony."

Selene didn't feel cold and stony. She felt hot and irritated. "Can I help it if I'm not an extrovert like you?"

"Of course. That's the great part about no longer being fully immortal. It's true that we have to keep some link to our old identities now that we don't have real worshipers. But we can define that connection for ourselves. That means we can be pretty much anything we want. This isn't like the old days, when mankind cast us in the image they desired. They made me a thief and a liar and a seducer of women, with fleet feet and a prodigious phallus. But I don't *have* to be all those things anymore. Though before you can ask—yes, I still have the enormous penis." He winked at Selene's obvious discomfort and gave his handkerchief another twirl. "But I don't lie or cheat half as often as I used to."

"You still sow plenty of mischief. That train stunt was completely unnecessary. If you don't watch out, you'll wind up as unhinged as Father, living in a cave and dining on bats."

"Me, mad? I'll leave that to the rest of the family. Look, I got all the good stuff. I *like* most of the attributes they gave me. You, on the other hand, definitely got a bum deal. Virginity and hunting." He made a loud retching sound. "Both things that were last in style in the mid-nineteenth century. I'm actually surprised you aren't already fading away."

"I *chose* to be the chaste Huntress," she retorted, ignoring his last comment. Until she figured out who was causing her transformation, she didn't want the other Athanatoi to know about her increasing power.

"Sure, maybe you sat on Father's lap and asked for a bow and hounds, just like the stories say. But was that really your idea to begin with? Or did men just need a Goddess of the Hunt? And could they imagine her any other way than silent and celibate and deadly?"

Dash's words reminded her of Theo's theories—casting the gods as figments of society's imagination rather than as autonomous beings. She knew there was some truth there, but she wasn't yet willing to admit how much. "So you're blaming my worshipers from millennia ago for my social 'inadequacies'?"

"No! I'm blaming *you*. You could be anything, and you're still a taciturn prude with no interpersonal skills." *He's right,* Selene thought, not bothering to protest. "They used to call you She Who Leads the Dance," he said thoughtfully. "Whatever happened to that epithet? Might be a little more fun than the Relentless One."

"I led *nymphs* in dances after the hunt. I knew how to deal with them. Mortals are harder."

"Please. Mortals just want to do whatever makes them feel rich and beautiful. It's *im*mortals you have to worry about. We've had too many millennia of resentment and overweening pride. So think carefully about what you're going to ask Cora. The Goddess of Spring is pretty touchy, you know, and you're not known for your subtlety."

"True. I find old habits hard to break, just like the rest of the Athanatoi. You, for example, are still a pain in my ass. And Cora—I think she's resurrecting her old Eleusis cult."

"Oh-ho! You think an Athanatos is involved in the murders?"

"I know it," she said grimly.

"Then how come you don't suspect me?"

"You said yourself, on the phone this morning, you had nothing to do with Eleusis. More important, you were in L.A. only a few hours after the last murder. Even with your private jet, that clears you of suspicion." The tracks ahead of them began to curve. "This is where the line loops around to head back uptown again?" she asked.

"Yup. Check it out." As they rounded the bend, an abandoned station came into view. The ceiling widened into a graceful barrel vault supported by fifteen tiled arches in patterns of green, white, and black, interspersed with leaded glass skylights. Brass chandeliers hung from the ceiling, their bulbs dark. Dash jumped up onto the stretch of platform beside the track. A green and orange mosaic sign on the terracotta wall read "City Hall."

"I forgot all about this station," Selene whispered. It seemed wrong to speak loudly in this perfectly preserved remnant of the past, a shrine to a city long since gone, where every public space was designed to impress visitors with its sheer ornate beauty.

"I haven't been here since they stopped using it in the 1940s. It looks pretty good, considering."

"After they renovated it, they wanted to reopen it as a historical curiosity. But they never did, supposedly because of security concerns after 9/11."

"Supposedly?"

"Well, really, a certain uncle of ours kept sabotaging the work. He convinced the crew that the station was either haunted or structurally unsound and they've pretty much left it alone ever since. Now the motormen see it as they drive the trains around the loop, but no one ever visits."

"So this is where the Receiver of Many calls home?"

"Naw. This is too public for our uncle—since he doesn't actually receive much of anyone these days. This is more like the foyer." He walked over to the "City Hall" sign and dug his fingers into the mortar around the edge of the ceramic "H." The entire letter swung upward, revealing a small button underneath. He pressed it firmly, maneuvered the "H" back into place, then turned to stare up at the chandelier. He smiled and waved at the lightbulbs. Suddenly, an exhalation of air sounded from behind them. A jagged section of tiles swung open to reveal a narrow spiral staircase stretching deeper underground.

"I guess they're home," Dash said cheerily.

"Of course you didn't check first," Selene grouched. Still, she followed him into the dimly lit passageway. For the first time in her long life, the Huntress entered the Underworld. She would have to trust the Conductor of Souls to get her out again.

Chapter 24

RECEIVER OF MANY

After walking down at least five stories, deep enough to bypass all the sewage and electric lines, Selene watched Dash squeeze through the mouth of a roughly hewn tunnel stretching westward. The tightly enclosed space made her sweat. She tried to calm herself by thinking about the fresh air above. They must be passing underneath City Hall Park, right by the Mayor's Office and the Tweed Courthouse. The tunnel continued for probably three hundred feet before ending at a small door. Dash pushed it open and Selene crowded beside him into the tiny room on the other side. Another heavy door on the far side remained closed. "This is like an airlock," Selene said, her claustrophobia growing.

"That's exactly what it was," Dash nodded, rapping four times on the door. "Pneumatic subways don't work if you let the air out."

"You mean the experimental subway from the 1870s? The one with the fancy waiting room? It only operated for a few weeks, then I thought the city destroyed it."

"Mm-hm. But urban legend collectors have been looking for

it for decades." He lowered his voice to a conspiratorial whisper. "Maybe some even found it. But anyone who manages to enter the realm of the dead, as you know, never returns to tell the tale." He waited just long enough for Selene to start worrying that he was telling the truth. "Kidding! Uncle Aiden's a pussycat." He pecked her on the cheek and turned to leave.

"Where do you think you're going?"

"You didn't think I was going in with you, did you? I'm the *Psychopompos*. The *Conductor* of Souls, not their babysitter. Have fun accusing the most fearsome son of Kronos and his wife of leading a homicidal Mystery Cult. I'll be back to pick you up when you're done, but I try to keep my visits to the Underworld to a minimum. Safer that way."

"What?"

"Come on. Big strong goddess like you." He winked. "You'll be fine." But despite his cavalier attitude, Dash left with all the speed his name implied.

Before Selene could go after him, the heavy door before her swung open. Selene shifted her backpack so she could reach her bow more easily. She was prepared for a three-headed guard dog or perhaps a cadaverous boatman. Instead, a middle-aged woman stood in the doorway, squinting suspiciously.

Selene suppressed a gasp of dismay. She should've remembered that, like Leto, Persephone would fade faster than one of the Twelve. Still, the transformation was shocking. Demeter's beloved only child had once had hair as yellow as wheat sheaves, dewy skin, and a body so irresistibly nubile that Hades himself had emerged from the Underworld to steal her away. Now, Cora's hair was brittle, her lusterless eyes sunken, and the flesh hung slack from her arms. She wore a pink chiton richly embroidered with flowers. It couldn't have been cheap, but it looked tawdry compared to the simple linen she'd worn in her prime.

"Cousin, it's me..." Selene ventured. "The Huntress."

Cora's eyes lit up. "Oh yes, we've been expecting you!" She called back over her shoulder, "Dearest! Aiden! The party's starting!"

Cora opened the door wider. Selene hesitated a bit. *What party?* she wondered. *What am I getting myself into?* She followed Cora into a long, vaulted chamber. Ornate gas brackets cast the room in a warm glow that reminded Selene how much better everything had looked before the advent of electricity. The floor gleamed with alternating black and white wooden planks, covered here and there by oilcloths of mauve Victorian bouquets. In the center of the chamber, a fountain jetted water in a tinkling arc. "As Time Goes By" echoed through the room from a baby grand in the corner, its keys flashing beneath invisible fingers.

"Do you like our ghost?" Cora asked as they passed the piano. "He's very good, isn't he?"

Selene murmured a noncommittal assent, her skin prickling. Then she noticed the power cord running out of the back of the instrument. A player piano, that was all. But Cora didn't seem to be joking. How far gone was she?

Cora prattled on. "I've been getting ready for the party, although good fruit this time of year is hard to find. You know, I'd heard you were living in the city these past few hundred years, but I guess, well...we just don't run in the same circles. In fact," she added with a saccharine smile, "last time we met, you were trampling a field of flowers with your rowdy band of nymphs and dogs. Or was it dogs and nymphs? With your followers, it was always so hard to tell."

Before Selene could retort, Cora continued her onslaught. "I'll have to lend you something to wear, of course. That leather jacket and those baggy pants will never do. You'll look much better in yellow anyway." Selene bit back a snort of disgust.

"No, no, it's no bother. We have plenty to spare. We've done very well for ourselves, as you can see. Isn't it beautiful?" She swept an arm across the lavish room. "Aiden lets me do all the decorating, of course." *Of course,* thought Selene. "Do you like the flowers?" Cora went on. "I thought they'd be a nice touch for the Great Gathering." She stopped to primp one of the many wilting pink bouquets tumbling from every surface. Selene breathed shallowly, trying not to gag at the smell of rot.

Cora opened a narrow, iron-studded door at the far end of the waiting room and led Selene into a stone-walled chamber. No pink or mauve here. Only black and gray—colors of the eternal night. A fire burned in a soot-stained hearth by the door, casting flickering shadows across the walls and floor and making the room uncomfortably warm. Despite the medieval décor, a modern sprinkler system peeked from the ceiling, and computer monitors covered the walls, each displaying jagged colored lines of oil prices and stock indices. Behind a vast desk, the Receiver of Many sat in a throne-like leather armchair. Even seated, he loomed over the room, impossibly tall. In the firelight, the pinstripes on his black suit glinted like shards of dark purple amethyst. Beneath his long black hair, his face looked as pale and gaunt as a cadaver's, but his skeletal appearance didn't mean he had lost his powers—as the Lord of the Dead, he'd always resembled his charges. In fact, he displayed none of his wife's frailty. Mankind's worship of money had only increased over the centuries, and he had clearly benefited in his other role as the God of Wealth.

Selene scanned the rest of the room, looking for danger. No swords, guns, or bows, but in a large glass case lay a dark Greek helmet with long nose and cheek guards. *Hades's Helm of Invisibility,* she remembered, *forged by the Cyclops for the war against the Titans. Probably doesn't work anymore.* Either way, as long as it stayed safely in its case, it shouldn't be a problem. Of more concern was the seven-foot-long wooden staff mounted beside it. On top of the staff perched the bronze figurine of a bird. Hades' scepter had always served more as a symbol of his dominion than as a useful weapon, but that didn't mean the bird's wickedly sharp beak couldn't draw blood.

"See who's come, my love!" crowed Cora, sitting on the corner of the desk and gesturing Selene to a narrow wooden chair beside the fireplace. "I'm sorry our first guest couldn't be someone more fun," she whispered loudly in Aiden's ear. She pecked him on the cheek. *At some point,* Selene thought, *I'll have to figure out when she got so nice to him. Last thing I knew, she was his eternally miserable sex slave.*

"Offer our guest some refreshment, my love," he said, stroking her hand with one long bony finger.

"Oh! How could I have forgotten?" Cora moved to a credenza against the wall and lifted a platter of overripe pears and browning apples toward Selene.

"No, thank you. I just ate." Selene perched on the front of the chair, ready to flee if necessary.

Cora frowned. "But you must!"

"No really, you know I prefer meat." *I also prefer not getting trapped in the Underworld by eating the food of the dead.*

"What kind of party will it be if you don't eat something?"

"I'm not here for the . . . party."

Cora's face fell. Aiden just sounded angry. "Then why *are* you here, Huntress?"

No use dancing around the point. The Lord of the Dead wasn't known for his patience.

"Because someone's brought back the Eleusinian Mysteries and is sacrificing innocent women—those I'm sworn to protect—as part of the rites. The hierophant leading the cult is no mere mortal—he's an Athanatos of significant strength." Selene fixed her uncle with an accusatory gaze. "Is it you, Hidden One? Have you revived the Mysteries in the hopes of bringing back Cora's youth and beauty?"

Cora gasped indignantly, her hand reaching for the drooping flesh of her neck.

"How dare you," Aiden seethed. "My beloved is young and beautiful until the end of time!" Selene could swear she saw a glint of red sparks within the black depths of his eyes.

She tensed, ready for a fight. "Perhaps love has blinded—" she began. But she instantly regretted her candor when her uncle rose from his desk, his hands clenching into fists.

Cora moved to stand behind her husband, clutching his wide shoulders like a shield. "Why's she being so mean?"

"I just want to know if you're involved in the murders," Selene said carefully. She eased her hand into the backpack at her feet, feeling for an arrow.

Aiden raised a long arm to silence her. "You dare insult my wife," he said with quiet intensity. "You dare accuse us of participating in forbidden rites." His voice grew louder. "Such impertinence!" He pounded the desk before him. "Why would I bother seeking strength that way? Power approaches my very doorstep all on its own!"

Selene kept her voice calm, but her fingers closed around an arrow shaft. "So you're not using the rites to—"

"I don't have time for this!" Cora huffed, suddenly more annoyed than offended. "There's so much to do for the party and here comes the Huntress with her terrible clothes and her worse manners, talking about things she knows nothing about. The Eleusinian Mysteries reversing millennia of decline! Hah! It doesn't work that way. The Mysteries didn't have that sort of power, not since the ritual changed."

"What do you mean, changed?" asked Selene.

"I don't remember exactly," Cora said with an impatient pout. She emerged from behind her husband. Aiden patted her hand and slowly lowered himself back into his chair. It seemed as long as Cora was happy, her husband's temper remained in check.

Selene released the arrow in her bag and made a mental note to play nice with her cousin.

Cora moved to the credenza and plucked a few slices of fruit from the tray. "You know how those old memories are," she insisted, popping a withered piece of apple into her mouth. "No one ever wrote down the original rituals. No one even *talked* about them. So all I have now are vague, hazy images. Grain. A crown."

"Then maybe they *did* once involve human sacrifice. Maybe that's what originally gave them power."

"Oh no, no. How gory! We'd never condone it. I may have forgotten the details of the cult, but I'd remember if we received offerings of *human flesh*. Maybe your hierophant's just killing women because he doesn't like them. Or to get back at humanity for abandoning us. I can see the temptation—mortals are such ungrateful little mammals. But their deaths can't be adding to the power of the ritual—certainly not."

Selene felt a weight lift from her shoulders. If the original Eleusis cult hadn't included murder, then hopefully she was right that the killings themselves had nothing to do with her own strengthening. She must be gaining power from some other aspect of the ritual. But if the Goddess of Eleusis herself didn't know what gave the rites their power, who would?

"So you're not involved, but have you been talking to anyone about the Mysteries? Helping them re-create the rites? What about your mother?"

"She hasn't mentioned anything to me. And she would if she knew anything, because she writes me letters *all* the time. As if forcing me to live with her for nine months of the year on her filthy Peruvian farm weren't bad enough," she said with a sniff. "I'm old enough to live my own life with my husband, but a deal's a deal, you know." She lifted a mushy hunk of pear to Aiden's lips and he slurped it from her fingers. Cora used her sleeve to tenderly wipe the juice from his dark beard.

"The gods' memories are long," Selene said, her expression carefully neutral. She was determined not to get involved in a squabble between Persephone and Demeter that had clearly persisted for centuries.

"But even gods can change," Aiden said softly, his eyes fixed on his wife.

Cora rested her lips against his forehead. "Even gods can learn."

Right. You learned how to be a pampered housewife with no self-respect, Selene thought, repressing a grimace. "If it's not your mother, who else could be doing this?"

"The Sky God always envied our Mysteries, but of course, he's probably still in his cave," Cora mused. "The God of War's still floating around somewhere, running a mercenary army in Africa, I think, but I doubt he's bright enough to come up with a new cult for himself. Of course, the Smith's awfully clever, but he's not really the murdering type, now is he? I would say Asclepius, since he's got a connection to our cult, but the poor man died long ago. Then again," Cora considered, "the Wine Giver is really your best bet. When he joined the Mystery, it changed. He siphoned off some of the worship and offerings for himself. We haven't seen him in centuries, but I wouldn't put it past him to bring back our cult and keep it all to himself. He was always jealous of Mother and me."

"An Athanatos can *change* a cult?" Selene asked eagerly. "Take it for himself?"

"The Wine Giver did. He told his own story alongside ours, then added his own attributes to the ritual. You'd have to ask him the details." Cora turned to Aiden. "Speaking of wine, my love, did you put in that order for the Dom Pérignon?"

"You know I prefer something darker. Champagne's a little...bubbly...for my taste."

Cora slapped him playfully on the arm. "Oh, you. *Bubbly* is exactly right! Just like me! And you love *me*, don't you?"

As the couple jabbered on, Selene began to form an idea: If

Dionysus had taken the cult once before, perhaps Selene could seize it now. Not for herself, but for Leto. She could create a new ritual with Leto's attributes, remove the gratuitous human sacrifice, and maybe...just maybe...bring her mother a little more strength.

"Ooh!" Cora exclaimed, interrupting Selene's musing. "I've got it! Maybe the hierophant is your twin! Asclepius was his son, after all, and the Bright One was always poking around Eleusis, trying to figure out what we were doing. Oh, I do hope it's him!" Cora clapped her hands with delight. "If he's so worried about bringing back his powers, then he must already be fading! How wonderful!"

It's true, Selene realized with a shiver. Paul was the perfect suspect. He still retained much of his own strength, but at the hospital, he'd made his terror of death clear. He'd flatly refused to succumb to the fading. Also, he already had a ready-made cult of thanatoi musicians following his every move. Most telling, he was the only god who might care enough about Selene to include her in the ritual. And he said he'd do anything to help Leto—maybe this was his attempt. *But kill innocent women? He must know Mother would never allow that—not even to save herself.*

Cora turned to Aiden. "Do you hear, dearest? The God of Music will be here soon! And to think, I was so worked up about having enough entertainment."

"Whoever the hierophant is," Selene said, "whether the Bright One or the Wine Giver or some other deluded relative of ours, he must be stopped. He's turning my city into a charnel house."

Cora giggled suddenly. "You were always so funny. A *charnel house*. So doom and gloom. I mean it's in very bad taste, of course, but a few dead mortals...what's the difference? They all die anyway."

"These are innocent women. They're under my protection. I will stop the hierophant—whatever it takes." There was work to do. Make a new cult to save her mother, then destroy the murderous one terrorizing the innocents. Selene had no time to waste. She rose to go.

"Silly Huntress! You can't leave!" Cora pushed Selene insistently on the shoulder until she reluctantly sat back on the chair. "And why would you want to? See how cozy it is here?" She crossed to the fireplace, warming her hands over the flames despite the uncomfortable heat in the room. "You can just stay here beside the fire, we'll drink a little wine, have a little chat, and you can just wait for your Athanatoi hierophant to show up on his own. He'll be here soon for the Great Gathering, along with everyone else. You can confront him then. It will add such drama to our little party!"

Selene cleared her throat, beginning to wonder if Cora and Aiden were more deluded than truly dangerous. "There hasn't been a Gathering of the gods since my father summoned us to announce the Diaspora from Mount Olympus."

"But now the gods are dying," Aiden intoned, "and when they do, they will come here, to our realm in the Underworld, just as all the dead do."

Surely there is no real Underworld anymore, Selene thought. *We die and we disappear into nothingness. And there's definitely no way dead gods wind up in the waiting room of a defunct pneumatic subway.* Then again...she had a sudden image of all the nymphs and long-forgotten minor gods, whiling away their days among the flowers and the music. If there was any chance, however unlikely, of seeing her companions once more...

"So those who have died already," she couldn't help asking, "they're here somewhere?"

"They pass through for a while," said Aiden with a grave nod, "then disappear into Elysium, or Tartarus, or Khaos."

She was almost afraid to ask her next question. "And...Orion?"

"He was denied an afterlife among his own kind."

Her heart sank. "Then where is he?"

"Where you put him. In the stars. At least to begin with. Who knows where his spirit resides now? I have no control over the fate of those you give to the heavens," he said with a touch of pique. "But the rest, as soon as they die, will arrive in my realm. And when they do, they will be under my power. *I* will become the King of the Gods," Aiden continued. He spoke with the confidence of one either very wise or completely delusional. "Your father stole the crown long ago when he divided the universe among his brothers. He made me Lord of the Underworld and seized the Sky for himself. Now, finally, I can rule over him, over his children, over all the Athanatoi."

"And I'll be your queen." Cora batted her eyelashes. "You, Huntress, can be my first handmaiden," she added, as if granting a great boon.

Selene scowled, more sure than ever that she needed to get out of Aiden's lair, and soon. The Gathering might just be a figment of his imagination, but she didn't want to stick around to find out. "Sorry, but I have things to do on Earth before I'm ready to consign myself to the Underworld."

"*Consign* yourself? She speaks as if our home were a prison," Cora said. "And I worked so hard to make it beautiful. Tell her she can't leave."

"Oh no, I have to," Selene said, thinking quickly. "If the cult is actually working, and the hierophant tells the other Athanatoi, then the fading will stop. We'll all remain in the world above. You don't want that to happen, do you? Who will come to your party? It'll be just the three of us for eternity."

Cora wrinkled her nose. "How awful."

"I couldn't agree more." Selene stood up and slung her backpack onto her shoulder.

She'd nearly made it to the open door when she heard Cora humming thoughtfully. "Oh bother, I've changed my mind. You can at least help me pick out the new drapes. Sit back down, Huntress."

"Sorry, Cousin." Selene smiled politely and kept walking. "Next time you want me to come to a party, send me an invitation."

Cora gasped. "What's she doing? Make her stay!"

"You *will not leave*." Aiden pressed a button on his desk. The iron-studded door slammed shut in Selene's face. She whirled toward her uncle. He rose once more from his desk. "Will you obey your elder, *Artemis*?"

"Not unless you make me, *Hades*," she seethed.

"Make her! Make her!" Cora shrieked, tugging on her husband's arm.

The Lord of the Dead smiled faintly, the red sparks now unmistakable in his eyes. Selene wondered if the flames might leap forth, charring her to a husk. He raised his hand in a gesture of command. *"Come, Cerberus!"*

Uh-oh. Selene spun toward the sound of clattering nails on the floorboards, expecting to see the enormous three-headed hound who had guarded the exit from the Underworld in days of old. Instead, she faced something far more monstrous. Racing through a small hatch in the wall were a wolfhound, a pit bull, and a Doberman, their collars lashed together. The tangled, scarred, slavering trio lurched toward her, their eyes rolling with pain and terror. Before she could free her bow, the pit bull lunged, snapping razor-sharp teeth inches from her thigh.

With a growl, Selene aimed a knee squarely in the pit bull's chest, cracking its rib and knocking the dog loose. The instant she was free, she lifted her arms above her head, leaned forward, and hollered, *"I am the Lady of Hounds!"* Then she snarled, low and long, until she could feel the foam frothing at the corners of her mouth. The three dogs cowered before her, whimpering as they lowered their heads. She placed one booted foot firmly on the pit bull's head, pressing it into the ground. Reaching into her backpack, she pulled out her bow, assembled it in an instant, and nocked an arrow. The other dogs tried to get away, their legs scrambling for purchase, but the rope around their necks held them tight. The sight of their drooling mouths enraged her. No hound could attack its Mistress and live. She raised her bow for a killing shot.

The Doberman let loose a long, piteous howl. Selene shot the arrow.

The point sliced neatly through the rope. Whining, the three dogs struggled free and skittered back through their hatch and out of the room. She wheeled toward Aiden's desk. "How dare you—" she began, her bow at the ready.

But he wasn't there. Selene's gaze flew to the glass case that held his helm and scepter. Empty. *Oh, Styx.*

Chapter 25

THE HIDDEN ONE

Searching the room in vain for any trace of her uncle or his bird-tipped staff, Selene backed up until she could feel the heat of the hearth on the backs of her legs.

Cora skipped to the corner of the room, where she could watch the proceedings from safety. She giggled maniacally. "Oh, this is just *thrilling!* Get her, my love!"

Selene ignored her and sniffed deeply, trying to catch the Hidden One's scent, but the stench of dead flowers and moldering fruit overwhelmed her senses. She aimed at the center of the room and hoped for the best. "Not another step, Uncle. My arrows might not kill you, but they'll hurt like hell."

"Like *hell!*" Cora squealed. "Do you hear? As if the Lord of the Underworld is scared of *that!*"

"If I can't see you, I can't aim," Selene warned. "No guarantee I won't take out an eye."

Aiden's voice came from somewhere ahead of her, thrumming with the power only a son of Kronos could command. "*Sit down.* You may not leave until I allow it." With only the slightest movement of air as a warning, something sharp and hard struck

Selene on her arm just as she loosed an arrow. The shaft flew wide, clattering harmlessly against the stone wall.

With a curse, she snatched another arrow from her bag and held it behind her back, dipping the tip into the fireplace.

"She's going to set us on fire!" Cora screeched.

"Not quite," Selene muttered. Without bothering to use her bow, she flung the flaming arrow toward the ceiling, where it struck one of the sprinkler heads. A fine mist of water filled the room—revealing an Aiden-shaped outline of raindrops. Howling with rage, he swung at her, but she noticed the gap in the water move toward her and raised her bow to block his staff. She parried another blow, and another, her gaze fixed on the twisting path of the droplets.

"My dress! It's silk!" Cora whined, patting at the dark stains spreading across her gown.

If I'm here another second, I'm going to throttle her, Selene thought as she blocked one more strike, then swung for Aiden's head with all her strength. Her gold bow clanged against the invisible bronze helm, sending a numbing shock through her bruised arm. Aiden's watery outline swayed before her—then collapsed to the ground with an unmistakable *thud.* Seizing her chance, Selene shot an arrow at the button on Aiden's desk, and the iron-studded door swung open. She dashed out of the stone chamber, into the gaslit waiting room, and past the ghostly piano—now playing a mournful dirge. Then she heard the squish of wet footsteps fast approaching. Aiden was back.

She sped toward the exit, slipped into the airlock, and slammed the heavy door closed behind her.

Dash, leaning casually against the wall of the tunnel, jerked upright when he saw her.

"Don't say a word," she warned him. "Just *run.*"

Dash didn't need to be told twice. "Hope you're still the Swiftly Bounding One!" he called over his shoulder as he sprinted ahead.

As they tore down the tunnel, Selene could hear the pneumatic door swing open behind them. Dash glanced backward. "I don't see anyone!"

"That's because he's wearing his Helm of Invisibility!"

"*What?* It still *works?* My winged sandals are about as useful as a pair of heels!"

Selene could hear Cora faintly whining and then, so loud it sounded like he was only steps behind them, Aiden's sudden roar: "This is your home, now, Huntress! *You must return!*"

"This is *not* good," Selene called up to Dash.

"Don't sweat it!" He spun around to talk to her, running backward all the while. "We've just got to get aboveground. Father's old curse still works—Aiden's powers fade when he leaves the Underworld." His smile dissolved as he looked past her. "Oops. Wet footprints. He's gaining on us."

"Then turn around and run like a normal person!" she snapped. Dash obeyed, picking up speed as they neared the spiral staircase. Together, they clattered up the five stories and back into the abandoned City Hall subway station. They shoved the secret door closed behind them, knowing it would only delay Aiden for a moment. Selene pointed up to the faint light trickling through the foggy, century-old skylights.

"We're not exactly aboveground, but will sunlight do the trick?"

Dash gave her a pained smile. "Maybe?"

Selene drew her bow and shot a single arrow high overhead, knocking one small pane from the intricately leaded skylight.

"Hey, watch it!" Dash cried, shielding his head from the tumbling glass shards.

"Watch the door instead!"

She shot out a second pane right beside the first. The thin stream of sunlight grew an inch thicker. Dash threw himself against the tiles, but his boyish frame was no match for Aiden's strength. An instant later, he tumbled aside when the wall burst open—just as Selene shot out a third pane of glass.

For a moment, the sunbeam streamed directly into the doorway, illuminating only the empty passageway beyond. Then, with a strangled cry, Aiden materialized. He raised his staff as if to ward off the light and glared at Selene, his eyes still fiery beneath his helm. But even as she watched, his strength ebbed. His posture grew stooped; the flesh of his hands withered. He lowered the staff, as if it had suddenly grown too heavy for him to wield. Then, as the sparks faded from his eyes, he pulled off his helm as if it crushed his skull. Beneath it, locks of gray now streaked his black hair.

Even in his weakened state, Selene stood firm, a single arrow aimed directly at her uncle's throat. He squinted in the light, his eyes flicking from the skylight to her. "I'll see you before long," he hissed, stumbling backward into the tunnel. As he stepped out of the sunlight, he donned the helm once more—and disappeared completely.

Dash struggled to his feet and slammed the door shut.

Only then did Selene lower her bow.

Dash grinned at her. "So not a heartwarming family reunion, I take it?"

"You think?" she flared, breaking down her bow and stowing it in her pack.

"Do I want to know why you're soaking wet?"

"No."

"And is that blood on your coat?"

She looked down at the hole in the arm of her leather jacket. "Just a scratch from that stupid bird scepter."

"But a scratch from a divine weapon. Doesn't heal like other wounds do."

"Great. I'm so glad I came down here. Super productive."

"Come on, sourpuss. You didn't learn *anything* useful?"

"Only that I can cross Uncle Aiden off the list. He's too weak aboveground to be the hierophant. He's also gone completely mad. He and Cora think we're all going to wind up joining them in the Underworld for some huge party when the fading kills us. They wanted me to stay and become a guest."

Dash rolled his eyes. "He never did learn to take the whole 'Lord of the Dead' thing less literally. Don't worry, I'll sort it all out next time I visit," he went on, as cheerful as always. "They like me. You, on the other hand..."

"The feeling's mutual, trust me." She leaped down onto the subway tracks and started walking back toward the Brooklyn Bridge station. "I've got no reason to ever speak to them again— they don't know anything about the cult. Too obsessed with their party preparations. I need to find the Wine Giver and the Bright One instead. You'll need to take me to them."

Dash trotted along beside her. "Sorry sweetpea, the Wine Giver's the one brother who's managed to slip past me. I don't even know what he's called these days, much less where he lives."

"Maybe he's just been too drunk to bother reaching out?"

"Yeah, or too distracted in other ways. They don't call him 'The God with Balls' for nothing."

One half brother with a huge penis, another with giant testicles. No wonder I've never gotten along with my family.

"Then what about my twin?"

"You don't know where he lives?"

"We haven't been close."

"Still? Well, then, sweetie, I don't think I can tell you."

"What do you mean?"

"Do you want me giving out *your* address to every immortal who asks?"

"Of course not."

"Exactly. He's a minor celebrity in the indie music scene in case you haven't noticed, so his address isn't exactly listed. I have to check with him first. Do you want me to do that?"

"No," she answered quickly.

"Ah-ha! The Delian Twins are at it again!"

"Well, you've been a real help," she grumbled. She was beginning to find Dash's rules suspiciously arbitrary.

"You asked me to bring you to Cora, and I did."

"What happened to her anyway? I thought she was supposed to *hate* being mistress of the Underworld! You should've seen them cooing over each other."

"She didn't change, I don't think," Dash replied. "Prissy and vain like always. What changed was the Receiver of Many. After centuries of living with a woman who hated him, he finally mended his ways. He repented. He tried to respect her. And she forgave him."

Selene snorted. "I'd never forgive someone for doing what he did."

"That's the thing about living for millennia. A mortal couldn't forgive—they don't have enough time. But when you've been around as long as we have, sometimes there's a way to make peace." He looked at Selene pointedly.

"If you're talking about me and my twin, forget it." She picked up her pace. "Now if you could move a little faster, I've got things to do aboveground."

"I'm just saying, Cora and Aiden probably have the best marriage of anyone in our family."

"I guess we just aren't made for commitment," she shrugged. "We're good at celibacy or promiscuity. Not much in between."

"I used to think the same thing. But times are changing, Selene. *We're* changing."

"I'm not about to give up my virginity," she seethed.

"Not even for that new bad boy associate of yours?"

Selene refused to even respond. But she couldn't help the sudden image of Theo that sprang to mind. Sitting beside him in the movie theater, she'd wondered what it would feel like if he grabbed her hand. At the same time, she was horrified that he might try.

The subway track beneath her feet began to vibrate. She shot Dash a worried glance. "You got a plan for not getting us run over?"

"It would be awfully humiliating to escape the Underworld only to get flattened by the Number 6 train," Dash agreed. "Thankfully, the Conductor of Souls wouldn't let that happen." Across the tracks, a single dim bulb illuminated a battered metal door. He grabbed the handle. Then paused, rattling the padlock. "Um."

"What happened to all your powers, God of Thieves?"

"Fine." He gave her a petulant frown. "The turnstile trick is an electronic transmitter I got from the Smith."

The subway train's headlight appeared ahead of them, a white pinprick growing steadily bigger.

"Move." Selene retrieved her lock picks from her backpack and set to work.

"I mean, if I'd brought my picks, I could totally have done that."

Selene snorted as she sprung the lock. Just before the light from the train could reach them, she hauled open the door and slipped through. They climbed a ladder, heaved open a manhole cover, and emerged on a quiet side street.

The Goddess of the Moon blinked in the sudden sunlight, grateful for once to emerge from the dark.

Chapter 26

MOTHER OF TWINS

A last water lily, striated pink and purple, floated in the fountain pool of the Conservatory Garden in Central Park. It lay with its petals unfurled, each a tapered ladle to scoop up the last rays of the setting sun. When darkness fell, the petals would close, only to open again with the dawn. A symbol of rebirth and renewal, of secrets concealed and revealed, of color too bright and form too beautiful for the mortal world. A lotus.

Soon after exiting the Underworld, Selene severed the flower's stem with a single slice of her pocketknife and lifted it from the water.

At New York-Presbyterian, Selene woke the frail woman in the hospital bed with a gentle kiss.

"Mother," whispered Leticia, staring at her daughter with cloudy eyes.

Selene could barely remember her grandmother Phoibe, Titan goddess of the moon, but she knew of her black hair and pale skin.

"No, I'm your daughter," she said gently.

"Phoebe?"

When she'd inherited dominion over the moon from her grandmother, the Huntress had taken the name "Phoebe," meaning "Bright One," just as her twin was called Phoebus for his association with the sun. But she hadn't gone by the name since a brief stint as Phoebe Hautman in New Amsterdam nearly four hundred years before.

"I'm not Phoebe or Phoibe, Mother."

"But I thought, for a second, you brought the moonlight in with you."

"I'm Selene now. Not Selene the Moon. Just Selene DiSilva." She wasn't surprised her mother could see a glimpse of her divine aura, just as the child at the movie theater had, but it saddened her. It meant Leto was approaching the border between worlds.

Her brow furrowed in confusion. "Artemis?"

Selene swallowed. "Yes, it's me." When they approached the end, the gods relinquished the mortal monikers they'd assumed and reverted to their true selves. For Leto, Selene had ceased to exist. Only her divine daughter remained.

"See what I've brought you," said Selene, pulling a length of dark purple linen from her bag. "I know it's not perfect, but it's the best I could do on short notice." Carefully, she helped her mother sit up and draped the fabric around her face so it covered her short gray hair.

Leto's eyes seemed a little less cloudy next to the jewel-toned cloth, and Selene could almost imagine that she still had long, chestnut hair underneath. "You see, Mother, it's a veil for Leto, Goddess of Modesty. And here..." Selene drew forth a small palm frond and wrapped Leto's hands around it. "For the Mother of Twins, who stood beneath the Sacred Palm on Delos in her travail and birthed the Bright Ones into the world." Next she pulled a box of dates from her bag. She ate half of one, gluey and oversweet, and fed the other half to her mother. "The date sustained you then, let it sustain you now."

Leto chewed slowly, painfully. "Why, Artemis? Why do you remind me of a past I cannot have again?" she asked.

"Because you can. I think I've figured it out, Mother," Selene explained, unable to keep the excitement from her voice. "There's a cult. A new one. It's using my attributes in its rituals, and it's bringing me power. I'm growing stronger, not weaker. I feel almost like myself again."

"Like yourself?" her mother asked wearily. "You've had so many names over the centuries... do you even know who you are anymore?"

"I know I'm your daughter," Selene said, her throat tight.

Leto stroked Selene's cheek, her fingers dry and cracked. "They called you She Who Helps One Climb Out. Do you remember?"

"Of course. Not my most melodic epithet."

"You've always lifted me from hardship. Just by your presence. Just by your love. You don't have to rescue me from death."

"But I will, Mother," Selene insisted. "If it can be done. I swear it by Gaia below and Ouranos above and by the dropping water of the River Styx. I swear it with the strongest and most awful oath of the blessed gods."

Leto gave a resigned sigh. "I've never stopped you from doing what you wanted."

"Then don't start now. You can see my radiance; you know it's working. Tonight, we're going to create our own rite, using your attributes. Then maybe I can bring you back to health, as well."

"I'm long past saving, Deer Heart."

Selene refused to listen. She took the last sacred object from her bag. The lotus flower. She laid it carefully on her mother's torso, where it dwarfed Leto's narrow rib cage with its outspread petals.

Leto touched a velvet petal hesitantly. "So beautiful," she whispered. "But not mine. Hera holds the lotus staff."

"But there were some vase paintings that showed you with it, remember? The lotus is the royal symbol, and in my eyes, you are always a queen." She kissed her mother on the forehead. "Now come, there's one more step in the ritual."

Selene lifted her mother out of the bed and set her on her feet. Leto stood on trembling legs, one clawlike hand clutching her daughter's arm, the other holding on to her IV pole. Selene was shocked to see how short her mother had become. Her head barely reached Selene's shoulder. Selene placed the lotus flower atop the pole, and draped the hospital blanket over Leto's thin frame like a cloak. Together, they left the room, taking one excruciating step at a time.

It took nearly twenty minutes to walk down the hall, into the elevator, and out onto the floor above. Long before they arrived at their destination, Selene regretted what she'd done. Leto could barely stand, and each step only weakened her further. "Almost there," she murmured encouragingly, taking more and more of her mother's weight until she was nearly carrying her.

They came to a large window that overlooked an interior room. "Do you see?" said Selene. "I've brought you to your temple."

Leto rested a hand upon the glass, staring fixedly at the infants within.

Selene looked over her mother's shoulder at the nursery, waiting for the babies to show some recognition that the Goddess of Motherhood stood before them. Surely, they would turn toward her, or cry with joy, or at least wriggle a little more. But they merely lay there, fast asleep, their pruney faces scrunched with annoyance at being thrust into the world. Selene found them completely unappealing. Yet when she looked at Leto, a new glow illuminated her mother's features.

"It's working," Selene whispered. "You look stronger already."

Leto turned to her daughter, her eyes clear. "Not stronger, my child. But content. Thank you for bringing me here. I can go happily now, remembering that mothers still labor and children still arrive without me."

"Happily? Knowing you're not needed?"

"Is that not what all mothers want?" Leto asked softly. "For their children to grow up and live their own lives?"

Selene couldn't respond to that, only clutch her mother's arm a little tighter.

Leto gazed at her daughter, a silent entreaty in her eyes. "Your brother was here earlier," she said finally.

"Oh?" Selene tried not to sound suspicious.

"He brought some other boys with him. They played a song for me."

"That's nice," Selene said carefully. "Did he mention anything about...trying to make you stronger?"

"I think he finally understands that he can't. But he hoped the music would bring me peace. And it did."

That sounded innocuous. But then again, would Paul really tell his mother if he were killing innocent women? Leto would never condone such barbarity.

"He also said he missed you," Leto went on.

"I'm sure."

"He's only ever tried to protect you. You know he would do anything to keep you safe."

That's what I'm afraid of, Selene thought with a shudder.

"When I'm gone, you're going to have to let him back into your heart."

Selene said nothing. She wouldn't make promises she couldn't keep.

"Now take me back," Leto commanded, her voice stern even as she slumped weakly against her daughter. "I've heard of those two women who were killed. One a child—a sick child. The nurses talk of nothing else. I know what you carry in that pack of yours, Huntress, and I know you have work to do tonight."

"But Mother—"

"Now, Artemis," she whispered. "I can barely stand."

Her eyes brimming, the Protector swept the Gentle Goddess into her arms and carried her back to the hospital bed.

Chapter 27

THE HIEROPHANT PART II

Lying beneath the writing snakes, the hierophant had dreamed.

Twin stags stand with heads lowered and antlers crossed. One spear pierces them both, and from the wound pours the blood of four women. One stag falls and the other remains, stronger and more glorious than before.

A gift from Asclepius—a dream to heal his tortured soul.

When he'd awoken, with the snakes' whispers still echoing in his brain, the girl still hung from the ceiling, long dead at the hands of his *mystai*—but he felt her life force trickling through his own veins. She'd been weak, sickly, but not without power. Sammi Mehra possessed a tenacity unmatched by the other children in her ward. She wanted desperately to live. The hierophant doubted her tests had shown it yet, but she'd finally started winning her long battle with the disease. In a few months, she would've been well.

Suddenly, he remembered another dream from that night—flying through the air at a gymnastics event, spinning once, twice, then landing lightly on the mat to a thunder of applause. Such a simple dream, a girl's dream, loosened from her mind as she slipped into unconsciousness. He would not feel pity. Her life had served a far higher purpose than anything her mortal mind could imagine. What was the too-short future of a single girl compared to the eternal glory of an immortal?

Now, deep underground, he held a green glass flask to the firelight and watched Sammi's blood swirl with Helen's. From Sammi, he gained determination and courage. From Helen, brilliant intelligence and unquestioning faith—a rare combination. Tonight, another woman, young and pure, would add her life's essence to his. Her blood would hold special magic: *kharisma*. Modern mortals defined charisma as mere personal magnetism. But the ancients derived the word from *karis*, "grace," meaning a talent divinely conferred. A hint of the godly ran through the veins of those with such talents, giving their blood extraordinary power.

The thought sent a shiver of impatience down the hierophant's spine. He could almost taste the blood of tonight's sacrifice upon his lips. But the steps of the ritual must be obeyed in order—the *Pompe* must begin here, in a long-forgotten chamber where the dead lay nearby, guarding the secrets of mortality.

The first offerings waited in cages nearby. Their brains could not comprehend their place in the ancient ritual—but they could feel fear. The hierophant breathed in the odor of their anxiety, reveling in the power it gave him.

"Remove the sacrifices," he said to his gathered *mystai*. While the cage doors clanged open, he turned to his most trusted acolyte and placed the glass flask in his hands. "One cannot achieve everlasting life without knowledge of death," he explained, his voice resonating with the tone of command. "The blood we have harvested carries within it the power of the living and the dreams of the dead. Tonight we add more. Tonight we grow closer to the end. And to the beginning."

In a few hours, he would finally show himself to the city. Fear would course down its filthy streets and through its crowded tenements. Terror would hurtle along the fetid underground tunnels and up the counterfeit majesty of skyscrapers, invading every corner of the city. One by one, the mortals would realize the extent of their vulnerability. And as they did, he would grow ever more invulnerable.

He stoked the fire before him and made a silent promise. *Before rosy-fingered Dawn lightens the sky, I will turn this soulless city into a god-fearing realm.*

Chapter 28

SWIFTLY BOUNDING

By the time Selene left her mother's hospital room, night cloaked the city. She glanced at the crescent moon where it hung between buildings, its horns yellowed by smog. *Hear me, Grandmother Phoibe, Bright Goddess,* she prayed. *If you still exist somewhere among the heavens, then answer my plea. Tonight I go to save a mortal life, but tell me it's not too late to save your daughter Leto as well.*

The moon was still and silent. No voice bright as starlight pierced her mind. Phoibe was long gone. Only a rocky sphere remained, orbiting the earth without the aid of any goddess. *If I could still guide it across the heavens,* Selene thought, jogging down Fifth Avenue, *I might be able to look down and see the hierophant at work. But something tells me that particular power is never coming back.* From what she'd learned of astronomy, she wasn't sure how she'd ever done it in the first place. She'd lived too long among mortals to understand the consciousness of a god anymore.

She'd have to find the killer the old-fashioned way: lots of legwork and a little bit of luck. And if she found him—*when* she found him—she'd force him to save her mother. She'd stop the murders, seize his power, and turn his cult of destruction into a cult of salvation.

The chatter on her police scanner indicated that, despite their skepticism, the NYPD couldn't risk rejecting Theo's tip out of hand: Officers watched every graveyard in Manhattan and even some in the boroughs. Still, she heard no mention of any suspicious activity. For an hour, she willed herself to stay patient, flipping between the precincts' different frequencies as she paced a rough circuit between the old Sephardic graveyards in the West Twenties and the Marble Cemeteries on Second Street.

Selene fiddled with the scanner. Still nothing. She spotted the unmarked cop cars parked near the various graveyards and the suspiciously sedentary "homeless" people near the cemetery gates. But nothing else. Over the course of the night, her relief at not running into Theo had evolved. At first, she blamed him for suggesting she patrol the graveyards at all. Now she secretly wished he were there to keep her company. Finally, she gave up and called his cell.

"Where are you?" she demanded.

"Where are *you*?"

"I'm watching the graveyards, where do you think?"

"I gave up waiting for you to call and came down to Trinity Cemetery. I'm unemployed, remember, so I've got plenty of time for stakeouts."

"Where are the assholes we're trying to catch? Are you *sure* they're going to be at a cemetery?"

"As I explained, the pattern of evidence—"

"Right, right. The NYPD are surveilling all over the—hold on." She turned her attention to the scanner. *"Respond to Duane and Elk 10-75 P."* At first, Selene assumed the additional units were being summoned to an unrelated patrol. Then she recognized the address and swore softly.

"What is it?" asked Theo.

"They're watching the old eighteenth-century African slave burial ground downtown."

"Why didn't I think of that?" Theo sounded distraught. "There must be others like that—graveyards covered up for centuries without visible tombstones."

"Dozens. They're under our feet, under the subway, under all the buildings."

"Shit. You're right. But how many people know enough New York City history to find them?"

"I wouldn't put it past this hierophant." Many of the city's immortals had called the city home since at least the nineteenth century. They'd remember graveyards long past. "They could be *anywhere*." She felt suddenly overwhelmed. Even with her preternatural speed, she'd never be able to search every part of the city. *Another woman will die, and I'll be no closer to helping my mother.*

"Let's look at this piece by piece," Theo said, his voice steady. "It can't actually be *any* defunct cemetery. It has to be one that's somehow still accessible. Maybe one that's connected to the subway or some other underground access so they could get close to the graves."

"New York City has over four hundred subway stations," she snapped. "And those are just the ones currently in use. You've got to give me something more, Theo. Tell me again—which cemetery did they use in Athens?"

"Kerameikos. It stood right outside the main entrance through the city walls—the Dipylon Gate."

Selene remembered it now. Many a time, the Huntress had watched in dismay as the mortal masses passed through the gate's two soaring portals, leaving the wilderness behind for the pleasures of civilization. If Manhattan had a Dipylon Gate...

"Grand Central." Sixty-seven tracks carried seven hundred fifty thousand people a day into and out of the city through the train station. "I remember there's an old burial ground—a potter's field for the poor—somewhere near Grand Central, but I don't know exactly where."

"The entrance to the city. Brilliant, Selene," Theo crowed. "Let me check on my phone..."

She'd attended a burial at the potter's field in 1849, but the city had looked completely different. She had no idea exactly where the field would lie on today's grid of city streets. The burial bore no relationship to Hamilton's stately Trinity Church funeral; it had been for a servant girl, Taryn O'Clare, one of her few friends over the centuries. Usually, the Huntress abandoned her companions before they could abandon her, but Taryn had died young, taken by the cholera epidemic. The Huntress had stood in the rain at the funeral, whispering her own rites as the Catholic priest chanted his. She could still see the white linen shroud sliding into a ditch of unwanted dead. She might have bought Taryn O'Clare a better resting place, but it wasn't in the Punisher's makeup to care about what happened to mortals after they died. Before her own fading had accelerated, death wasn't something she spent a lot of time thinking about.

"Are you thinking about the pauper's graveyard at Forty-ninth and Park?" Theo asked. "Wikipedia says the Astors bought up the land in the late 1800s and put the Grand Central train tunnels through it and the Waldorf-Astoria hotel on top."

"That's the one. It's perfect."

"But it doesn't have any underground access," Theo protested.

"Yes it does." Selene had personal experience with the tunnels beneath the hotel.

"Then I'm on my way," said Theo.

"Don't even think about it," she snapped, hanging up on him. The last thing she needed was a clumsy mortal getting in the way of a confrontation between gods. He would only get himself—or her—hurt.

Selene had only been in the Waldorf-Astoria once, in 1944. She remembered the year clearly because it had been one of

Franklin Roosevelt's visits to New York during World War II. Like the other Olympians, she'd stayed far away from the conflict. It was the first time mortals had truly acted like gods, ravaging earth and sea, massacring men and women by the millions, harnessing the power of flight and farseeing. The gods had stood in the shadows, realizing once again that they'd been permanently replaced. Not by the Church, this time—but by the Machine.

One of Roosevelt's bodyguards had gotten a little overzealous with a young woman he'd picked up at the Waldorf's bar. The girl left the hotel bruised and weeping, nearly bumping into a tall, black-haired woman in a pencil skirt and sensible shoes.

Now that same woman sprinted up Park Avenue to the Waldorf. The freight elevator was still there on the Forty-ninth Street side of the building, right beside the entrance to the hotel's underground parking garage. She ran her hands along the seam between the doors. Welded shut. Probably forgotten for decades. But Selene remembered where the elevator led. Deep beneath the hotel, a little-known private "presidential" railroad siding known as Track 61 had once served VIPs. Trains could pass through Grand Central terminal without stopping and discharge their passengers under the Waldorf so they wouldn't have to contend with the unwashed masses. For Roosevelt, the secret siding provided a way of leaving the city without the public witnessing his crippled body being lifted onto the train. The platform sat directly on top of the old potter's field.

That day in 1944, Selene had followed the president's bodyguard down the freight elevator, but lost him in the mass of Secret Service men readying to depart on the underground train. Even the Far Shooter wouldn't take on so large a crowd. The abusive bodyguard escaped her bow that day. When she saw the same man three years later, smoking a cigarette on a lonely street corner in the West Village, he wasn't so lucky.

The elevator might be defunct, but when Selene pushed on the adjacent fire-exit door, it swung open easily, as if someone had already picked the lock.

Cursing, she assembled her bow on the run and dashed down the narrow staircase to a dark, abandoned platform. She could feel, rather than hear, trains passing in the distance. The blur of far-off headlights provided just enough illumination for her night vision to function. Arrow nocked, she came to a halt, spinning this way and that, sniffing the air. No scent of man. Only stale air mingled with oil and grease. Then, suddenly, a faint whiff of blood from an old train car. Midnight blue. Just like all the Roosevelt-era Presidential coaches. Had one really been sitting on this siding for the past seventy years? She padded up to it. The smell of blood grew stronger, but she heard no movement inside the car. Bow in one hand, she hauled on the door with the other. It slid open with a rusty squeal.

She stepped inside. No light of any kind penetrated the boarded-up windows. Even with her newly keen vision, she couldn't see in such darkness. She stepped forward cautiously into the silent black. Her foot slipped, pitching her forward onto her hands and knees into slick wetness and knocking her bow from her hand.

Styx, she cursed silently, belatedly fumbling for the flashlight in her pack. She flicked it on. She was kneeling in a wide pool of blood. Not a woman's blood, by the smell of it, not even a human's. *Probably more pigs or boars,* she reasoned. She bent close to examine the puddle. In a violent attack, blood would splatter and smear the surroundings as it projected from the wound, even if the victim didn't thrash or move. But the droplets around the pool formed near-perfect circles with barely a spatter, meaning they'd fallen from a distance of no more than eight inches, as if someone had opened an animal's vein—or from the size of the pool, its throat—and let the blood pour onto the floor.

The animal sacrifice would only be the beginning. The men may not have captured another human victim yet, but Selene was willing to bet they were about to.

She sniffed again at the blood. Still fresh. They couldn't have gotten far. Rising to her feet, she'd gathered her weapon and prepared to leave when two spots of glowing yellow a few feet away caught her eye. Instinctively, she raised her bow with one hand as she swung her flashlight toward the yellow glow with the other.

In the cold circle of light, a dog's face stared up at her. For a second, she thought it was Hippo. It had the same square skull and floppy ears. She took a deep breath to calm herself—Hippo was safe at home. The large mutt lying before her clearly had no owner. Patches of mange covered its wide back; its tail was flea-bitten. And despite its shining eyes, Selene knew the dog was dead. The dog's mouth was closed and its head lolled to one side as if it died peacefully, but the wide gash in its throat told a different story. She knelt and sniffed at its mouth. Anesthesia. They'd drugged the dog before they murdered it. She wasn't sure whether to feel relieved that it had died without suffering or infuriated that the hierophant had used modern medicine to simulate a willing sacrifice.

She stepped back, widening the circle of light across the train's floorboards, and fury overwhelmed all other emotions. A dozen dead dogs lay in front of open cages, making a rough semicircle around the perimeter of the train car. Their unseeing, unblinking eyes shone red and yellow and green in the dark. Most were smaller than the large mutt. Easier to carry, no doubt. The smallest was a puppy, only a few days old. When she lifted it from the pool of its own blood, it fit into the palm of her hand, its chin wobbling on the tip of her finger.

Theo had said tonight's *Pompe* began with sacrifices to Demeter and Persephone. But the Goddess of Grain and the Goddess of Spring would shun such an offering. This massacre of dogs could only be meant for the Lady of Hounds.

"Are you trying to worship me or punish me?" she begged in a rough whisper.

Selene put down the puppy and shone the flashlight on her own trembling hand. She clenched her fingers, pressing her nails into her palm, hoping the sudden pain would banish her fear. She could almost hear the voices of Sammi Mehra and Helen Emerson: *He's killed all you're sworn to protect. Now he's coming for you. Beware, Huntress, lest you, too, become prey.*

"Don't worry about me," Selene said aloud as her rage burst into flame. "He's the one who should be afraid."

—◦—

"Stop here!"

Theo tossed some bills at the cabbie and dashed out of the car. "Did you see a super-tall woman in a baseball cap come by?" he demanded of the hotel doorman.

But before he could get an answer, Selene burst around the corner, nearly running into him.

"I thought I told you not to come!" she said furiously. She was even paler than usual.

"This is dangerous, Selene. I'm not letting you do this alone."

"I can take care of myself!" As she pushed her hair out of her eyes, she left a greasy red smear across her forehead.

"Then what's this?" He grabbed her hands, turning the bloody palms upward.

"It's not mine." Her hands trembled, and he instinctively grasped them a little tighter.

"Another woman dead?"

She shook her head. "Just animal sacrifices." As she described the scene, her voice quavered. Finally, she pulled her hands away from Theo. He merely moved to grasp her shoulders instead.

"It's going to be all right," he said, fighting the urge to pull her into his embrace.

She stiffened in his grip. "Do you think I need to be *comforted*?" she snarled. He dropped his hands. "I'm *angry*, Schultz. And I'm not going to be 'all right' until we find them. They can't have gotten far. *Think*. Where would they have gone?" Theo had never seen her so filled with rage and urgency—emotions he'd mistaken for fear. Her silver eyes glowed in the light pouring from the heat lamps beneath the Waldorf's awning, and her gaze banished his tenderness. He felt honed, sharp and bright and ready for battle.

"*Pompe* means procession. So they're moving. From the cemetery, they would have traveled to Demeter's temple."

"Okay, a temple. A church maybe?"

"Maybe." The pieces didn't fit right—not yet. "Why would a pagan cult associate itself with Christianity? Besides, it's got to be somewhere public, and churches aren't open this late."

"You said they tell lewd jokes, remember, to ease Demeter's sorrow? A comedy club then?" she pressed. "A theater? Maybe somewhere televised, so they can reach the biggest audience?"

"Televised?" Theo looked down at his watch. He felt the blood drain from his cheeks as the puzzle piece finally slipped into place. "It's midnight. It's Saturday."

"So?" she demanded.

"*Saturday Night Live*. It broadcasts from Rockefeller Center. That's only three blocks away."

As swift as arrow flight, Selene took off down the street. Theo took a deep breath, then, like an acolyte with his priestess, followed in her wake.

Chapter 29

UNTAMED

"I need to get into the *Saturday Night Live* taping," Selene said again, fighting the urge to seize the Rockefeller Center security guard by the collar and shake him.

"*SNL*'s already started airing. No tickets, no entry," the guard recited, his stern tone undermined somewhat by his chipmunk cheeks and obvious youth.

Selene glanced across the lobby at the security stanchions blocking the elevators. She'd hoped to get up to the eighth floor without making a scene. That way, in case her suspicions were wrong, she'd be able to continue the night's hunt without the cops stopping her. But if she had to knock the guard out of the way and bust through the stanchions, she would.

Just then, Theo tumbled through the lobby's revolving doors. "Did you find—" he started to ask, but his question quickly devolved into a gasped curse. Selene followed his stunned gaze to the televisions on the far wall.

A young black woman in a sequined gown and a Michelle Obama wig stood on the set of *Saturday Night Live*, her face contorted with terror. Sooty tears streamed down her cheeks as her mascara washed away.

"That's Jenny Thomason," stammered the security guard. "Newest member of the cast... She's just a kid."

A short man in a hooded yellow cloak stood with a knife held to her throat. A wooden mask covered his face—the grotesquely carven rictus of Comedy. The camera zoomed out, revealing three other men in identical masks and cloaks. One leveled a short knife at a group of cowering actors in the corner of the set. Another played a small hand drum. A third pointed his weapon offscreen, as if warding off interruption of their ritual.

And in the center of the set, holding aloft a green glass flask filled with dark liquid, stood a taller man in a purple cloak. He wore the mask of a warrior hero—an exaggerated visage with a curling wooden beard and fiercely drawn eyebrows.

"The hierophant," Theo whispered. Selene nodded dumbly.

Rage boiled within her. Ancient. Untamed.

In the lobby, alarm bells screamed to life, then a voice boomed over a loudspeaker, *"This is an emergency. Please follow lockdown procedures and shelter in place. Await further instructions from police officers or Rockefeller Center Security."* As the message repeated, the young guard's walkie-talkie squawked urgently, calling for all available security personnel to proceed immediately to the eighth floor. In a single fluid leap, Selene jumped over the entrance stanchion and sprinted to the nearest elevator bank. She slipped inside, jabbing repeatedly at the Door Close button even as the guard, three of his fellow security officers, and Theo wedged themselves in beside her.

"You can't be in here," the young guard insisted as the doors shut. "And you—" He pointed at Theo. "Aren't you the guy—" The doors opened on the eighth floor, and animalistic screams drowned the guard's protests as a mass of terrified audience members swarmed the elevator.

Head lowered, Selene slammed her way through the crowd, heedless of the frustrated cries of the guards as they tried to keep order. She didn't know if Theo'd be able to follow her, and she didn't care.

She reached the main entrance to the studio just as the large double doors slammed shut in her face. She heard a chain clatter through the handles on the other side. She pounded on the doors, but they held tight.

"A hillbilly takes his twelve-year-old daughter to the gynecologist for her first exam." Selene's head shot up, looking for the source of the rasping voice. *Speakers on the wall,* she realized, *broadcasting the show from inside the studio.* The *Pompe*'s lewd jokes had finally begun.

"The gynecologist asks, 'Is your daughter sexually active?' The man thinks for a moment and replies, 'Naw, she mostly just lays there like her mother.'" A drum punctuated each word. Not the snare drum accompaniment to a comedian's punch line, but a slow, steady beat, like the tolling of a funeral bell.

With a cry of outrage, Selene flung her shoulder against the doors. They swung open a crack before slamming back, held in place by the chain. But in the instant they opened, she saw that Jenny Thomason was still alive, clutched in the initiate's grasp.

The hierophant's voice went on, calm and confident. *"What's the definition of the perfect virgin?"* He waited a beat, as if for comedic effect. *"She's three feet tall, toothless, and there's a flat spot on the top of her head where you can set your beer."* Selene kicked at the door, revealing a glimpse of the *mystes* pressing the knife closer to Jenny's throat as the hierophant screamed, "Don't turn off the cameras or we'll kill her!" Then, his composure restored, he continued with his jokes.

"What's the worst part about having sex with a six-year-old?"

Selene gave up on the door and rushed down the hallway, looking for a back entrance to the stage. The voice followed her as she ran.

"Getting the blood out of the clown suit."

She found her way backstage, where costumers and production assistants huddled beneath dressing tables. The rasping voice droned on and on, the drumbeats keeping time.

"How do I get onstage?" Selene demanded of a scrawny makeup artist.

"Be careful! They said if we moved, they'd kill Jenny!"

"Let them try," she growled. "Just show me the way in."

He pointed to a nearby door. "They locked it from the other side."

Suddenly, the hierophant's voice ceased, replaced by those of multiple men, chanting with surprisingly intricate harmonies to the steady pounding of the drum.

"Pheromen touto to partheneion thuma . . ."

"What the fuck is that?" whimpered the makeup artist.

Horrified, Selene didn't think twice about translating aloud: "We bring this virgin sacrifice, so that our god might flourish with her blood."

She took a running start and hurled herself against the door. She could hear a faint splintering on the other side.

"Here!" The makeup artist had come out of hiding to offer her a fire extinguisher. But Selene had already kicked the door open on her own.

She burst onto the set just in time to see the yellow-cloaked man's knife slip into Jenny's neck. The hierophant held the flask to her throat, collecting her blood. The other actors screamed. Then blackness as the lights in the building snapped off.

The shuffling of booted feet told her the hierophant and his followers were on the move, dragging Jenny with them. Through the actors' panicked shouting, she heard the clatter of a falling chain as the security guards finally broke through the main entrance. They poured through the doors, their flashlight beams zigzagging wildly across the set. But the cult had disappeared.

Dodging the guards' lights, Selene stepped onto the stage,

sniffing the air for Jenny's fear. Finally, she caught a whiff of the pheromone, sharp and pungent. She followed her nose, moving quickly into a back service corridor, then opened the door to a pitch-black stairwell.

She could hear footsteps, a few stories down. Swiftly, she reached into her backpack and assembled her bow. She didn't need any light to know how the pieces fit together. She took a step forward, nearly tripping on Jenny's fallen wig. Then, with one hand on the wall to guide her way, she moved down the stairs in complete silence, taking them three at a time.

Before long, she saw wavering lights up ahead; the initiates had brought flashlights to ease their way. She grabbed four arrows from her pack, slipping them between the knuckles of her right hand. Two flights later, the cult members came into view. Two of them carried Jenny's limp body between them. Then, for a heartbeat, the hierophant crossed into a beam of light—Selene loosed her first arrow. He dodged out of the way, faster than any mortal ever could. Then he laughed. A cold, cruel sound. A second later, Selene rolled the second arrow from one finger to the next and shot again—but he plucked it from the air as if it were a paper airplane.

He gestured for his acolytes to stop their flight.

"Let the woman go," Selene said, willing her voice to be calm.

The hierophant's wooden mask, made horrific in the glancing light and shadow, betrayed no emotion. "Why?"

"Because you may be able to pluck arrows from the air, but I doubt your companions can." Hoping she was right, she swung around and sent the third arrow sailing into the thigh of an initiate. He grunted and fell to his knees, nearly tumbling forward. "You need them, don't you?" she went on. "A Mystery Cult with only a hierophant isn't much of a Mystery Cult. Let the girl go, or I shoot again." He tilted his head, as if considering. "Too slow," she snapped, firing the last arrow into the initiate's stomach.

Before she could grab another arrow, the hierophant lunged forward to rip the bow from her hands. *He's strong. Stronger than I*, she realized with a shock. Then, a screeching of metal, the twang of a string, and her golden bow lay broken upon the ground. She cried out, as if her soul itself had snapped in two. But the hierophant gave her no time to grieve. He still had her arrow in his fist. He pressed its point up against her throat. She could barely breathe. Her voice squeezed past, thin and weak.

"Are you trying to make me stronger? Or trying to kill me? Make up your mind." The arrowhead nicked her skin. A trail of wetness ran down her neck to pool between her collarbones.

"I'm not going to kill you. I couldn't. Not with this." He tossed the wooden arrow on the ground and reached over his shoulder. Only then did she notice the quiver hidden beneath his purple cloak. "Now *this*—this could kill you." In the slanting illumination from the flashlights, the arrow in his hand glinted silver—just like her twin brother's divine shafts.

"Apollo," she hissed. "Is that you?"

He brushed the arrowhead against her cheek, as gentle as a lover's touch. But his voice still rasped like sandpaper on skin. "Very smart, Artemis."

Of course. Paul would do anything to stop the fading he feared so much. The drummer, the harmonic chanting—the four *mystai* must be his three band members and his manager. The worship they showed for their frontman already bordered on idolatry; someone as charismatic as her brother could easily manipulate those feelings into the blind obedience *mystai* owed a hierophant.

"I should've known you'd let Mother die while making yourself stronger," said Selene. "Now speak to me in your true voice. Show me your true face. Let there be no lies between us. Not anymore."

But he just laughed, a dizzy cackle.

He's gone mad, she realized. *Like our father. Like Hestia. It won't be long before I lose my mind, too, if I haven't already. Maybe we were crazy to begin with, thinking we were gods in a world of men.* She closed her eyes. *He wants to save me and kill me at the same time,* she thought with a sudden icy calm. *So we have always been, loving and hating all at once, for millennia. It was always fated to come to this.*

She opened her eyes, searching the carved face for some sign of the man she'd known so well. "I'm not scared. Death comes for us all. We are Athanatoi no longer."

A sudden pounding of footsteps on the stairs above. The *mystai* swung their flashlights wildly toward the disturbance, but Selene didn't dare look. An instant later, the hierophant groaned sharply, and she managed to twist her head an inch to the side.

Theo stood, teeth bared, one end of her broken bow in his hands, the other embedded in her attacker's side. The hierophant lurched away, the silver arrow in his fist slicing across Selene's abdomen. Before she could fall, Theo grabbed her arms and pressed her body close. "I gotcha," he murmured, turning their bodies so he stood between her and the hooded men.

"Help me," the hierophant demanded of his acolytes, still using the low rasp that disguised his melodious voice. The three *mystai* who could still walk dropped the actress's body on the ground and moved to their leader's side.

"I'm fine," Selene hissed to Theo, pushing him away. She blinked in the swerving flashlight beams—the sharp alternation between light and dark played havoc with her night vision. But there—she spotted the other half of her broken bow on the ground. The end that had once slid so effortlessly into the handgrip lay twisted and torn. A small voice in her head—her mother's voice, she realized—begged her to be merciful. But Leto had also understood that the Protector had a job to do. Selene's code was clear: murder for murder. Apollo might be a god, but that didn't make him exempt from the Punisher's justice. Selene snatched up the piece of her bow and swung it toward him.

The *mystes* who'd sliced Jenny Thomason's throat, shorter

than the others, but broad and solid beneath his cloak, stepped in front of her blow. The ragged metal sliced into the murderer's shoulder. He grunted but did not cry out. Another initiate, this one with a hand drum slung over one shoulder, grabbed her from behind. She broke his grip easily.

Hair whipping across her cheeks, she spun and lashed out with her leg, the blunt heel of her boot catching her assailant in the chest. Now a third man rushed toward her, a knife extended. She batted it away with the broken end of the bow, then brought the sharp point up to strike him in the neck. He choked and stumbled to a halt just as Theo jumped onto his back and the two men collapsed in a pile of flailing limbs.

Now the drummer and the stocky murderer were on Selene at once, swinging with their flashlights and knives. She struck out with one end of the bow and then the other, knocking aside their weapons. Even when her bow landed on their flesh, they merely moaned and winced, then came on like zombies. She wondered if they were drugged—maybe with the *kykeon* potion so central to the Mystery. Theo's sudden grunt of pain distracted her attention for an instant, allowing the drummer to grab her. Before she could break free, the stocky one kicked her injured side. She fell to the ground with a cry. From the corner of her eye, she watched a booted foot swing toward her face.

"Enough!" gasped the hierophant from his position by the wall. "This is not the time. Leave her and get me out of here!"

Abruptly, the men stopped their attack. Jenny's murderer and the drummer hurried to their hierophant and lifted him in their arms. Theo's assailant retrieved the man Selene had shot. As they continued down the staircase toward the basement shopping concourse and subway entrance, Selene dragged herself unsteadily to her feet.

"Are you all right?" Theo asked from the corner, where he stood clutching his stomach.

"We can't let them—"

A faint moan interrupted her. Jenny lay slumped on the landing where the *mystai* had left her. Theo crawled toward her. "She's alive, Selene!"

Ignoring him, Selene turned to follow the initiates.

"Leave them!" Theo cried. "If you don't go get help, she'll die!" He cradled Jenny's torso in his arms, pressing vainly against the flow of blood from her neck. Selene stood frozen, torn between her desire for revenge and the desperation in Theo's voice. "Hurry, Selene! What's wrong with you?" he shouted, breaking through her paralysis.

What's wrong with me, indeed? She fled out the nearest door, nearly bowling over a young policewoman. "I found her. She's in the stairwell. Hurry!" She didn't warn them to stop the subway trains leaving Rock Center. Didn't tell them to block off the entire concourse level. This was still her fight. Her hunt.

Selene dashed back down the stairs into the underground concourse, flying by the shuttered Starbucks, the newsstand, the Ben & Jerry's. No sign of her twin. No sign of his *mystai*. Then to the subway station. No MTA worker manned the entrance booth this time of night, just MetroCard machines and man-high turnstiles. It would have been hard to get two wounded men through, but not impossible.

She sprinted from one train platform to another, fighting the late-night crowds of theatergoers and tourists. "Have you seen a group of men in yellow cloaks? Or a tall man in purple robes?" she begged as she ran. But people mostly shook their heads and stepped away, alarmed by her battered face and the piece of twisted gold metal in her hands.

She heard a downtown F train rumble out of the station before she could get down the stairs, then watched in frustration as an uptown B departed while she was on the downtown track. She cursed loudly and slumped over, breathing heavily and wincing at the pain in her slashed abdomen. They were gone. No sign of blood on the ground; no smell of fear or triumph in the air.

She thrust the broken piece of her bow angrily into her pack and stumbled as fast as she could back out of the subway, up the stairs, and toward the landing where she'd left Theo and the girl.

Just then, she felt a strange jolt of adrenaline pump through her veins. The unbearable pain in her stomach grew a little less fierce, as if the healing process had already begun. Last night in the shower she'd felt a similar rush of energy—just before the sudden healing of the cut on her face. On that same night— probably at that same instant—Sammi Mehra stopped breathing.

Selene felt a wave of despair as she realized what had just happened: The human sacrifice *was* making her stronger. And Jenny Thomason was dead.

Chapter 30

THE LADY CAPTAIN

Someone had gotten the lights back on. Selene watched over the heads of the EMTs as they pried Theo's bloody hands from Jenny's body. "I tried," Selene heard him say. "I tried to save her." A young policewoman gently helped Theo to his feet and led him through the crowd of medical personnel.

As they passed Selene, the policewoman said to her, "We'll need to ask you some questions after an EMT looks at your neck, okay?" Selene nodded, putting a tentative hand to the nick on her throat. It came away bright with blood. When the policewoman turned away, Selene lifted her shirt to glance quickly at the larger wound across her abdomen. Not as bad as she imagined; she'd stopped losing blood in the rush of power after Jenny died, and a wide scab already covered half the gash. The remaining wound, three inches long and glistening red, had missed her organs, but still sent waves of stabbing pain through her side. She pulled her leather jacket tighter to conceal it. Made with Apollo's divine arrow, the injury wouldn't respond to the paramedic's interventions anyway.

As she followed Theo and the policewoman toward the lobby, Selene leaned in toward her partner, her mouth a hairbreadth from his ear. "You don't know me," she whispered. "There were no arrows, and I'm not a PI." He turned toward her, his eyes red-rimmed and dazed. He looked like he might protest, but something in her face must have stopped him. He nodded wearily then hung his head and allowed himself to be led away.

An EMT led Selene to the lobby and sat her on a bench as he dabbed at the wound on her neck. Selene looked at the TVs mounted on the wall, each tuned to a different NBC affiliate. On every station, newscasters hovered outside 30 Rock, their faces creased with concern. And over and over, they ran the footage of Jenny Thomason in the hierophant's arms. They didn't show the stabbing, but Selene couldn't help replaying it in her own mind.

She died so I might grow stronger. Can I ever forgive myself for that? Once, she might not have cared about the life of a mortal. She found thanatoi frustrating, confusing, and annoying in equal measure. But over the millennia she'd come to admit that without their worship, their faith, their need, she might not exist in the first place. Mankind might tell stories of how Zeus commanded the gods to mold the first human beings, but in truth, the creation stories themselves came from the minds of men. So thanatoi created Athanatoi who created thanatoi...an Ouroboros, a snake eating its tail, no end, no beginning. Selene's entire life, her very being, lay entwined with those who worshiped her. And now she knew that without the deaths of three innocent women, she would still be weak, vulnerable, an Athanatos with no power at all. *And without Theo,* she realized, *I would have died tonight.*

The EMT covered the wound on her throat with gauze. "From all the blood, I figured you really got hurt," he said. "But it's barely a scratch. Still, keep it covered for a while until it heals completely. Anything else hurt?"

"No."

"You sure? You're sitting funny."

"I'm sure."

"Why don't you just take off your jacket and let me have a peek?"

"You come near me and I'll rip your hands off."

"Whoa!" He stood up. "I'm just trying to help, miss."

Selene stood, then caught the edge of the bench when a wave of dizziness passed through her. Instinctively, the EMT reached out to her. She snapped her teeth at him like a rabid dog.

He backed up, eyes wide. "Can I get some help over here?" he called across the lobby.

"What's going on?" demanded a croaking voice.

Selene turned toward the approaching woman, instantly recognizing her narrow-hipped stride.

The EMT gestured toward Selene. "This woman was present at the scene—"

But her old friend Geraldine Hansen wasn't listening. Mouth slightly agape, the captain just stared at Selene.

"You look—my God—just like..." She shook her head slightly, as if to clear it. The EMT stopped speaking. He glanced from one woman to the other, confused.

Selene fought the urge to flee, forcing her mouth into a polite, bewildered smile.

The gray-haired captain blinked twice, and Selene noticed her chest heave slightly with a suppressed sigh. Geraldine looked away. Suddenly, she was all business. With calm, cordial authority, she told the EMT to check the actors and crew in the dressing rooms for signs of shock. Then she gestured for a weedy, olive-skinned cop to come join her, saying, "Get out a pen, Officer, and take down this woman's statement."

When she finally turned back to Selene, she acted as if nothing unusual had occurred. "You must be the woman who attacked the perpetrators." Geraldine introduced herself as a member of the Counterterrorism Division, and Selene nodded warily. The captain hadn't seen "Cynthia Forrester" in nearly forty years. Hopefully, she'd blame her sense of recognition on foggy memories.

"Counterterrorism? Do you think terrorists are involved?" Selene asked with an attempt at wide-eyed innocence.

"I'd say killing a woman on TV in front of ten million viewers qualifies as terrorism, wouldn't you?" She put her hands on her hips. "Although exactly what kind of terrorism remains to be seen. We still don't know what language they were speaking."

"It was Greek," said the weedy cop at her side. Selene glanced at his badge: Officer Christopoulos. "I only made out a few words here and there, and the pronunciation was weird. Sounded like Ancient Greek maybe."

The captain grimaced. "Then there're going to be a lot of questions asked at the Greek Consulate tonight. Now, Ms. Di-Silva, I understand you were up on the eighth floor when the murder took place. Tell us what happened."

I just wanted to see the show, Selene decided. *When I saw what had happened on the TVs in the lobby, I wanted to help. I pursued the murderers while a tall guy in glasses tried to save the actress, but it was too late and they got away.* But before she could begin, the captain continued, "And we'll need to get some fingerprints, if you don't mind, to compare against those at the crime scene."

Selene's heart did a quick somersault. In all the commotion, she'd forgotten to wear her gloves. Even if they didn't match her prints to the old 1970s police database, the new computerized system would store them for perpetuity, making her life of anonymity nearly impossible going forward. Her only option was to prevent them from fingerprinting her in the first place. She briefly considered making a run for it, but discarded that idea for about a dozen reasons, mostly to avoid getting shot. Instead, she thought of the way Theo had breezily talked their way out of any number of difficult situations. She squinted at the captain's nametag. "Did you say *Hansen*? Not *Geraldine* Hansen, by any chance?"

"That's right."

"Oh! I've always wanted to meet you." She thrust out her hand and tried her best to dazzle the captain with a wide smile. "Cynthia Forrester was my mother."

Geraldine gave a tiny gasp. Christopoulos looked at the captain in alarm, as if he'd never seen her show surprise. "That's remarkable," she said finally, taking a step closer to Selene as if to get a better view. "I knew you looked familiar. You could be her twin."

"I get that a lot."

The captain took Selene's proffered hand. Her grip was as strong and sure as Selene remembered it. Christopoulos began to click his pen compulsively, ready to take her statement, but Geraldine waved him away and instead motioned Selene to sit beside her on the bench.

"Your mother was the best shot in the Policewomen's Bureau." Her stern face dissolved for a moment into that of the excited young girl the Huntress had known so well. "Make that the best shot in the whole damn department, and you know back in the seventies they barely let us ladies practice on the shooting range. She's the reason I joined the force in the first place."

"So you remember her," Selene said. "I wasn't sure you would."

"How could I forget? She was an inspiration to all of us. When they kicked her off the force, well, I don't mind telling you, a lot of us thought about quitting in solidarity."

Usually, Selene tried not to think about the ignominious dismissal. But she'd never forgotten the looks on the faces of her fellow policewomen when she'd walked out of her captain's office without her badge. A few might have thought she deserved what she got, but most couldn't bear to think ill of Cynthia. She was a hero among them; they followed her not unlike the nymphs had followed the Far Shooter. Young Geraldine Hansen had clutched Cynthia in a brief, tight embrace. "Don't you let them do this to you," she whispered fiercely. Back then, her voice had been high and light. "If you're not good enough for them, then how can any of us be?"

"You're a good cop, Gerry," Cynthia had whispered back, surprised by the desperation in her young friend's voice. "Better than me. Don't give up." At the time, she didn't realize that she spoke in a voice long unused—that of a goddess commanding her worshiper. Now, forty years later, Selene knew Geraldine had obeyed.

Time had carved deep creases between her brows and beside her thin mouth, but her eyes still gleamed a bright, steely gray, undimmed by the hard years of fighting crime and sexism. Despite her sternness, Gerry reminded Selene a little bit of her mother. They'd both grown old dedicating their lives to causes far greater than themselves. "You're a captain now?" she said softly. "I'm sure my mother would've been very proud of you."

"You're talking about her in the past tense."

"My mother died years ago." Selene shuddered involuntarily at the palimpsest of images: Leto on her deathbed, herself as an old woman. *This is the problem with lying,* she thought, *reality alone is hard enough to grasp.*

Geraldine sucked at her upper lip for a moment, the only concession she'd give to grief. She'd never been demonstrative. *Hard as nails,* the men had called her. "Poor Cynthia. After she left, I tried to find her, looked everywhere, staked out her apartment. They'd indicted her by then and there was a warrant out for her, of course, but I wasn't going to arrest her, just talk to her." She spoke nonchalantly, but Selene noticed the way she scratched angrily at the callouses on her palm. Even after so many years, this was a fresh wound. "But she'd disappeared completely. Like she'd never existed in the first place. How'd she die, if you don't mind my asking?"

Selene wanted to give Cynthia a heroic death. But that seemed like the biggest lie of all. "The doctors never really knew what was wrong. A slow fading away."

"I'm sorry to hear that." Geraldine patted the breast pocket of her suit, as if searching for the comfort of a smoke, and then dropped her hand limply back onto her lap. "I'm sorry if I'm staring at you," she continued with a slight, uncomfortable laugh. "You look the same age your mom was when I knew her. You're so like her. Mannerisms, voice, everything. It's uncanny."

Selene's heart raced a little, but she reminded herself that Geraldine Hansen was a cop. A good cop. Cops didn't look for supernatural explanations. The fact that Cynthia and Selene could be the same person would never cross her mind. Still, for a fleeting moment, she wished it would. She wanted to tell her the truth. *I'm so sorry, Gerry,* she'd say. *I saw you outside my old apartment. But I'd already left the West Village, changed my name, my entire identity. I couldn't be Cynthia anymore. I never even bothered to say good-bye to you. What did I care for the emotions of a mortal?* She wanted to make it up to Geraldine. Instead, she had no choice but to lie once again.

Selene launched into her planned recital of the night's events. She left out the most important part, of course—the identity of the hierophant. Not that Geraldine would've believed it.

"And this Theodore Schultz?" the captain pressed. "The man we found with Jenny Thomason's body?"

"Is that his name? Thank goodness he showed up. I'd probably be dead if it weren't for him. Someone should give that man a medal."

Geraldine frowned. "Are you aware that Mr. Schultz is a person of interest in the murder of the Columbia professor?"

"He threw himself between me and an armed man. Then he went to Jenny Thomason and tried to save her life." She leaned a little closer to the captain. "My mother always told me that sometimes the cops get it wrong. They did with her. And they have with Theodore Schultz."

Geraldine nodded slowly. In the ensuing silence, Christopoulos approached the captain. "Should I take Ms. DiSilva to fingerprinting?"

Selene shut her eyes briefly and clutched the side of the bench. She Who Leaves No Trace wasn't about to disregard her own epithet.

"Are you okay, hon?" Geraldine asked. Selene opened her eyes at the unexpected endearment.

"Just a little woozy is all. It's been a very long day." She groaned softly and pressed a hand to her head. "I think I need to lie down."

"Of course."

"Perhaps I could go by my local precinct tomorrow and give my prints there?"

"Yes, that'd be sufficient." Geraldine lent Selene an arm and hauled her easily to her feet. She turned to the other officer. "Will you get Selene a cab?"

"Oh no, please, I'll be fine."

They shook hands one more time. As Selene left the building, she could feel Geraldine's gaze on her back.

Selene didn't go far. She stood on the far side of the plaza, hidden in the shadows of an awning, watching the crowds of reporters milling around 30 Rock. Before her, the iconic bronze Prometheus statue presided over the empty skating rink, a torch held in his upraised arm. The piece captured the Titan at his most defining moment—granting mankind the gift of fire. Soon after, Zeus had punished him for sharing the gods' sacred flames. He chained Prometheus to a rock and commanded an eagle to devour his liver. Every time the Titan healed, the eagle returned, over and over again, day after day for eternity. The story was a sharp warning to anyone who sided with mortals over their fellow gods. *As of today,* Selene realized with a shudder, *that means me.* The thought scared her, but her resolve held firm. Her twin could not be allowed to get away with the murder of innocents.

Unfortunately, a broken bow and wooden arrows couldn't help her—only a divine weapon could stop Apollo. And if she could find one—and that was a big *if*—she'd need to be strong enough to wield it. She glanced beneath her jacket once more. The bloodstain covering the left side of her shirt had dried to rust. She peeled the shirt up gingerly, wincing as the fabric stuck to the torn flesh of the still-angry wound. There was only one way to heal it completely.

But first she would wait for Theo.

The moment after he'd struck her assailant hung in her mind, bright and sharp. The hard grip of his fingers on her arms, the rippling beat of his heart against hers as he moved to shield her from harm. His own fear supplanted by his concern for her. And his eyes, brilliant in the light from a waving flashlight. Until that moment, she hadn't realized they were the bright green of new-sprung leaves.

<hr />

At the concourse-level food court, Theo sat huddled under a foil blanket like an earthquake survivor. He was in shock, so the EMT had said, but otherwise only bruised. He stared blindly at the coffee list behind the Starbucks counter, but all he could think of was the blood caking his hands.

"Mr. Schultz." A wiry older woman took a seat across the table. "Or should I say Professor? What's more appropriate?"

He remembered the lady captain from the hospital crime scene. "I think the finer points of etiquette died about when Helen did. How about just Theo?"

"I'm Captain Hansen from the Counterterrorism Division. And I think you know Detective Brandman." She gestured over Theo's shoulder.

His least favorite cop stood just behind him. *Hovering like a vulture,* Theo couldn't help thinking.

"Since he's been your primary contact with the department so far, I've asked him to join us." She motioned Brandman to sit.

"How're you feeling?" the captain asked Theo. "You've had quite a night."

"I seem to be making a habit of it."

The woman smiled briefly. "You've bitten off a bit more than you can chew, no?"

Theo looked again at the blood caking his hands. "Yes, I suppose," he responded mechanically. *But I'm still alive. And I'm still one step ahead of Brandman, so I'm not doing so bad.*

"You like playing the hero, it would seem," she said, not unkindly. "The other woman at the scene reported that you saved her life and that you tried to save Jenny Thomason."

"The other woman? You mean—" He stopped himself, remembering Selene's warning. "The one who tried to take out five armed men all by herself?"

"Yes. She spoke very highly of your actions. May I ask how you wound up here? You told Detective Brandman that the killer would attack a cemetery next."

Theo explained that there had once been a burial ground beneath the Waldorf. Hansen's eyes widened. She called over another officer and gave instructions to investigate the old train platform. Then Theo went on, explaining about the *Pompe* ritual and how he'd known to look for a public display of lewd jokes. His story didn't make complete sense without admitting Selene's part in it, and he felt bad claiming all the credit when she'd found the cemetery, but his weariness precluded any clever lies.

"One of the stagehands said she overheard the men saying that if they got separated, they'd meet up tomorrow, 'somewhere the masks would be more appropriate.' Any idea what that could mean?"

"The masks... huh. Well, they're copies of ancient theatrical comedy masks. Chorus members in Athenian plays wore large wooden masks to make their voices resonate—not only for the audience, but within their own heads as well. It let them submerge themselves in the character. I had a roommate back in grad school at Harvard who had a reproduction mask that he'd picked up on a trip to Greece. He used to wear it around at parties. He was...let's just say he was eccentric. But I tried it once, and it works. You feel like you're inside your own mind, even as your voice is projected outward. The cult initiates are probably doing the same thing, subsuming themselves within the ritual."

Brandman snorted. "Or they just don't want to be recognized."

Theo went on as if he hadn't heard. "To the Greeks, plays were more than entertainment—they were sacred rites to honor Dionysus and Apollo. So the masks aren't appropriate for a place like this." He forgot his aching body as he considered this new piece of evidence. "Normally, tomorrow night's *Pannychis* would take place in a field near a 'well of beautiful dances,' but I wouldn't be surprised if they used a theater instead. That way, they can incorporate Dionysus, the God of Wine and Theater, who was worshiped along with the other Eleusinian deities. I gave Detective Brandman an outline of the Eleusinian Mysteries if you want to see it."

"I've been pursuing Mr. Schultz's leads, ma'am," Brandman said tightly. "The cemetery tip he gave us, as you can see, was a dead end, but somehow *he* still managed to be in the right place at the right time. This time, he even beat the cops here. A bit suspicious, in my book."

"Any more suspicious than you leaking my name to the press?" Theo flared.

Brandman pointed a stubby finger at Theo's chest. "I did no such thing. Do *not* accuse me of breaking protocol." His eyes darted to the captain, whose icy stare rivaled Selene's. "It wouldn't surprise me if the professor himself tried to convince some reporter of his crazy theories and it backfired on him."

"Crazy theories?" Theo spluttered. "Are you mad? Didn't you see the video of the killing, Detective? That was Ancient Greek

they were speaking. A goddamn human sacrifice on network TV. And I'm the one who had to hold the woman in my arms while she died." Theo clenched his hands together to stop their trembling. "I warned you they'd kill again."

Brandman leaned forward, his face inches from Theo's. "Don't you dare try to blame this on me."

"Detective!" Hansen barked. Brandman sat back, but from the furious look on his face, Theo could tell he didn't appreciate being silenced—especially by a woman. "Do you have any evidence, *any evidence whatsoever*, that points to Professor Schultz's involvement?"

"The professors in his department have all testified to his emotional instability after Helen Emerson left him and to his continued erratic, sometimes violent behavior."

"My *what*?"

"And *I* can certainly testify that he led the police on a goddamn wild-goose chase tonight while the murderers struck again. Half the police force was standing around guarding a bunch of corpses while a real crime was taking place on the other side of town. Just put the pieces together!"

"I thought you built a case on *facts*, Detective," Theo said, trying to sound as calmly furious as Selene would have. "Isn't that what you told me once?"

Brandman glowered at him. "Who better than a classics expert to dress it all up in Greek?"

Theo laughed loudly. "Well, you've got the wrong classicist. But if you're going to arrest me, just get it over with."

"We're not going to arrest you, Professor Schultz," Hansen interposed calmly. Theo let out a breath he hadn't realized he was holding. "At least," she added with a tight smile, "not at this juncture. And we will certainly pursue the possibility that a theater will be involved next." She turned to Brandman, who tugged at his mustache with undisguised agitation. "As of right now, Counterterrorism is taking lead on the investigation into the Emerson, Mehra, and Thomason murders. Your assistance will be invaluable, Detective, but I need you putting your energy toward capturing the men who are terrorizing our city, not the man who almost stopped them."

The detective opened his mouth to protest, but Hansen raised her hand for silence. "Sometimes the cops, even the best-intentioned ones, get it wrong. That's something I was recently reminded of. And I don't intend to forget it again anytime soon."

Chapter 31

SHE WHO ROAMS
THE NIGHT

The cops led Theo out a side exit to avoid the swarms of reporters hovering around the building's main entrance. They released him at Sixth Avenue and Forty-eighth Street and advised him to go home and get some rest. Keeping his head down, he walked obediently toward the subway, but then stopped at the entrance. Somehow, he couldn't bear to be underground right now. He walked instead toward the illuminated red steps in the middle of Broadway, seeking somewhere to rest.

Even at four in the morning, a few tourists stood on the freestanding staircase, gazing at the carnival of Times Square spread out around them. Theo collapsed at the top of the stairs and leaned his head back toward the night sky. The last few hours had been like something out of a nightmare. He didn't know where Selene was; maybe she'd simply disappeared again. Nothing about her made sense. *First, she carries around a bow and arrows like she's some comic book superhero. Then she nearly runs out on Jenny Thomason instead of trying to save her life. Finally, she asks me to lie to the police about knowing her—which, although I can't really explain why, I did. I'd be better off never seeing her again,* he reasoned.

Yet when a woman's low voice called his name, his eyes flew open and his pulse raced in anticipation. *So much for wanting to be rid of her.*

"So." Selene stood on the step below him, her arms folded and her backpack held loosely at her side. "They let you go."

He blinked at her. The EMTs had bandaged the arrow wound on her throat, but blood and grease still streaked her face.

"Just. They had a lot of questions." He tried to feign alertness but wound up slumping farther down on the stairs.

"At least they didn't arrest you again."

"Whatever you told Captain Hansen seemed to have convinced her I'm not a threat. So I owe you for that."

She sat down beside him on the glowing step. The red light from below flushed her pale cheeks with color. Despite the foot of space between them, he couldn't help remembering what she'd felt like in his arms. He fought a sudden desire to feel that way again.

"The captain seems smart," he offered. "And not just because she thinks I'm innocent. I've got a good feeling about her."

Selene merely nodded.

"You really don't like cops, do you? That's why you didn't tell them you were a private investigator."

She shrugged.

"You're not really an official PI, are you?" he asked gently.

After a moment, she shook her head. "I don't have a license. But women come to me. I try to help them."

Theo's imagination churned. She must have been the victim of abuse at some point. That would explain why she spent her time tracking men, why she seemed so vulnerable yet so impenetrable, why she didn't believe the cops could be trusted—even why she told the Persephone abduction tale with such passion. Suddenly, her behavior didn't seem so crazy. "I didn't tell them anything about you . . . or us."

"Good. I have a history in this town," she said. "I sort of like to stay off the grid."

"What happened?" He had to ask, although he suspected the conversational topic was off limits.

Selene remained silent for a long moment, but then, to Theo's surprise, she began to tell him. "There was once a policewoman with the NYPD who was so good that other women clamored to join just to be like her. On her first street patrol, she chased down two bank robbers, leaving her fellow officers in the dust. Tackled them both simultaneously, handcuffed one, and knocked the other unconscious. Then, after a year, they decided to pair her with a male partner. Charles Augustino. Chaz." She wrinkled her nose. "First day out, they responded to an assault call in Hell's Kitchen not far from here—a prostitute and her john having it out on the street corner. She insisted she'd been underpaid. The john swore up and down he'd never slept with her in the first place, that he was the victim of extortion. Each claimed the other had struck the first blow. Woman had a black eye and a bloody lip. Chaz handcuffed her anyway."

"For what?"

"Prostitution's illegal, even though most cops don't bother arresting the women. But Chaz pushed the prostitute up against his cruiser. The policewoman saw his hand linger between the prostitute's legs and then he grabbed her ass. When the woman spit in his face, Chaz slapped her, hard, and she collapsed onto the roof. So the policewoman pinned her partner to the ground and twisted his arms around her baton. She told him to apologize to the woman, and he refused. So she turned him around, stood him up, and broke his jaw with her fist."

"She sounds like a hero."

Selene shrugged. "As he fell, he hit his head on the car's fender. She hadn't meant to kill him. But she wasn't sorry she had."

Theo let out a low whistle.

"By the week's end, she'd been discharged from the force and indicted on charges of second-degree murder. But she disappeared before they could catch her."

"And this policewoman was..." *You,* Theo thought. *Go on, admit it.*

Selene met his eyes. She paused for a moment, as if deciding how to answer. "Cynthia Forrester."

"I see." "DiSilva" was simply the Italian version of "Forrester"—they both meant "of the forest"—and the name "Cynthia" was, like "Selene," an epithet of the Greek Moon Goddess. If she'd gone through the trouble of changing her name, her story was even more complicated than Theo'd imagined. "When was this?"

She looked away again. "Nineteen seventy-three."

"Oh" was all Theo could say. What he'd taken to be a confession now seemed like a lie. He'd been sure Selene was the policewoman in the story, but if she'd been a cop in 1973, she'd be over sixty by now. Impossible. Once again, just when he thought he'd begun to understand her, she defied comprehension. *Maybe someday I'll crack the mystery,* he thought, stealing a glance at her profile. Despite the bandages, she looked even younger than usual. As if the night's tragedy, which made Theo feel very old indeed, had only rejuvenated her.

"Now you see why I don't trust men," she said. "Or cops."

You can trust me, you know, he wanted to say. But for once, he held his tongue.

They sat silently for a moment more, gazing down Broadway. The giant LED screen above the ABC Studios at Forty-fourth Street streamed breaking news footage of Jenny Thomason's murder. Suddenly, the image of a dour man with messy fair hair and round glasses flashed across the screen. It took him a moment to recognize his driver's license photo. He realized sitting in the most public place in the city was monumentally stupid. Only dumb luck and dim lighting had prevented anyone from noticing the "Pervy Professor." But he feared that if he moved, Selene would disappear. So he sat there, his hand inches away from hers. Usually, he could feel a chill emanating from her flesh. But tonight, he felt warmth.

He almost jumped when her hand slid into his.

"You saved my life, you know." She stared at the ABC news footage, not meeting his eyes. "So much for not taking needless physical risks."

"Uh—I just—" he began. But then he stopped. *I guess I did.* "It wasn't exactly 'needless.'"

She tightened her grip. "You said yesterday that if we were being attacked, you'd run away."

"If *I* were being attacked, I'd run," he said with a laugh. "But if *you* were..." He felt the smile fall from his face.

At last, she turned toward him. For an instant, their eyes met. Then she pulled her hand from his and looked away. *Here it comes. She's about to walk away again.*

But she didn't. She just flared her nostrils and said, "Your clothes are covered in blood."

"So are yours." Her jacket had fallen open. "Holy shit, are you wounded?"

"It's not my blood," she said quickly, pulling her jacket closed again. He heard an unaccustomed tremble in her voice.

"Here." He shrugged out of his overcoat. "You must be cold." To his surprise, she accepted it. It was too big in the shoulders. He smiled. "You look like a little girl playing dress-up in your mom's closet." She drew a sharp breath. *Christ, I've said something stupid. She probably has issues with her mother.* Sure enough, she rose and started down the staircase.

"You can't just leave in my coat, you know," he called after her.

She paused for a moment, her back to him. "Then come with me."

Theo hesitated. If he obeyed, there'd be no denying to himself that he wanted something more from this strange woman than just help tracking down Helen's killer. Gabriela would tell him not to be an idiot—Selene was dangerous. He'd almost definitely get his heart broken. More to the point, if today's activities were any indication, he might get himself killed. But somehow, he still ached to follow her. Theo remembered his fear with Helen—he'd worried that she would cling too tight, demand too much. But despite the challenges she posed, Helen hadn't shaken his own understanding of himself and the world—she'd only reinforced it. Her unquestioning adoration made him feel strong and smart. Selene, on the other hand, often made him feel weak and awkward. Yet on some level he welcomed those feelings of inadequacy: They pushed him to try harder, reach further, risk more. And that meant he wound up feeling stronger and smarter after all. Being with Selene wasn't scary—it was downright terrifying. Not to mention intoxicating and exhausting. Yet he didn't want it to end. Not yet.

Theo levered himself off the stairs and fell into step beside her. *Taking needless risks seems to be par for the course these days,* he reasoned. *Why stop now?*

Chapter 32

GODDESS OF THE WILDERNESS

They walked in silence up Broadway to the southern border of
Central Park. Selene showed no signs of stopping. "So where
to?" Theo asked finally.

"There's a place in the park that I go sometimes when something like this happens. Up around 100th Street."

Forty blocks. All thoughts of a romantic tryst flew out of his
mind. He wasn't going to make it. His feet hurt. He'd been up
for twenty-four hours. His glasses had pressed two indelible
commas into the bridge of his nose. He smelled like old sweat-
pants. He put his hands on his hips and cracked his back. "I'd
love to come, but I—"

"Let's take a cab."

Theo knew she preferred to walk. "Really?"

"This time of night, the cabbies might be desperate enough
to ignore a little blood."

"Well, here—" Theo pulled a rumpled tissue from his pocket
and dabbed at the blood and grease on her forehead. Her eyes
followed his hand, but she didn't move away. "Sorry, I'm about
to act like my grandmother, but..." He dabbed the tissue with

his tongue, placed one finger on her chin to steady her head and wiped a bit more firmly, careful not to press too hard near her bruises. "Tell me if I hurt you." She smiled, as if at a secret joke. Her eyes were very close to his. The piney smell of her filled his nostrils.

They entered the park at its northern tip, next to a large pond surrounded by weeping willows and spreading sweetgums. After the chaos in Midtown, it felt like stepping into another world. A raccoon froze at the pond's edge, a fish clutched in one hand-like paw. Theo tried to move as silently and gracefully as Selene so he wouldn't disturb it. He'd been to this pond many times—it wasn't too far from Columbia—but he'd never dreamed of this secret, predawn idyll. Selene veered off the path to follow a narrow, rushing stream into the unlit North Woods. Theo fell a few steps behind, unsure of his footing.

Finally, deep in the woods, Selene stopped on an outcropping of boulders beside the stream and waited for him. He peered down at the seven-foot-high waterfall below them. It cascaded between granite shoulders into a small, shallow pool of frothing white. He'd never known such a place existed in the heart of the city. *Perhaps it didn't until this moment. Maybe she conjured it from thin air, and if I were to return tomorrow, there'd be no trace of it,* he mused, glancing at Selene.

Now that they'd stopped moving, he missed his coat. He clasped his arms around his chest. Selene jumped down the surrounding boulders and crouched at the foot of the pool, staring into the shallow water as if looking for answers.

Theo squatted beside her, elbows resting on his knees. "I've been tracking this cult, thinking I understand it," he said after a moment. "And then tonight...when Jenny Thomason...God, when they put that knife in her...I realized I still can't answer the most fundamental question of all. Why? Why murder these women?"

A tremor slid across Selene's face, and for a moment, Theo

was afraid she might cry. Instead, she took a shuddering breath and said, "Because the hierophant believes it will make the rite more powerful."

"Just because it's more gruesome? More dramatic?"

She shook her head wearily. "You claim all ritual is metaphor. But this cult is different—they're translating symbolic action into something real. At Eleusis, the clay vulva was just a *symbol* of fertility, right?"

Theo nodded. "Yes. And the burnt offerings, the 'sacrifices,' were also symbolic: The ancients gave the fat and the bones to the gods but kept the rest of the meat for themselves—they never relinquished food necessary for their survival."

"So using actual flesh goes beyond metaphor, beyond ritual— it's a *true* sacrifice—the greatest offering you can make to the gods."

"I remind my students that the Greeks didn't take their religion so literally. But I guess our hierophant doesn't know that. You're right—he probably thinks he can do it better than the ancients did." Theo rubbed the point of his chin, intensely thoughtful. "But why 'empower' the rite in the first place? They really believe they can tap into some sort of ancient juju? Helen was a scholar, not a fanatic."

Selene raised an eyebrow. "A scholar with a hidden *lararium*."

He winced. "I can't help feeling somewhat responsible. I've always claimed Greek religion has some advantages over monotheism. But I never dreamed she'd take it so far. To think Helen would actually embrace paganism...it's so absurd, so sad."

"The ancients created a civilization unparalleled for its time—maybe unparalleled for *all* time—and they did it while believing that immortals walked among them. Maybe Helen wasn't so crazy after all."

"No, Greek civilization benefited specifically because they *didn't* take their own myths literally."

"That's your own bias talking," Selene said sternly. "You like the Greeks. You don't believe in the gods. So you think they didn't either. That they were somehow too 'advanced' for something you consider superstition."

For once, Theo was silent.

"Yet," she said more gently, "when you prayed by the riverside the day we met, you spoke in Ancient Greek."

He shot her a surprised look. "I wasn't praying."

"No?"

After a moment, he said, "I guess after spending so many years studying the Olympians, I do feel some spiritual connection to them. God—you know, the one with the capital 'G'—has always been a bit unknowable for my taste. So abstract. Athena and Zeus and Hermes and Apollo... they're just human enough to make us think we have some agency in the world, and just divine enough to remind us we can't really control our fates. Maybe you're right... maybe the world was a richer place when mankind believed they lived in the same realm as gods. So I guess, on some level, it was a little like a prayer." He gave a rueful snort. "You realize you're making me rethink everything I've been teaching and writing about for the last ten years."

"You're welcome." She rose from her crouch. "Now let me show you something."

He followed her to a low pile of rocks on the far side of the pool. There, a thin rivulet of water emerged between two stones.

"Montayne's Fonteyn." Then she gestured to the larger waterfall behind them. "The waterfall's manmade, you know, in the 1870s. That and the stream, too. But this spring is older. It's the last natural water source left in Central Park. It used to flow into a creek, Montayne's Rivulet, but when they designed the park, they cut it off to create the waterfalls. All the lakes and ponds and streams in Central Park are full of New York City tap water now. There's a pump house where they can just turn it on or off.

Except this one. A little bit of Montayne's Fonteyn still finds its way into the stream up here. A last bit of the natural world." She cupped a hand beneath the spurting water and took a long drink.

"You sure that's safe?"

"You just attacked five armed men and you're worried about a little spring water?"

"Death by knife wound is faster than death by *E. coli*." But he knelt down anyway and took a quick sip. The water tasted faintly of iron and mold. "Tastes like New York."

"It *is* New York. The very heart of it." She stood and walked to the edge of the pool at the waterfall's base. "Drinking from the spring cleanses your insides, but bathing in running water from a stream's the only way to purify the body. So in you go."

"You can't be serious. That water would freeze the balls off a brass monkey. I'll catch a cold and die."

"You don't catch colds from cold."

"True, but it weakens the immune system—" He stopped himself before his pedantry got the better of him. She'd probably read the same *New York Times* column he had. Too many conversations among the city's intelligentsia devolved into recitations of articles everyone had already read. His relationship with Selene should be different. He stumbled across the boulders to join her. Kneeling, he cupped his hands, still stained with the actress's blood, in the freezing water.

"You have to get your whole body in. You read the classics. Don't you understand ritual purification?"

"Selene—"

"You've been polluted by their filth," she interrupted fiercely. "Wash it off, Schultz."

He was about to protest further, but stopped himself. *I already followed her up here. Why would I turn down the chance to get wet?* The entire situation was completely absurd. Who ever heard of skinny-dipping in Central Park? But since when had Selene been anything but extraordinary?

"Christ," he muttered, hopping precariously on one foot to pull off his shoes and socks. Standing on his tiptoes to avoid the chill rock beneath his feet, he pulled off his blazer. While unbuttoning his shirt, he realized belatedly that he'd misbuttoned it that morning, leaving one shirttail hanging drunkenly off-kilter. Then he yanked his undershirt over his head, catching the neckband on his glasses for one embarrassing moment and emerging static-charged and tousled. Throughout it all, Selene just stood, arms folded. Her gaze was no longer stern, but he could see the tension in her jaw. Finally, he stood shivering in only his corduroys; she looked away, a hint of disgust in the flaring of her nostrils. Theo glanced down at his own bare torso. He was no longer the gangly, acne-plagued teenager he'd once been—cords of muscle defined his flat stomach—but hunched over with cold, his chest seemed concave once more. *Might as well get this over with.* He fumbled with the zipper on his pants and tugged them off in another stunning display of imbalance. Perhaps he should be glad Selene had stopped watching. He'd forgotten until he looked down that he was wearing his yellow C-3PO briefs, an old birthday gift from Gabriela that made him look like a cross between a male stripper and a space robot. He didn't hesitate to doff the offending garment and splash noisily into the pool. If only it were a little deeper, he might be able to regain a shred of modesty. As it was, the water only came to mid-thigh.

"Go on, all the way in, or it doesn't work," Selene said quietly. He looked over his shoulder. She still wasn't watching him. Instead, she sat hunched over a small pile of branches. He took a deep breath. "And don't scream," she warned just in time.

Theo stayed under the waterfall for about five seconds, his teeth clenched together the entire time to squelch the rising holler that would no doubt bring hordes of park police to their little hideaway and put him right back into custody—this time for indecent exposure. He splashed back out of the pool hissing,

"*Shit shit shit shit it's cold cold cold.*" Selene was laughing now— not her usual dry chuckle, but the splendidly absurd, unbridled honk he'd heard only once before. She held out his incriminating briefs. He pulled them on with even less grace than he'd yanked them off, then crouched down beside the low fire she'd made.

"We're not going to burn down Central Park, are we?" he asked as he dried himself hurriedly with his shirt.

"Trust me. I've done this a thousand times." She shrugged out of his overcoat and handed it back to him. He pulled it on gratefully, enjoying the faint scent of cypress that enveloped him.

"You're like a homegrown Prometheus, huh?" he teased. "Bringing fire to man despite the gods'—or should I say the park commissioner's—proscriptions."

She chaffed her hands over the flame. "Prometheus did what he did for love of mankind," she murmured, suddenly serious. "I'm not sure why I do what I do."

"What do you mean by..." He wanted to understand. She was being cryptic, as usual.

She swung her head toward the trees. "Do you hear that?" she asked, her voice low.

"What?" he whispered back.

"There's a rabbit in there."

"You're not going to kill it, are you?" he asked, alarmed and fascinated at the same time.

"I don't have a bow anymore, remember?"

Theo thought it was grief that tightened her mouth this time, not anger. "But you can hear a rabbit?" No matter how he strained, he heard nothing but an indistinguishable rustle of leaves in the wind.

"I can hear the raccoon returning to its den in a log by the stream," she said softly, her eyes fluttering shut. "I can hear a rat rustling in the undergrowth. I can hear a hawk winging its way above our heads." Theo looked upward. He saw only the dark outline of branches against the dim glow of the light-polluted sky. "I can hear the slow crawl of worms through the mulch. I can hear the small cry of leaves as they wither and die and glide gently to the earth. I can hear the pull of the moon on the water."

Theo couldn't decide if Selene was insane or inspired. He let his eyes fall shut and tried to listen as she did. Yes, there was the small sound of an animal in the brush. If he concentrated very hard, he could distinguish between the wind blowing through the branches and the wind blowing through the leaves upon the ground. There—a bird cheeped! And the waterfall, of course; he could hear the white rush of the water. And a softer sound, the burble of the stream that fed it. For an instant, he felt his awareness swing outward—he was beyond himself. At once as large as the universe and as small as the insect crawling across his bare ankle. Then the roar of an airplane overhead snapped him back to his own shivering form. He opened his eyes. Selene was staring at him. The sudden warmth of her gaze made him tremble all the more.

"Your turn," he said, suddenly bold.

"Hm?"

"Ritual purification." He nodded back at the waterfall. "Your idea."

Her skin grew, if possible, even paler. Her silver eyes narrowed.

"Right now," he said softly when she didn't move, "you remind me of your namesake. Homer said the Moon Goddess was mild, but I've always thought she'd be fierce. Fierce and lonely." He left the challenge hanging and forced himself to say nothing more. He stayed silent and calm, the way he imagined one might stalk a bird of prey who at any moment might lash out—or fly away.

"You can't..." she began finally. "You can't look." He'd never heard her stammer before tonight. Maybe he was rubbing off on her just as she was on him. He was pretty sure he came out ahead in that trade.

"I promise," he said, turning his back.

He heard her baseball cap fall to the ground. Then the whisper of her shirt against her skin. He tried to give her some privacy—to not imagine each layer as it fell from her flesh—but he couldn't help it. The hum of a zipper and he knew her pants were off. He couldn't hear her walk away, but the pine scent disappeared, followed by the quick splash of footsteps into the pool.

◄○►

Selene watched the running water flow over the small cut in her arm from Hades's scepter. Nothing happened. Even the power of the wild couldn't overcome a divine weapon of such potency. But the wounds from Apollo's silver arrow presented less of a problem—perhaps because the Smith had forged the shaft in the modern age. When she turned to let the water rush over her abdomen, the flesh knit back together before her eyes, leaving only a long red scab. She sighed with pleasure at the lessening of pain and turned her face into the waterfall. Icy and hard, the water slammed against her cheeks and lips, scouring away the night's terror. She felt the bandage on her throat come loose and touched the miraculously unbroken skin beneath. She knew Jenny Thomason's death had made her own healing possible—a cruel irony for a goddess dedicated to protecting young women—but she couldn't let guilt overwhelm her. She hadn't asked for her twin to commit such heinous acts. In fact, she'd done everything in her power to stop him. *Or did I?* she wondered. *Did I hesitate? Did I let him escape, without even knowing what I did?*

She ducked her head fully under the torrent, drowning out the accusatory voices in her own head. The water flattened her hair like a seal's and muffled the sounds around her. Only then, in a protective cocoon of water, did she dare think about Theo, sitting on the rocks less than ten paces away. She shuddered, afraid he was watching her. Then she realized, with an even deeper terror, she actually *wanted* him to look. Her mind returned again and again to the same image, no matter how she tried to banish it: Theo, his muscles clenched in the cold as he stepped from the water. The flat planes of his chest, the corded veins of his forearms, the tracing of light hair across his stomach. *Must I be so alone with my questions? My guilt?*

She walked forward through the fall, leaning her palms against the granite and breathing the damp air between water and stone. The waterfall cascaded down her back like a cloak. Before she could stop herself, she whispered a single command, so silent only the rock could hear: *Theo, come to me.*

And then he was there.

She could feel him behind her, just beyond the wall of water. Slowly, hands at her sides, body uncovered, she turned. He looked like an image from a dream, his outline wavering behind the thick stream of water. He was wearing his pants again, unmindful of the water lapping at his legs, but he'd left his glasses behind. She could see his green eyes shining at her, wide with astonishment.

Selene passed a hand through the fall, the water encircling her wrist like a foaming bracelet. Theo took it and drew her slowly toward him. She passed through the water and into his arms.

"I couldn't help but look," he whispered.

She said nothing. How could she blame him for following the command of a goddess?

He reached a finger to her abdomen, touching the scab very gently. "Someone hurt you," he said, his voice tight.

"An old wound," she lied, shuddering beneath his touch.

He moved to the cut on her arm. "And this? It's still bleeding a little."

"A scratch from one of the *mystai*. It doesn't hurt."

He didn't remove his fingers. Instead, he ran them, very lightly, up her arm, to her shoulder, and down her back. Before she could pull away, he bent his forehead to hers. The tip of his sharp nose rested in the hollow of her cheekbone. He moved closer, folding her into his arms. Together, they breathed. With each exhalation, her guilt receded, the night's horrors dimmed. With each inhalation, she felt herself melt a little farther into Theo's embrace. Thanatoi and Athanatoi, past and future—all of it faded away in the heat of his touch. They stood like that for a long moment before Theo moved, just a little, so that his lips were only a breath away. She knew his kiss already, like a prophecy long foretold. *It will be soft, as gentle as his heart. He will wait for me, and only when I'm ready will he let me feel his hunger. And once we begin, we will not stop.* Unconsciously, she moved her hands along his shoulder blades. Theo breathed in sharply and tipped her chin toward him so he could meet her eyes. The desire she saw there sent an answering tremor through her body. But in the instant he bent toward her, she stiffened and drew back. Hurt flashed across his face, quickly hidden beneath a crooked smile of understanding. He brushed a strand of wet hair from her cheek, then folded her in his arms once more. She rested her cheek against his collarbone so she wouldn't have to meet his eyes.

"You're glowing," he said, finally breaking the long silence.

"It's just the moonlight sifting through the water," she murmured.

"Maybe." He sounded unconvinced. "Or maybe I'm dreaming."

Maybe Theo was right. That would make it easier to explain, easier to bear. "We're both dreaming," she said softly, her lips moving against his neck in the closest thing to a kiss she could allow. "So there's no reason we can't stay right here."

Chapter 33

SHOOTER OF STAGS

Selene had lain beside the stream in Central Park until sunup, not sleeping, just marveling in the feel of Theo curled behind her, his arm thrown across her side, his fingers intertwined with hers. Even now, as she walked back to her house in the hazy light of dawn, she could still feel the cold stone against her bare thigh and the caress of his breath against her neck.

Heat flushed her body so suddenly that she halted in the middle of an intersection. Dimly, she registered a honking taxi swerving around her. Then, just as abruptly, a cold knot tightened her chest, spreading out its tendrils of icy panic. *Where is the Punisher now?* she wondered. *Who have I become that I invite a man to watch me bathe rather than punish him for even daring imagine such a thing?* Until last night, only one man had ever seen her naked—a memory made sharp by the poet's retelling.

The waterfall's mist casts rainbows across the forest pool, deep in a sacred grove. After a long, hot hunt, the spray beckons, irresistible. I discard my tunic on the rocks. Beside it rests the carcass of a she-bear, my arrow still lodged in the flesh of its throat. I kneel and cup my hands in the foaming water, washing away the dust from my face and arms. One pull on the ribbon around my forehead and my hair tumbles free to tickle the small of my back. With a contented sigh, I wade through the shallow pool to stand naked beneath the pounding water. No stag's breath or hare's step heats my blood—only oblivion awaits beneath the water's white roar, mercifully dulling my senses. I throw back my head and open my mouth. The water tastes of wildness. Of purity. I drink deep.

A fish brushes my calf. Unable to resist, I bend to snatch it. But as I move my head from the waterfall's roar, I hear it—a branch snapping in the underbrush. The fish slips unharmed through my fingers. I remain bent over, staring at the water, my face hidden behind a curtain of black hair for another moment. Listening.

There it is. The absence of sound. A held breath.

When I fling back my hair and stand erect, the held breath becomes a strangled gasp. There is a flutter of movement between the branches of a juniper.

Acteon.

He's tracked me for days with his six matched hounds. The best-bred pack in Boeotia, he brags. Many mortal men seek the Huntress, but none have kept pace. Until today.

I step through the swirling water toward the juniper tree. "Show yourself, son of Aristaeus and Autonoe." My voice carries above the rushing water like the baying of hounds. No mortal can resist the command it carries.

Acteon steps from the thicket. When last I glimpsed him racing across the plain, he'd been a youth with the straight back and bright eyes of one trained by the centaurs and favored by the gods. No longer. Shuddering with shame, shoulders hunched, he stands before me, his lids lowered.

"Now you turn away," I say, my voice hard. "But from the shadows, you dare to look upon me at my bath. Is that not so, thanatos?" The thought disgusts me, enrages me. Deep within my breast, it even scares me. "No man may look upon my flesh and live." I raise a dripping arm in accusation. "Only the animals may see me unclothed. Don't you know that? So despite your beard and your spear, you must not be a man after all."

He looks up. If he'd kept his head lowered in submission, perhaps he could have avoided his fate. Perhaps. But he meets my stare, and for an instant, defiance flashes in his eyes. I snarl like the she-bear. Then I flick my wrist.

Antlers grow like forked saplings from the young hunter's head. His sandals fall from new-sprung hooves. A short tail waves furiously from the small of his back. He opens his mouth to scream. Only a stag's bugle emerges.

With a sharp whistle, I summon Acteon's hounds from their hiding place amid the trees. The dogs dart across the earth, tongues lolling with excitement. I read their thoughts in the lift of their tails and the sheen in their eyes. They will bring down this new-made stag for the glory of their master. The lead hound leaps upon the animal's back. Another closes its jaws around the stag's throat. The beast stumbles and falls beneath the onslaught. I watch, unmoved, as Acteon's eyes, still clear and blue despite his metamorphosis, meet mine. Within his new skin, his mind is still a man's. I cannot read his thoughts as I can an animal's, but there is no mistaking the horror in his gaze.

My heart stone, I step from the pool and pick up my chiton before the spreading blood can stain the white linen. I leave the glade without a backward glance.

For Selene, the world had always been divided in two. Male and female. Sun and moon. Day and night. Thanatoi and Athanatoi. Her icy rage had kept the two separate, balanced, safe. But the moment Theo had pulled her through the waterfall, those lines had blurred.

She began to jog, then to run, hoping that if she ran fast enough, she could escape the questions that tormented her. She felt as if the ghost of her past life and the vision of her possible future both ran behind her, their steps heavy and insistent. If she slowed for an instant, one would catch her, and she couldn't bear to succumb to either.

Legs blurring with speed, she sprinted toward the familiar, lonely house and the dog who awaited her there. *That's all I've ever needed. A hound at my side and prey to hunt. Love has only ever brought me heartache. I need anger. Hatred. Vengeance. These are the emotions that bring strength to the Relentless One.*

It wasn't hard to summon such rage. She need only think of Jenny Thomason and Sammi Mehra and Helen Emerson. She banished Theo's green eyes from her mind; instead, she saw her twin's golden-brown gaze looking down upon his victims as their lifeblood drained away.

I will not think of past or future, she determined. *Only the hunt.* As she pounded up the stairs of her brownstone, Selene looked up at the slowly lightening sky. Even as the sun rose, the moon, a faint white crescent, looked on. *Brother and Sister together,* she thought, *watching the Earth below.* She paused on the stoop, not even winded. *This was the hour in centuries gone by when Apollo and I crossed paths guiding moon and sun across the heavens. Tonight, we'll meet once again. This time, I will be prepared. I will be strong. This time, he will not escape.*

When she walked into her apartment, Hippo nearly bowled her over. Burying a hand briefly in the dog's fur, she allowed herself a single moment of comfort in Hippo's uncomplicated love. Then she pulled off her jacket and shirt and checked herself in the mirror. She put a small bandage over the unhealed cut on her arm. There was no trace of the wound in her neck, and the large scab on her abdomen already seemed a little smaller than it had after bathing in the waterfall. *What have you done, Brother?* she wondered. *Do you even know that you're healing me as you seek to destroy me?* Maybe, despite their long separation, the twins' destinies were so inextricably linked that Apollo's cult benefited his sister whether he wanted it to or not. She traced the smooth flesh beside her eyes where the faint crow's-feet had once appeared. The scowl line, too, had disappeared from between her brows, although whenever she thought of her twin, it came right back. *If I kill you, does all this go away? Do I return to my slow demise, or do I rush toward senescence like Mother?*

She leaned against the hall table, steadying herself. Her lips curled in self-loathing. *How many fears can I allow to overwhelm me? Have I already forgotten my vow to be strong?* Then her stomach rumbled with a raw, physical ache that pulled her from her self-pity and sent her toward the kitchen. As her body strengthened, her appetite continued to grow. After a quick meal of three defrosted rabbits, Selene could think straight again.

She called her twin's cell phone. Unsurprisingly, he didn't pick up. "I don't know what kind of sick game you're playing," she hissed into his voice mail, "but I'm warning you right now, I *will* hunt you down. You may have gotten away last night, but don't think you can hide from me again. You will be punished for what you've done, no matter what womb we shared."

But despite her strong words, she had no idea where the Bright One was. And now that he'd revealed himself to her as the killer, she knew he wouldn't casually drop by during hospital visiting hours. He wouldn't be easy to find. Still, she had no choice but to start looking.

She withdrew the broken half of her bow from her pack and called Dash. Again, no answer. "Things are going from bad to worse," she grumbled to his voice mail. "Add 'new bow' to the list of things I need from the Smith. And don't ask why."

She threw a few kitchen knives into her bag. Behind her winter coats in the hall closet stood an old javelin she'd picked up years ago. It wouldn't kill Apollo, but it might slow him down. The ancients hadn't called her Hurler of Javelins for nothing.

Chapter 34

THE FACE THAT LAUNCHED A THOUSAND SHIPS

When Theo awoke to the harsh morning light and the prodding toe of a park gardener, Selene was gone. He'd never thought he'd sleep, not with Selene naked and unkissed in his arms, but lust had finally succumbed to exhaustion sometime before dawn. She'd left his coat tucked carefully around his torso. A strange touch of solicitude for someone who'd abandoned him, again, without a word of explanation.

As he walked out of the park, he reached for his phone, thinking to track her down. Then he stopped. Hadn't he learned from his experience with Helen not to get involved with fanatical women? Thoughts of his ex-girlfriend brought him spiraling back to reality—today was the memorial service.

Back in his apartment, Theo took a hot shower. He tried not to compare it to the waterfall from the night before, but every time he closed his eyes, he saw the sinewy curves of Selene's body, white in the moonlight. He could still feel the weight of her in his arms. She hadn't been marble at all—heat flushed her skin despite the waterfall's chill, and while muscle corded her arms and back, her breasts felt like velvet against his chest.

Forcing aside the memory, he put on fresh clothes for the first time in days. His best khakis, a button-down, and a dark blazer. His discarded shirt bloomed poppy red in his laundry bin, reminding him that last night's wonders had come on the heels of its terrors. Had he really stabbed a man? Grappled with another? Held Jenny Thomason in his arms as her blood seeped over his hands? He would never forget the grim rattle, the sudden quiet, the limp weight.

Tonight would be the *Pannychis*, the Nightlong Revelry. After that, the two climactic *Mysteriotides Nychtes*. If they didn't stop the cult soon, more horrors lay in store. And if he was going to face the murderers again—assuming he could find them in the first place—he needed to be armed. He thought of Selene's bow and wished for an equally impressive weapon of his own. Then he laughed at himself and packed his outlines, a pen, and his laptop into his satchel. *Not exactly a sword and shield,* he thought ruefully, *but about the closest to Golden Age heroics I'm going to get.*

A large photo of Helen sat on an easel at the front of the auditorium in Earl Hall. She graced the assembled crowd with a small, enigmatic smile.

Theo spotted Ruth Willever, Helen's roommate, leaning against the back wall, far from the university administrators and faculty. He and Ruth had become friends through Helen, and they remained close even after the breakup. The young woman peered up at him with bloodshot eyes, as if she hadn't slept since the murder. He hugged her lightly; she seemed so frail that he feared squeezing too hard. They stood together in silence as a long parade of professors and students spoke of the woman they'd both loved.

Theo's fellow faculty members stood on the dais with Helen's colleagues from the Archeology Department, staring out over the mourners. Martin Andersen, a gangly crane with a bobbing crown of sparse gray hair, looked appropriately grim. He wore an ascot around his neck; pretentious on anyone else, on him it looked appropriately anachronistic. Chairman Bill Webb, standing with his usual praying mantis stoop, whispered something to Nate Balinski. The cocky grin of a satyr flashed across Nate's face, quickly suppressed as he rose to introduce a slide show in Helen's honor. Fritz Mossburg, the only who who'd shown Theo any real sympathy recently, was nowhere to be seen.

Helen's favorite Sarah McLachlan song began, slow and mournful, as images flashed across the drop-down screen: her as a young woman at the front of a lecture hall, standing beside a photo of the Rosetta Stone. Sitting on a camel before the pyramids at Giza, with Ruth standing awkwardly nearby. Performing in some high school Shakespeare, a teenager in doublet and hose, her hair a brighter yellow than when Theo had known her. A towheaded child building an elaborate castle in a sandbox.

Beside him, Ruth began to shake. Gently, Theo took her by the elbow and led her out of the building. They sat together on the grass, huddled close as the wind sapped the sun's warmth. Theo couldn't help thinking that Helen would never see the sun again.

"How're you holding up?" he asked finally.

"Shitty." Ruth swiped at her eyes with the cuff of her hoodie. "You?"

"The same. But I've had some practice turning off my emotions where Helen's concerned. That makes it easier, I guess. Or sadder. I'm not sure." He laughed bitterly. "She'd be so disappointed. She always knew her mind. None of this emotional ambivalence." Blinking furiously, he fought against the sudden sting of tears, then finally gave up and let one spill down his cheek.

"You don't seem emotionally ambivalent to me," Ruth offered, pressing a tissue into his hand. "You know, I've always wondered why you didn't fight to get her back. If I were you, I would've punched Everett in the face."

He frowned. "I find the entire idea of fighting over a woman absurd. She makes up her mind, and we abide by her decision. Who can knock out whom seems beside the point. Anyway, we were never right for each other. I knew that early on, I just didn't have the balls to admit it."

Ruth stared down at the grass. "I'm sure you'll find someone, someday. Someone who's perfect for you."

"I'm not sure anyone's perfect," he replied. "I think the best we can hope for is someone who makes us a better version of ourselves while we do the same for them. And I'm not sure I liked the man I was when I was with Helen. Maybe that's why everyone thinks I had something to do with her death."

"What?"

Theo winced. "I guess you didn't hear I was a suspect for a while there." He went on before she could protest. "Don't worry, I've pretty much been cleared." As she listened, aghast, he explained his difficulties with the police and his theories about the investigation. "Right now, I suspect Helen's killers are headed to some Dionysian theater ritual. But I have no idea which theater out of the hundreds in the city."

"Why don't you ask your colleagues if they have any suggestions?" Ruth gestured to the professors filing out of the hall beside the other mourners.

"They all think I'm deranged for even pursuing it. How about you? Got any ideas?"

"Not a clue. I'm a microbiologist, remember? You saw that picture of me and Helen in Egypt. I was afraid of the camel and too claustrophobic to go into the pyramids. I'm not good with ancient civilizations. Why not call up that crazy grad school roommate of yours instead? Wasn't he into cults?"

"Dennis?" Theo shuddered.

Ruth chuckled. "The look on your face! Is he really that awful?"

"The last time I saw him was a few years after I got my Ph.D. He was still there, of course—this was before he transferred to NYU—and I'd gone back to do some research in their rare books library. I was walking through Harvard Yard. It was winter, like ten degrees out. Everyone's all bundled up, walking as fast as they can to get out of the snow and the wind. And there he is, dangling out of a fifth-story window in Widener Library, shirtless, incredibly hirsute, and drunk off his ass. He starts shouting my name. *'Where you been, dude?'* Like he hasn't seen me for a few days instead of a few years. And now everyone in the Yard is staring at me. *Then* he starts rubbing his nipples."

Ruth was laughing now, hard.

"It's not funny," he protested with mock indignation. But it was, and he was glad of it. The pain had left Ruth's eyes for the first time.

"*Then* what did you do?"

"I just kept walking like it had never happened and swore— on Jesus, the saints, and the Olympians, too—to shave my chest if I ever got a pelt like his."

Ruth wiped her eyes. Whether her tears were from laughter or grief, Theo wasn't sure. Probably both. She took a shaky breath and asked suddenly, "How're we ever going to get over this?"

Theo felt his smile collapse. "I don't know if we ever will," he answered truthfully. "But I went to the river where they found her, and I said good-bye. It helped. A little. You want to go back in and try?"

In the empty auditorium, they stood halfway down the aisle, gazing at the photo of Helen. Theo forced himself not to look away. Ruth was moving her lips. Praying, he realized. After a long moment, she squeezed his hand and gave him a tremulous smile. "Yes, better. A little."

A sudden movement in the front row caught Theo's eye. A hunched figure, hands threaded through his wavy black hair.

Ruth followed his glance. "Everett?" she whispered. Theo nodded. She made a small sound of distress. "Do you think I should..."

"I'll do it."

She surprised him with a quick peck on the cheek.

"What was that for?"

"You're a good man, Theo."

He felt a stab of guilt. What would she think if she knew he and Helen had slept together only a few months ago? But he didn't have the heart to reject Ruth's compliment. She needed to believe people were still kind. He hugged her, more firmly this time, and she left him alone with Everett. And Helen.

Everett glanced up as Theo sat beside him. "All those people crying over Helen as if they really knew her," he said. "But they didn't, did they? Not the way we did."

"I'm not sure if anyone really knew Helen," Theo said carefully.

Everett shot him a surprised look. "What do you mean?"

"Did you know about the *lararium* in her office?"

When Everett shook his head, Theo described the shrine. "Helen's obsession with her work went beyond academic passion. She really *believed* in the gods."

"She was always talking about them—Apollo and Persephone especially—but I thought it was just part of her research."

"Research she never showed you."

Everett shook his head miserably. "Is that how she got mixed up in this awful cult? Through some delusional religious belief?"

"If you know anything about the people she got involved with," Theo begged, "you've got to tell me. It's gone beyond

Helen now, and the more information I have, the more chance of stopping them before another woman dies."

"I don't know anything. She would disappear for hours, sometimes even a few days, but she said she was just thinking or writing. If she was actually sneaking off with other people... God, I didn't think she'd lie to me about that."

At the sight of his colleague's tear-filled eyes, Theo's stomach clenched. What would Everett do if he knew Helen had lied about meeting *him?*

Suddenly, Everett clutched his stomach, as if he might be sick. "You all right?"

"It's not really physical. More like heartbreak, I think. I was just starting to believe she's really gone. Now I'm wondering if she was ever really here to begin with."

Theo swallowed his guilt and put a comforting hand on Everett's arm. He'd wanted to spare Everett this pain. "She loved you. You can be sure of that. *A flood tide*—that's what she called it when she met you."

"I should've kept her safe."

Theo shook his head. "Don't blame yourself. I used to feel responsible for her, too—but we have to respect her enough to believe that she knew her own mind. The only one responsible is the man who took her passion and twisted it into something dangerous. The man who killed her."

Everett nodded, too choked up to say anything more. Theo went on quickly, "Look, I'm sorry to hash this out with you. I know it's shitty timing. Bill would be furious if he knew I was bringing this up."

"Bill and Martin and the others just want this to blow over before their reputation is wrecked," Everett managed, swiping away his tears impatiently. "If Helen got involved in some Greek cult after she started hanging out with the Classics Department, it doesn't look too good for them, does it? They'll do anything to protect themselves. But you—you've been trying to help." He sat up a bit straighter and looked at Theo with new intensity. "I don't care what Helen did, what lies she told. I loved her. And you're right, she loved me. That much I have to believe. So you're not going to stop looking for her killer, are you?"

"I don't...I don't know if I can." Theo picked at the seat cushion beneath his legs, suddenly unsure of himself. "I'm working with an investigator, and she does this all the time. Hunts down evil people. It's addictive." He turned his gaze back to Everett. "I've never done anything like this before. You'll have to forgive me if I sound like a pretentious prick, but my life feels *real* somehow for the first time. Like it finally matters. Like I have a job to do."

"Like Heracles. Fated for some higher purpose."

"Yeah? The cops keep trying to get me to stop. You said the same thing the other day."

Everett grabbed Theo's shoulder. "I was an ass. You've done more for Helen than anyone else. I think we all underestimated you. You can find the bastard who did this to her. I believe in you."

Theo found himself caught in Everett's dark stare, flattered and embarrassed at once.

"Well, I'm only going to succeed if I can figure out where they're going tonight. It's a theater, that's all I know. The cult is up to the seventh night of the Eleusinian Mysteries, the *Pannychis*, and since it was traditionally performed at the 'well of beautiful dances,' that could mean Lincoln Center. The ballet performs there, and it has that famous fountain."

"Yes, but that fountain's too public," Everett said thoughtfully. "After last night, they have to do something hidden again, something secret, or they'll be caught too easily. Where was this ancient well supposed to be?"

"Close to the Bridge of Jests from the *Pompe*—the *Saturday Night Live* studio."

"Huh. Well, what if the 'well' is metaphorical? All of Broadway is like a fountain of beautiful dances, isn't it? It's got a lot more theaters than Lincoln Square *and* it's closer to Rockefeller Center. I say look in Midtown again."

"You may be right."

"You sound surprised."

"I just...I'm astonished someone actually wants to help."

"I should've believed you from the beginning," Everett said, pounding his own thigh angrily.

Theo hesitated. He didn't want another partner, especially not one who might kick his ass if he found out about his illicit night with Helen, but he needed all the help he could get. "Do you want to come with me? I'm going to track down a possible cult expert."

"God, I wish I could. But Helen's brother and sister are due in today. They're accompanying the casket back home for the funeral, and I promised to help with all the arrangements. But I'm not going to let you down again, Theo. I promise. I'll keep thinking about your 'well of beautiful dances.' If I come up with something more, I'll let you know right away." He clasped Theo's hand in his usual bone-crunching grip.

"A hidden theater in Times Square is somewhere to start, at least." Theo heaved himself out of the seat. "You going to be okay here?" Everett nodded. "Take care of yourself. And...thanks. For your faith in me." *I don't deserve it. Not from you. Not yet, at least.*

As he walked out of the hall, he texted Selene: *Think we might need a hidden Bway theater. Whatever that means. Going to visit a Bacchic scholar. Might help.* He sent her Dennis's name and address, then hesitated for a moment, but finally decided to add, *Not sure where you are, but it'd be great to have you there.* His thumb hovered over the Send button. Just the thought of seeing Selene lessened some of the grief and confusion he'd been carrying around all morning. He erased the last line of the text, changing it to: *Would love to see you.*

A sudden memory of her body, all smooth skin and taut muscle beneath his fingers, raised the hair on his arms. He thought of Helen, an open book he'd failed to read. Then Selene, so full of secrets, yet he felt he already knew her. Impulsively, he changed the text once more. *Would love to love you.* Thoroughly disgusted with himself, he erased the last line entirely and just pressed Send.

Chapter 35

HE OF THE WILD REVELS

By the time Theo'd walked up six stories to Apartment J, the sitar music blaring through the door drowned out his panting. He went to knock, but the door swung open at his first touch. Currents of booze and pot and incense and sex wafted toward him.

"Hello?" he said, raising his voice over the din.

Dimly visible through the clouds of smoke, a young man reclined on a battered leopard-print couch with a naked woman slumped against each shoulder. He wore a loosely tied silk robe that did little to hide his expansive, hair-covered body, puffy with the effects of lassitude and drink. At Theo's greeting, he looked up groggily, his dark eyes bloodshot.

Theo cleared his throat. "HEY, DENNIS, IT'S ME!"

Dennis pushed himself off the couch and stood, swaying slightly. The two women—undergrads from the look of them—slumped in place, their chins resting on their chests.

"Hey, dude...come in, come in. What's up?" Theo's old roommate slurred. Theo couldn't really hear the words, but he got the gist.

"Well, I know it's been a long time—" he shouted.

"Whatever, dude, it hasn't been that long, has it?"

Theo shifted his weight uncomfortably and shouted back, "Well, yes, it's been *ten years.*"

"That's nothing, bro. You want something to drink?" Dennis moved slowly over to a well-stocked bar in the corner.

"*It's two in the afternoon.* I think I'm okay!" Dennis always brought out his most priggish side. Theo felt like he'd never left grad school. If he wanted to get any help, however, this time he'd have to resist hiding in the bathroom when Dennis tried to lure him into vice.

"Still got a stick up your ass, Schultz?" Dennis gave him a familiar, disappointed frown. "Loosen up, it won't kill you."

"Okay, but *just one.* Maybe a beer?" he said hopefully.

"I got my own special brew," Dennis demurred, handing Theo a Goya Peach Nectar bottle filled with something that looked distinctly unlike juice. The smell wafted toward him, sickeningly sweet, like fruit gone bad.

"You know, I'm a *professor up at Columbia* now so I've got to stay sober to *teach class later today,*" Theo shouted over the music as he gazed suspiciously into the bottle in his hand, aware of just how lame he sounded. At least Dennis didn't seem to remember it was Sunday.

"Way to go, Theo." While Dennis spoke, Theo walked over to the stereo and turned the volume down just enough so he could hear and be heard. "I'm impressed. You must have finally learned to play the game, kiss the right asses, huh?" Dennis continued. There was no malice in his voice, but his apathy made the words sting all the more. "Just like good old Nate Balinski. Tenures and titles, while I've got tits and ass. Still think you made the right choice? You let Nate know anytime he wants to party again, he should come on by. I miss that little shit-kicker."

This really was just like old times. Dennis always did like Nathan best. Theo hid his ire with a tentative sip of the brown liquid. The drink was like honey fire. Delicious and warming and stinging all at once. Some of his frustration melted away.

Dennis fell back on the couch. He draped a naked woman over his lap so Theo would have a place to sit down.

"Look," Theo began, trying to sit very straight so he didn't accidentally stare at the woman's breasts or legs or any other part of her that was bared before him. "I just thought maybe you could help me with a little problem."

"You need uppers? Downers?"

"Not that kind of problem." He reached into his satchel for his laptop. "See, I know you're an expert on neo-pagan Greek cults..."

"You mean fraternities?"

"Uh, no. I was thinking more like Dionysian throwbacks. Specifically, the Eleusinian Mysteries. Maybe you can take a look at this outline I've made of the ritual. Then let me know if any of the local pagan groups might possibly be mixed up in the gang that murdered the *SNL* actress last night."

"What the fuck, dude? You trying to get me kicked out of grad school?" Dennis didn't sound particularly angry at the thought, just amused. He took a big swig from his own jar of brew and then a long puff on a joint.

"Nothing could get you kicked out," Theo couldn't help retorting. "Certainly you've slept with enough students and gotten enough minors drunk, but NYU still lets you stay."

"That's because they *need* me, dude." True, Dennis was the most gifted scholar of Ancient Greek and Latin whom Theo'd ever met. He seemed to have extraordinary insights into the ancient mind. No program could bear to let him go, even though he was easily the most profligate grad student in history.

Theo downed another swallow. It tasted good. Really good. He'd forgotten just how delicious Dennis's concoctions were. "So you don't know anything?" he asked again, less urgently this time. His laptop slipped out of his hands.

"Look, bro, I don't get out of the house much. When I do, yeah, I sometimes go for some retreats upstate. We do some singing, a little drumming, a lot of dancing. You know. Some shrooms. Some weed. All totally natural, see. No gory shit."

The sitar music came to an abrupt halt. Only the soft snores of one of the passed-out women broke the sudden silence. Dennis looked up in surprise. Selene stood stiffly before the stereo, her arms crossed.

"No gory stuff? Are you sure about that, *Dennis*?"

"Who're you?"

Theo made a feeble effort to rise. "This is my friend Sel—"

"Celia," Selene interrupted, glaring from beneath the low brim of her baseball cap. "Really, Dennis? No drunken rages? No tearing limb from limb? I'd think a guy like you might be into that."

"I don't know who you think I am, sweetheart, but—"

"I know exactly who you are."

"I doubt that." Dennis smiled. He retrieved a remote control from under a pile of old pizza boxes and turned the music back on. He cranked the volume and leaned back, eyes closed.

Theo felt the wailing music vibrating deep in his bones like some seismic event. He took another swig of the liquor. He nodded in time to the music, and the motion made the world slip a little before his eyes. The woman on Dennis's lap opened her eyes a slit. Huge pupils. Like she wanted to take in every bit of light.

"You're in my sunbeam," she murmured, and slid off Dennis's lap to stretch herself, catlike, over Theo's. He had a distinct impression that this wasn't what he wanted—her limbs were too round, her hands too soft, her hair too blond and too long. Then she arched her back and purred, and he no longer cared that she wasn't the woman he sought, only that she might give him what he needed. The sun lit the strands of her honey-colored hair into fire, but it felt like cool water on his fingers. One of his hands slid down her spine, stroking every knob like keys on a piano. He could almost hear the music radiating through her skin. Could see it pouring off her in waves of color.

A drum joined the sitar, a rolling, vibrating, liquid drum, speeding the blood in his veins. Now he was playing the woman like an instrument, his hands fluttering and patting and pounding on her ribs, her thighs, her ass.

"Schultz!"

Theo squinted through the haze of smoke and lust. Someone was calling him. Celia? Who was she? Had he come in with her? Surely not. No woman so beautiful could be with him. He beckoned her onto the couch. There was room for one more.

The woman with the honey hair had flipped onto her back and was slowly pulling off his blazer, then pushing up the shirt underneath. Her tongue followed her fingers, tracing a wet line from stomach to chest. He groaned and wove his fingers once more into her hair, pushing her face more firmly against him. He was shirtless now, and her breasts pressed against his stomach. Dimly, he heard a door slam shut. Celia was gone. He forgot her in an instant.

On the other end of the couch, Dennis lay entangled with the other woman. Theo took another swallow of liquor, then poured a splash in the cup of the woman's collarbone and licked it clean, the salt and sweat only intensifying the flavor.

Dizzy, he poured the rest of the drink onto the crotch of his own pants. The woman lapped greedily at the twill. After lying beside Selene last night, unable to do more than hold her, the woman's tongue felt like the promise of manna to a starving man. Theo was pounding her back again, playing his song. He felt his voice, unused since seventh-grade choir practice, rising up to join the sitar's melody. He closed his eyes as the woman began to tear at his pants. "There's a button..." he began half-heartedly. Some small part of him remembered he'd bought these pants at Macy's and they were his only khakis left without stains and maybe he shouldn't let them be ripped apart, but then that little spark of reason was extinguished in a wave of ecstasy as her tongue found his flesh.

Then he was flying. Literally flying. He opened his eyes and the ground was spinning beneath him. His feet were off the ground. He spread his arms wide and watched the world pass by.

Then he watched it come rushing toward him. *Too fast, too fast!* he thought just before he slammed into the ground.

———◄◊►———

Selene had to resist kicking Theo while he was down. He looked so pitiful lying on the sidewalk where she'd dumped him. She contented herself with prodding his bare rib cage with the toe of her boot until he rolled over onto his back.

"Wake up, you idiot."

He cracked his eyelids. His pupils were still dilated, his eyes unfocused. He threw an arm across his face and groaned in the sunlight.

"You'll survive. You just had too much to drink."

She'd almost left him. She'd made it about two blocks before turning around. If their roles were reversed, she realized, Theo never would've abandoned her, no matter how furious he was. And if she hadn't rescued him, who knows how long it would've taken him to escape the apartment? Bacchanals could go on for days. She was shocked he'd ever made it through grad school at all with "Dennis" for a roommate. It gave her new respect for Theo's strength of character—a respect currently challenged by the fact that his fly was open, revealing bright orange underwear and an unmistakable bulge that filled her with equal parts anger and...something else she'd rather not name.

Theo finally sat up. He peered at her, still shielding his eyes, and then rubbed his face so hard she was afraid he'd tear it off. "Did I? Holy Roman Empire..."

Now she knew he'd truly lost it.

He retched a little. "I know better than to drink his shit..."

She refused to help him up. A goddess expects proper homage from her worshipers, and it took all her willpower not to accuse him of betraying her with the woman upstairs. He heaved himself onto all fours then finally lurched to his feet, swaying slightly. "I didn't think you were coming," he managed.

"I got your text." It'd been too good to be true. A Bacchic expert named Dennis Boivin? The God of Wine was as predictable as the rest of the immortals. "Dennis" meant "servant of Dionysus." "Boivin" was derived from Old French, meaning "Wine Drinker." His presence in New York City wasn't actually that surprising—many of the gods wound up in large metropolises, drawn to the aura of power they projected.

Theo patted his bare chest distractedly. "My shirt?"

She shrugged and lifted one disdainful brow.

"And oh, God, my pants." He zipped his fly, but the button at the top came off in his hands. A huge wet stain spread from his crotch. "That's not what it looks—I don't think—it was just that girl—"

"Schultz. Stop talking. If you're going to let some woman put her mouth all over you, that's your business. It's clear that's what you really want—you don't need to be ashamed of it." She spoke with careful insouciance, hoping he couldn't hear the anger lying just beneath the surface.

"What?" He blinked and shook his head as if trying to clear it. "No, that's *not* what I want. *She's* not what I want."

She snorted, trying not to fixate on the implication of his words. "You certainly weren't pushing her away."

"You're angry with me."

"Only because you're wasting time." She glared at him, silently commanding him not to push her further.

But whatever power of compulsion she'd summoned beneath the waterfall had faded in the light of day. "Last night—" he began.

"No." She held up a hand. "Don't."

Theo frowned at her. The expression looked out of place on his features. She wondered if her own face looked so sour when she scowled. No wonder men were afraid of her.

"The hierophant's not going to wait for you to explain yourself and neither am I," she went on before he could protest. "We need to keep moving."

He gestured to his damp pants. "Well, I can't walk around like this."

"It's the East Village. No one will notice."

That wasn't precisely true. They'd already gotten their fair share of stares from tourists and eye-rolling from locals.

"Please? Come on, the shirt I can do without." From the appreciative stare of a passing Goth girl, Selene guessed he was right. "But the pants. I look like a homeless runaway."

"You fit right into the neighborhood."

"I'll have to go buy something." He reached into his back pocket. Then into his front pocket. Then, frantic, into his back again. "My wallet. I think it fell out."

"More likely, Dennis stole it."

"He wouldn't do that."

"No?" Selene sighed. Even gods weren't immune from the needs of the almighty dollar. Dionysus could easily make a fortune selling his wine or his drugs, but he'd never had any common sense. She'd warned her father not to let him onto Olympus, but Zeus had been as enthralled by his liquors as everyone else. If it weren't for stony-eyed Athena, who insisted Dionysus not serve his drinks to the gods, they might all have fallen into a stupor for the next three millennia. Now it seemed "Dennis" was a petty criminal, a New Age acolyte, an eternal grad student, and possibly her twin's accomplice. She wouldn't know for sure until she went back and confronted him—as one child of Zeus to another.

"Oh no. It's not just my wallet. I left my bag up there. My computer, everything. I didn't even realize—"

"I'll go back and get it."

"It's not safe. I'll do it."

"*You* can barely stand up straight. And *I'm* not stupid enough to drink anything." In no mood to be swayed by his concern for her, she left him there, shivering and shirtless. Served him right. Still, she could hear his teeth chattering from halfway down the block. Sighing, Selene dropped her backpack, yanked her belt from around her slim hips, and pulled off her flannel shirt. She tossed them both to Theo, picked up her pack, and marched back to Dennis's building in her tank top.

Chapter 36

HE WHO UNTIES

Selene opened the apartment door without knocking. The music no longer blared. The two naked women sprawled, unconscious, across the floor. The man she knew as Dionysus sat on the couch alone, a joint hanging from the corner of his mouth, riffling through the contents of Theo's wallet.

"Find anything interesting?"

"Wha—" Dennis looked up, his face bright red. Even the god of shamelessness could feel embarrassed about stooping so low.

"Just give me the wallet."

"My friend gave it to me, don't you remember?" he soothed, puffing smoke toward her.

Selene leaped over the coffee table and onto Dennis's chest like a pouncing cat, her knee pressing his solar plexus, her face an inch from his. "I said, give it to me."

"Kronos's balls..." Understanding flashed across his face. "I didn't recognize you."

She rolled off him, snatching Theo's wallet as she went and shoving it securely into her pants pocket. His computer lay on the floor; she stowed it in his satchel and slung the bag over her shoulder.

"Artemis—"

"Don't use that name," she snapped, glancing at the two women.

"No worries, sis, they can't hear a thing."

"What'd you give them?" She sniffed at the open Goya bottle on the table. "Let me guess. *Kykeon*. What did Theo call it? The 'specialty cocktail' of the Mysteries. Gets people to do your bidding, huh?"

"Just helps them do what they really want to do anyway."

"Disgusting." She slammed the bottle down.

"Oh? You get mortals to obey *you* by pointing arrows at their throats, if I remember right. My way's a bit more humane. And much more fun."

Selene whipped a kitchen knife from her bag and leaned over the couch, holding the point to the pulsing vein in the side of his neck. "Yeah, but my way's also effective. And not just on mortals." Dennis didn't even flinch. "Tell me where your thyrsus is." The Wine Giver's pinecone-tipped staff was clumsy and inelegant, but any divine weapon was better than none.

"Oh, babe, my thyrsus is way too big for you to handle." He waggled his eyebrows suggestively. Selene pressed the point of her blade closer to his skin. He laughed in her face, and she winced in the eye-watering fumes. "Chill. It's not here. Haven't seen it since I lent it to an undergrad for her production of *The Bacchae*. I'd swear it on the Styx, but since the river probably doesn't exist anymore, guess you'll just have to take my word for it."

She pushed herself away from him and paced the filthy room, moving aside piles of pizza boxes and dirty laundry with her toe. As unlikely as it seemed that Dennis would leave his last remaining divine attribute just lying around, it was even more unlikely that he'd let a mortal use it as a theatrical prop. Still, with Dennis, anything was possible. She rummaged through his closet, nearly coughing in the overpowering stench of weed and fermented fruit.

"Told you. It's not here. Now will you get the fuck out?"

She moved closer to him and pointed her knife once more in his direction. "Tell me this. Did you give *kykeon* to my twin so he could control his men? Is that how he got a bunch of hipster musicians to murder three innocent women?" she demanded.

"The word 'lunatic' must have been invented for you, *Moon* Goddess. I assume you're talking about that crazy shit on TV last night, but it wasn't me. I don't get off on death and destruction." He crossed his arms behind his head and leaned back more comfortably into the leopard-print upholstery. "Sex and drugs are more my thing."

"Just because you didn't wield the knife doesn't mean your hands are clean. Your drink is helping the Bright One revive the Eleusinian Mysteries—which just happen to have a connection to Bacchanalian worship. You can't resist the chance to get strong again."

"Strong again? There's a good old Bacchanal every night in every bar across the world. The others may be fading, but plenty of mortals still worship the almighty bottle. So don't look at me. I've been happily holed up here with Tanya and Bree for the past few days. Haven't left the apartment." He reached beneath his robe to scratch lazily at his famous balls.

Selene's stomach heaved with revulsion. "I don't trust you for a second. Where else would they have gotten their hands on *kykeon?*"

"Oh, please. I teach that recipe to anyone who asks. Why be greedy?" He held out the bottle to her.

She scowled and shook her head. "And we think the next ritual will be in a theater. Any explanation for that?"

"Get real. Every fag and hag in this city loves theater. That doesn't make them my minions. Not like my lovely maenads here." He leaned down to put his hand on Tanya's—or perhaps Bree's—bare buttocks and began to rub desultorily. "And Apollo presided over theater, too, in case you've forgotten." He yawned cavernously. "Besides, why would I bring back the Eleusinian Mysteries when I was the one who destroyed them in the first place?"

"What do you mean *destroyed* them? You were worshiped by them!"

"Yeah, but that wasn't my idea. You think I liked hanging out with *Persephone*?" He feigned a resonant snore. "You know drunk maenads are a hell of a lot more fun than prissy harvest goddesses."

"Then you joined the Mysteries because they gave you power."

"Naw, my own cults were more than enough for me. I joined because *Dad* made me. Because our all-powerful father was shitting his pants with fear."

"I don't believe that."

"No? In the old days—like the *really* old days, like *pre-Olympian* days—the Eleusis cult only allowed female hierophants. They worshiped only the Earth Mother, like all big ol' labia and boobs and bellies, you know?" He mimed an enormous pair of breasts on his own hairy chest. "Demeter and Persephone tapped into those beliefs when they took the cult over."

"So? Why would Father, the King of the Gods, fear worship of an ancient goddess?"

"*Because* Demeter and Persephone weren't just coasting along, living on the cult's burnt offerings. They were actually getting *more* powerful every year." He paused to flick some ash from his joint onto the coffee table, not bothering to use the ashtray sitting a foot away. "Their new power came from their ancient connection to the Earth Mother, see, something completely outside the Olympian realm—outside *Dad's* realm. He couldn't stand that sort of challenge to his dominance, so he wanted to get rid of the cult. He couldn't actually eradicate it, since it was mankind's creation in the first place, and he couldn't overtly threaten Demeter and Persephone, since he's such a pansy around the women in his life. So he asked *me* to steal the cult from Persephone and Demeter, just as they'd stolen it from the Earth Mother, and then weaken it so it was no longer a threat. Of course, I'd do it all subtle-like, so they wouldn't realize until it was too late."

"You? Subtle?"

"I've got all kinds of talents, babe," Dennis said, flicking his tongue lasciviously. Selene felt her stomach roil. He laughed, not bothering to wipe the drool from his chin.

"Just keep talking before I do something I might regret," she said stiffly.

"Oh, you wouldn't regret it, I promise." He patted the couch invitingly. Selene just glared. He chuckled. "Your loss, babe. Okay, where was I before I started dreaming about finally popping that overripe cherry of yours?" Before Selene could punch him, he went on. "Right, I changed the cult. First I put in male hierophants and added my own *hiera*. Made them tell my story alongside Demeter and Persephone's. Then I introduced this shit." He lifted the Goya bottle. "Once they drank it, the *mystai* would do whatever their new hierophants told them to do. And the hierophants, of course, did whatever *I* told them to. Everyone still loved the Mystery—it's amazing how many revelations come from hallucinogenic stupor"—he waved the Goya bottle cheerfully overhead—"but it no longer carried true power. Not since I told them to stop the original rituals."

"*Original* rituals... right. The ones Cora *insisted* she couldn't remember. You mean human sacrifice."

"Oh-ho! The secret's finally out! And you make it sound so distasteful."

"It's the ultimate forbidden act! That's what we were always told!"

"But didn't you make Agamemnon sacrifice his own daughter before you'd let the winds blow him to Troy?"

"That's a *lie*. I withheld the winds from the Greeks to *stop* the Trojan War, not so some idiot king would kill his virgin daughter. I am the *Protector* of the Innocent, not their destroyer. It was Homer who dreamed up the human sacrifice for the *Iliad* and everyone's remembered it wrong ever since."

"Are you sure? You know our memories aren't really our own."

"I'm sure." But, of course, she wasn't.

Dennis stretched, looking bored, and took another swig of liquor. "Well, let's just say our aunt and cousin weren't quite as scrupulous as you. We can't all be uptight virgins, right?"

Selene ignored the dig. "So Cora *did* know about the sacrifices."

"She did once," he acknowledged. "But not anymore. Dad didn't want anyone knowing about the old rituals, so my hierophants made their initiates take an iron-clad oath of secrecy. One whisper of the human sacrifice and, sayonara, off with your head. So no one ever wrote about it, ever talked about it, or even thought about it, and mankind forgot. And you know how that goes—Persephone and Demeter eventually did, too. Funny thing about our memories of godhood, right? Unless we hold on to them for dear life, or the poets sing the tales, those memories just slip away. But I remember 1694 like it was yesterday. I spent the night floating in a fountain filled with five hundred gallons of rum punch and—"

"Spare me the details. Are you sure there's not some way, any way at all, to gain power from the cult without the killing?"

"I can see what you're thinking." He put on a prissy, high-pitched voice that sounded nothing like Selene's. " 'Ooh, I'll just steal my twin's new cult, but I'll make it all cute bear cubs and moonlight and happy lesbians and maybe we'll shoot a stag or two. And then I'll be stronger, but no one will have to get hurt.' Well, forget it, sister."

"It's not for me," Selene growled. "It's for my mother."

Dennis's face softened. His mortal mother had been burned alive as she witnessed Zeus's unleashed radiance. He'd never known her. "Look, I wish I could help you."

"I tried putting my mother's attributes into a ritual," she said tightly. "Veil, date palm, infants, lotus...they didn't do anything."

"That's because attributes alone don't work. I mean, in the old days, all kinds of worship contributed to maintain our strength, but if you want to actually *reverse* millennia of decline? Sorry, babe. No human sacrifice, no dice. And you've got to do it right."

"And what exactly does 'right' mean?"

"In Eleusis, the priestesses chose a new man to crown as their Corn King every year. They'd feast him, fuck him, make him bless their fields and flocks. Then, in the fall, the *mystai* killed the King during the climax of the *Mysteriotides Nychtes*. They plowed his blood and bones into the earth to guarantee a good harvest. Figured that when he was reborn in the grain, they'd be reborn in spirit. They used to say it gave them a deeper understanding of all kinds of shit—life, death, you name it. And here's the really crazy thing: it *worked*. A few of the *mystai* even inched toward immortality. One lived to be a hundred and twenty, and might have lived longer if her jealous boy toy hadn't stabbed her in the spleen. Another died at a hundred and thirty-three, but only because she fell off a rooftop during the *Pannychis* revelry."

"They were making thanatoi into Athanatoi?" Selene would never have thought her girlish cousin capable of such a feat.

"Yup. Why do you think Eleusis was the most popular cult in the ancient world? And Demeter and Persephone made themselves more powerful in the process. Oooh, I see that glimmer in your eye. Sounds tempting, doesn't it? Just a few murdered innocents and you might never age again. Maybe bring your mom back to strength, too."

"My mother has spent her life as a midwife, bringing mortals into the world. She'll never consent to sending them back out of it again—certainly not in her name. And neither will I." But even as she spoke so firmly, a cold serpent of doubt slithered through her stomach. Hearing Dennis describe the ritual so matter-of-factly made it all sound so easy, so simple. Is that how Apollo felt? Just follow the steps, ignore your conscience, gain unlimited power?

"If this is such a forgotten secret, how does my twin know about it?" Selene demanded. "Did you tell him about the Corn King? Or did Father?"

"Fat chance. Me and Dad swore never to tell. Too dangerous— to everyone. Why do you think he's in that cave? He knows he holds the key to bringing back his own power, but he can't bring himself to do it, and it's driving him, literally, out of his mind."

"Since when has he shown such restraint?"

"True. The man's worse than me when it comes to chasing mortal ass. And trust me, if it just meant the lives of a few thanatoi and Dad could be marshaling his storm clouds again, he'd be fucking the Corn King himself. But there's a catch, see? After we changed the Eleusinian Mysteries, something interesting happened..." He took a long drag on his joint and then spread his arms as if drawing aside invisible curtains. "Civilization itself. Ta-da! The Golden Age of Athens, the whole shebang. Little did we know, but if you take away mankind's hope of ever gaining immortality through some primitive, bloody rituals in a hidden cave, they start to use their own intellects and talents to improve things in the here and now instead. They build beautiful temples for Dad, write some *very* dirty plays for me, compose some pretty rocking poems for Apollo. And as they changed, so did we. That vision you have of yourself all clean and perky in a neat white tunic, bouncing around Crete with your shiny bow? Well, before Eleusis got civilized, you were probably running around in half-rotten furs, ripping your prey apart with your bare hands. You don't remember because it was a whole different life, one erased by the myths they've told of us since. But trust me, no one wants to go back to that. Then again... you are the Goddess of Not-Civilization." He squinted at her through the haze of his own smoke. "Maybe I shouldn't have told you. You might *want* to regress to blood and gore."

She shuddered. "The good old days are one thing. What you're describing sounds a bit untamed even for me."

"Oh, good. Because if Dad found out I told you, he might finally leave that cave and bring down some thunder and lightning on my ass. Or not. Whatever. Seems Apollo knows the secret anyway, so it doesn't make much sense to keep it quiet anymore." He flipped one of the young women over with his foot and ran his toe up her bare thigh. "Did I unravel enough mysteries for you, babe? 'Cause if you don't mind, I've got more pressing matters to attend to."

The sight of the naked girls, the noisome smell of old food, and the musk exuding from Dennis's robe made her want to vomit. This at least was one thing she had no moral ambiguity about. "Clean those girls up and put them back where they belong." Selene's knuckles were white on the knife handle.

"Take it from He Who Unties—it's time to loosen up." He snorted at his own pun.

"I said put them back." She brandished the knife once more. "Do as I say. I am still your elder."

"You were always stronger than I, Artemis, but I know how little homage mortals pay to hunters these days. You look pretty good for your age, but you must be weakening." With a speed she didn't realize he possessed, Dennis sprang from the couch and grabbed her wrist, his fingers like a vise.

"Get off me," she demanded. His eyes were no longer clouded. She should've remembered drink could have no effect on the God of Wine unless he willed it to. He looked at her almost quizzically, daring her to prove herself. Her arm was beginning to hurt. He twisted her wrist violently and the knife fell from her numb fingers.

Selene grabbed his arm with her other hand and pulled. Nothing. He only smiled. Their strength was perfectly matched.

"Give me back that wallet," he said. "Being a perpetual grad student doesn't pay very well."

"Too bad." She lashed out at his chest with all her force. He remained upright, unmovable. They stood there in silence for a moment, glaring at each other. Then she heard slow footsteps on the stairs. She knew the sound of Theo's tread, even when he was stumbling with drink.

"Ah, here he comes again, the fucker," Dennis said, looking toward the door. "I should've known he'd show up someday with one of my irritating siblings. Trust a Makarites. We can never stay away from one of his kind, can we?"

Selene felt her jaw drop.

"Oh! You didn't realize what he was? Always so blind, babe!" Dennis threw back his head and laughed. She seized the opportunity. In one fluid movement, she spun and kicked, nailing him hard in the groin. He screamed and fell to the ground, clutching his legendary balls.

"Selene, are you okay?" Theo panted, staggering into the apartment. "What was—"

She pushed him back out the door and grabbed his hand to drag him down the stairs. "What's going on?" he demanded. "Did you get it? I heard—"

"Keep moving!"

She pounded down the steps, forcing herself to go just slow enough so Theo could keep up. From somewhere behind them, she heard Dennis's ragged scream: *Artemis! Artemis!*

Chapter 37

ARTEMIS

They dashed down the subway entrance. Hearing an uptown train approaching, Selene jumped the turnstile without missing a stride. Theo, on the other hand, stopped to fumble in his pocket. Before she could drag him bodily over the turnstile, he'd found his MetroCard and swiped through. Together, they jumped through the subway doors just before they slammed shut.

Panting so hard he could barely speak, Theo sat with his head slumped between his knees. Selene was breathless, too: not from the exertion, but from Dennis's revelations.

Theo finally looked up. "Artemis, huh?" He smiled a little.

Selene felt a strange rush in her veins. She realized with a start that she'd never heard her real name on Theo's lips before. It terrified her that she liked it.

"I don't know what gave him that idea," she said lightly.

"Maybe the fact that you're six feet tall, run like the wind, carry a bow, and look like a goddess." Theo smiled tipsily. "There's power in naming, you know. That's why the gods had so many epithets. I think I'll call you Artemis, the Eater of Much Pork, the Owner of Scary Mutt, the Protector of Professors." He was flirting with her, she realized. She felt the heat in her cheeks and watched a corresponding flush creep up Theo's neck.

Dennis had called him a Makarites—"Blessed One." In ancient times, the Athanatoi used the term for heroes who earned the gods' favor through extraordinary deeds of bravery, such as Theseus or Heracles. Since the Diaspora, a Makarites earned the title not through battling supernatural monsters but through his or her own ability to understand the gods on a profound level— whether through study or artistic endeavor. Besides a brief surge in the Renaissance and another in the Neoclassical period, when artists brought Greco-Roman mythology to life for a new audience, Makaritai had been exceedingly rare. With her penchant for avoiding mortal entanglements, she'd never even met one before. But she knew that when they did appear, the gods were irresistibly drawn to them. *It would explain how Theo wound up with an Olympian for a roommate,* she realized, *and why I can't seem to stay away from him either. Last night in the park, perhaps I let him hold me not because of who he is, but* what *he is.* And was his attraction to her equally involuntary? Of course he desired her—no thanatos stood a chance when a goddess came into his life. *Maybe he doesn't actually like Selene DiSilva at all,* she considered, fighting back a surprising pain in her chest. *Maybe, like Acteon and all the others, he's just blinded by Artemis. Last night, I commanded him to come to me in the waterfall. What choice did he have?*

She let out an exasperated groan, and Theo looked over at her quizzically. Then the blood drained from his face. His smile vanished. Selene followed his gaze to the livid welt encircling her wrist like a tattoo. "He hurt you," Theo said, his voice tight. "I know Dennis is dangerous. I should never have let you come with me to his place."

"You didn't *let* me, remember? It was my choice. It's fine. It'll fade." *Sooner than you think possible,* she thought, *and for reasons I can't bear to admit.* She crossed her bare arms so her wrist was hidden beneath her armpit. But would she prefer to be weak again? Could she bear it? She looked around at the subway car as if she'd never ridden in one before. The mortals sat, half-asleep or jittery with energy, despondent or ecstatic but mostly apathetic. Above their heads, ads for light beers and teeth whitening competed for space. Ways to make a temporary existence a little less painful. To improve the constantly deteriorating human form. What would she give to save herself and her mother from such a fate? For an instant, she imagined herself at the riverside, watching Helen Emerson pray for justice to a goddess who refused to hear her pleas. Then she imagined slicing through Helen's soft flesh. A wave of nausea rushed from Selene's stomach to her throat. She leaned her elbows on her knees and swallowed, hard.

"Selene, are you okay?" Theo's hand, warm on her upper back, rubbed in gentle circles.

"Yeah." She straightened up, her decision made. "Just making sense of everything."

Theo withdrew his hand and gave her a wry smile. "Good luck. I feel more confused than ever."

"That could be because you're drunk."

Theo laughed sheepishly. "Have you forgiven me?"

He asked so easily. He couldn't know that forgiveness did not come easily or often to the Punisher. And yet even as she started to say she couldn't, she realized she already had. She looked away and nodded.

"Good." He held his arms out straight before him. He looked absurd: The cuffs of her flannel rode high on his wrists, the buttons strained across his chest, and her belt did nothing to hide the stain on his still-damp trousers. "You didn't happen to grab my shirt while you were up there? As a peace offering?"

"No. Sorry." But she wasn't. Somehow she liked seeing him in her shirt. "But here." She handed him his satchel and pulled his wallet from her pocket.

"Thank God," he said, checking over the contents of his billfold.

"You certainly have interesting taste in friends."

"Dennis is a real asshole. Always was. I should probably report him to the cops, but one case at a time, right?"

"Well, at least we learned something from him."

"About my own stupidity?"

"We already knew about that. But now we finally know exactly why the cult's using human sacrifice. They're not just translating symbols into literal acts. They're actually following a more ancient version of the Mystery. When I went back, Dennis told me all about it. Turns out the priestesses in Eleusis used to kill off a yearly Corn King to appease the Earth Goddess."

"A Corn King? You mean a man chosen to represent the fertility of the harvest? Fascinating. None of the extant sources mention that—then again, Dennis was always uncannily good at this sort of thing. It fits into an old theory by James Frazer in *The Golden Bough*—that most Greek myth is derived from cult ritual involving the annual killing of a king." Even drunk, Theo still sounded like a professor. "It's an early version of what becomes the Christ story. The king takes on the sins of the community and dies in their stead so that everyone else can prosper. The theory's been widely discounted, though."

"Dennis sounded pretty convinced. He also claimed that at some point, the Mystery evolved to a more sanitized version, replacing human sacrifice with Dionysian worship and *kykeon*—which he thinks he figured out how to brew. That's what you were drinking up there. If the hierophant also knows the recipe, that may explain how he's controlling his *mystai* so effectively."

Theo whistled appreciatively. "Who knew a drunk stoner like Dennis could be so useful? Ruth was right to remind me about him."

"Ruth?"

"Helen's roommate. I saw her at the memorial service this morning."

"How was that?"

"Devastating." He chewed his lip as if to stop himself from saying more.

An unfamiliar discomfort nibbled at her, somewhere deep in her chest. He caught her staring.

"It was a long time ago," he said, as if he'd read her mind. "Helen and me. I'm not pining for a lost love, just a lost friend. I want to find out who's doing this."

"Theo..." She didn't know how to tell him that she knew exactly who the hierophant was.

"If you're about to tell me to get lost, don't," he said, his smile belying his stern tone. "And don't run away again. You're not getting rid of me that easily." He threaded his fingers through hers. Selene looked up into his eyes, bright and green and incredibly warm, and she knew exactly whom Apollo would choose as his Corn King.

Chapter 38

LADY OF THE STARRY HOST

Selene ripped her hand from Theo's just as the subway squealed to a halt. Before he could protest, she ran out of the car, through the station, and up into Grand Central Terminal. She could hear Theo following her into the soaring main hall of the station. The clamor suddenly subsided as the chamber's echoing marble expanse muffled and distorted thousands of voices at once. The sound reminded her of her godhood, when the prayers of the faithful came to her in a layered, muted cloud, one barely able to be sorted from the other.

The air in the hall was different, too, whooshing up from the underground train platforms and subway tunnels and coursing against the painted ceiling far overhead before swirling down once more to brush past her cheek as gently as a kiss. As gently as *his* kiss.

She stopped. *Orion took me in his arms and pressed his rough, wind-burnt lips to mine. I ran my hands through his black curls. I loved him. Grief was my reward. Apollo took him away. Now, once again, I've walked into the trap my twin has set. Again, he uses my feelings against me. He says he wants to protect me, but in truth he cannot bear to see me happy.*

"Selene, what's wrong?" she could see Theo mouthing, but the rushing of blood in her ears drowned out his words.

She looked up.

A painting of the heavens arced across Grand Central's vaulted ceiling. Gilded stars ornamented with line drawings of the constellations hung against a sky blue background. Aquarius, pouring starry water above the ticket counters. Pegasus, breaching through a cloud. Gemini, side by side. And there, so far overhead that she needed to crane her head to see him—Orion. The stars were still there, right where she'd put them. One for each shoulder. One for each leg. A gilt row of three stars for his belt and a star for his sword.

She could still hear Apollo's footsteps as he ran through her sacred grove, bringing her the news that would change her life forever.

"Moonshine, Moonshine! Did you hear of Merope? A man took her by force beneath the poplars."

I seize my bow and my golden arrows, my cheeks hot with wrath. "Who would dare touch my sacred companion?"

"Orion. The man you call friend."

I, most graceful of goddesses, stumble with shock, my bow flying from my grasp, my knees slamming against the hard ground. My twin picks up my weapon and places it once more within my grasp. He holds out his hand to lift me up, but I brush him aside. "Orion wouldn't betray me! He left here only a day ago with promises of fidelity." I sound like a child, a lovelorn maiden, but I cannot bear the news. I have not yet given Orion my body, but I have given him my soul. When he left the grove, he pressed his lips against mine. A secret promise. He vowed that when he returned to me, he would bear a surprise. The only other man I've allowed so close to my heart is the one standing before me—Apollo, Leader of the Muses, Healer of the Sick, the Bright One.

"You know how these half mortals are. They cannot be trusted," my brother says.

"You speak the truth?"

Apollo narrows his golden eyes. "From the womb, I have cared only for you. I would not lie."

We stalk through the forest, over hill and across streams, seeking our prey. I find it easy to hate, easy to believe my Hunter is false. I have so little practice with loving.

Three times, Apollo drives the sun across the sky. Three times, I guide the moon from one horizon to the next. And then we find him. Lying on the shore of the limitless sea, where his father Poseidon rules the deep. I look upon his broad shoulders, the familiar easy grace of his pose, his head pillowed on his crossed arms, his long legs stretched out before him.

I nock a golden arrow to my bow, the shaft in my fingers as light as it is deadly. I hesitate for one moment only. Just long enough to remember the taste of his lips. Then I let the arrow fly.

At the thrum of my bowstring, my Hunter sits up and turns away from the sea. His eyes meet mine, wide with shock and disbelief. For an instant, I doubt his guilt.

The arrow pierces his heart.

Theo was shaking her shoulders, calling her name.

"Catasterismi," she breathed, as if that were an answer to his panicked pleas. Her eyes did not leave Orion's gilded form on the ceiling above.

"Catasterismi?" he repeated. "What? Selene?" He gripped her arm, hard. "Look at me!"

She blinked once and dragged her eyes away from Orion and back to Theo.

Face pale, Theo took a step back as if he'd been struck. Selene wondered vaguely what she'd done to make him so afraid. Then she realized she was crying.

"Oh my God. I'm sorry, I didn't mean to yell at you. Really, don't—"

"It's not your fault, Theo."

Suddenly, she didn't want to lie anymore.

"It's *his*." She pointed to the ceiling, but did not look. Theo craned his neck back.

"Him? Orion?"

"*Catasterismi.* It means 'the placings of the gods among the stars.'"

"I know what it means, I just don't understand why it's so important. Is it a clue? What did you figure out?"

She shook her head slowly. "Only what I should've realized before. That the hierophant will come for you next."

"Why? I'm no virgin maiden, I hate to break it to you."

Selene didn't smile. "Because everyone I care for is destroyed. And that...that means you." She pressed onward as she saw his eyes widen. "And that's *not* a good thing," she insisted before he could speak. "It's a terrible thing. You have to stay away from me. Get on a train and leave the city. Go far away where he can't reach you."

Theo smiled, gently at first, trying to look comforting, but soon he was beaming. His eyes were very green in the slanting sunbeams pouring through the windows high above. "You care about me, huh?" he said softly, as if he hadn't heard any of the rest of her little speech.

"And that's a bad thing," she repeated.

He nodded, still grinning. "Terrible."

"Yes, terrible."

"Sure. Mmm-hmm." He moved toward her, his smile aglow. *One more step,* she realized, *and he'll kiss me.*

She stepped back, one hand raised in warning. "No, Theo. You don't understand." She could feel Orion's eyes on her still. Her tears sprang afresh.

"What's wrong?" Theo asked, suddenly all concern.

"I've been trying to tell you," she snapped.

Then she turned on her heel and fled.

———◇———

For once, Theo didn't go after her. He stood among the swirling crowd, watching her go, shocked more by his own reaction than by hers. He'd expected her to run away—he just hadn't expected it to hurt so much.

The adrenaline of his escape from Dennis's apartment dribbled away, leaving him hollow, exhausted, and still slightly drunk. *Maybe if my head were clearer, I'd understand what Selene was trying to tell me,* he thought. *I feel like all this time I've been unable to hear a conversation she's trying to have with me. And now, when I'm finally listening, she no longer wants to speak.*

Slowly, he wended his way toward the exit, determined to head toward the Broadway theater district. With or without Selene, he wouldn't give up the hunt for the hierophant. *She said I'm in danger, but what else is new?* He'd been in danger ever since she'd walked up to him in Riverside Park and pulled him into her world. Only now losing his life to a murderous cult didn't seem so important—not when he'd already lost his heart to Selene DiSilva.

Just before he could exit the terminal, a woman's voice called his name. Chest tight with anticipation, he swung toward the sound, sure Selene had come back for him. But the young woman before him was short, black, and holding a gun leveled at his chest.

Chapter 39

THE DELIAN TWINS

This is what I'm good at, Selene thought, dodging the crowds on the sidewalk, keeping her eyes on the bright lights of Broadway up ahead. *Hunting, punishing. Not loving. Never loving.* She banished the image of the pain and disbelief in Theo's eyes and slammed a door closed over her heart. She didn't have a choice. The only way to save him was to abandon him. Then, with or without a divine weapon, she needed to face Apollo.

It came as no surprise when her cell phone registered that she'd missed a call while underground in Grand Central: Her twin had always known when she was thinking of him.

"Come quickly," Paul said in the message, his voice thick. "She's holding on for you, but it won't be much longer now."

It was obviously a trap. But if it meant the chance to confront her twin tonight, then it was a trap she would gladly enter.

Paul Solson lay on the narrow hospital bed with his mother cradled against his chest. Leto's breathing, quick and shallow, barely stirred the thin blanket swaddling her narrow frame. She still wore the purple veil Selene had brought her, but the lotus flower lay shriveled and brown on her lap. No tubes snaked from her arms; only a single wire emerged from beneath the blanket, connected to a monitor on which a silent green line jerked erratically with every Titan heartbeat. Trap or not, Paul had spoken true. Their mother was dying.

"You came," he whispered as Selene entered. "I didn't think you would."

She hesitated at the doorway, unsure what he meant. He didn't think she'd come to their mother's deathbed? He didn't think she'd come to challenge him? He hadn't even looked at the javelin in her hand. It was as if he hadn't seen it.

"You didn't save her," she said, more entreaty than indictment.

He shook his head, his face crumpling with grief.

Leto's eyes fluttered open. When she saw Selene, the merest hint of a smile curled her lips. Slowly, she turned her hand over so it lay palm up on her son's arm. An invitation.

"Whatever has been between us," Paul said softly as Selene hesitated by the door, "whatever harm I've done to you, be with me now. For her. For me. I can't do this alone."

Selene's grip tightened on the javelin as she readied herself to fling his words back in his face. But her mother silenced her angry retort with the faintest of whispers: "Come to me. Let us be a family." In the words, as quiet as breathing, lay the ineluctable command of a mother to her daughter.

Deep inside Selene, a thick heaviness, a long-brewing despair, finally broke through in a crack of thunder. Tears sprang like lightning flashes, blinding her, and the sudden storm of misery washed away the hard edges of her anger, leaving her shuddering and hunched beneath its pounding force. She staggered forward, dropped her weapon, and knelt at the bedside. With her face pressed against her mother's skeletal hip, she listened to her heartbeat grow ever slower.

"Tell me about Delos," their mother whispered at last. A final request from a goddess who'd never asked for anything.

Selene lifted her head and reached for her mother's hand.

Her brother took a deep, shaky breath.

"O far roamed Leto, heavy in travail," the God of Music began to sing. Selene recognized her twin's favorite poem: the *Homeric Hymn to Apollo*. "But none dared receive her—"

"Not in their words," Leto interrupted, her voice barely more than a breath. "Yours."

Selene raised her head. The desolation she saw in her brother's face reflected her own. They had always been opposites, she and her twin, but together they had once formed a perfect whole. She knew him better than she knew herself. When he wore a mask in his role as hierophant, she couldn't trust anything he said. But now, with his face, so like her own, revealed before her, she saw the truth. No matter what he had done, what he had planned, the tears that swelled his eyelids and streaked his cheeks were as genuine as her own. And so, if Leto wanted to hear of an earlier time, before her children had grown to despise each other, then the Delian Twins would give her that gift. But what was their story? *Do we even have memories besides those mankind has given us?* she wondered. *Delos is so faint. So far away. The recollections of a different person in a different age.*

Selene took a deep breath, reaching into the past. "I remember the palm tree beside the Sacred Lake," she began finally. "When we visited it, you would tell me how you walked across the dusty rocks with me, a newborn infant, on your hip. Wracked with pain, for my brother refused to leave your womb. And I spoke my first words, pointing to the one spot of green in the middle of the island, and told you to seek the trees, for they were our friends." Leto's eyes closed, but Selene knew by the smile on her lips that she still heard. "From that time on, every year, we returned to bless the sacred date palm that you'd grasped in your labor, when the Bright One came forth into the world."

"You had a temple there, right next to ours." Paul took up the story. "The *Letoön*. Always bathed in sun. So much sun. That was my gift to Delos and to you."

"We went as priestesses, to listen to the supplicants at your shrine." As Selene spoke, the old memory returned to her, surprisingly vivid. She could smell the sunbaked stucco on the walls, the sweet smoke of burnt offerings rising from the brazier, the salt tang of the ocean wafting through the colonnade. "A woman, heavy with child, crouched at the foot of your statue. You sat beside her and laid a hand on her shoulder. With a tear-streaked face, she told you she'd lost her first three children to miscarriage and stillbirth and had come to ask the Mother of Twins for a healthy babe. You turned to look at me, and I could see in your eyes that she would never bear a living child. Yet you clasped her head against your breast and stroked her hair, as you've done so often for me. And you whispered in her ear— you said, 'You will be a mother to many, for true motherhood lies in the heart, not the womb.'" Leto nodded imperceptibly as Selene continued. "We saw her again, years later. She'd lost her child, but started a home for orphans. I'd never seen a woman so content, so fulfilled. You did that for her, Mother."

"She was only one of many," said Paul. "Remember, we'd walk through the streets, casting blessings like coins among the crowd."

"All those people, crammed into an island only a few miles square," Selene remembered. "All come because we'd made Delos holy." At its height, her birthplace had not been that unlike Manhattan, she realized. No wonder she'd always felt at home here.

"We'd climb to the top of Mount Kynthos, where Father's temple stood."

"The wind rushed from the sea on all sides, whipping our clothes and our hair, so strong it almost lifted us from the mountainside."

The twins spoke as if they'd never been separated, thoughts and memories intertwined.

"As a child, I thought I might learn to fly if I let the whirlwind take me," said Selene, "but you, Mother, held me down and said even a goddess must learn her limits." *You were right. Even still, I forget that lesson. Even still, I throw myself into danger.*

Paul picked up the memory once more. "The sea cradled our island in its vast blue bowl, with the isles of the Cyclades set into their circle along the horizon. Naxos and Mykonos and Paros, all larger, more fertile, but none so sacred as our island."

"Delos, the center of the world."

And with that, Leto took one last breath, deeper than the rest, and let it out in a contented sigh. Selene didn't need to look at the monitor to know that the green line had grown as still and flat as the Sacred Lake on a windless day.

Delos was never the center of the world for us, Selene realized. *She was.*

Somewhere on the floor above, Selene could hear the infants in the nursery wailing. In her death, Leto had found the power she'd long ago lost in life. The new mothers began to moan in response, then to cry with great wracking sobs, although they knew not why. The cries grew in strength until the very walls began to vibrate. Nurses scurried toward the sound, wondering what terror stalked their charges. *Not terror,* Selene thought. *Only lamentation. The Goddess of Motherhood is gone.* The mourning reached a crescendo as Selene's own sobs came ragged and quick. Then the mothers and children subsided into quiet tears and hiccupping sighs, and Selene, too, found she could breathe again.

Soft rubber footsteps entered the room. A loud click as a nurse turned off the monitor. Selene could feel her taking in the scene: two children clasping their dead mother in their arms. The nurse said nothing, but left them to their grief. Never before had Selene felt such pity in a mortal's gaze. What would Theo do if he could see her now? She'd told him to leave, but would his compassion draw him to her anyway? She longed for his arms around her, easing her sadness. *No,* she thought, pulling away from the bed. *Theo can't come to me. As long as Paul lives, it's too dangerous.*

She stood slowly, as if struggling from sleep. The God of Healing lay motionless on the bed, Leto still clutched in his arms. Eyes closed, tears streaming across his lips. Finally, Paul pressed a kiss to Leto's forehead. He rose from the bed with his mother still clasped in his arms like a swaddled child. He looked at Selene then, and she read the silent question in his eyes. *What do I do now? What does one do with a dead god?* She reached to take Leto from him. She needed no supernatural strength to hold her mother's frail form. Gently, she laid her on the bed and arranged the purple veil over her hair. She would not cover her face. *They'll cremate her,* Selene decided. *And I will break the old prohibition. I will bring her ashes back to Delos, where we were happiest, and scatter them from the summit of Mount Kynthos so the gentlest of goddesses might overspread the world once more.*

After a long moment, she spoke. "I've seen photos of Delos as it stands today." Paul stared at her blankly. "The yellow glow is gone," she continued softly. "The walls are bare gray stone now, the roofs long burned away, the upper stories collapsed. Our temples are only broken columns and foundation stones. A torso and a hip of your colossal statue, left behind among the weeds by looters. It's all gone."

"Is there not already enough grief in this room? Why remind me of how far we've fallen?"

"Because you want to bring it back. Don't you? Return to an age of unlimited power. Divine omnipotence. And you'll do anything to make it happen. Even if it means denying everything we stand for."

His eyes narrowed. "What're you saying?"

"You couldn't save Mother. I think I could have forgiven you, if you'd done it all for her. Whether you intended it or not, you've strengthened me instead. But I'd give it all back. Every ounce of strength, every second of speed, I'd give it all back after tonight if I could have her with us again. But first, I'd use it for one more thing—to bring you down."

She picked up the javelin from the ground and leveled it at Paul's heart.

"What do you think you're doing?"

"I don't care that it's not a divine weapon. I'll find a way to kill you before you hurt anyone else. Before you drag this city further into chaos. You don't have your bow now, do you? You should've known better. Should've brought it to defend yourself."

"I haven't used my bow for more than target practice in a hundred years!"

"I saw the silver arrow, Apollo, the night you and your sycophantic bandmates murdered Jenny Thomason. You admitted it! Stop lying to me."

Like a cloud passing before the sun, the God of Light's eyes darkened. He reached toward the chair behind him. Selene grasped the javelin a little tighter, ready for a battle worthy of epic. *Sing, Muse,* she thought. *Sing of the duel between twins. Let heaven shake with the cries of Sun and Moon. Let the stars weep as Phoebe and Phoebus, Bright Ones, grow dim.*

Chapter 40

THE EPIC HERO

Shortly after Detective Freeman had arrested Theo, Brand-man arrived at the Grand Central police station. He pulled up a chair next to the bars of Theo's holding cell and sat down. The younger detective stood beside him, her hands planted on her hips.

"Knew we'd catch you sooner or later," Brandman said. "We've had an APB out on you all day."

"What's this all about, Detective?" Theo asked, trying not to rattle the bars in frustration. "Captain Hansen said I was cleared of suspicion."

"That was before this." He pulled a photo from a file folder on his lap and held it up so Theo could see. A footprint in soft earth. "Size twelve. Bass brand, Albany model. Inner right heel worn down. Found next to Helen Emerson's body. Perfect match to a pair of shoes found in your office, with corresponding mud in the soles." Theo felt his stomach clench. "And we've got the forensic reports back from the Mount Sinai Hospital basement." He held up two evidence baggies. "Hair from the Sammi Mehra crime scene," he said, waving one bag. "And matching sample from the comb in your apartment."

"You searched my apartment? My office?" Theo tried to swallow, but his mouth had gone dry.

"We got warrants this morning," volunteered Freeman. "Right after we learned that you'd gone to Natural History yesterday and threatened one of the employees—while in possession of a stolen prehistoric tooth."

"But I wasn't in Riverside Park until after you'd already finished investigating the scene. I went to pay my respects that afternoon, that's all. And I never stepped foot inside the hospital."

"Uh-huh. And what about this?" Brandman removed a paper from the folder. Theo recognized it with a sick sense of dread. Helen's note from the box under his bed. "Seems your relationship with the deceased wasn't quite as long ago as you claimed. One more fling, huh, for old times' sake, and then she said goodbye for good. Makes sense you'd be looking for revenge after she played with you like that."

"That's crazy. I—"

"And then, of course, there's this." He pulled one last sheet from the folder. The mangled shreds of Helen's photo from his office desk drawer, now carefully smoothed and taped back together by the detective with the same care Theo had once shown reconstructing papyri fragments.

"I know how that looks, but—"

"Occam's razor, Professor. Or should I say, *lex parsimoniae*?"

"I haven't even told you about the Corn King..."

"You're drunk, Professor. I can smell it on you. And before you start blaming a Corn King or a Watermelon Queen or anyone else, save your breath. I've had enough of your theories. You're getting sobered up, then I'm bringing you before a judge. End of story."

"Let me speak to Captain Hansen. She'll listen."

"She's out with a small army of cops, following your latest lead," said Freeman.

"Extra patrols in Times Square, Lincoln Center, the Public,

Radio City, and every other goddamn theater in the city, looking for your cult," Brandman added. "But I say they'll turn up somewhere in Harlem at a church service or down at the South Ferry terminal or smack dab in the center of City Hall. Anywhere but where you say they'll be."

"I'm not part of the cult."

"No? Then how did you know they'd be at some TV studio?"

He could've told Brandman about his relationship with Selene. Taken some of the focus off himself. But even after she'd just walked out on him, he refused to violate her wish to remain anonymous. He'd vowed to be worthy of her trust. Nothing could change that. "I've told you how I found it. Research. Context. Putting the puzzle pieces together and seeing the pattern."

Brandman stood and took a step toward Theo, fists clenched. Theo didn't flinch. Before the cop could say anything more, Theo moved close to the bars so he could look down at the shorter man. "Detective Brandman, I know we've had our differences, but we both want to stop any more killings. You can question my motives all you want, but you have to admit I've been pretty good at finding these guys. Last time, I was too slow and they murdered Jenny Thomason. This time, I intend to find them before it's too late." Theo looked Brandman straight in the eye. Somewhere in this cynical, distrustful cop was a man who'd spent his life trying to serve the people of New York.

"Jake..." Freeman began. "He might be—"

"Forget it. I'm not letting him back on the streets."

And then, just as Theo decided all hope was lost—a knock on the door. A uniformed cop handed Freeman Theo's cell phone and whispered something in her ear. At the same time, Brandman's phone rang.

He turned his back on Theo and answered the call. "Brandman here. Yes, just picked him up. Course I've got a warrant, Captain. And DNA evidence placing him at the Emerson and Mehra crime scenes. And don't forget that Jenny Thomason's blood was all over him at Rock Center. And you believe that... No, I haven't—yes, he's—right away, ma'am."

Ending the call, the detective swung back toward Theo. "Wipe that smile off your face, Professor. You're not cleared yet—not in my book. But it seems Professor Martin Andersen called up and told Geraldine Hansen that you couldn't have murdered Sammi Mehra because you were with him the whole night at his apartment, discussing Helen's case."

Theo almost opened his mouth to protest but then snapped it shut again. *If Martin wants to save my hide, who am I to stop him? Maybe he feels guilty that the rest of the department has been bad-mouthing me to the police.*

"Captain Hansen's in Times Square," Brandman went on, "checking out the Duke Theater, where they've got a production of *Oedipus Rex* going on. She wants you there. So let's see your hands." Theo obeyed, sticking his hands through a horizontal slot. Brandman cuffed him.

"Hey! I thought Hansen told you to set me free!"

"She did." Brandman unlocked the door and led Theo out. "But I don't trust you, Schultz. Somebody's lying here. Remember those puzzle pieces you keep talking about—well, they don't fit. Not anymore. So you'll stay in cuffs until I say otherwise." He began to march Theo out of the room, but Freeman stopped him with a hand to his shoulder.

"Jake," she said quietly, "seems Schultz's phone's been buzzing like crazy. Someone's trying to tell him something." She handed Brandman the phone.

"Let me see that," Theo said, sure it was Selene.

Brandman ignored him and scrolled through the text messages. "From Everett Halloran," he said aloud. "'Try the Liberty Theater on Forty-second Street. It's been abandoned for years.'" He scowled at Theo. "What's this all about?"

"He found it? It was his idea in the first place," Theo explained. "To look for a hidden theater. Come on, Detective, you don't really think I'm guilty, do you, if Helen's *fiancé* trusts me? Now let's stop wasting time and get to that theater."

"Captain Hansen said I should take you to the Duke, and that's exactly what I'm going to do," Brandman said, slipping Theo's phone into his pocket. "If she wants to go on a goose chase with you, let her."

From the backseat of Brandman and Freeman's car, Theo watched the lights of Times Square flash up ahead. Even with the detectives' siren blaring, they made no progress. Traffic stood still around them. "What's going on?"

"Your buddy Geraldine has blocked traffic into and out of Times Square," Brandman replied. "That hasn't happened since September eleventh. Everything's a goddamn terrorist attack to these people."

"But we've got to hurry. The rituals begin at night. It might've already started."

Brandman honked his horn, but the cab driver in front of them only turned around and waved his hands in frustration. In a traffic jam like this, there was simply nowhere to go. The detective pulled at his mustache for a moment, then turned off the car, leaving his lights flashing. "Freeman, stay with the vehicle." He got out and opened Theo's door. "Come on, we're walking." He held Theo by the elbow and propelled him down Forty-second Street. Before long, they ran up against a crowd so large it blocked the sidewalks entirely. "She's going to get people hurt," Brandman muttered. He tried to force his way through the crowd, but to no avail. He detoured downtown a block and dragged Theo through the south entrance of the Times Square Hilton.

"Shortcut," he explained.

Brandman was almost through to the Forty-second Street lobby exit when Theo skidded to a halt, staring at a photo on the wall.

"Detective! Wait!" He gestured to the photo. Teal walls, battered red seats, a faded, ancient show curtain hanging from the peeling proscenium. The photo looked recent, but the theater was clearly very old. The caption underneath read, *Liberty Theater*. "Where is this?" Theo begged the hotel doorman. "Please, it's urgent."

The doorman pointed to the wall on which the photo hung. "It's right there. Behind the wall. They can't destroy it because it's landmarked, but it's been boarded up for years, and now it's covered by Madame Tussaud's Wax Museum next door."

"Come on." Brandman pulled Theo's arm, trying to drag him away.

"Hold on!" No way he was going to be this close to the hidden theater without checking it out. "Has anyone gone in tonight?"

"Well, yes, actually," said the doorman. "A team of architects and contractors. They're going to turn the theater into a restaurant next year. They came to look around."

"Five men?"

"Four. And a woman," added the doorman.

Brandman stopped pulling on Theo. "Goddamn it."

"How do we get in?" Theo demanded.

"It's not open to the public, sir."

Before Theo could grab the doorman and shake him, Brandman flashed his badge. "Show me the entrance. Now."

"Right there." An innocuous double door. It could've been a custodial closet.

Brandman placed his ear to the door. "Drumming," he whispered. "Very faint." He requested backup on the radio.

"We've got to get in there *now!*" Theo insisted.

"Not until backup arrives with—" A shrill scream emerged from inside the theater. Brandman drew his gun from the holster inside his suit jacket. He met Theo's glance. "All right, I'm going in." He put his hand on the doorknob, then looked back at Theo, annoyed.

"You can leave me out here," said Theo. "Hook my handcuffs

to a pipe or something while you face a bunch of angry cult initiates all by yourself. Or you can take me in with you and let me help translate whatever Ancient Greek they're spouting."

Brandman growled. "If you make a sound, or warn them in any way, I will put a bullet through you, do you understand?"

Theo nodded. "We're on the same side."

"We'll see." Brandman nodded to the doorman. "Do not let anyone through this door except the NYPD, got it?"

The cop opened the door and slipped inside, gun in one hand and Theo's elbow in the other.

———◁◦▷———

When Selene's phone chimed, she nearly laughed. How typical: an epic battle of ancient deities, interrupted by the most mundane of twenty-first-century intrusions.

"Are you going to get that?" Paul asked.

Selene didn't answer, just circled around the bed toward him, unwilling to hurl a javelin over their mother's prostrate form. Paul held a guitar case in one hand.

"Is that where you keep your bow?" she asked, judging how fast he could open it.

"It's where I keep my guitar." He held the case like a shield in front of him. "I'd rather it not get stabbed, but better it than me."

"Don't bother playing innocent. You tried to kill me last night."

"Why would I try to kill you? We're day and night. Civilization and wildness. One without the other is meaningless."

"I've lived without you in my life for a long time now. A more permanent parting won't be too hard to take."

Paul flinched. "Is that how you really feel? After everything we've been through together? I've only ever tried to protect you."

"Yet you've brought me nothing but grief."

Paul's eyes flicked to the woman on the bed. "Thank you for

waiting until she was gone to say that. She couldn't have borne it—you know how she always wanted us to reconcile."

"Only because she didn't know what you really are."

"And what am I? God of Light who no longer controls the sun? God of Music who loses his voice after the third week on tour? God of Healing who can't even save his own mother?" Tears sprang afresh to his eyes. "Even when all my other names were meaningless, I was still the Son of Leto. And if Mother were still alive, I would fight to save myself, for her sake. But now, if I'm not even the Delian Twin anymore..." He shrugged. "I'm not sure what point there is to any of it." He lowered the guitar case slowly. "So go ahead, Artemis." He closed his eyes, but the tears still came, streaming down his cheeks like rain. "Put me out of my misery. I'm sure that javelin will do the trick—I'm not really divine, any more than you are."

Selene tested the weight of the shaft. Her phone chimed again.

Paul groaned and cracked opened his eyes. "Please get that. It's ruining the solemnity of the moment."

One eye still on her brother, she reached for her phone with her left hand, intending to turn it off. Then she saw who'd sent the text.

The cult's at a theater hidden behind the Times Square Hilton and they've got another woman, it read. *I'm going in after them, but if I don't make it out, then it's up to you. Don't let them win, Selene. Do that for me, at least.*

Selene stared at the text for a moment longer. Then she looked up at her brother. He stood with his guitar case hanging by his side, his eyes still puffy and red, resigned to death. "You're not the killer," she said softly.

"I can't believe you thought I was. I am my mother's son, you know."

———◇———

Darkness swallowed Theo and Brandman as they entered the theater's lobby. Drumming rolled swiftly from somewhere nearby, stirring Theo's already racing heart. Brandman had consented to give him his phone back, although he still hadn't removed Theo's cuffs. Theo wondered what Selene would do when she got his text. On the one hand, he didn't want to drag her into danger. On the other, he desperately wanted her to show up with a new bow and kick some ass.

The chanting began. Brandman tugged on Theo's arm. "What're they saying?" he breathed into Theo's ear.

He translated the Ancient Greek in a whisper: "We sing to celebrate the Maid, that she might bring forth new life from the earth." Then a soft, high-pitched singing began. A woman's voice, tremulous and thin. "That's not Greek anymore. I don't know what it is," Theo murmured. "It doesn't even sound Indo-European."

Theo heard a click. Brandman had drawn the safety on his gun. "So they *are* terrorists."

"I don't know if..." Theo began, but Brandman had already released him. He could see the man's outline very dimly, black on black. A tiny amount of orange light seeped through a crack beneath a nearby door. Brandman eased the door open and slipped through, his gun raised. Theo followed right behind, despite Brandman's stern gesture to stay put.

The two men crouched behind the last row of seats, peering down the aisle toward the cavernous bare stage. In the center, a small fire hissed and crackled, illuminating the figures around it in grotesque shadow. Only four men now, not five. The one Selene had shot in the stomach at Rockefeller Center had likely never recovered from his wound. As before, they wore cloaks and monstrous wooden masks. One danced in a frenzied circle to the beat of another initiate's drum. The hierophant, tall and broad in his flowing purple robes, stood watching with a bronze sword clasped in his hand. The final *mystes* pointed a knife at the woman, who faced the back of the stage, her wrists bound behind her back. Six stiff braids of curly black hair surrounded her skull like a melting crown, swaying in time to her choked, tear-laden song.

"We have to help her," Theo hissed.

"Not without backup."

"You're just going to let them—"

"I'm one gun versus four armed men."

"Just shoot them!"

"I'd risk hitting the woman."

Theo was tired of excuses. He scuttled out from behind the seats on his elbows, cursing the handcuffs, and half crawled, half ran down the aisle. Immersed in their dance, the *mystai* never even turned his way. The woman's song grew suddenly louder, more desperate, and Theo had the abrupt realization that it was Navajo. Then the woman revolved in her dance until she faced the audience. She lifted her head. Gabriela opened her tear-filled eyes and met Theo's stunned stare.

———◄○►———

Selene felt as if she'd regained the use of a limb long atrophied. She'd learned over the years to compensate for her twin's absence. To forget how lonely she was, to force away the memories of music and companionship. "Come with me," she said now, holding out a hand to her brother. "We were always stronger together."

Paul collapsed back into the chair beside his mother's bed. "To do what?"

"To save Theo Schultz."

"Theo?" Paul's eyes narrowed. "Wait...you mean the *Pervy Professor*, who's been all over the TV? Pale. Tall. Skinny."

"He's not *skinny*. He's stronger than he looks. And right now he's walking into a trap."

"Since when have you cared about the fates of thanatoi?" he demanded.

I don't know, she thought. *Maybe since Theo Schultz reminded me how to laugh.* But she said simply, "Maybe since I've become one."

"Or since you've fallen in love with one."

"What?"

"I've known you since we shared a womb. Yours was the first face I saw, even before Mother's. I've only seen that look on your face one other time—when you spoke of Orion."

"Don't you dare say his name. Not after what you did to him."

"You can't have it both ways," he said with a bitter laugh. "You can't ask for my help and still refuse to forgive me. I did what I did because if you slept with Orion, if you broke your vows of virginity, you'd have been banished from Olympus. Lost all your powers."

"It was *my* decision to make. Not yours."

"Fine. But I'm not about to help you rescue some mortal so you can sleep with him and ruin your life."

"I'm not going to *sleep* with Theo. He's a *friend.*"

"With your nymphs gone, I've been your only friend, Moonshine, don't you remember? No one else could understand you. No one else could love you with all your faults. Except Mother." He took Leto's hand in his own, stroking the tracery of empty veins. When he looked up at Selene once more, his eyes were hard. "Don't you see? We couldn't save her. We can't save ourselves. The Fates have spun the thread of our lives, long and shining like the heavens, and now their shears hover above us, ready to snip. So go ahead, Selene. Waste your last days on a mortal. But I'm not going to help."

—◦—

Theo held a finger to his lips to stop Gabriela from calling out his name. He stared at her hard, willing her to hear his unspoken promise: *I will get you out of this.* He crawled closer to the stage. Now he could feel the warmth from the flames.

The tall hierophant stepped out of the circle and approached Gabriela with his bronze sword. She stopped her song with a strangled gasp.

"Keep singing!" the man cried. She obeyed, stumbling and stuttering over the words. He reached for a handful of her black curls, sliced off a hank, and tossed it into the fire. Then he drew his blade across Gabriela's left wrist. She screamed. A third man rushed forward with a flask to collect the blood.

Theo had no plan. No weapon. It didn't matter. He dashed toward Gabriela.

Detective Brandman beat him to it.

Gun raised, the detective vaulted over the orchestra pit. "Police! Hands in the air!"

Gabriela crouched down with her hands over her head.

"Block the door!" the hierophant shouted. One of the *mystai* jumped off the stage and sprinted up the aisle to obey.

Theo hollered a wordless battle cry and rushed the hierophant, but a skinny *mystes* tackled him before he could reach the priest—they crashed to the stage in a tangle of limbs and robes. Theo slipped his cuffed hands over the man's head and clasped him in a bear hug. Somewhere, dimly, he heard a crash as one of the initiates overturned something to block the entrance to the theater. Then pounding and shouts as the police tried to get inside. *God, please hurry,* Theo thought.

"Drop the weapon, *now*, or I will shoot!" came Brandman's cry.

An instant later, gunshots pocked the air. Theo risked a glance at the detective. With Gabriela clutched in one arm, Brandman aimed his gun at the hierophant. Every time he fired, the hierophant swung the blade in an arcing blur, deflecting the bullet. Brandman fired one more time. The hierophant raised his sword again. This time, the bullet ricocheted off the weapon and back toward the cop, striking him in the chest.

The detective pitched forward, carrying Gabriela with him. Her head slammed the ground with a sickening thud. She lay unmoving in Brandman's arms, a pool of blood widening beneath them.

"NO!" Theo screamed, lurching toward his friend. The *mystes* slid from his grasp, but Theo didn't care. Someone tackled him from behind. He slammed face-first into the ground, a bony knee jabbing his spine. Theo's cuffed hands were trapped beneath his body. He wriggled uselessly in the man's arms.

"Just in time, Theo," whispered a familiar voice in his ear. "But did you have to bring the cops? Why do you always have to throw a wrench in our plans?"

Theo twisted, searching out the man behind the mask. But he didn't need to see his captor's pockmarked face to know that Bill Webb, esteemed chairman of the Columbia Classics Department, held him in his grasp.

On the other side of the stage, the stocky *mystes* started to move toward Gabriela's prostrate form. A lock of red hair peeked out from the edge of his mask. *Nate Balinski,* Theo realized. *But why is he doing this?* He struggled in vain against Webb's grip, wondering how a man with cancer could restrain him so easily. Then he nearly gagged as the smell of rotten fruit wafted toward him on Webb's panting breath. *They're too drugged with kykeon to feel any pain. Jesus, they've been drinking it all week,* he realized, remembering the glasses of "scotch" Fritz Mossburg, Nate Balinski, and Martin Andersen had toted through the office.

Police sirens pierced the air as the sound of splitting wood echoed from the lobby. Everyone froze.

"Leave the woman," ordered the hierophant. Theo knew that voice. It no longer rasped like it had the night of the *Pompe*. But its rich, melodious timbre filled him with dread.

The hierophant stepped toward Theo and gripped him on the shoulder. A familiar, overlong, manly clasp. Then he pushed back his purple hood, revealing an elegant tumble of black curls, and removed his mask.

Everett Halloran's dark eyes glinted in the firelight.

"We've got the sacrifice we need right here."

Chapter 41

THE LAUREL BEARER

Selene arrived in front of the Hilton just in time to see a team of paramedics emerge from the lobby, supporting a short, full-figured woman whom Selene recognized, with a shock, as Theo's friend Gabriela.

Selene pounded the top of the police barricade. "Tell Captain Hansen that Selene DiSilva's here and has crucial information for her," she told the sergeant standing guard. "Tell her she has to let me through." She tried to sound rational, but she had to use every ounce of will not to grab the policeman's baton and throttle him with it. Captain Hansen appeared, looking like she hadn't slept in days.

"Somehow, I'm not surprised to see you here, Ms. DiSilva."

"Where's Schultz, Gerry?" Selene demanded. "Is he okay?"

The captain raised her eyebrows at the old nickname. "We have no idea."

"What?" Selene's heart skittered. "He was here, I know."

"He and Detective Brandman were on their way to meet up with me when they interrupted the cult inside an abandoned theater. Right under our noses, but we never would've found it. But Gabriela Jimenez said both men risked their own lives to save her. I'm afraid the detective was shot. He didn't make it. And the last thing Ms. Jimenez remembered before she blacked out was Schultz being held on the ground by one of the perps."

"I need to get inside." One thought tormented her: *It's my fault Theo went in there without me to protect him.*

"He's not in there," the captain said. "We searched the entire theater. There's no sign of any of them. I'm not letting you into the crime scene, Ms. DiSilva, and don't even *think* about breaking in this time."

"I don't know what you—"

"A Dr. Gregory Kim from Natural History contacted us earlier today. He'd been inexplicably unconscious for the last twenty-four hours or so, but when he woke up, he reported that a tall, black-haired woman had impersonated a police officer and then returned a specimen that had been stolen, we now believe, by members of the cult. We got the surveillance tapes from the museum, showing you and Professor Schultz entering the building yesterday afternoon." Her face remained stern, no hint of a smile on her lips. Selene could only be grateful they didn't have footage of her zip line exit. That would've been even harder to explain. "There's a lot you're not telling me, Ms. DiSilva."

"Are you going to arrest me?" Selene tensed her muscles, ready to flee or fight. She wouldn't let anything stand in the way of finding Theo.

Geraldine stared at her for a moment. "I don't think your mother would thank me for that."

"No."

"I think she'd want me to focus on tracking down these killers instead. When it came to men who hurt women, she was relentless." She allowed Selene a familiar smile, tinged with sadness. "And so far, you and Professor Schultz have provided our most reliable leads. You're a mystery, young woman."

"I guess it runs in the family."

She sighed. "Before you go, Ms. Jimenez wants to talk to you." She escorted Selene to where Theo's friend sat beside a solicitous paramedic. Before Gerry turned to go, she said, "And next time you feel like playing cop, you should take the Police Officer Exam. We could use a good woman like you."

"I'm fine, I'm fine," Gabriela was saying, batting at the EMT's hand as he waved two fingers in front of her face. Gauze encircled her left wrist. "Just a mild concussion and a little loss of blood, for Christ's sake." She looked up as Selene approached. "Where the fuck have you been?"

"What do you mean?"

"I thought you were Theo's *partner* in this. At least that's what he seemed to think. Where were you?"

"We had a disagreement," Selene said stiffly.

Gabriela stood up from the back of the ambulance. "I said, lay off," she barked at the paramedic who tried to hold her back. "If you want to straitjacket me, go right ahead, and I'll have my lawyer sue you." The man backed off, hands raised in submission. She turned to Selene. "You need to find Theo."

"That's why I'm here. Who were the men who captured you?"

"I have no idea. They showed up at my apartment in hoods and masks and disguised their voices. I asked them—why me? And they said my death would be the perfect punishment for Theo."

"I don't understand . . . Why're they targeting him?"

"I thought you'd know the answer to that." Gabriela was nearly shouting. "What have you gotten him mixed up in?"

I don't even know anymore, Selene realized. She'd thought Paul would choose Theo as his Corn King because of her feelings for him. But if Paul wasn't the hierophant, who else would be jealous enough to target her new friend? *Unless Theo's kidnapping has nothing to do with me.* Perhaps his role as a Makarites, a title he earned through his own years of passionate study, made him a prime candidate for sacrifice. Dennis had said the gods couldn't stay away from a Blessed One. *If that's true,* she thought, *Cursed One would be a better name.*

"Can you tell me anything else about the cult members? Height? Weight? Eye color?" Selene asked Gabriela. "Did any of them seem unusually tall or strong?"

"Look at me! I'm five feet tall and haven't been to the gym in about...oh that's right...*ever*. *Everyone* seems unusually tall and strong to me. Besides, I was a little distracted by the whole being tied up and almost sacrificed part."

"If you don't know anything, then I need to go." She started to walk away.

"Go where?" Gabriela demanded, stopping Selene in her tracks.

"Anywhere. Everywhere." She knew nothing about the hierophant anymore, nothing about his initiates. She didn't even have a clue where the climactic *Mysteriotides Nychtes* would take place. But she knew talking to Gabriela wasn't getting her anywhere.

"Great. Sounds like a plan," Gabriela sneered. "Try thinking like Theo instead. And I don't mean the reckless, impulsive, always getting himself into trouble version of Theo. I mean the version that was the youngest tenured professor in the history of Columbia Classics. He'd start at the beginning and trace the whole story so he could see where it's headed next."

"He always thought Helen's research would have all the answers. But we never found it."

"Did you look in her apartment?"

"The cops had the place surrounded."

Gabriela gave her an incredulous glare. "I saw you *zip line* out a sixth-floor window. You're telling me you're scared of a few cops?"

"I wasn't quite myself at the time."

Gabriela waved a bandaged arm at the dozens of police officers bustling through the streets. "It looks like the cops are busy at the moment anyway. So I don't care who you have to knock unconscious, or how many doors you have to break through—just go save my friend."

After stopping by her house to pick up Hippo, Selene made her way to Helen Emerson's apartment.

A timid voice answered her knock, asking what she wanted.

"It's about Helen," she explained to the closed door.

"I don't want to speak to any reporters," came the muffled reply.

"I'm not a reporter. I'm a..." Selene stopped before she could say "private investigator." "A friend of Theo Schultz." Hippo woofed softly at the closed door.

The young woman who opened it looked like she'd been crying for days. Her lank brown hair hung in a messy ponytail, and she wore an overlarge sweatshirt and pajama pants. "I've been watching it all on TV. He was really kidnapped? Is there any news?" she asked breathlessly. "Have they found him yet?"

"No. That's why we need your help." Selene introduced herself and her dog.

"Ruth Willever," the woman whispered in return, holding out a tentative hand toward Hippo. The dog sniffed cautiously at her fingers, then at her fuzzy blue slippers, and finally gave Ruth's palm an approving lick.

The woman ushered Selene to a canvas couch, taking the rattan footstool for herself. Hippo moved to lie at Selene's feet, but she gave the dog a subtle prod so she'd go to Ruth instead. From long experience, Selene knew the dog would make talking to Helen's roommate easier—while she growled at men, Hippo acted like an adoring puppy with most women. True to form, she sat her shaggy bulk next to the footstool and laid her massive head in Ruth's lap, eliciting a faint smile.

"The reporter on the news said there was no sign of Theo. Do you really think you can help find him?" Ruth said.

"I'll never forgive myself if I don't."

Ruth gave her a quizzical look, then turned her gaze back to the dog. She scratched behind Hippo's ears. "At least now they know he's innocent. I can't believe they ever thought otherwise."

"You never doubted him?"

"He's a good man. One of the best. And Helen might not have known it, but she traded down when she fell for Everett." Her voice had fallen to a whisper, as if she were afraid to say even that much.

Selene wondered if Ruth had ever told Theo how she felt about him. The thought made her cheeks hot. She forced herself to speak gently. It was less of a trial than usual.

"I need to find Helen's research, Ruth. It might have the clue we need."

"The police searched her room already."

"Do you mind if I take a look?"

It was a small chamber, immaculate despite the police search. A pristine white coverlet offset colorful Turkish pillows on the double bed. A small whitewashed desk, bare of papers, books or photos. Selene opened a drawer. Empty. "The cops took everything," Ruth offered from the doorway. She hadn't put a toe over the threshold. Looking around the bare room, Selene felt hope slip away. There wasn't much time left. Hippo brushed past Ruth and came to sit by Selene.

"What about you, Hippolyta?" Selene asked softly, stroking the dog's head. "Any ideas? I could use some help here." The dog dutifully began to sniff around the room, snuffling from one end to the other. She barreled under the bed, nearly lifting its legs off the ground.

"They looked under there," said Ruth. But Hippo would not be dissuaded. She snuffed a little longer, then began to whimper.

"She's probably just smelling a mouse in the walls," Selene said, not daring to hope. "Come on, mutt, get out of there and let me see." Hippo scuttled backward, and Selene shifted the brass bedstead farther into the room. The dog whimpered again and pawed at one of the floorboards. The edge of the narrow plank was chipped, as if by a blunt tool. Selene dug a key out of her pocket and levered up the floorboard. The faint smell of bay leaves wafted into the room. There, beneath a bundle of dried laurel, lay two thick sheaves of papers. *I should've known,* Selene thought. *Theo said she liked hidden compartments, secret ciphers.* The first document contained images of papyri fragments—thousands of them—all painstakingly pieced together to form an imperfect whole. Beside the Greek characters were Helen's own translations. The other stack of papers contained only her cramped script. The cover page read:

A MYSTERY SOLVED
THE BIRTH, DEATH, AND REBIRTH OF THE ELEUSINIAN MYSTERIES
by Helen Emerson

Selene sat back heavily on the floor and began to leaf through the stack. In the lower left corner of each page was a number: five hundred and twenty-three pages of tiny, nearly illegible script. Selene glanced out the small window. The sky glowed pastel blue. "Ruth, I'm going to need your help." She held out the second half of the papers. "I can't read all of this fast enough."

"I'm just a scientist," she demurred.

"This isn't exactly my field either. Just tell me if you see any clue about the location of the Telesterion—the Hall of Completion where the climax of the Mystery, the *Mysteriotides Nychtes*, takes place."

Ruth stepped cautiously into the room and sat beside Selene on the floor. Neither woman dared disturb the neatly made bed. They began to read.

After a few hours, her eyes burning from squinting at the minuscule writing, Selene decided Helen's paper would've revolutionized the study of Ancient Greece—if she'd lived to publish it. Everything was just as Dennis had revealed. In the first chapter, she explained that she'd found evidence within the Oxyrhynchus papyri that the Greeks in Eleusis had once practiced human sacrifice as an integral part of their religion, killing a Corn King every year to appease the Earth Mother, and later, in homage to Demeter and Persephone. Then, the cult transformed, replacing human sacrifice with Dionysian worship and *kykeon*. Although the Eleusinian Mysteries continued until Emperor Theodosius outlawed them in the fourth century AD, Helen hypothesized that the later, tamer version of the ritual was no longer a truly transformative experience.

Ruth gasped, interrupting Selene's reading. Face white, she held out a page.

" '*Only by re-creating and reenacting this earlier version,*' " Selene read, " '*not the sanitized alternative written about in previously recognized ancient sources, can modern scholars hope to understand the Mystery in its full power. Accordingly, this chapter will outline a New Eleusis Mystery with which we might test this hypothesis, unlocking a force long forgotten.*' "

"It was her idea," Ruth whispered. "No wonder she kept it hidden."

Selene nodded dumbly, reading ahead. " '*The original Mystery Cult, before its taming, gave nearly supernatural healing powers and longevity to its initiates. At its strongest, it may have even granted them immortality. Performed correctly, the New Eleusis rite could do the same.*' "

Oh you foolish girl, Selene thought. *You had no idea the quest for an eternal life would cut your own so cruelly short.*

The outline of Helen's new cult mirrored the events of the last few days, with a few notable exceptions. The *hiera* she suggested all related to the Earth Mother, Demeter, Persephone, and the other traditional Eleusinian deities: piglets, grain, and snakes. She made no mention of murder or mutilation during the beginning of the ritual. The targeting of virgins, the sacrifice of hounds, and the use of the boar tusk must have been the hierophant's idea.

As she skimmed over the descriptions of the first seven nights of the ritual, Selene borrowed a map of Manhattan from Ruth and spread it out before her. *Be like Theo,* she thought. *Look for the pattern, the hidden meaning on the opposite side of the vase. See how the pieces fit together.* Swiftly, she inked a dark mark on each crime scene: first the Met, where the robberies had occurred on Day One of the ritual, then the others, ending with the Liberty Theater. Six sites so far. *But seven days of Mysteries,* she realized. She pulled out the napkin with Theo's outline on it and found the missing day: the *Agyrmos,* the public gathering announcing the ritual's formal beginning. It would've taken place the night before Helen's murder, but she and Theo had never identified its location.

"What did Helen do the night before she was killed?"

"She went out before sunset. I was asleep when she got home, but it must've been after two a.m. The next morning, she seemed excited. She was...glowing almost. But she wouldn't tell me what was going on. Said it was a secret. A lot of things had become secret. These last few months I hardly saw her. She'd always been single-minded about her work, but this was unusual, even for her. She was always holed up in her room, off in the library, or out with Everett."

Selene turned back to the papers. Helen wrote that the *Agyrmos* must take place in an open space, as close to the center of the city as possible. To conjure the theatrical rituals of the ancient world, an outdoor amphitheater would be best.

She looked back at the map. The center of the city was Central Park. And there in the middle of the park, not far from the Natural History Museum, was the Delacorte Theater, a large amphitheater best known for its free Shakespeare performances every summer. In the fall, however, the amphitheater stood abandoned. A late-night gathering on its stage might escape notice. She marked the location on the map.

She kept reading, skipping forward until she reached the

eighth and ninth nights of the rituals, the *Mysteriotides Nychtes*. The papyri had revealed that the early, pre-Olympian version of the Unspeakable rituals that formed the rite's climax would've taken place in a natural underground chamber, a symbolic representation of the Earth Mother's womb. Helen believed that the Golden Age Athenians had built their Telesterion above this original site. But in order to be true to the ritual's more ancient origins, she argued that the climax of the New Eleusis Mystery should take place, once again, in a cave.

"Huh," Ruth said, pulling a photo from between the manuscript pages. "I wonder why she put this in here."

"Let me see." A picture of Helen and a dark, broad-shouldered man so handsome Selene had to catch her breath.

"That's Everett," Ruth was saying.

"No. It's not." Selene took the photo, her hands trembling, staring at a face intimately familiar—one she never thought she'd see again.

"What do you mean?" Ruth snatched the picture back. "How would you know? I've known him for a year—it's definitely him."

Selene looked down once more at the map before her.

That's when she saw the pattern.

Riverside Park in the northwest, Mount Sinai Hospital in the northeast, the old cemetery beneath the Waldorf in Midtown East, the hidden Liberty Theater in Midtown West. The Metropolitan Museum of Art and the Museum of Natural History strung through the middle of the city on either side of Central Park, with the Delacorte amphitheater between them. A star for each broad shoulder. A star for each strong leg. Three stars for his belt.

Only the sword was missing.

The hierophant was no god. Only the son of one.

The Hunter had returned.

Chapter 42

HURLER OF THE JAVELIN

Icy water dripped onto Theo's cheek. He woke with a start, surfacing from a dream of murdered women only to plunge into a waking nightmare. Handcuffed and gagged, he lay on damp stone, his pulse racing. Another cold drop struck his face. Rolling out of the way, he realized his captors had tied a rope around his ankles and secured it to an iron ring hammered into the rock wall. He could only move a few feet in either direction.

Looking around at his stone prison, Theo couldn't help thinking, *See, Brandman, they may not have used it for the* Asklepia, *but there* is *a cave in Manhattan.* At least, he hoped he was still in Manhattan. *The only thing worse than being kidnapped would be being kidnapped* and *spending the night in Staten Island.*

Mortared stones plugged most of the tall, narrow entrance, but a low opening admitted a thin sunbeam. *They must've knocked me unconscious, and I've been passed out all day,* he realized. Fighting the sense of growing panic, he tried to take stock of his surroundings. Birds chirped nearby, and he thought he could hear the lapping of water. Through the cave's mouth, he glimpsed the bottom of a narrow staircase hewn into a rock face, descending

into muddy, leaf-strewn ground. *A cave in a park then,* he surmised. He opened his mouth to scream for help, then remembered the duct tape across his lips. He tried shouting anyway, but
only a weak moan emerged. He beat the ground with the heels
of his shoes, but the muffled thuds would never carry. Theo
struggled against the metal handcuffs and the ropes around his
ankles, but to no avail.

Finally, exhaustion and fear left him motionless, helplessly
watching as the sunlight crept across the ground, turning from
yellow to gold to orange. When it disappeared entirely, the cave
plunged into twilight. *The cult will come for me soon,* he realized.
No use calling for help any longer. Sane New Yorkers didn't
wander in parks after dark. *Only deranged classicists bent on torturing their least favorite colleague.*

His fellow professors' roles started to fall into place. Bill Webb
wanted to lead the cops astray. That's why he'd worked so hard
to implicate Theo. Nate Balinski must have learned how to brew
kykeon from Dennis during one of their old grad school parties.
Fritz Mossburg worked as a part-time consultant at the Met; he
would have had access to the stolen vases. His absence from Hel-
en's memorial service now made sense—he must have been the
initiate shot in the stomach at Rockefeller Center. Likely he was
now dead, hence the presence of only four men at the Liberty
Theater. Martin Andersen—awkward, harmless Martin—had
used the shoes he'd borrowed from Theo to make the footprints
at Helen's crime scene. Any one them could've gotten Theo's
hair off the back of his desk chair and planted it in the hospital
basement. And Everett? Passionate, loving, charismatic Everett? He had played it all perfectly—luring Theo right into his
clutches. But *why*? Why would any of them join the cult in the
first place?

Theo leaned back against the damp wall, slowly thumping
his head against the stone. *If I knock hard enough, I could knock*

myself senseless again. Maybe then I won't notice when they kill me. Would that be better? Had Helen known she was about to die? He realized suddenly that Brandman never told him whether she was already dead when they cut her apart. *Will Everett kill me first? Or cut off my cock while I watch? Burn it maybe. A sacrifice to the gods. That would be more in keeping with the tradition of the Mysteries, I suppose.* Even facing death, he was still trying to figure out the scholarly angle. He laughed at himself, the sound a choked, muffled cough through the duct tape. Someone watching would've thought he'd lost his mind. *At least laughing's better than pissing myself with fear.*

Footsteps outside the cave. He crawled forward on his knees and elbows as far as the rope would allow, but could see nothing in the darkness except the faint outline of the narrow entrance, a dark slightly less chthonic than that within the cave. *Be like Selene,* he thought, *HEAR!* Yes, he could hear more than one set of footsteps descending the stone stairs. Three, maybe, he wasn't sure. Slow, deliberate, loud. Not Selene, then. *How absurd that I still think she's going to rescue me. She has no idea where I am.*

The bright circle of a flashlight beam skittered across the bottom of the step and into the cave, seeking him out. He squeezed his eyes shut as the light found his face, holding up his bound hands to block the sudden glare.

"Still alive, then," said a voice he recognized as Nate Balinski's. "Hasn't died from fear, at least."

Theo lowered his hands and blinked away the colored haloes in his vision until four hooded figures materialized before him. Three wore identical wooden masks crowned with false black hair. On the night of the *Pompe*, they'd worn the face of Comedy. Tonight, Tragedy's grotesque, twisted frown stared out malevolently from beneath their hoods.

Theo could tell one *mystes* from the other by their bearing: stocky Nate, gangly Andersen, and stooped Webb. Everett, of course, towered over them all in his purple robes. Once again, he wore the mask of an invincible warrior hero. *Fitting,* Theo thought grimly, *since despite limping off after I stabbed him with a broken bow two nights ago, he shows no signs of injury.*

Everett squatted in front of Theo and removed the gag.

As soon as he could move his lips, Theo demanded to know where Gabriela was.

Nate Balinski spoke up. "Who knows? We left her at the theater."

"If she's hurt..." Theo began.

"You should be worrying more about yourself," came Everett's cool response.

"You don't need to wear those masks, you know," said Theo. "I know who you are."

"Very smart, Theo-*bore*, as usual," Nate said, leaving his mask in place.

"How could you? Everett—you of all people. How could you kill Helen?"

"I had no choice. She had a role to play, just as you do." Everett's dark eyes glinted behind the mask.

"Oh? What role is that?"

Everett chuckled. "You're a Makarites, Theo. Didn't you know?"

"A *what?*"

"And that makes you the best bait I could ask for."

"If you mean Selene—"

"The woman with him at Rockefeller Center?" interrupted Bill Webb. "The one who killed Fritz?"

"That's one thing our genius here never figured out," said Everett, rising to his feet. He turned to his *mystai*. "She's not really a woman."

"You could've fooled me," said Nate. "Did you see the legs on that chick?"

"No, she's not a woman at all...she's a god. And so am I. Or at least, I will be." Everett pulled off his mask and flashed Theo a dazzling smile. "As soon as we kill our Corn King."

◄o►

Phoebe Hautman first visited the sacred cave in the middle of Manhattan in the midst of a blizzard in 1643. She'd been hunting along the edges of the lake when the winds kicked up. The biting cold pierced through her leather leggings and fur cloak, chilling her nearly impervious skin. The snow wouldn't kill her, but it would make for a deeply unpleasant night. She walked along the shore of a narrow cove, looking for shelter. That's when she saw the firelight beckoning through the tall, narrow cleft in the rock. She snuck to the edge of the cave entrance and peered inside.

A dozen Lenni Lenape sat huddled around their fire in a tight circle, shoulder to shoulder. Although Phoebe couldn't understand their chant, she felt a familiar, tingling tug that told her they sang to the aspect of Kishelemukong who helped them in the hunt, begging for sustenance in the depths of winter. Slowly, she entered the cave like an answer to their prayers, holding out the carcass of a white fox as an offering. They took her in without question. If they thought it strange that a white woman dressed and hunted as a man, they didn't show it. They had long ago accepted the inscrutability of Europeans.

This was a holy place, their shaman told her in his broken combination of Dutch and English. Close to the heart of the Earth, its narrow opening like a woman's cleft, its wide chamber like a mother's womb.

Phoebe returned often to the cave, even after the last Lenni Lenape had left the island. Eventually, Dianne Delia made the same pilgrimage to sit in the last ancient sacred space in Manhattan. When the city leaders built Central Park in the 1860s, the "Indian Cave" became a popular tourist attraction. Decades later, Officer Melissa DuBois patrolled it regularly. In 1929 alone, the NYPD arrested 335 men for unwanted groping in the cave's shadowy depths. In part due to the patrolwomen's protests that the place had become a magnet for perversion, the city walled up the cave in the 1930s and removed it from maps of the park. Now, few people knew it had ever existed.

The Huntress hadn't been to the cave in eighty years, but she remembered where it was, at the tip of a narrow cove on the north end of the lake, just south of Central Park's Great Lawn. Not far from the Delacorte amphitheater. Right where Orion's sword would fall. The constellation would be complete.

The sun had set by the time Selene entered the tangle of woods above the Lake. The place was a favorite destination for dog walkers during the day, but this late at night, with the chill of autumn in the air, she had it to herself. She sprinted down the curving paths, hurrying toward the two men who loved her.

Barricades labeled "Restoration in Progress. Please Keep Out" blocked her way. Orion wasn't taking any chances that a passerby might stumble upon his ceremony. She vaulted the barrier and continued to run until she saw a glimmer of moonlight reflected off the cove to her left. There, nearly hidden by the surrounding trees, rough stone steps descended a steep hill into darkness.

Javelin ready, Selene crept down the stairs. Sure enough, someone had removed the bottom portion of the stones blocking the cave entrance. She stopped with her toes brushing against the square of firelight pouring from the opening. *I am no wild girl tonight,* she reminded herself. *I will not rush headlong into the fray.* With only her javelin and kitchen knives, she'd be vulnerable to attack, and she couldn't predict Orion's reaction to her appearance. He'd almost killed her at Rockefeller Center, yet he could not have forgotten their love, any more than she had. What would it be like to look once more upon his face? To catch his dark gaze in her own? Her heart raced at the thought. She knew Orion deserved to die for the murders he committed, but for once, she ignored the imperatives of her own code. If she could forgive her brother for his crimes, didn't she owe Orion at least that much?

The voices of the *mystai* rose through the cave's mouth. *"Legomena,"* they chanted. *Things Said*—the first of the Unspeakable rites that marked the Mystery's climax. In Helen's description, the hierophant told the tale of Persephone's abduction. *But not tonight,* Selene thought, remembering Dennis's explanation of how to steal a cult. *Tonight Orion will tell our story.* As shadows swept past her, she could imagine the *mystai* dancing in a circle, masked faces awful in the firelight, eyes bright as they waited for the epiphany.

"They say that Orion was of gigantic stature and born of the earth." Her lover's voice, deep and warm. The Hunter. "But Pherecydes says that he was a son of Poseidon and Euryale. Poseidon bestowed on him the power of striding across the sea, but he was killed by the arrows of the Delian twins, and died with a wish upon his lips." Hearing him now, Selene felt an almost irresistible pull. For a moment, she imagined rushing into his arms. Surely, he wouldn't kill Theo if she asked him not to.

"But even as Orion's spirit took its place among the stars, blue-haired Poseidon took pity upon his son and sent the waves to carry his body to his watery lair. With a blast of the triton, Poseidon granted his son his heart's desire. Immortal he would rise from the sea. Immortal he would walk through the woods. Immortal he would seek his revenge upon his enemies. Now he shares the gift, bestowing immortality on those who follow him. You, my *mystai*, will grow strong by my side."

An incredulous guffaw broke the rhythm of the chant.

Selene's heart skittered. *Theo.*

"*This* is the fabulous Mystery?" His hoarse voice was nearly unrecognizable, but his sarcasm was unmistakable. "It's *plagiarism*. He stole the beginning of that from Apollodorus, for God's sake."

"Shut up, Schultz." Not Orion's voice now, but one of the *mystai*. His speech was slightly slurred. *They've already drunk the kykeon,* she realized.

"I get it, Bill," Theo went on, undeterred. "Everett promised you he'd cure your cancer with his little 'immortality ritual.' And you, Martin—did you think he could bring back your dead wife? Nate, you've always been an arrogant prick, so why not make yourself even more powerful than you already think you are? But surely you all don't believe the lies he's telling you!"

"Theo." Orion was deadly calm. "If you interrupt the ritual again, I will be forced to put the gag back on."

"Oh, sorry, don't let me interrupt. This is fascinating, really."

"I'm sure you won't be bored once it's your turn to participate."

"Yippee. Do I get a mask, too? Maybe something a bit more flattering—I don't pull off the dour tragedy thing that well. And of course, you'll have to teach me the dance steps. Unless my participation is purely sacrificial, in which case learning choreography seems like a waste of my last moments on earth."

"Don't sell yourself short," said Orion with a hint of his old charm. "You've been essential to my plans from the beginning. You made the perfect suspect, the aggrieved ex-boyfriend—thank you for distracting the police all this time. You kept them off our tail just long enough to reach the end of the ritual. It almost backfired, of course—we couldn't let you actually get taken off to jail. But a well-timed call to Captain Hansen solved that problem. You're welcome, by the way. Of course, the cops will be of no concern after we finish with you tonight—they won't be able to hurt me. No one will."

"Try untying me, and we'll see if you're right. I—" Theo's voice cut short, devolving into muffled protest. Orion had heard enough.

Once again, the Hunter took up the chant. "Tonight we sing of love found, then lost, then found once more. Tonight we sing of death defied and power restored. Tonight we sing of revenge."

Theo gave another smothered protest.

"I said *do not speak*!" Orion cried. Selene heard him drag something—or someone—across the ground, heard his indrawn breath and then the dull clap of flesh striking flesh. Theo moaned. Another strike, this one on bone. Then the thud of a fist punching soft tissue. With each strike, Selene's dream of rejoining her Hunter slipped farther out of sight, banished by her growing rage.

"ENOUGH." She ducked through the entrance, stepped into the light, and hurled the javelin.

She'd meant to stop him, to wound him, but as Orion tumbled forward, she saw the weapon had pierced clean through his heart.

In giving the Hurler of Javelins back her unerring aim, the Hunter had doomed himself to die at her hands.

Chapter 43

THE HUNTER

Selene saw Theo lying beside the fire. He gave a muffled shout of relief through his gag as he met her eyes. Livid welts marked his face. Blood trickled from a wound on his forehead.

Then Orion groaned and levered himself slowly off the ground, pushing his initiates aside so he might see Selene. For the first time in millennia, she looked upon him face-to-face. *How long have I imagined the touch of his lips on mine?* Her heart hammered in her chest. *He is dream become flesh.* Her javelin protruded through the bloody fabric of his cloak. *Yet I've killed him again.* She swallowed a cry of despair.

Ignoring the wound, Orion held out a plaintive hand toward her. "My love. You've come." His voice was as strong and smooth as ever.

She shook her head, fighting the overpowering urge to go to him. "You were hurting Theo. I—I couldn't let you do that." She blinked away stinging tears and stumbled backward, made clumsy by shock. The *mystai* moved behind her to block her way, the whites of their eyes wide behind their masks. She pulled a knife, ready to strike them down.

"You can't protect the Makarites any longer." Orion threw

back his shoulders and drew the javelin through the front of his chest in one smooth movement. Theo gave a bewildered moan through his gag.

"This"—Orion held the bloody javelin aloft—"cannot kill me. But I forgive you for trying. You wouldn't be the one I love if you did not send your grievous shafts." He granted her a brief, sad smile. "Saturday night, the wound in my side lamed me for a day. But every moment, I grow stronger." Calmly, he turned to face his *mystai*. "Behold! The Mystery is almost fulfilled."

He shrugged off his cloak and spread his arms. A neat round hole pierced his rib cage just between the swelling muscles of his bare chest. With every heaved breath, the wound grew smaller, the tissue knit closed, until finally he stood unscathed, his black eyes luminous.

A flash of light drew Selene's attention to her own hand. Only then did she realize that the kitchen knife trembled in her grasp. Relief rushed through her, making her weak. *He lives. And with him lives hope.* Surely, if she could just explain that the rituals were so dangerous even Zeus himself feared their return, then Orion would stop the killing, and she wouldn't have to destroy him once more.

Orion took a step toward her. The firelight played across the chiseled planes of his torso. She could smell him now, his sweat conjuring wild oregano crushed underfoot, heat rising from the dusty island hills, the musk of deer and boar clinging to the leaves of a cypress tree.

"It was you," she breathed. "The night after I learned my mother was dying, I lay in my bed beside my open window and dreamed you held me while I slept. But it was no dream, was it?"

"Every night for eternity I dreamed of holding you. I finally gave in."

"But how? How have you returned from the dead?"

"My father granted my wish for immortality at the moment of my death. My body fell to the bottom of the sea, but my soul stayed in the heavens where you'd put me. So I hung suspended between man and constellation for an eternity, moving through vast, frozen emptiness, crawling through endless tunnels of fire to reach this plane of existence once more." He shuddered. "Again and again, I wanted to give up, to let myself become nothing but myth. But I kept fighting—because of you. Every time you looked at the heavens and thought of me, dreamed of me, remembered our story, I moved one step closer to regaining my place in the world. Finally, many years ago, my body washed up on the shores of the Hudson, pulled here by your love. I emerged, my eyes opened, and I saw the stars above me. I claimed my soul once more. And now, finally, I am here, ready to claim something far more precious—you."

Slowly, he laid a warm hand on her arm. Before she realized what she'd done, she lowered the knife. With his other hand, he touched her cheek, her forehead, traced a lock of her hair to its blunt tip. "You are changed, my love," he said in a voice for her alone. "But still ravishing."

But he has not changed at all, she thought. *He is still the most beautiful man I've ever seen.* "You've found me. You're here. Now you can stop this madness. You don't understand what you're doing, Orion. The rituals are evil, dangerous. They will return us to a time of barbarism. So let Theo go."

He chuckled. A patronizing, indulgent sound that only increased her unease. "I did not struggle for millennia to be by your side just to have us both fade away because the thanatoi refuse to pay us homage. Look." He touched her stomach, tracing the scab of Saturday night's wound through her shirt. "Look how your ichor flows."

"Ichor is for the gods," she retorted. "I only have blood in my veins."

"Not for long," he whispered, his breath like a cool salt wind blown from the sea. Before she could react, he pulled the knife from her hand and threw it to one of his initiates. "There's no need to fear me," he promised. But in that moment, she did. She looked deep into his eyes and saw not love, not devotion, but madness. Like her father, like Cora, like so many of her old companions, Orion wandered adrift in a new world that had no room for ancient myth. And he would stop at nothing to make a place for himself once more. Reasoning with him was futile. Her hand clenched on empty air, desperate for a weapon.

He turned to his acolytes, lifting his arms as if he would raise the men to immortality through gesture alone. "Come, my *mystai*. The rite continues. *Dromena!*" The cloaked initiates repeated the word with almost sexual excitement. Then they removed their masks, and Selene recognized Bill Webb and the older, skinny professor she'd met at Theo's office. She knew the third man, probably also a professor, by his stocky build. He had slipped his knife into Jenny Thomason's throat.

Selene looked to Theo. Eyes wide with bewilderment and terror, he met her gaze.

With a single sharp pull, Orion snapped the rope that tied Theo to the rock wall, then dragged him across the stone floor to the fire. Selene moved to stop him, but Orion held out the flat of his hand. "If you come closer, I will hurt him." She stood frozen as Theo tried to right himself, but the ropes around his ankles and the handcuffs on his wrists left him twisting helplessly on the ground.

"You sweet, sorry fool," Orion said, not unkindly. "You thought you'd get away with it—sleeping with Helen behind my back. Ah, you didn't think I knew?" He crouched beside Theo, speaking only for him. "She kept no secrets from me. My power scared her, and she fled to you for a night. But once you've been with the son of a god, there's no going back to a mere mortal. Not for Helen. And not for *Artemis*." Orion patted Theo on the head as if he were one of the hounds in his hunting pack. "It all works out perfectly—as a Makarites, your sacrifice will carry more power than that of a normal mortal. More power even than a girl with *kharisma* like Jenny Thomason. You're why I found my way to Columbia in the first place—I knew only a Blessed One might know enough of the gods to help me come back to full strength—and I dared not seek help from the immortals. But then another Makarites came into my life—one far prettier than you. My lovely Helen had the answers I needed. She wanted to recruit you into the cult, you know. Wanted to share the gift of immortality with you. I might have given you that—spared you despite the power of your blood—but then you both betrayed me. She took you back into her arms, and you went willingly. That night, you signed your death warrants, my friend. You both had to be punished for your disrespect, you understand that. Her sacrifice began the rite. Yours will end it." Theo groaned, struggled even harder against his bonds. "Shh... be still, Theo. You still have time left in this world, because tonight I'll show you mercy. For the *Dromena*, you may play me, the Celestial Hunter, as I lay upon the shore, made helpless by my love. And *I* will be Apollo, the Gilded God. Tonight the true story will be told. This is *Dromena*. This is *Things Done!* Come, my Good Maiden," he said, standing and turning to Selene. "You know your role. The beginning of our story is known to all. But the end... only we know that."

The *mystai* formed a ring around the fire, with Selene, Theo, and Orion in the center. Orion nodded briefly to Webb, who pulled a bottle full of amber liquid from beneath his cloak. Selene turned her head away. "I won't drink that." She'd never partaken in Dionysus's drinks—not even the more innocuous ones. The *kykeon* would have more powerful effects on her than on someone accustomed to intoxication, and she had no intention of clouding her mind.

Orion slipped an arm around her, his grip like a steel cord encircling her ribs. "I've inhaled the burnt offerings all week. Do you see how strong I've become?" He forced the bottle between her lips and the warm, honey liquid poured down her throat. "I would make you as strong as I am." Even as his eyes grew hard with cruelty, he spoke as if coaxing a wild deer into his net. "Drink, drink, my love." She spluttered and choked, but the liquid slipped past her lips. On the ground, two professors knelt over Theo. The stocky one held him down while the skinny one removed his gag and poured the amber *kykeon* into his mouth.

When Orion released her, Selene stood swaying, blood rushing in her ears, the liquor's fire clouding her sight and setting her skin aflame. Orion thrust an arrow into her hands. Except he wasn't Orion anymore. In the haze of *kykeon*, he had transformed into Apollo—his black hair turned blond, his dark eyes golden. She looked to the ground, where Theo had lain a moment ago. Now the figure of Orion lay in his place, helpless before her. As if he'd been felled by an arrow. A voice in her ear chanted, *"Dromena, Dromena."* She shook her head violently, fighting the memories, but the *kykeon* burned through her veins.

A part of her knew she looked at Theo, not Orion, and that he merely repeated the words another whispered in his ear— a sick tragedy enacted by an unwilling puppet—but the drink transported her to a different age. She was back on the shores of a sapphire sea.

A single gold arrow stands wavering in his chest, but still Orion lives. He is half-mortal, true, but his father is a son of Kronos and he is not easy to kill. With my twin by my side, I walk toward him, the wet sand dragging at my feet. My Hunter lies with his face toward the heavens, his bronze sword far from his grasp. Many times, I have lain with my cheek against his heart. Now I watch the blood pulse from his wound in the same familiar rhythm.

"My love," he whispers as the red bubbles from his mouth. "What have you done?"

"You shamed me," I say, willing my voice to remain cold. "You, who said you loved me. You forced my companion Merope to be yours."

"No." He drags his hand to press against his bleeding heart. "I came

to the shore to speak with my father Poseidon, that he might grant me immortality as Zeus granted it to Heracles." His eyes, so often glowing with the thrill of the hunt, are now bright with tears. "Then I could marry you, Artemis. Chaste or not, I'd be your faithful companion until the end of the world."

"You lie," I spit. I meet his eyes. The black eyes of the man I loved. Or are they green? I do not look away. It doesn't matter if his eyes are those of a god's son or a mortal man. I cannot trust anyone.

I pull another golden arrow from the quiver upon my back. I fix my eyes upon my target's throat.

"SELENE!" A voice from the present snapped her from her trance. For a moment, her vision cleared. Theo lay beneath her, fighting through the haze of *kykeon* to scream her name. She followed his gaze to the arrow in her own hand, poised above his neck, ready to strike.

"Do it, my love, just as you did then," urged Orion. "You killed me once. You thrust the arrow through my throat with your bare hands. Now do it again. So I might rise stronger than ever."

"SELENE, it's *me!*" Theo begged once more. She shook her head once, twice, then let the arrow clatter to the ground.

"Theo . . ." she whispered. *"I'm sorry . . ."* Then she stumbled, weak-kneed. Orion caught her, pressing her gently against him.

"Give him more," he commanded with an angry glance at Theo. The skinny acolyte splashed more *kykeon* across Theo's face while Webb held his jaws open. His eyes slid out of focus and he quieted once more.

"You haven't saved him. The story's not over until he's dead," Orion whispered in Selene's ear. Her eyes fluttered open and closed as she struggled for consciousness.

"Continue!" Orion said, louder this time, his voice dropping into a hierophant's thrumming tone of command. Selene felt the present wobble around her as the *kykeon* regained its hold, engulfing her in the past.

"You've done what you must, Moonshine," says my twin. "Your lover was a raper of women."

Merope, beloved nymph, defiled companion, runs panting to the shore and falls upon my feet. I crouch beside her, pulling her into my embrace.

"I'll never let anyone hurt you again," I promise her. "You were right not to trust Orion."

"No! Please, Artemis, I've run all this way to stop you," the nymph tells me, breathless. "He's innocent! He was faithful to you. It is your brother who has betrayed you."

The world spins. Cold dread captures my breath. A true memory. Not the outline of the story as told by the ancients. The memory as I lived it. The memory I can never forget.

Apollo's voice, usually as warm as the sun itself, is cold and hard as he comes to stand beside me. "You are the Virgin Goddess. I had to save you from throwing away your chastity, and your godhood along with it. I must be the only man you will ever love." He grabs my hand and presses it against his heart.

I rip from his grasp. "I will never forgive your lies." I strike him once. Red blooms upon his cheek. His eyes turn hard.

I race back to the shore, for just as a goddess takes life, so she may give it back again. But I'm too late. My Hunter's body is gone, claimed once more by his father the Sea.

In my grief, I pull forth eight arrows. One by one, I shoot them into the sky, placing my lover in the firmament to be worshiped for eternity. Hoping that somehow, someday, the Fates will bring us together again—even if it means I, too, must die to take my place beside him in the stars.

Chapter 44

THE CORN KING

Theo awoke trussed like a pig on the floor of the cave. A headache hammered against his skull with a fury he hadn't experienced since the worst of his grad school hangovers. Stabbing pain radiated along the bridge of his nose where his glasses had gouged a deep trench while he slept. He worked his bruised jaw from side to side for a moment, struggling to remember why he wasn't dead.

A single beam of red sunlight inched across the ground. As he watched, it narrowed to a fiery sliver then vanished, thrusting the cave further into twilight. *Sunset?* he marveled. *Again? Have I slept away an entire day? Or is everything I remember from yesterday a dream?* The latter seemed more likely. Charming Everett Halloran an invincible psychopath who styled himself the Greek hero Orion and believed Selene was the goddess Artemis? He ran his tongue along his cracked lips, grateful they'd left the duct tape off. *Kykeon-induced hallucinations,* he decided. *That's the only explanation.* Trying to ease his aching ribs, he rolled over.

Right into Selene.

He realized he'd never seen her sleeping before. She looked younger and more vulnerable than he'd ever seen her. Long, dark lashes brushed her high cheekbones. Her full lips were parted, just a little. *She came back for me,* Theo thought. *Just as I would have for her.*

"Well, you're not a hallucination," he murmured.

Selene's eyes snapped open.

Theo had a million questions for her, but one came first. "Did I dream the part where they left Gabriela at the theater? Please tell me she's okay."

"She's fine. I left her telling off the police and infuriating the paramedics."

"Thank God."

"Your detective friend wasn't so lucky."

"Shit." Theo's heart sank. "It's my fault. He wanted to wait for backup."

"From what I've heard, if you'd waited another minute, Gabriela would've been the sacrifice. With Brandman, the cult had the killing it needed to complete the *Pannychis*. He died to save her. There are worse ways for a cop to go."

Theo nodded, but he couldn't escape the heavy mantle of guilt. He'd gotten Brandman killed, put Gabi in danger, and now Selene's life, too, was in peril.

"Stop feeling guilty and let's get the hell out of here." Selene moved to stand, but the fetters on her ankles and wrists kept her teetering on her knees. "By the Styx…" she muttered, pulling fruitlessly at the ropes.

"That reminds me… You're not a goddess, are you?"

"Don't be ridiculous," she shot back.

"Oh, good. Just checking. And Everett—I know Helen thought he was God's gift and all, but he's not actually *immortal*, right? I have a vague recollection of your throwing a spear through his chest and him just plucking it out again."

"It was a javelin. What kind of classicist are you?"

"One currently more concerned with surviving the night than with identifying ancient weaponry. Sue me." He forced a short laugh, but fear slid down his spine and wriggled into his stomach.

"You know Everett's name means 'strong as a wild boar' in German, right?" she said with a hint of pique. "We should've known this was all about Orion."

Theo levered himself to an awkward sitting position. "I only speak Greek, Latin, and a smattering of Acadian. German just makes me think of Nazi movies." He looked at her more closely. "I don't remember much about last night, but I could swear you and Everett knew each other."

Selene grimaced. "We did, once. A long time ago."

Something in her expression made him ask, "Did you *date* him?"

She snorted. "In a manner of speaking. It didn't end well."

"And now he wants you back?"

"I guess."

"But you're not..."

"He tied me up and left me in a cave. He's killed three innocent women. He would've killed Gabriela if you and Detective Brandman hadn't shown up. So no, I may have a terrible track record with men, but even I'm not *that* damaged."

"Ah. Good." Theo's mind whirled. Why did Selene sound like she was trying to convince herself? How had she met Everett in the first place? And why would he start a cult to win her back? But one image stuck in his mind. "And the javelin thing? Am I crazy? Is he really invincible?"

"He's very strong. But no, he's not invincible. *No one* is invincible anymore. He's a performer—you saw the masks. That stunt with the javelin was just a cheap theater trick. It only seemed real to you because of the *kykeon*—it plays havoc with your brain."

"He called me a Makarites. A 'Blessed One.' And Helen, too. Any idea why?"

"No," she said shortly. But he had the distinct impression she was lying. "I told you, don't trust anything you remember from last night."

"But you're here. That's real." He recalled something else: Selene, standing above him with an arrow and refusing to strike. Even drugged with *kykeon*, she'd protected him. The knot of terror loosened a little as he watched her now. "You came to rescue me, huh?"

"I came to catch the hierophant." She looked away swiftly, staring out through the cave opening. Theo forced himself not to say anything. He watched the flaring of her nostrils and waited. She looked down at her bound wrists. "And also to rescue you." She blushed. "I'm sorry, Theo." She spoke so softly he could barely hear her, and with a stiffness that hinted she wasn't used to apologizing. "I thought if I left you, you'd give up on me—go escape somewhere safe. I should've known you'd run right into danger instead."

Theo allowed himself a moment to enjoy her sudden bashfulness. Then another to imagine what he might do if they'd left him unbound. *Don't say it, Theo,* he admonished himself.

"If I could reach you, I'd kiss you," he said anyway.

Selene shifted a little and wove her white-knuckled fingers together. "Why? I didn't rescue you very well."

"It wouldn't be a gratitude kind of kiss."

Selene's gaze snapped to his.

She's afraid of me, he realized with a start. *At least that's one advantage to being tied up: She can't run away this time.* "But only if you wanted me to."

Her gaze softened. In the darkening cave, her eyes seemed to glow. "Let's just concentrate on getting out of here, shall we?"

Theo looked through the cave opening. Twilight painted the leaves and shrubbery in shades of gray. At any moment, Everett and the others might appear, and any chance he had of ever kissing Selene DiSilva—or any other woman, for that matter—would be over. "Shouldn't the cops be here by now?"

"The cops?"

"You did tell Captain Hansen where you were going, didn't

you?" His stomach tightened once more. "Please tell me you didn't think you could take down an entire cult all by yourself."

Selene shrugged, averting her eyes once more.

"You're not really a goddess, remember!" Theo groaned.

"I brought Hippolyta."

"Oh. Good. I'm sure one woman and a dog are more than a match for four drugged madmen. And where is this canine crime fighter? Is *she* calling the police?"

"I didn't want her to get hurt so I let her off leash and told her to run home."

"Ah. Well at least one of us is safe." He ignored her unamused frown. "I don't suppose you have a phone you can reach?"

"He must have taken it out of my pocket last night."

"So there's no plan."

"I'm supposed to be Artemis, remember? Not Athena," she snapped. "I'm not great at planning ahead."

Theo stopped himself from a snarky retort. The last thing he wanted was to fight with her. "Well, it's sunset again. That means the Unspeakables will keep going. Can you remember how much they got through last night? It's all so fuzzy."

"*Legomena* and *Dromena*."

"So tonight is *Deiknumena*, 'Things Shown.' To be honest, I'd rather not see them, whatever they are."

"At least we know what to expect," she said. "When they captured you, I went to Helen's apartment. I read her manuscript."

"Everett told me it was on her missing laptop."

"Everett lied. Big surprise. My canine crime fighter sniffed it out."

"And what did it say?"

"That all this was Helen's idea in the first place."

He shook his head. "She may have been a little eccentric, but there's no way she condoned *human sacrifice*. Torturing virgin girls. That's not the woman I knew."

"Everett added the virgin killing because he's trying to transform Persephone and Demeter's cult into one worshipping Orion and Artemis instead, and virginity is Artemis's attribute. But Helen's not blameless. Far from it. She wanted to re-create the original Mystery—the one Dennis told me about, complete with the sacrifice of the Corn King."

"That would be me."

She could only nod.

"But why?"

"You yourself said the Mystery provided the answers to life's greatest questions. Helen thought the only way to uncover that lost wisdom was to perform the ritual as it was meant to be."

"So if I remember correctly what Everett said last night, the long-forgotten answer to 'how to live a better life' is…become immortal?" He shook his head. "Helen used to talk about the myth of Tithonus and the Dawn. Said she wanted me to live forever by her side. But I never dreamed she was serious about it. I guess she decided Everett would make a better grasshopper."

"Immortality…" Selene snorted disdainfully. "Immortality doesn't teach you anything about how to live, because you never learn how to die."

"Well, no worries on that front. I have a feeling my colleagues are going to teach me that lesson pretty soon." It was getting harder and harder to maintain his sense of humor.

"Yeah, I recognized Bill Webb. And the skinny old guy—he was the one Hippo barked at that day at your office. I thought she just wanted his sandwich, but looks like she recognized his smell, after all."

"That's Martin Andersen. And the other's Nate Balinski. Seems they couldn't resist Everett's promises any more than Helen, or Bill, or anyone else. Except you, that is. I seem to recall that he tried to get you to kill me last night during the *Dromena*. Thanks, by the way, for refusing."

"Anytime," she said with the ghost of a smile.

"But tonight's his last chance to consummate the ritual.

Nothing's going to stop him from sacrificing me." The roiling fear in his gut had settled into a clenched numbness. "And you're telling me I have Helen to thank for this."

"I think, maybe, she did it for love. I bet after Everett drugged her with *kykeon*, she believed anything he told her—even that he was the mythological Hunter reborn."

Theo shook his head. "Pure lunacy. She must've known she could never publish her work—the university would've had her committed—but she kept going anyway."

"Because Everett persuaded her it was the only way to make the mythical Orion fully immortal."

"And she was willing to sacrifice me for *that*? For *nonsense*?"

"There's nothing in her paper that implies *you* had to be the king. Choosing you as the sacrifice is just payback for your little fling with Helen."

"But *someone* was going to die."

"Love makes people do crazy things."

Theo didn't know how to respond to that. *I guess that explains how I wound up handcuffed in a cave in the middle of Manhattan, about to be killed. Love for one woman inspired me to start this chase. Love for another led me to its end.*

————◇————

Selene tugged uselessly at her ropes. Even with her renewed powers, she couldn't break the thick hemp. Finally, she succumbed to frustration and stooped to asking for help.

"Apollo, Phoebus, *Alexikakos*, *Boedromios*. Bright One, Protector from Harm, Rescuer," she whispered, so low Theo wouldn't hear. "You denied me once, but come to me now. I'm in danger, Sunbeam. I need you."

Even with their bond as twins, she doubted Paul would hear her invocation, not from so far away. And even if he did, even though she used his real name, he would likely still refuse her request. He'd made it perfectly clear in the hospital that she was on her own.

Water dripped in the back of the cave. *Father lives in a place like this,* she realized. *Huddled among the stalagmites. Alone and afraid.*

The cave grew dark, but she could still see Theo. A dim profile. Sharp nose, pointed chin. The faint glint of his glasses as he turned to speak.

"I hate to bring this up." His forced lightness couldn't hide his terror. "But I'd rather not die tonight."

"Me neither." *I will not give up as my father has. I will not abandon my duty to Theo, to the women of this city—nor to my fellow Athanatoi either. If what the Wine Giver told me is true, I cannot let this cult succeed.* She pulled at her hempen fetters one more time, calling upon the cave, the rock, the trees, for strength. *I am the Goddess of the Wild,* she thought angrily. *This is* my *space.* But she only succeeded in chaffing her wrists further.

Disgusted, she let loose a long, angry scream. The roar of a bear. The howl of a wolf.

Theo whistled in appreciation. "Someone might hear *that.*" But no intrepid passerby shouted back. No police siren signaled a rescue. The only sound was the rustling of some creature in the leaves outside the cave. "Looks like only the squirrels know we're here," he said after a while.

"Theo. That's a brilliant idea."

"What?"

"Shhh." Selene closed her eyes, reaching for an ancient, primal knowledge she'd possessed long ago. She squeaked. Once. Twice. The rustling noise came closer. She chittered softly. The almost imperceptible click of claws on stone. Close enough now to make out overlarge black eyes, big ears, furry tail. A field mouse. She'd been hoping for a rat. In the old days, she would've summoned a bear. Still, it was better than nothing. Slowly, she moved her hands toward the mouse, squeaking soothingly. She tried to communicate the most basic of ideas—*Come, there's food.* She couldn't remember anything more complicated. The mouse's whiskers twitched rapidly as it approached, sniffing. It crawled hesitantly onto her hand, then up her wrist to the hemp rope, where it sat down and began to gnaw. Theo gave a small gasp of astonishment but, for once, remained silent. Praying for enough time, Selene held her hands still while the mouse worked. His teeth were awfully small.

Approaching footsteps sent the mouse scurrying with only half the rope chewed through. *It might be enough,* she hoped, working the bonds, feeling the new give in the rope.

"I may say things to Everett that sound crazy," she whispered hurriedly to Theo. "But just go with it, okay?" *If the Fates are kind, maybe I'll get out of this without having to explain that everything Orion said is true.*

Chapter 45

UNDYING

The Hunter entered the cave, a flaming brand in one hand and his bronze sword in the other, moving with his usual supple grace.

"Came alone this time?" Theo challenged. "Left your friends getting drunk at the Faculty Club?"

Orion ignored him. He knelt and placed the torch into the charred remains of the fire pit. With two rushing breaths, he blew life into the flames. In the sudden blaze, Selene looked at Theo. His glasses were askew, his hair a tangled nest, one eye nearly swollen shut. But he caught her gaze and held it.

"Don't do that." Orion sheathed his sword, took Selene by the shoulders, and turned her to face him. He sat so their eyes were level. "Look at *me* now. Look at me and see me."

She forced herself to resist the pleading in his gaze. "I see a monster."

A flash of hurt narrowed his eyes. "I see a goddess."

"Everett, you idiot—" Theo began.

"My name is *Orion*," the Hunter shot over his shoulder. "As it has been since my father Poseidon named me. As it was for millennia, while I hung between life and death, waiting for my father's promise to come true. And it will be for eternity once I take my place among the Athanatoi. Helen did the research. Nate knew the recipe. Martin found the Caledonian Boar. From there, it was like tracking a deer through muddy ground." He turned back to Selene. "I just had to make sure that Artemis could follow my trail as easily."

"You left Helen there in the river, because you knew I would come by."

Orion smiled and stroked her hair. "I know your habits, my love. I left just enough clues so that, at the end, you'd come to me."

"Is that why you used the tusk and the vase with my picture on it as your *hiera*? To keep me interested?"

He laughed shortly. "No, I knew once you had the scent, you'd never give up the hunt until you caught your prey. I used the tusk and the vase because your story is my story. And because, by including them in the ritual, I could bring you power. Then, when you finally found me, you'd understand that I'd do anything, anything at all, to save you, to love you, to spend eternity at your side. Last time, your twin tore us apart. This time, nothing will stop us. Can you imagine how much more glorious you'll be when you've stood above the flames and inhaled the burnt offerings as I have? When you've witnessed the revelation of the *hiera*? Then, when the final sacrifice is complete, we will both be fully immortal. Your limbs, your beautiful, strong limbs, will never wither and weaken. You will never die, Artemis. I will save you, make you into the goddess you once were. We can leave this filthy city—go anywhere in the world. The boreal forests of Canada, where bear and moose and elk still roam. Africa, to run side by side hunting antelope across the savannah. We could even go back to the sacred grove at Ephesus, my Far Shooter. Things will be as they always were."

Selene could indeed imagine it. A return to power. To glory. To love. Could it truly be that easy? "The Wine Giver said the cult would send us back into barbarity. Maybe even bring civilization crumbling around us."

Orion's mouth tightened. "After all this time...haven't you learned that your brothers are liars? I'm the only one you can trust." He leaned toward her and pressed his forehead against hers. "I was so hopeful on the shore that day, waiting for my father. I knew he'd grant my wish once he saw the depth of my love for you. I dreamed of your white legs sprinting through the forest." He pressed his nose beside her ear and breathed deeply, the sound resonating in her head like the rush of waves. "Of the smell of your hair. Like cypress on a summer day." He placed his fingertips on her jaw. "Of the feel of your skin beneath mine. Always cool, like the underside of a leaf." He ran his fingers down the length of her neck and rested them gently on her collarbone. "I would kiss you, right here, and we would be together, forever." Even as her mind screamed in protest, Selene felt her body stir at his touch. Try as she might, she couldn't deny that all she'd wanted, for so long, was to feel his arms around her once more. It had been more than two thousand years since she'd been kissed.

Orion pulled back just enough to look her in the eye. His face no longer held its tinge of cruelty. His eyes, warm and dark, bored into hers. "You killed me then, Artemis. But I came back from death itself to be at your side. Don't kill me again by turning me away."

Finally, she whispered aloud the words she'd dreamed of for millennia: "I trusted my twin more than my love. I've lived with regret for so long it's like a shield, keeping the world at bay. Break through," she begged. "Tell me you forgive me."

"I never blamed you," he said, his mouth very close to hers. "I knew even death could not keep us apart." Orion showed none of Theo's restraint. He simply claimed her for himself. He pressed his warm lips to hers. Selene felt as if the corner of her heart that had been stone for so long finally melted back into flesh. Vaguely, she heard Theo protesting in the background. As if in answer, Orion clasped her head in his hands and kissed her deeper, his mouth firm and gentle all at once. His arms snaked around her, clasping her so tightly she could barely breathe. When he broke the kiss, her mind still reeled.

"Tell me you'll be mine," he pleaded.

She rested her bound hands upon his cheeks, feeling the familiar, rough scratch of stubble, the bold contours of his jaw. A single tear rolled down his cheek to rest upon her thumb.

Gently, she brushed it away. "I have *always* been yours."

"Selene, what are you—"

"Quiet, Theo."

Orion kissed her once more. "You won't regret this." He smiled, his eyes aglow. "You've made me happy for the first time in an age." Hungrily, he kissed her cheek, her throat, her eyelids.

When she could think again, she held out her hands to be untied.

"Not quite, my love, I'm sorry. Not until the ritual is complete. Then...then you'll never know bonds again." He rose swiftly, leaving her still shuddering from his kisses, and walked to the mouth of the cave to summon his *mystai*.

———◇———

Theo watched Everett with Selene, growing more furious by the second. *Did I really tell Ruth I didn't believe in fighting over a woman? It must not have been the right woman, because I feel like I could rip out his throat with my bare hands.* Unfortunately, the cult members had other ideas.

At Everett's command, Nate pulled a fresh roll of duct tape from beneath his robe. Webb and Andersen grabbed Theo under the arms, dragged him to the center of the cave, and stood him on his feet. "Guys," Theo begged, wobbling from the ropes around his ankles. "You don't need to do this. You're drugged, don't you see? You wouldn't do this otherwise! Can't you see that I—"

Leaning close, his breath reeking of *kykeon*, Nate slapped the tape across Theo's mouth. "I can't tell you how often I've wanted to do that." Unmasked, the initiates appeared more terrifying than ever. Now, Theo couldn't pretend that Everett had turned them into powerless automatons. The familiar faces leered around him, their smiles tilted toward madness, but their eyes cold. *Perhaps they started this unwillingly, but now they know what they're doing,* Theo admitted. *And they're enjoying it.*

Webb placed a wreath of cypress boughs and barley sheaves on Theo's head. They started to chant a wordless, meditative harmony. Then the dance began, a shuffling circle of awkward men, made terrifying by the polished bronze blades in their hands, winking and flashing in the firelight. Theo looked toward Selene. Everett had removed the ropes around her ankles, and now she stood, staring intently into the flames. She hadn't met his eyes since Everett had kissed her.

Everett put an arm around her shoulders. "I know you care about Theo," he said gently, "but he's our chosen Corn King, crowned and blessed. A Makarites, the most powerful sacrifice we can offer." Selene didn't protest. He brushed a knuckle across her cheekbone. "The strength you've gained so far will stay with you, no matter what happens tonight. That is my gift to you. But to become an invincible goddess again, to make myth into truth—Theo must die." He kissed her lightly. "Then, as long as we repeat the Mysteries every year, we will live forever."

How can Selene just stand there, Theo wondered, *when Everett speaks of an eternity of murdered innocents?* He screamed a muffled, wordless protest through his gag.

Everett turned at the sound. "You've been a selfless friend, Theo." He spoke with his old easy charm. "Even willing to be kind to the man who stole your girlfriend. I know you won't fail me now, when it's so important. You will die to save Artemis, won't you? So she may return to glory as an immortal?" He ripped the duct tape from Theo's mouth.

Theo's lips and cheeks burned where the tape had ripped his bruised skin. But he forced himself to ignore the pain and meet Everett's eyes. "No. But I would happily die to save Selene."

Everett laughed. "See, my love! He doesn't know you at all. I thought maybe you would've told him the truth, as I did Helen. She gave the ultimate sacrifice so she might help me."

"That's a *lie*." Theo strained at his handcuffs, aching to strangle him. "Helen didn't sacrifice herself willingly. You *murdered* her."

Everett shook his head. "No, my friend. Helen understood. She didn't even know she was being punished for her infidelity. She thought it was a great honor." From a pocket, he drew out a small, white gold ring. The edges of the Greek key caught the firelight as he turned it slowly between his fingers. "Not at first, of course. She thought me mad, as you do. But then I showed her I could run faster, climb higher, jump farther, and heal more quickly than any human. You saw it last night with your own eyes, yet you still refuse to believe. Helen was not so foolish." He sighed regretfully and slipped Helen's ring onto his pinky finger. "A beautiful girl. And so smart." He patted Theo roughly on the shoulder. "She knew that thanatoi have only one role. To serve the gods who made them. She gave up her life for mine, knowing what I was."

Theo started to protest, but Selene cut him off calmly. "And now Theo knows what *I* am." Still she did not look at him.

"Selene—"

"No, Theo. There's nothing you can say. Better not to speak."

"Listen to Artemis," Everett said, replacing the tape on Theo's mouth. He took one of Selene's bound hands in his and kissed it lightly, then turned to his acolytes. "Bring forth the *hiera*!"

From a duffle bag, Martin Andersen withdrew the stolen bell-krater: a large pottery vase with three red stags leaping across its black surface. Nate produced the familiar bottle of *kykeon* and poured its contents into the larger vessel. Holding the bell-krater by its two handles, Andersen drank deeply, then passed it to the other *mystai* in turn. Before he drank, Webb raised the vase high. "To immortality," he intoned. Nate went last, then moved to force the drink down Theo's throat, but Everett told him to stop. "I don't want Theo's mind clouded. Last night, he couldn't trust his own eyes. I want him to go to his death believing."

"You don't need to—" Selene began.

"Hush, my love. You're going to be worshiped once more. Don't you realize?"

Nate carefully poured a thin stream of *kykeon* into the flames. "A libation," he chanted in Greek. "For Dionysus, who taught man to make the drink which brings revelation." Next, he pulled from his cloak a green glass flask brimming with dark liquid and handed it to his hierophant. Everett swirled the liquid so it glinted redly in the fire's glow. "From the first sacrifice, we reap faith and intelligence," he said, uncorking the flask. "From the next, tenacity and courage." He paced around the fire, splashing the blood in a circle as he went. "From the *Pompe*, charisma and beauty. And from the last, loyalty and ferocity." *That's Gabriela's blood he's talking about,* Theo realized. He shouted unheard curses against the duct tape.

Everett spilled the last drop of blood onto his finger, then placed it on his tongue, closing his eyes for a moment in pleasure. "These are the gifts of the sacrifices. May they make us strong."

Then Martin Andersen turned to his duffel bag and removed a large, unglazed terracotta vessel shaped to look like a basket, its base roughly decorated with painted grain. Theo recognized the Met's stolen *kalathos*. Reaching within, the professor withdrew the long, curved tooth of a Hell Pig. He held it aloft and chanted, "We call upon the spirit of the Boar, sacred to the Hunter and the Huntress." He threw the tusk into the flames, where it sputtered and began to char.

Bill Webb took his turn. He leaned over the *kalathos* and removed the body of a yellow-headed snake, a dead loop of taxidermy with cotton balls for eyes. "We call upon the spirit of the Snake, creature of hidden truths, sacred to Asclepius, who grants life to the dead." Another precious specimen disappeared into the flames. Next, a bundle of dried wheat. It sparked and popped in the fire. "We call upon Demeter and Persephone, goddesses of grain, goddesses of life, goddesses of death. Let us be reborn."

Finally, Everett revealed the last of the *hiera*. He drew it carefully out of the *kalathos* and held it in the palm of his hand. A pale diamond of flesh, drained of blood. Crude black stiches had sewn Helen closed. Unlike the other sacrifices, Helen was not a virgin—so Everett had made her one. Theo retched against his gag.

Everett betrayed no emotion. "We call upon the Virgin Goddess, Artemis, she who protects the pure from harm, that she may restore our fragile bodies and cleanse our corrupt souls." He dropped the offering into the flames. Each curling hair caught fire, a hot orange nimbus quickly charred to black.

Everett moved closer to the flames, inhaling the smoke through his mouth as if imbibing it. He drew Selene to stand beside him. "Breathe. Let the offerings give you strength, as they have done for me." Theo wasn't surprised to see her obey. Little could surprise him anymore. Selene stood with her mouth open and eyes closed, sucking in the smoke with great, wheezing gasps. Suddenly, her hands began to shake. Blood flooded her cheeks and her eyes snapped open.

Everett knelt before Selene like a supplicant and took the hem of her shirt in his hands. He lifted it slowly, just to the bottom of her rib cage, and pressed a long kiss against the red scab that ran across her stomach. When Everett pulled away, the scab was gone.

"It works," Selene gasped.

"I told you." Everett pressed her palms to his lips. "This is just the beginning." He drew his sword and pointed it at Theo.

"No, my lover," she said, raising her bound hands before her. She flung her arms wide, breaking free of the ropes. Theo winced in the bright silver light that suddenly flooded the cave. He could barely see Selene through the glare, but he could hear her voice, thrumming and deep, vibrating in his skull like the words of a prophet.

"This is where it ends."

Chapter 46

THE RELENTLESS ONE

"What are you doing?" Orion demanded, shielding his eyes from the glare of Selene's divine radiance. "We have to complete the ritual!"

"I am the Protector of the Innocent." She moved to stand by Theo, glaring at each of the *mystai* in turn, daring them to challenge her. "Saving him is my birthright."

Orion stepped back as if struck. His face slackened with the same look of disbelief he'd given her when she thrust an arrow through his throat on the shore of the sapphire sea. The same look she'd spent so long trying to forget. "You don't...you can't..."

"You made me choose. I choose him."

Orion shook his head, incredulous. "You only want him because he's a Makarites. You can't resist the allure of a mortal who remembers the gods."

"No. Whether he is Blessed or not, I *choose* Theo. I choose his brilliance. I choose his empathy. I choose his laughter."

"But he's dust. Have you forgotten? Every second of his life is spent hurtling toward death, his body disintegrating even as you watch. His mind is mortal, finite. Even as a Makarites, he's unable to comprehend your true glory. That's what you choose over *me*?"

"There was a time I would've chosen you over anyone, anything," she said, unable to keep the regret from her voice. "Why didn't you come to me then? Why wait for so long?"

"I wanted to come to you in my full glory, not a pale shadow of the hero I'd once been. I knew you'd never condone the killing of innocents, and I couldn't let you stop me before my transformation was complete. Maybe before, in the old days, you would've overlooked the murders, but I know how you've changed, even if you don't." The pleading left his voice, replaced my something hard, accusatory. "You've grown soft. You've come to care for those you protect. Still, I thought that if I waited until you could see for yourself the power I could bestow, then you wouldn't be able to say no."

"Then you didn't really know me at all."

"But I would give you an eternity of power." He opened his arms as if expecting her embrace. "How can you resist that?"

"I've already had it," said Selene, unmoved. "I don't need it any longer." Orion dropped his arms. His sword hung loosely at his side. *Leave here,* she begged him silently. *Disappear back into my memories, where you will stay forever beautiful and brave. Let me forget the monster you've become. Let me finally find happiness without you.*

Then Orion lifted his head, and she knew with a sinking heart that the fight had just begun. No longer was he the yearning lover of old, nor the fierce companion of her youth, but a creature neither god nor man, a monster wracked by millennia of bitterness and resentment, disappointment and fury. "So be it." He turned to his *mystai* and said very calmly, "Kill them both."

From the corner of her eye, she saw Martin Anderson lurch awkwardly forward with his knife outstretched. In a flash, she punched him in the jaw with her right hand and ripped his knife away with her left. Martin stumbled backward, moaning and spitting blood. She brandished the knife at the other two *mystai,* who froze in place. Only then did she allow herself to look at Theo. Her divine radiance cast a cold light across his bruised face, but his gaze was still warm. Despite the duct tape silencing his words, she could read the message clearly in his eyes: *Whatever you're planning, I'm with you. Just lead the way.*

"Don't just stand there," Orion commanded his acolytes. "Complete the sacrifice!"

Nate lunged toward Selene, who sidestepped him easily, then knocked the knife from his hand with a well-placed kick. At the same time, Theo ducked under Bill Webb's slash, then came up to head-butt his chairman soundly in the forehead. Neither of the *mystai* took long to recover, not with their *kykeon*-enhanced strength. She tensed for a renewed attack. *Let them come,* she thought. *They are mere mortals against a goddess.*

Then a muscled arm snaked around her chest from behind, pinning her in place. "You can't stop this," Orion hissed in her ear. He held his sword to her neck. "Now drop the knife, my faithless lover, and watch my *mystai* complete their work." She ignored him, slamming her booted heel into his shin and twisting in his grasp. Implacable, he swung his sword, striking at her knife and knocking it from her grip. With the flat of his blade, he forced her head toward Theo.

The *mystai* had him in their grip again. Handcuffed and bound, her friend had no hope of fending off all three of them at once. A cold fist of dread seized her heart, and she realized that despite all the danger of the past week, she'd always believed, deep inside, that she could protect him from harm. Even when he'd been kidnapped, she'd known somehow she would find him, save him, no matter what it took. And now he stood only a few feet away, and though the burnt offerings had granted her more strength than she'd known in years, she was helpless to prevent what was about to happen.

She continued to thrash desperately against Orion's embrace, heedless of the sword's kiss on her throat. "Go on! Kill me now. Make *me* the sacrifice if you must." But Orion just stood behind her, wordless and unyielding. "You can't, can you?" she taunted, her cries edging toward hysteria. "You're weak, Hunter. You drug your followers. You bind your sacrifice. You lied about Helen. She didn't go happily to her death. She fought with everything she had! And when she died, she prayed to *me*, never to you. She begged me to avenge her—and her prayer will not remain unanswered!" But her words were wind and Orion stone.

Martin and Nate gripped Theo by the shoulders while Bill Webb, a red welt on his forehead, held a knife aloft. He looked to his hierophant for the final command.

Theo's eyes sought Selene's. Even now, she knew, he held out hope that she could rescue him. *My brilliant professor—you will die a fool, believing in a goddess who doesn't deserve your faith.* Then Orion nodded to his acolyte.

Webb thrust the knife into Theo's heart.

A high-pitched keen like a hawk in distress reverberated through the cave. An instant later, Selene realized she was screaming. Orion released her and she fled to Theo's side, dragging his body into her arms. His blood seeped through her clothes and pooled against her skin.

She ripped the gag from his mouth and tore the cypress wreath from his head. He looked up at her, his green eyes still bright.

"You can't die," Selene said. "I won't let you."

Blood bubbled through Theo's words. "Just try to stop me."

She kissed him. Through the blood. Through her tears.

He smiled. A faint shadow of the dimpled grin she knew so well. "Worth it...for that."

She kissed him until his lips went still and his body grew limp. Only then, as he lay lifeless in her arms, did she allow herself to admit the dreams she'd had for him. *I'd kiss you beneath the stars, and we'd swap stories of the constellations,* she thought, brushing a lock of hair from his eyes. *You'd take me to the movies, but I'd watch you more often than the screen, loving the way you smiled with delight.* She kissed the corner of his mouth. *We'd climb mountains and swim in cold streams. You'd learn to enjoy it, and I'd learn to laugh as easily as you do. Then, someday, when the time was right, and I knew you'd understand, I'd give you my real name.* She closed his eyes, then leaned her forehead against his and whispered, "And then, perhaps, if I was very brave and you were very patient, I'd give you myself."

A burst of laughter ripped her from her mourning. She looked up to see Nate grinning and flexing his biceps. "It worked!" he crowed. Martin took off his glasses and blinked, as if astonished that he could see without them. Bill Webb straightened and ran his hands along his throat, feeling for a tumor that was no longer there.

In that moment, the power of the sacrifice blazed through Selene's veins, leaving her trembling in its wake. The cave grew brighter as her aura intensified. She felt the glow burning around her now, cold flames licking her skin. Very carefully, she laid Theo's head on the stone floor. The strength she'd gained from the burnt offerings was nothing compared to the force now pulsing within her. Dimly, she recognized that something fundamental had shifted, cracked, reformed—granting her unbounded strength while, at the same time, destroying the kernel of humanity she'd both cherished and resented for millennia. She could barely feel grief at Theo's loss, couldn't remember the touch of his arms around her or the warmth of his smile—all those human memories had been suddenly burned away within the fiery outrage of an offended immortal. Artemis the Untamed rose to her feet and faced Theo's killer. Webb stood, laughing and smiling with his comrades, Theo's blood still red on his hands.

The chairman turned to face her, waving his bloody knife. "You can't hurt us now. Look how strong we are!"

"Now it's your turn, Artemis," Orion said. He looked younger than he had a moment before. His muscles even larger, his skin glowing with a hint of his own divine radiance. A god indeed. "If you won't live by my side, you won't live at all."

Artemis began to laugh. A crazed, piercing howl, more fury than mirth. The *mystai* grew silent, watching her uneasily. Orion raised his sword and took a single step toward her.

Her laughter stopped as suddenly as it had begun. She pointed an accusing finger at her lover of old. "You should have killed me when you had the chance."

She lifted her arms above her head, palms to the sky, feeling like she could ride the moon once more. "I am Artemis, the Relentless One," she roared. "I am the Punisher, the Huntress, and no man can escape my justice."

Orion curled his lip in disdain. "You had none of those titles until *I* gave them back to you."

"They are my names and always have been." She remembered what Theo had once told her: There was power in naming. "I am an Olympian, the Daughter of Leto." She curled her fingers toward the ceiling of the cave, feeling the moonlight pouring on the rock above. "I am Phoebe, granddaughter of Phoibe. I am Selene, Moon Goddess." She opened herself to the power of the heavens and felt it rush through her like a waterfall. She grabbed hold of the light and *pulled*. Outside, the lake itself moved with the moon's force, sliding toward its mistress until it lapped over the shore. Water, spotted with algae and smelling of loam, flowed into the cave. Artemis felt it seep through the soles of her boots and rise to her ankles. She took a deep breath and reached for another name, another power. "I am the Mistress of Beasts and the Lady of Hounds." Somewhere in the park, she heard a dog's howl, dimly familiar. Then, farther away, a furious roar, rolling across the park with the rumble of thunder. The grizzly bears in the Central Park Zoo, proclaiming their fealty.

Artemis sensed the initiates moving cautiously toward her, armed once more with their bronze knives. "Remind your followers—I am the Shooter of Stags and the Huntress of the Wild Boar, but men are my favorite prey."

"You're alone and unarmed," Orion scoffed. "I still have the divine sword my father gave me. I'm stronger than I've ever been. You will fall tonight, and I will cease to be tormented by what I cannot have."

"You forget that I am the Lady of the Starry Host." Even now, she could feel the heavens pulsing above, giving her strength. "And you are nothing but a constellation I created."

Orion snarled like a wounded animal. He lunged toward her, sword outstretched for a killing thrust. Then, with his blade a few scant inches from her chest, a silver arrow burst like a shooting star through the side of his stomach. He stopped in his tracks, staring down at the glimmering shaft in disbelief.

Artemis turned to see Apollo, the Bright One, standing in the mouth of the cave, Hippolyta prancing in place beside him.

"She's also the Bearer of the Bow," her twin said, tossing his sister a perfect golden weapon and a quiver of gleaming arrows. "And she's not alone. Not anymore." Beside him stood Dionysus in ripped jeans and a stained undershirt, holding his six-foot-long thyrsus, a pinecone-tipped staff covered in twirling vines. Hermes, wearing a slim linen suit and a gaily colored silk pocket square, carried no divine weapons. Just a semiautomatic pistol in each hand. And there, nearly hidden by the shadows, a barrel-chested figure with a massive hammer in one hand. He limped forward on shriveled legs, leaning heavily on a titanium crutch. Hephaestus, the Smith.

Orion gripped the arrow in his flank and fell back against the wall of the cave, his sword still held tightly in his other hand.

He looked at Apollo, his face suffused with rage. "My betrayer, the Gilded God," he hissed. "I have waited millennia for my revenge." He dove at his old nemesis. Artemis moved to stop him, but the *mystai* stood in her way, knives flashing in the last remnants of the firelight.

Hippo bounded to her mistress's defense. With a yelp, Martin swung his blade toward the lunging dog. Faster than thought, Artemis nocked a gold arrow to her new bow and sent it through the old man's throat. Hippo toppled him to the ground, her growls drowning out his death rattle. With a desperate cry, Nate tackled Artemis from the side. She shrugged off his attack, then watched impassively as Hermes shot two bullets through his chest. Somehow, the professor managed another staggering step toward her, only to be felled by a single stroke of Hephaestus's hammer, which broke his kneecap with a gravelly crunch. Nate splashed into the shallow water. Before he could scream, she stepped on his head, pushing his face into the water and holding it there. He thrashed and choked, but she ignored him, turning her attention instead to the battle at the cave's entrance.

She watched Apollo fire arrow after arrow at Orion, who, despite his wound, batted the shafts from the air with the flat of his sword, forcing her twin to dodge and shoot at the same time. Unlike his sister, the Bright One had never learned to hold more than one arrow in his shooting hand at once, so Orion easily kept pace with his onslaught.

Hermes turned away from the professors to join his brother in the fray, shooting at the Hunter with reckless abandon. The first mortal-crafted bullets bounced off Orion's newly strengthened skin harmlessly. He caught the next bullet on his sword, sending it whizzing back toward Hermes so quickly even the Many-Turning One couldn't dodge it completely. The bullet grazed the arm of his suit, ripping a long slash through the linen. With Hermes's weapons doing more harm than good and Dionysus useless—he merely leaned drunkenly on his thyrsus, watching the proceedings with mild amusement—Apollo would need his sister's help to defeat Orion. But first, Theo's killer had to die.

Bill Webb stood trembling, his back to the cave wall, staring aghast as Nate quickly drowned in three inches of water and Martin choked to death on the blood welling from the arrow shaft in his throat. The chairman looked up at Artemis, dropped his knife, and kneeled before her. Hippo sprang toward him, and Hephaestus raised his hammer, but the goddess stopped both her protectors with an upraised hand. "No. He's mine."

Bill's eyes rolled from Hippo's slavering jaws to Hephaestus's massive weapon, then finally to Artemis's stony face. He held up his hands in supplication. "Mercy, Gentle Goddess."

She drew the string taut and aimed her shaft at his face. "Theo would've shown you mercy," she said slowly. The force of her godhood left her memories of Theo washed out and dim, like a photo bleached by the brilliance of the sun—but she knew that much.

"Yes! For Theo! Do what he would've wanted!"

"For Theo. Indeed." She sent a golden arrow through his eye and into his brain. Webb swallowed once, twice, with a familiar birdlike jerk, then collapsed.

"Moonshine!" Paul hollered. "I'm running out of arrows!"

She turned to him calmly, bemused by the panic in his voice. Didn't he realize she was invincible? Orion didn't stand a chance.

She narrowed her eyes, watching the pattern of Apollo's shots. "Do you remember how we used to hunt?" she called to him. That memory, one she thought long forgotten, returned bright and sharp, even as she could no longer recall the sound of Theo's laughter. Twin gods in chariots of gold and silver, racing across the plains of Attica, arrows flying like rain, striking down those who offended, those who defied. The ghost of a smile crossed Apollo's face, even as he dodged another arrow ricocheting off Orion's sword—he remembered, too.

She raised her bow and nocked a row of three arrows to the string. "Then hunt with me now."

At her cue, Apollo shot his last silver shaft at Orion's calves. Arms raised, the Hunter leaped upward to dodge the arrow, just as Artemis sent her own gold arrows hurtling through the cave, right into his path. One flew into his left wrist and another into his right, shot with such force that they knocked him backward and pierced the stone behind him, pinning him to the cave wall. At the same instant, the third arrow struck the bronze sword with a sharp clang, tearing it from his hands. It fell, dented and misshapen, to the ground.

Only Orion's harsh breaths broke the sudden silence. He hung limply from the wall, his body dangling as if crucified. His feet swung weakly, looking for purchase, but the ground was just out of reach. Blood slid in torrents down his arms from the arrows in his wrists, two red rivers joining the stream still pulsing from the wound in his side.

Apollo looked from the helpless Hunter to the victorious Huntress. "You want to do it, or should I?"

Artemis stared down at the golden bow in her hands, then up to Hephaestus. His arms and chest retained their colossal girth, but gray peppered his bushy hair and deep crags marked his coarse face. He'd already moved firmly into middle age. "You made this."

"Special order." His voice was deep and rough—a slow tectonic attrition. "Dash said you needed it."

She nodded slowly. "A divine weapon to kill a divinity." She nocked an arrow to the string, but held it loosely at her side. She looked once more at Theo's fallen form. Then, finally, she lifted her eyes to Orion. He struggled against the arrows in his wrists, trying to pull his flesh past the fletching, then gasped with pain and hung still once more. Artemis felt no pity.

She raised her bow, focusing only on the swell of muscle above his heart. Hippo barked sharply, urging her mistress on.

Orion didn't cry out or beg for mercy. He merely shook his head, more disappointed than afraid. "You should be grateful. You're stronger than you've been in millennia. You would kill the man who gave you such a gift?"

She searched her heart for any joy at what she'd become, any gratitude, any last remnants of love for the man before her, and found only emptiness. "Not a gift. A curse."

"You're wrong. Don't you see?" he insisted bitterly. "I've given you the power to bring your sweet Theodore back to life."

Artemis's fingers faltered on the string. "What did you say?"

From the corner of the cave, Dionysus spluttered with laughter. "You were right, Apollo, I'm glad I came. This is finally getting interesting." He lifted his thyrsus and pointed it at his sister. "Go on, Artemis, bring back your man, if you can. But Orion left out one teensy weensy detail. I warned you—the only way to get stronger is human sacrifice. If you reverse the sacrifice, you'll lose all that lovely strength. And let me say, that radiance looks damn good on you, so think twice before you give it up."

"Don't listen to him!" Orion protested, but Hephaestus silenced him with a threatening wave of his hammer.

"Orion's setting a trap," Apollo begged. "He wants you vulnerable again so he can hurt you. Please, Moonshine, why would you return to weakness now that you know strength?"

"Because I finally know what real strength is," she said, lowering her bow. "And this isn't it. This is power, this is rage, this is Artemis...but I've lost *Selene*. I've lost Theo. If I can bring them back, I will. I *must*."

"Are you sure?"

"Yes. And you're going to help me."

Chapter 47

SHE WHO LEADS
THE DANCE

Apollo shook his head. "I told you before that I won't help you destroy yourself."

Artemis tried to keep the fury from her voice. An Athanatos was no mortal, to be ordered about. "I once knew love and you took it away. You owe me."

"I didn't come for this."

"Then why *did* you?" she seethed. "Why answer my summons?"

"At the hospital you asked me to help you save Theo. But in your prayer, you asked me to help you save yourself. I would do anything for you, how many times must I tell you that?" he asked, his voice rising with impatience.

"Then do this. You're the God of Healing. Help me bring him back." Before her twin could protest, she went on. "I don't care if it takes away my supernatural powers." They were hard words to say—even harder to mean—with such strength thrumming within her. "The goddess I've become," she explained, "is the version Orion and his acolytes have worshiped. Heartless, cruel, *desperate*. Willing to sacrifice anything, *anyone*, to regain my strength."

"So you want to be *powerless*?"

"No." She didn't want that. Merely the thought of returning to the vulnerable woman she'd been a week before made her tremble with fear. Power beckoned her like a siren's call, but she stopped her ears and fought through the haze of vindictiveness, fury, and bloodlust, to find the faint spark of humanity that still glowed within her heart. If she stayed a goddess much longer, it might be quenched forever. "The key to understanding life's meaning...it's not immortality like Helen thought. It's *mortality*. I've been wandering this city, this world, for millennia, acting out a role I don't even know if I chose for myself. Now, Orion would remake me again, with all the worst parts of Artemis and none of the best. I can't let that happen. This time, *I'm* making the choice."

Apollo's golden eyes filled with tears. Then he nodded and lowered his bow.

The twins knelt beside Theo's body. The professor lay upon the cave floor, blood smeared across his lips from Artemis's kisses. The warmth had already drained from his face, leaving it cold and still, a marble death mask that barely resembled the man he'd been.

The God of Healing placed one hand on Theo's head and one on his bloody heart, just above the knife. "I'll try," he said, meeting his sister's eyes, "But I don't think I have the power anymore."

"I'll help you. I am the Relentless One who brings swift death, but I could also once give life and help bring children into the world." She placed her hands on either side of Theo's face. "Tonight I am more powerful than I have been in an age. As you shared my mother's womb, now may you share my strength."

Apollo closed his eyes and moved his lips silently. Then he took a deep breath and held it. His smooth brow furrowed. Nothing happened. He let out the breath with a heaving gasp. "I'm not quite strong enough. Maybe this isn't going to work."

"*No.* Try again."

Apollo's face twisted with sadness, but he yanked the knife clear of Theo's body and pressed his palms against the wound, stanching the slowly oozing gash. He began his silent chant. When he took a breath, Artemis did, too.

"I am She Who Helps One Climb Out," Artemis whispered into the silence. "Take my hand that I may pull you from death, Theodore. I am She Who Leads the Dance. Follow me."

She reached out with all her senses. She heard the wind in the trees. A hawk overhead. The drip of Orion's blood upon the ground. The breathing of the divine family around her. The thump of Hippo's tail on the stone floor. She felt the air stir in the cave. She sensed the movement of a mouse nearby. Once more, she summoned wind and water, animal and bird, moon and stars. The power of the wild surged through her and into her twin, who sent his own sharp heat back to her, a tongue of unquenchable fire made only stronger by the foaming river of her strength. Silver and gold, day and night, sun and moon, a maelstrom of energies swirled within her, burning and freezing at the same time until she feared her corporeal body would burst and only her immortal spirit would remain.

Then it all stopped.

She heard the water ebb back into the lake. She could no longer feel the moonlight above. All her senses went blank, as if someone had pulled a shroud over her mind. Only the pulse of a vein against her fingers broke through.

Selene opened her eyes. Theo stared back at her.

Her brother gave a small gasp of surprise. Hippo barked happily, then started sniffing Theo as if he were a newly discovered treat.

Memories flooded back...the feel of his hand in hers by the riverside, the sound of his laughter as he crawled across his office floor in a safari hat, the look in his eyes as he took her in his arms beneath the waterfall.

Theo raised a shaky hand to Selene's cheek. "Goddesses don't cry," he murmured hoarsely. "No, don't look away."

She opened her mouth to protest, but one look at Theo's awe-struck face and she found that for once, she couldn't lie.

"I'm not hallucinating this time, am I?" He looked down at the bloody crust on his chest where the knife had been, watching it scab over before his eyes. "How did you—"

"Apollo and I healed the wound," she admitted. Despite her dulled senses, her strength remained. Calmly, she tugged at the handcuffs around his wrists until the steel snapped beneath her grip.

"Wow." He struggled onto his elbows, looking down at the twisted metal. "I finally catch a break, huh? Just what you need when you get stabbed by your ex-girlfriend's insane fiancé—an Olympian god to bring you back to life." He laughed weakly, then groaned and clutched at his chest.

"Whoa there, hero. You're going to need to take it slow for a little while." She helped him ease back onto the ground.

He reached for her hand. "Selene...I..."

Paul's strangled gasp interrupted him. "Artemis. *Artemis.* Something's wrong."

And in that instant, Selene felt a wave of weakness wash over her. She flexed her hands, knowing with a terrifying certainty that all the power she'd possessed just a moment before had fled. Still on her knees, she swayed woozily. It took all her effort just to turn her head toward her twin. A streak of white ran along a curl of his hair. Paul held out his shaking hands toward her. "You didn't say it would weaken *me*."

Selene clapped her hands to her head, trying to banish the rush of dizziness. The cave suddenly grew darker as her radiance leaked away. Theo, still shaky himself, caught her as she slumped forward. Hippo whimpered piteously, staring at her mistress.

Paul rose to his feet, bracing his hands on his knees like an old man, and stumbled backward toward the cave entrance.

"We were connected," he said with a moan. "When your power drained, so did some of mine. You've got...you've got a white streak in your hair."

"So do you. I'm so sorry, Sunbeam," Selene managed. "I didn't know. I thought—"

Orion's wheezing laughter interrupted her. "Thank you, my Huntress," he said. "You finally avenged my murder." He looked to Paul. "Bringing the dead back to life has made you weak, Gilded God," he spat. He turned to the others. "Men follow musicians like dumb sheep, and their worship has kept Apollo strong. We must kill him *now*, before he recovers."

The Smith stepped forward, his hammer raised. "You think we'll let you harm our brother?" he rumbled.

"Oh yes. In fact, I think you'll do it for me."

Dash laughed. "You've been playing with mortals too long, Hunter, if you think you can get us to do your bidding."

"This is no joke, Hermes," Orion seethed. "Even you are not as powerful as you once were. No one is. I can change that."

The Smith glowered at him suspiciously. "How?"

"You stole one Corn King from death. Give me another. Give me Apollo. Once he's crowned and blessed, as Theo was, he'll be a sacrifice more powerful than even a Makarites—a sacrifice so great it would do more than bring Artemis and me back to strength. It would make you *all* truly Athanatoi once more."

"He lies," said the Smith.

"Tell them, Artemis!" Orion cried. "She had the power of a goddess again before she threw it all away. Sacrifice Apollo to the ritual and you, Hermes, will fly through the air on winged sandals. Hephaestus, your fading will cease, volcanoes will erupt at your command! Dionysus—you can bring men to madness or lust with a flick of your finger."

Dennis merely snorted. "Sounds like an average Saturday night in my apartment."

But Dash looked intrigued. "My sandals will work?"

Dennis lifted his thyrsus and pointed it at his brother. "Look at that. You're considering it. Damn, Dad was right. Give the gods hope of return and things get *all* kinds of fucked up."

"What do you say, Apollo?" Orion demanded. "Theo sacrificed his life for Artemis. Will you?"

Paul could only look from Dash to the Smith to Dennis, his expression panicked.

"Don't answer that, Sunbeam." With Theo's help, Selene struggled to her feet. "No one is sacrificing anything for me. Not anymore."

She turned to her brothers, unsurprised by what she read in their faces. Dash and Dennis eyed Paul curiously, as if mulling over the possibility of his demise. Even the Smith, usually one of the least bloodthirsty of the Olympians, looked at her twin with something like hunger. If they chose to listen to Orion, she'd be unable to stop them. By relinquishing her omnipotence and weakening Paul, she'd put him in great danger. Now it was up to her to save him by convincing the others to spare his life. She was used to urging people at the point of an arrow. *I'm no good at this,* she thought. *I'm no stitcher of songs, no weaver of words. That's Theo's gift, not mine.* As if he heard her, Theo laced his fingers through hers. His touch was a rope thrown right into her desperate hands. Through it flowed love and confidence, and most of all, hope. She gripped his hand a little tighter, then let it go and stood upright on her own. As the shock from losing her powers faded, her dizziness dissipated, and some of her strength returned. She took a deep breath and turned to her siblings.

"There will be no more killings. The cult is finished. And we must swear tonight that there will never be another," she began.

"Don't listen to her!" Orion interrupted. "Apollo's at his weakest right now—you must do it now if you have any hope of killing him before he recovers." Before he could say more, Theo retrieved the roll of duct tape from Nate's body and slapped a gag across Orion's mouth. Selene nodded her thanks, then continued.

"I see how you look at my brother even now, wondering if *maybe* it'd be worth it. One dead god and an eternity of power. But tonight's sacrifice would not be the last. Every year, the ritual must be repeated. More innocents dead. Not a god, you're thinking—you would only kill thanatoi after tonight. But each time we condone the murder of a guiltless mortal, we take one step further from our own humanity, one step closer to a version of ourselves better left in the mists of memory. We were heartless, cruel, fickle creatures, bereft of empathy, of true human emotions. Only jealousy, rage, lust, despair were left to us. I had forgotten until Orion brought me back to godhood. I could control the tides, that's true, but I couldn't control my own choices, my own memories, my own heart. Is that what you would return to? Long ago, Father put a stop to the sacrifices in the Eleusinian Mysteries when he decided we should cease to grant immortality to mankind. Tonight we must do so again, even though we deny godhood to ourselves as well. But if our millennia on earth have taught us anything, it's that the world changes, and we must change with it. You may yearn for what is lost. I prefer to see all that we have gained. I say this because... because I have never felt weaker than I do at this moment. But here, with all of you around me"—she looked at each of her brothers in turn and then at Theo, who stood just within reach, solid and strong and vitally alive—"I have never felt stronger either."

Shame creased the Smith's face. "She's right. What Orion offers comes at too great a price. We must learn to accept our new lives. None of us are perfect anymore. I've had a little longer than the rest of you to get used to that idea. We'll be all right."

Paul heaved a sigh of relief as Dash patted him on the back.

"You didn't *really* think I'd kill you for a pair of flying shoes, did you?" Selene thought Dash's grin a little forced, but at least Paul seemed out of immediate danger.

Dennis just rolled his eyes. "So everything's settled, then? Apollo, looks like you'll live another day—even if you are looking a little worse for wear."

Paul bristled and ran a hand self-consciously through the streak in his hair. "It was...a shock, that's all." He stood up a little straighter and met Selene's gaze. "If losing some of my powers is the price I must pay for getting my sister back, I do so willingly. I'm no thanatos yet, just a little...dimmed. It was bound to happen eventually." Fine words, but he couldn't hide the grief that pulled at his mouth.

Selene walked to her twin and leaned her forehead against his. They were exactly the same height. Very lightly, she kissed his tanned cheek, then stepped back to look him in the eye. "Do not despair. Whether gods or not, our lives still have purpose," she said quietly. She took his hand in hers and faced the others. "The mortals need us, even if they don't know it. And, most of all, we need each other. The Smith made me a bow and arrows to wield. The Messenger carried him word that I needed it. He Who Unties unraveled the truth of the Mystery. And you, Bright One, God of Healing, Son of Leto, Twin of Delos, brought the man I...brought Theo...back to life."

Hippo barked in protest. "She doesn't want you to leave her out," Theo said with a laugh.

Paul chuckled, and his mirth warmed Selene like a sunbeam on a winter's day. "True. Your dog found me wandering through the park and led me to the cave. I felt the pull when you invoked me, but turns out my directional sense isn't quite as specific as it used to be."

"That's that, then," Dennis said, yawning. "Sorry, Orion. Guess your plan didn't work. Seems we're not quite as desperate as you thought. Maybe try again in another hundred years or so."

"Now can we kill him?" Dash asked, spinning his pistols like a gunslinger.

"He doesn't look very dangerous," Theo interjected. "Shouldn't we just turn him over to the police?"

Selene looked at him incredulously. "You would spare the man who ordered your death? Who killed Helen?"

"He's unarmed. Helpless. I don't believe in vengeance killing."

"What do you say about that, Orion?" asked the Smith, tearing the tape from the Hunter's mouth. "This man would show you mercy, even now."

But Orion just spat at the ground before Theo's feet. "Don't do me any favors, Makarites. I'm one god you don't understand." With a cry of pain and fury, he twisted free of the wall, the arrows' fletching tearing great wounds in his wrists. He stumbled forward, drenched in blood, and dove toward the cave's mouth. Moving with surprising speed, Dennis swung his thyrsus at Orion's head, just as the Smith launched his hammer through the air. With a hollow thud, the heavy wooden staff connected with his skull, sending Orion sprawling on the ground, while the hammer struck him in the chest with an audible crack of breaking ribs. Orion fell with one arm flung behind him and the other trapped beneath his body. He lifted his head, his eyes unfocused, and let out a low moan. Dennis lowered his thyrsus with a smug smile.

Orion's face remained slack, but his left arm whipped out suddenly, reaching for his fallen sword. "Watch out!" Theo cried. He grabbed Selene's bow off the ground while she yanked an arrow from Bill Webb's fallen body. Just as the Hunter rose to his feet, Theo tossed her the weapon, his green eyes bright with urgency. Whatever hesitation he'd shown before had vanished. He might not believe in killing for revenge, but he would do anything to protect the people he loved.

Once before, Selene had killed Orion in a wild rage, only to regret it for the rest of her life. This time, as she nocked the divine arrow to her bowstring, her heart was stone within her breast. There would be no coming back for the Hunter, not with his father Poseidon out of reach. The thought gave her only comfort. She sent a golden shaft straight through his heart.

He blinked once, twice, and the sword slid from his fingers to clatter upon the stone. He swayed on his feet and looked up at her—his immortal love, his eternal Huntress. His face softened. His hate dissolved. Only anguish remained.

He sank to the ground, his dark eyes still glued on Selene, even as they clouded over. She knelt by his side and took his hand in hers. The gleaming gold and silver arrows jutted from his flesh in a parody of divine radiance. For a last few breaths, his mouth moved with a dry clacking sound, unable to form words of entreaty or accusation. Selene fought the grief that nipped at the edges of her composure as she watched an old dream die.

"I know," she said softly. "You killed for love. So did I." With a last, choking breath, he was gone. *I forgive you,* she admitted. *And I forgive myself.* Gently, she touched his eyelids, closing forever the gaze that had once captured her heart.

Chapter 48

THANATOS

Theo sat with his back against a tree for the next two hours, watching five mostly immortal Olympian gods cover up a crime scene. First Hermes had dashed off into the woods. Minutes later, he returned, his body blurring with speed before he came to an easy halt, casually brushing a few leaves from his impeccable linen suit and holding a shovel no doubt illegally procured from a park ranger's storage shed. Dionysus gave him a sardonic golf clap upon his return. Theo was finding it surprisingly easy to think of his old roommate as the Wine Giver. It made more sense than many of Dennis's other exploits.

Between the shovel and Hippolyta's strong claws, it didn't take them long to dig a ditch deep in the woods. They laid Everett's body—*Orion's* body—carefully inside. Hephaestus the Smith did something uncanny with a match and a jar of black goo that made the corpse burn nearly smokelessly. At Selene's direction—and with a little help from Dionysus, God of Wild Vines—they made the entire area look untouched and natural once again. Hermes and Selene, with their experience on the police force, inspected the cave and wiped any prints that would indicate someone other than the professors and Everett had been there. They removed the gold and silver arrows and Orion's bronze sword, but left the professors' knives. Before they burned the corpse, they pressed Orion's fingers against the knives' handles. Theo would explain that the professors had taken him to the cave, but he'd managed to escape before the ritual began. The cops would blame Everett Halloran, the mysteriously missing classicist, for killing his colleagues as part of their cult. *That much is true, anyway,* Theo thought. *Everett's the one who really killed them, with his flattery and his promises. They were decent men once. Or at least, they weren't evil. Soon, I'll mourn them all. But right now, I'm just glad it's over.*

Theo felt a little lame for not helping with all the burning and digging, but he *had* just died and been brought back to life. And they were gods, after all.

Finally, as the Olympians placed the final shrubs and branches on Orion's grave, the sky grew light. Now Selene sat beside him, a scant two feet away, her head thrown back against the trunk of a neighboring tree, her eyes ringed in dark circles. New lines creased her forehead. She wouldn't look at Theo.

"It's almost dawn," Theo said quietly. "The park crew will be here soon."

She nodded wearily.

"Artemis?"

"Don't call me that."

"Why not?" he asked a little giddily. "Isn't that your name?" It wasn't every day that Olympians stepped out of myth to stand beside him. It would mean reworking all his lectures on the "real" meaning of myths, but he'd deal with the philosophical ramifications later. For now, he might as well just enjoy it.

"That's the name of a goddess," Selene murmured. "I haven't been a goddess in a long time. Right now, I barely feel human." She raised a hand to the new streak of white in her black hair.

"You feel exhausted, and overwhelmed, and like you can barely stand?"

"Yeah."

"Well, that's exactly what being human feels like most of the time," he said with a laugh.

"I hate it."

"You'd rather have let Orion turn you back into a goddess?" He wasn't sure he wanted to hear the answer.

She finally met his eyes. "No. You knew, didn't you, that I hadn't really gone back to him?"

"I knew you weren't the type of woman to forgive someone who'd killed so many innocent people. And I'd begun to suspect, although I still couldn't believe it, that you weren't really an ordinary woman at all."

"What gave me away?" A hint of a smile brushed her lips.

"Hmmm. The talking to mice? Breaking steel handcuffs? Bringing me back from the dead? Something like that."

"I don't think I'll be performing many supernatural feats again anytime soon. That was my last hurrah for a while. Maybe forever."

He looked again at the white in her hair, the new creases around her mouth. "It weakened you to bring me back, didn't it? Without the sacrifice..."

"You died. I think we're even."

He laughed at her rueful smirk. *If she can smile, even when her entire future is in doubt, then I may have finally met my match.*

"In the cave..." he began. She looked away from him, but he pressed on. "You said you wanted me to kiss you."

"I kissed you before, don't you remember?"

"Doesn't count. I was almost dead, so I couldn't really enjoy it."

Her hands were shaking. "I've been lying to you all this time."

"Well, I wouldn't have believed the truth, so I can't blame you."

"I don't even know what the truth *is* anymore. I'm not a goddess. I'm not quite human. I've lived forever and sometimes still feel like a child."

"I know enough. I know you'd do anything to help a friend. I know you're brave and wild and lovely, and that you saw things in me I didn't know were there."

"Don't you see how dangerous I am?" She gestured to the cave. "Look what happened to the last man I was with."

"I think I can learn from his mistakes. You know…don't become a serial killer. Don't piss off your twin brother. Don't try to become immortal. I'm a quick study."

Selene started laughing. That beautiful, embarrassing honk, mixed with equal parts tears.

"Hey, Relentless One, you haven't answered my question."

She turned and gazed at him. Her silver eyes could still strike him speechless. Taking his face in her hands, she ran a thumb across his lips. Then she kissed him very lightly. "How's that for an answer?"

"Almost perfect."

"Almost?" She frowned.

He wrapped her in his arms and drew her close, ignoring the dull ache of the wound in his chest, and kissed her with all the passion and relief of a hero finally returned home.

Epilogos

THE GOOD MAIDEN

Day Ten. *Plemochoai*. Libations.

Sunset gilded the cross streets. New York glowed pink and orange, the buildings bathed in light. A crisp autumn wind stirred the trash into graceful pirouettes above the sidewalks. Passersby lifted their noses to sniff at the smoky air, dreaming of Halloween and Thanksgiving, then turned their faces back to the traffic and the crowds and barreled forth into the gloaming.

On the corner of West Ninety-seventh Street and Riverside Drive, the Delian twins stood side by side, watching the sun go down and the moon arise.

Under one arm, Selene carried a small white box. Paul held a bottle of wine. If it weren't for the solemnity of their expressions, you might have thought they planned on a picnic.

"You sure you want him here for this?" asked Paul. "He didn't even know her."

"But she would've wanted to know him."

Theo appeared across the street, Hippo nearly dragging him up the sidewalk. He finally let her run unhindered to her mistress, whom she greeted with a series of slobbering licks and bruising tail thwacks.

"Did she give you too much trouble?" Selene asked.

"Nope. We're old friends, right, girl?" Hippo looked at him balefully then returned to licking Selene's hand. "How was the funeral home? Everything go okay?" Selene raised the white box in answer. He turned to the other twin. "Hey...Paul. Good to see you again."

The Bright One hesitated for a moment, then shook Theo's proffered hand.

Dusk had already settled beneath the trees of Riverside Park. Selene led the way past the playgrounds and park benches, down the sloping path to the Hudson waterfront. They stopped at the boulders, not far from where she'd found Helen's body. Hippo splashed in happily. "No, girl, come on out. Not tonight." Panting, the dog scrambled back onto the rocks and shook a fountain of water and hair into the breeze. It took a moment for them all to regain the proper degree of gravity. But finally, Selene took a deep breath to steady herself and stepped forward to the water's edge.

She turned to her twin. "Come on, Sunbeam," she urged softly.

Paul uncorked the bottle. In a flashing ruby arc, the wine tumbled into the river. *"Sponde Letoi,"* the Bright One sang in the ancient tongue. *A libation for Leto.* "A libation for the mildest goddess. For the gentle Titan. For the mother of twins."

Selene took up the chant. *"Sponde Letoi.* For the goddess of Delos. For the consort of mighty Zeus. For the daughter of Phoibe, who lends her light to the stars and moon."

Then it was Theo's turn.

"Sponde Letoi." His Ancient Greek was as flawless as it had been the first time she'd heard him speak, on this very shore, at another memorial for another loved one lost. "For the mother of Paul and Selene. For the Titan who birthed two gods to shed light on the world, but who died as happily as any mortal mother might, in the arms of the children she loved."

Selene opened the box and tipped it toward the water. She'd changed her mind about bringing the ashes to Delos. Leto would want to be here, where her children lived and laughed and loved. A plume of ash swirled forth, curling and dancing on Zephyrus's breath. It flew high above their heads, falling and rising as gracefully as Leto's veil had floated on the breeze. Then, with a puff of wind, the ash dispersed, scattered to the water, to the trees, to the earth, to the sky.

Theo slipped his hand into Selene's and she slipped hers into Paul's. The three mourners stood in silence for a long time. Even Hippo sat quietly, her eyes fixed on the water, as the last of Leto disappeared from view.

I have never been so sad, Selene prayed to her mother. *Or so happy.*

Theo picked up Hippo's leash. "I'll let you two be alone, okay? I'll be under the trees near the exit whenever you're ready to go."

Selene watched him walk off down the path, Hippo trotting gamely at his side, until he was swallowed by the shadows of the woods.

"He's good to you," Paul said suddenly.

"He's good *for* me."

She reached for the bottle and poured the last of the wine into the river. "*Sponde Orioni.* A libation for Orion, the Hunter," she murmured. "Tortured by love, tortured by hate. May he rest now among the stars, finally at peace. And may he forgive me once more."

"Are you sorry he's gone?" Paul asked softly.

She shook her head. "I don't need a god." Handing the bottle back to Paul, she smiled ruefully. "I've got someone better waiting for me."

Her brother nodded. "You know, don't you, that this isn't the end of it. Dash is the Messenger, after all. Word of the Mystery's power will get out. Rumors will spread. Soon all the fading

Athanatoi will be clamoring for a chance at rebirth. And most will have no qualms about massacring mortals to get what they want."

"Then they'll have me to deal with."

"Protector of the Innocent, huh?"

"Always."

"Then you're going to have quite a fight ahead of you."

"And will you be there beside me?"

"Always."

Selene found Theo sitting on the grass beneath a towering elm, right on the border between the city and the park. Beside him, Hippo kept her eyes glued on a flock of geese, ready to pounce.

She slipped off her backpack and settled next to him on the ground. For once, Theo didn't speak, only took her hand in his.

Selene looked west, where the faintest traces of purple and orange still streamed above the horizon. The lights on the Jersey shoreline flickered like constellations across the river. Above her, the moon, a waxing crescent, began its ascent through a deep blue sky. Then she looked east, toward her city. Dog walkers and late commuters strolled the twilit sidewalks, heading home after a long day. Across the street, Selene could see the illuminated windows of apartment buildings. Inside, friends and families gathered to eat. Children played with their parents. Lovers flew to each other's arms.

"After I met you, I dreamt of lying with you in a moonbeam," Theo finally murmured.

Selene's insides clenched—pleasant and painful all at once—as he went on. "I didn't know it was you at the time. You were just a faceless dream woman. But sitting here with you, it's like déjà vu." His thumb brushed gentle circles across her palm. He laughed lightly before her embarrassment could make her pull away. "Sorry. I know you don't have a lot of time for sitting in moonbeams.

You've got to get back on the streets and find another crime to solve, another woman to protect, right?"

"Captain Hansen said I should be a cop again. For the third time."

"The *third* time?"

"Long story."

Theo just laughed. All day, she'd been saying the same thing. Some stories he'd demanded to hear right away. Others he'd consented to wait for. "Well, forget the badge. I like you better as a vigilante. It'll be easier for us to fight crime if we play by our own rules."

"Us? You want to help?"

"Just try to stop me."

"You realize I'm going to be confronting more bloodthirsty immortals in the future?"

"I'm a Makarites, remember? I've got a special connection to the gods. Might come in handy. Trust me, this is a dream come true."

"Is it?" Selene pulled her hand from his and turned to face him. "Am I just a dream to you?"

A dimple appeared on one cheek. "Moon Goddess. Huntress. Far Shooter. They're the dreams. I know my mythology. If I were to see you in all your glory, I'd be consumed by flame, left a charred husk of a man, blown to ashes by the wind. When you started glowing in the cave, I thought I was a goner for sure." He covered her hand with his own, his gaze suddenly serious. "I don't want the dream. I want Selene. With all her warmth and laughter." He threaded his fingers through hers. "And her ice and anger, too."

She settled back against the tree, her shoulder brushing his. With a sigh, Hippo rolled over to rest her head on Selene's lap.

"Did you really dream of lying with me in a moonbeam?" she asked finally.

Theo paused a moment. "Actually, I dreamt of making love to you in a moonbeam."

"Oh."

She could feel the heat of his skin through her shirt where their shoulders met. Finally, she answered his unspoken question with a kiss. Long and slow and full of hunger.

"Fierce." He smiled breathlessly. "I always said the Moon was fierce."

"Fierce and lonely. That's what you said." She kissed him again, softer this time. Theo's hands tangled in her hair as he pulled her closer.

"Not so lonely anymore," he said quietly when they finally drew apart.

"Come, Theodore." She stood and held out a hand to haul him to his feet. "I've been waiting for you for almost three thousand years. Would you ask me to wait any longer?"

"I wouldn't dare. You might get angry and turn me into a stag."

She took a step back, alarmed. Only then did she realize he was teasing her.

"You? More like a mockingbird. You've certainly got the tongue for it."

Theo chuckled briefly, but then cast her a nervous glance. "Wait... you're not serious, are you?"

Selene laughed, so loudly the passersby shot her worried looks. She didn't care. "Don't worry. I rather like you as a human." With a sly grin, she raised Theo's hand to her lips and pressed a kiss on his knuckles. "At least for now."

AUTHOR'S NOTE

The Eleusinian Mysteries were the most important religious ritual in ancient Athens and the surrounding area for almost two thousand years, until the Holy Roman Emperor Theodosius outlawed pagan rites in the fourth century AD. The veil of secrecy around the rites has led both to an absence of any definitive historical records of the events' details and to a surfeit of fragmentary allusions to the Mysteries in a variety of sources. Thus, our knowledge of exactly what transpired is hazy at best. Theo's understanding of the ritual's components is a loose conflation of many scholars' hypotheses, most prominently those featured in Jon D. Mikalson's *Ancient Greek Religion*, Mara Lynn Keller's article "The Ritual Path of Initiation into the Eleusinian Mysteries" in the *Rosicrucian Digest*, and *The Ancient Mysteries: A Sourcebook of Sacred Texts*, edited by Marvin W. Meyer. My apologies to these and the many other classicists who would no doubt find the version of the Mysteries presented in this book hopelessly simplistic.

The nature of the epiphany at the rite's climax is unknown and still a point of great scholarly debate. The presence in the *kykeon* of a hallucinogen not unlike LSD has been proposed in R. Gordon Wasson, Albert Hoffman, and Carl A. P. Ruck's *The Road to Eleusis* and would seem to explain the Greeks' powerful reaction to the ritual. That human sacrifice played a role is my own invention. The Oxyrhynchus Project has yet to discover any mention of such atrocities in its trove of Hellenic papyri (see Oxford's *Ancient Lives* project at www.papyrology.ox.ac.uk if you want a chance to do some decoding of your own). However, the Eleusinian Mysteries stretch back in time before the rise of Athens, to an earlier age in which, many have proposed, earth-goddess worship may have required a bloodier form of ritual than that practiced by the sophisticated citizens of the Golden Age.

While the details of the Mysteries are in large part hypothetical, the stories of New York City's past are all real. Alexander Hamilton's death, the formation of the Policewomen's Bureau in the 1920s, and the crime wave of the 1970s are all grounded in fact. So, too, are the majority of the locations in this book. The waterfall in Central Park's Ravine is easily visited. Franklin Roosevelt's presidential railroad car still sits on its abandoned platform beneath the Waldorf-Astoria Hotel, where, indeed, a paupers' cemetery once lay. You can see pictures of it in an informative article by Jen Carlson at gothamist.com. The hidden Liberty Theater exists, and was at one time inaccessible, although a recent renovation has transformed it into a not-so-hidden restaurant. Seeing the abandoned City Hall subway station is a cinch—just ride the downtown Number 6 line past the last stop and look out the windows as the train loops around before heading uptown. To visit Montayne's Fonteyn (barely a trickle these days) or the old Indian Cave (still walled up, unfortunately), follow the directions in Christopher Gray's excellent article "Scenes from a Wild Youth" in the *New York Times*. The Pneumatic Transit waiting room has, sadly, been lost to us, but it must have been a remarkable sight. Joseph Brennan describes it in great detail in his article "Beach Pneumatic" on columbia.edu.

Into these very real locations I've placed characters from myth that have only ever existed in the collective imagination of mankind. The tale of Orion and Artemis has no single definitive version—only fragments and allusions remain to us. In some, the two are chaste lovers. In others, he tries to rape her or one of her nymphs. In still others, he is a lascivious braggart, brought down by her rage. He dies when Apollo tricks Artemis into shooting him or, alternatively, when the angry goddess sends a scorpion to kill him. No matter the version, however, the story of the Huntress and the Hunter has always fascinated, perhaps because Artemis has always been one of the most paradoxical and intriguing figures in classic myth. For many, myself included, she has been a feminist icon: a woman warrior unhindered by societal norms, fiercer, swifter, and deadlier than any man. And yet, she is also a product of her time—consigned to virginity by a society that sees sex, love, and motherhood as incompatible with the fiercer aspects of her personality. As demonstrated by the plethora of epithets ascribed to her, Artemis is complicated and contradictory, beloved and feared. Wandering the dusty, sunbaked streets of Delos, past the ruins of her temple, you can easily feel the goddess and her twin beside you. It seems a short leap to imagine her walking through the streets of Manhattan as well. In some ways, she is immortal indeed.

Jordanna Max Brodsky
New York, NY
April 2015

Appendices

Olympians, Heroes, and Other Immortals

A note on spelling:

For the more ancient gods such as the Titans and primeval divinities, I've used the transliterated Greek spellings (Ouranos rather than Uranus). For the Olympians and others, I've used the more familiar Latinized spellings (Hephaestus rather than Hephaistos).

Aphrodite: Goddess of Erotic Love and Beauty. One of the Twelve Olympians. Born of sea foam after Kronos castrates his father, Ouranos, and throws his genitals in the ocean. Wife of Hephaestus and lover of Ares. Attributes: dove, scallop shell, mirror.

Apollo: God of Light, Music, Healing, Prophecy, Poetry, Archery, Civilization, Plague, and the Sun. One of the Twelve Olympians. Leader of the Muses. Twin brother of Artemis. Son of Leto and Zeus. Father of Asclepius. Born on the island of Delos. Called Phoebus (Bright One). Attributes: silver bow, laurel wreath, lyre. Modern alias: Paul Solson.

Ares: God of War. One of the Twelve Olympians. Son of Zeus and Hera. Lover of Aphrodite. Attributes: armor, spear, poisonous serpent.

Artemis: Goddess of the Wilderness, the Hunt, Virginity, Wild Animals, Hounds, Young Children, and the Moon. One of the Twelve Olympians. Twin sister of Apollo. Daughter of Leto and Zeus. Born on the island of Delos. Called Phoebe, Cynthia, Diana. Has more epithets than any other god, including Far Shooter, Huntress, Relentless One, Protector of the Innocent, and more. Attributes: golden bow, hounds. Modern aliases: Phoebe Hautman, Dianne Delia, Melissa Dubois, Cynthia Forrester, Selene DiSilva.

Asclepius: Hero-God of Medicine. Half-mortal son of Apollo. Worshiped in the Eleusinian Mysteries and many other cults. Attribute: a snake-twined staff.

Athena: Goddess of Wisdom, Crafts, and Justified War. One of the Twelve Olympians. Virgin. Attributes: helmet, shield, owl.

Boreas: God and embodiment of the north wind.

Cerberus: Three-headed guard dog of the Underworld.

Demeter: Goddess of Grain and Agriculture. One of the Twelve Olympians. Daughter of Kronos and Rhea. Sister of Zeus. Mother of Persephone. Patron goddess of the Eleusinian Mysteries, which retell the story of her quest for Persephone after the girl was abducted by Hades. Called Bountiful, Bringer of Seasons. Attributes: wheat sheaves, torch. Modern alias: Gwenith.

Dionysus: God of Wine, Wild Plants, Festivity, Theater. One of the Twelve Olympians. Son of Zeus and Semele, a mortal. One of the gods worshiped in the Eleusinian Mysteries. Usually accompanied by maenads (female devotees) and satyrs (male devotees, sometimes with cloven hooves). Called Bacchus, Phallic, He Who Unties, He of the Wild Revels. Attributes: grape vine, thyrsus (a pinecone-tipped staff), ivy, leopard. Modern alias: Dennis Boivin.

Gaia: Primeval Earth Divinity. Mother to all. Consort of Ouranos, the Sky.

Hades: God of the Underworld, Death, Wealth. Son of Kronos and Rhea. Brother of Zeus. Husband of Persephone. Called Pluto, Receiver of Many, Hidden One. Attributes: helm of invisibility, bird-tipped scepter. Modern alias: Aiden.

Helen of Troy: Daughter of Zeus and a mortal woman whom Zeus appeared to in the form of a swan. Reputed to be the most beautiful woman in the world. Her abduction instigated the Trojan War. In the late sixteenth century, Christopher Marlowe coined her most famous epithet, "the face that launch'd a thousand ships."

Helios: God and embodiment of the Sun. Also identified with Apollo, who has dominion over the sun.

Hephaestus: God of the Forge and Fire. One of the Twelve Olympians. Son of Hera, born parthenogenically. Lamed when thrown off Olympus by Zeus and walks with a crutch. Called the Smith, the Sooty God, He of Many Arts and Skills, Lame One. Attributes: hammer, tongs.

Heracles: Greatest of the Greek heroes. Also known as Hercules (Latin). Half-mortal son of Zeus. Completed twelve famous labors. On his death, he was made immortal by the gods and ascended to Olympus.

Hera: Queen of the Gods. Goddess of Women, Marriage, and the Heavens. One of the Twelve Olympians. Daughter of Kronos and Rhea. Sister and jealous wife of Zeus. Mother of Ares and Hephaestus. Known as "white-armed." Attributes: crown, peacock, lotus-tipped staff.

Hermes: God of Thieves, Liars, Travel, Communication, Hospitality, and Athletics. One of the Twelve Olympians. Son of Zeus and a nymph. Known as "the Psychopompos," the Conductor of Souls to the Underworld. Herald to the gods. Called Messenger, Luck-Bringing, Trickster, Many-Turning, Busy One. Attributes: caduceus (winged staff twined with snakes), winged sandals, winged cap. Modern aliases: Swifty O'May, Dash Mercer.

Hestia: Goddess of the Hearth and Home. Eldest daughter of Kronos and Rhea. Sister of Zeus. Virgin. Once part of the Twelve Olympians, but gave up her throne to Dionysus. She tended the sacred fire at the center of Mount Olympus. Called "The Eldest." Attributes: veil, kettle.

Khaos: Primeval embodiment of Chaos. From the same root as "chasm," the name means the void from which all other primeval divinities sprang.

Kronos: A Titan. With the help of his mother, Gaia (the Earth), he overthrew his father, Ouranos (the Sky), to become King of the Gods until overthrown in turn by Zeus, his son. Father/grandfather of the Olympians.

Leto: Goddess of Motherhood and Modesty. Daughter of the Titans Phoibe and Koios. Lover of Zeus. Mother of Artemis and Apollo. Chased by jealous Hera to the island of Delos, where she finally gave birth to her twins. Called "neat-ankled," Gentle Goddess, Mother of Twins. Attributes: veil, date palm. Modern alias: Leticia Delos.

Merope: A nymph. Sometimes identified as one of the daughters of Atlas, the Titan who holds up the Earth. Artemis's hunting companion.

Odysseus: Hero of Homer's *Odyssey*. Fought in the Trojan War, then took ten years to get home to his wife after many adventures along the way. Known for his cunning, cleverness, and eloquence. Mastermind behind the Trojan Horse.

Orion: Son of Poseidon and a mortal woman. Artemis's only male hunting companion. Some tales describe him as blinded and exiled after raping Merope, a king's daughter. Other myths say he raped one of Artemis's nymphs. He was killed either by a scorpion or by Artemis's arrows. Placed as a constellation in the sky. Called the Hunter.

Ouranos: Primeval Sky Divinity. Father of the Titans. Also called Uranus. Overthrown by his son Kronos.

Persephone: Goddess of Spring and the Underworld. Daughter of Demeter and Zeus. Wife of Hades. Worshiped in the Eleusinian Mysteries, which commemorate her abduction by Hades into the Underworld and her eventual return to her mother. Called Kore ("Maiden"), Discreet, Lovely. Attributes: wheat sheaves, torch. Modern alias: Cora.

Phoibe: Titan goddess of the Moon and Prophecy. Mother of Leto. She gave the moon to her granddaughter, Artemis, and the gift of prophecy to her grandson, Apollo.

Poseidon: God of the Sea, Earthquakes, and Horses. One of the Twelve Olympians. Son of Kronos and Rhea. Brother of Zeus. Father of Orion, Theseus, and other heroes. Called "blue-haired," Earth-Shaker, Horse-Tender. Attributes: trident.

Prometheus: A Titan. After molding mankind from clay, he gave them fire, despite the prohibition of the other gods. As punishment, the Olympians chained him to a rock and sent an eagle to eat his liver every day for eternity.

Rhea: A Titan. Goddess of Female Fertility. Queen of the Gods in the Age of Titans. Helped Zeus, her youngest son, overthrow his father, Kronos.

Selene: Goddess and embodiment of the Moon. Lover of Endymion, a mortal to whom Zeus grants eternal youth and eternal slumber. While Artemis has dominion over the moon, Selene is the Moon incarnate.

Tithonus: A shepherd boy loved by Eos, the Dawn. She begs Zeus to grant him immortality but forgets to ask for eternal youth. Eventually, he grows so old and shriveled that he's turned into a grasshopper or cicada.

Zephyrus: God and embodiment of the gentle west wind.

Zeus: King and Father of the Gods. God of the Sky, Lightning, Weather, Law, and Fate. One of the Twelve Olympians. Youngest son of Kronos and Rhea. After Kronos swallowed his first five children, Rhea hid baby Zeus in the Cave of Psychro. After coming to manhood, Zeus cut his siblings from his father's gullet, defeated the Titans, and began the reign of the Olympians. He divided the world with his two brothers, taking the Sky for himself. Husband (and brother) of Hera, but lover of many. Father of untold gods, goddesses, and heroes, including Artemis and Apollo. Attributes: lightning bolt, eagle, royal scepter.

The Eleusinian Mysteries

A Brief Outline

Day One: Procession of the Sacred Objects (*hiera*) from Demeter and Persephone's temple in Eleusis to the Acropolis in Athens. The objects were carried in a *kiste* (chest) and a *kalathos* (basket). (Note: This is often considered the "Day Before Day One," and the *Agyrmos* is counted as Day One. For simplicity's sake, I've counted the *Agyrmos* as Day Two.)

Day Two: Agyrmos, "the Gathering": The opening ceremony. Initiates (*mystai*) are given their instructions. The Sacred Objects are taken into Demeter's Athenian temple, accompanied by singing and dancing.

Day Three: Alade! *Mystai!*, **"Seawards, Initiates!":** Ritual cleansing of the initiates in the ocean south of Athens.

Day Four: *Heireia* **Deuro!, "Bring Sacred Offerings!":** Initiates offer suckling pigs to the goddesses. City-states bring tithes of grain to Athens.

Day Five: *Asklepia*, **"Feast of Asclepius":** The cult of Asclepius joins the rite. Initiates spend the night seeking "healing dreams," probably in the Athenian temple to Asclepius, built in a cave with a sacred spring.

Day Six: *Pompe*, **"Procession":** Hierophants (priests) and initiates process with the Sacred Objects from Athens back to Eleusis. They start at the Kerameikos Cemetery, then cross the Bridge of Jests, where jesters mock them with bawdy jokes. The *Pompe* is sometimes associated with Dionysus.

Day Seven: *Pannychis*, **"Nightlong Revelry":** Torch-lit dancing around a "well of beautiful dances" near Demeter's temple in Eleusis.

Days Eight and Nine: *Mysteriotides Nychtes*, **"Nights of the Mysteries":** Exact rituals unknown. Secret rites took place inside Demeter's temple at the Telesterion, the "Hall of Completion." The ritual included three components: *Legomena* ("Things Said"), *Dromena* ("Things Done"), and *Deiknumena* ("Things Shown"). Likely, the rites involved the display of the

Sacred Objects and a reenactment of the story of Persephone's abduction by Hades and her later return to her mother, Demeter. Initiates drank *kykeon*, a special potion, possibly consisting of barley water and pennyroyal. At the climax of the ritual, they received a holy, life-altering vision.

Day Ten: *Plemochoai*, **"Libations":** Initiates pour libations (offerings of wine or water) to the gods and to their ancestors.

GLOSSARY OF GREEK AND LATIN TERMS

Athanatos (pl. Athanatoi): "One Who Does Not Die" (an immortal).

Chiton: a long tunic worn in Ancient Greece.

Hiera: sacred objects.

Hierophant: head priest of a Mystery Cult, literally the "Revealer of Sacred Things."

Kalathos: wool-gathering basket.

Katharsis: catharsis, from *katharos*, meaning "pure." Release from strong or repressed emotions, often through experiencing tragedy in art or drama.

Kharisma: charisma, from *karis*, meaning "grace." A talent conferred by the gods.

Kiste: a chest or box.

Kykeon: special potion drunk in the Eleusinian Mysteries.

Lararium: a shrine in Roman homes honoring the household gods or protective spirits (*lares*).

Makarites (pl. Makaritai): "Blessed One."

Meandros: a decorative element common in ancient Greece, also called the "Greek key," named after the twisting path of the Meander River.

Mystes (pl. mystai): an initiate into a Mystery Cult.

Sex crines: hairstyle of six braids worn by Roman brides, denoting virginity.

Thanatos (pl. thanatoi): "One Who Dies" (a mortal).

ACKNOWLEDGMENTS

As an extrovert in an introvert's profession, I've found myself seeking out companions since the beginning of this journey. Luckily, I've been blessed with more than my share of friends generous enough to travel along with me.

Helen Shaw introduced me to the Eleusinian Mysteries and generously supplied me with ideas and inspiration, not to mention invaluable moral support, editorial help, comic relief, and unconditional friendship, throughout the entire process. If you found something especially clever or funny, you can probably thank her. The indomitable Dustin Thomason not only gave reams of helpful feedback, but his introductions, encouragement, and extraordinary generosity of spirit truly made the book possible. Tegan Tigani, my partner in creativity since the third grade, never balked at reading more drafts and sharing her publishing expertise. She is the best advocate and the best friend anyone could ask for.

My heartfelt thanks to my other readers: Jaclyn Huberman, Eliot Schrefer, Emily Shooltz, Christopher Vander Mey, Chandler Williams, Chad Mills, and John Wray. Great minds and great friends—you made *The Immortals* a better book, just as you've made me a better person for so many years.

Dr. Michael Shaw and Dr. Anne Shaw, classicists extraordinaire, generously provided most of the Ancient Greek translations and transliterations for the book. Any brilliance in Theo's work is theirs; any errors or inconsistencies are my own.

My undying gratitude to my tremendous agent, Jennifer Joel at ICM, who pored over every line of the book multiple times, always leaving the pages a little shorter and a lot better than when she found them. Her unerring eye and superhuman patience never fail to astound. Thanks as well to Madeleine Osborn at ICM, who carried the book to new heights at just the right time. Without the advocacy of my editor at Orbit, Devi Pillai, this book would never have seen the light of day. She believed in *The Immortals* when no one else did, and for that I owe her a debt that I can never fully repay. To Tim Holman, Jenni Hill, Lindsey Hall, and the whole staff at Orbit and Hachette, thank you for welcoming me, and Selene, into your world with such enthusiasm.

My family, both Brodsky and Mills, gave me the foundation of love and acceptance that makes creativity possible. My parents, Lewis and Cathy Brodsky, handed me *D'Aulaires' Book of Greek Myths* as a child, instilling a lifelong passion for mythology and storytelling, while my grandmother Tamara Rottino and her husband, Joe, provided the enthusiasm that galvanized me at the very beginning of this project. The entire Mills clan seemed to accept from the first that I would eventually get this book published; their matter-of-fact confidence made me believe it, too.

And finally to my husband, Jason Mills. My first, last, and twenty times in-between reader. The love of my life, the song in my heart. His own immense talent served as a goad, pushing me to prove myself. Every time I wanted to give up, he refused to let me. Without his tireless enthusiasm, unquestioning faith, insightful editorial comments, and knack for making a good cup of tea, I would have stopped writing after page two.

extras

about the author

Jordanna Max Brodsky hails from Virginia, where she spent four years at a science and technology high school pretending it was a theatre conservatory. She holds a degree in History and Literature from Harvard University. When she's not wandering the forests of Maine, she lives in Manhattan with her husband. She often sees goddesses in Central Park and wishes she were one.

Find out more about Jordanna Max Brodsky and other Orbit authors by registering for the free monthly newsletter at www.orbitbooks.net.

interview

What makes New York the perfect place for your immortals to live?

I grew up in Virginia, not far from George Washington's house at Mount Vernon, and spent a lot of time frolicking through the recreations at Colonial Williamsburg in a tri-corner hat. Then I went to school in Massachusetts, where reminders of Puritans and Patriots inhabit every corner. So when I moved to New York City just after college, my first thought was: *where's all the history?* Even though the Dutch settled Manhattan back in the 1620s, making it the oldest major city in the United States, it's grown and changed so much in the ensuing centuries that it often seems that there's no room for the past. But over time, I learned that if you look closely enough in places like Central Park, you can still find traces of the two things a goddess like Artemis craves: history and wilderness.

The park lies right in the heart of Manhattan's tumult, but inside the North Woods, the skyscrapers disappear from view. History springs to life: ruins from the war of 1812, a wall from a tavern built in the 1770s, even the remnants of the original spring that predates the park and fed the area's creeks. It's also one of the best bird-watching locations in the entire country. There are raccoons and hawks, waterfalls and cliffs. I loved the idea of a Goddess of the Wilderness who'd come to the island when it was all forests and swamps and has spent the last four hundred years watching that landscape disappear beneath streets and skyscrapers. Now she clings to the few patches of wilderness that remain, haunting the city's parks and reliving her own past.

Even though the city's inhabitants don't know it, Artemis has become New York's patron goddess, just as Athena was to Athens. She's lived in New York since it was New Amsterdam, and she's its staunchest defender. For all that the city's changed over the centuries, it's still a perfect match for her. New York is as paradoxical as she is: alive with energy and power, but dark, dangerous, and full of secrets.

Why the Greek pantheon? What about it appealed to you as a writer?

As a lover of both history and fantasy, I find Greek mythology irresistible. Most fantasy authors have to construct their worlds from scratch—mine comes ready-made, full of weapons, settings, costumes, ancient languages, poetry, legends, and religions. Yet it's also full of the historical details inherent in a real time and place. I didn't need to invent places like Delos or Crete—I could actually visit them. Yet, because we're talking about a civilization that flourished in the fifth century BC, scholars don't know everything about it; that uncertainty leaves plenty of room for an author's imagination to fill in the gaps.

As Theo explains in his lecture at the beginning of *The Immortals*, the myths exist in many different versions. There's not one "true" telling, which means I had room to find my own stories. And the heroes of the stories, the gods themselves, make great characters. They're superheroes, complete with special outfits and powers. But unlike the distant, amorphous gods of most modern religions, the Olympians are also profoundly human, capable of rage, despair, love, jealousy, and laughter. That's the paradox I wanted to explore.

Greek myths are full of interesting goddesses. Why Artemis?

Her impulsiveness, her temper, her bow and arrow, her implacable sense of justice—she's certainly the most exciting goddess. Unlike Hera or Aphrodite, she doesn't define herself in relation to men. Unlike Demeter, she's not constrained by her role as a mother. And let's face it, Artemis's ability to talk to animals and shoot things is a lot more fun than Athena's talents at weaving and pottery.

But Artemis's appeal also comes from her epithets: she's got close to three hundred of them, more than any other god. Each embodies a different, often contradictory aspect of her personality. As human beings, we each have at least that many names, even if we never articulate them. Like the gods, some of these titles are roles or personality traits we've chosen for ourselves—others have been thrust upon us by our friends and family. We can't help identifying with someone like Selene, who struggles to define her identity in terms of both her own sense of self and others' expectations of her.

When did you first know you wanted to write *The Immortals*— was it a specific image or scene that occurred to you?

I'd always wanted to write a book about Greek gods in the modern day, but it wasn't until I'd lived in New York for a while that Selene's character began to take shape. Whether you're walking in Central Park or sitting on the subway late at night, you're constantly surrounded by strangers. Visitors think people in my city are rude and mean, and that's simply not true. They're just closed off. Their aloofness is a survival strategy: a way to secure a little privacy among a throng of eight and half million people. I think it's human nature to start imagining what secrets might hide behind all those stern faces.

The very first scene I wrote was a prologue that I later cut from the book. I wrote it in the second person, speaking to the average New Yorker who might spot a silver-eyed woman on the subway and wonder about her story. Eventually, I make a direct address to a man who's attacked a woman in the park—he finds himself facing this six-foot-tall vigilante avenger who thinks she's a goddess. As a jaded New Yorker, that sort of confrontation doesn't actually sound so far-fetched.

What sort of research did you do for *The Immortals*? You studied history at Harvard, so that must have been a big help both in portraying Selene's past and Theo's world of academia, but what about the other elements in the book?

I had a basic background in mythology and had taken a few related courses at school, but I'd never heard of the Eleusinian Mysteries until I started work on the book. I was immediately struck by the rite's endurance. What sort of secret ritual lasts for two thousand years, much of that time in a highly literate society, and yet its rituals never get written down? I read everything I could, of course, but I also traveled to Greece and Italy to see many of the ancient sites and artifacts. I wanted to get a sense of what that world would've looked like, felt like, smelled like, when Artemis and Apollo lived there. I visited the sacred island of Delos and hiked to the top of Mount Kynthos; I trekked through the gorges of Crete; I walked through the Kerameikos Cemetery in Athens and down the Sacred Way. I learned a lot more than I could ever fit in one book—so I'm glad there's going to be a sequel!

Selene is particularly concerned about violence against women in this story. Would you describe this as a feminist novel?

Absolutely, although Selene herself isn't exactly a feminist in every sense of the word. Yes, she's strong, independent, fearless, and determined to assert a woman's right to live however she chooses. But those traits meant something different in Ancient Greece than they do today. In a patriarchal society, men couldn't conceive that a hunter and punisher could also be a mother or a wife. Artemis's only option is celibacy. Because of her background, Selene buys into this dichotomy—so in that way, she isn't really a feminist at all.

In the modern age, we no longer see femininity and ferocity as mutually exclusive. And we certainly don't think that sex necessarily equates to motherhood or marriage. When she meets Theo, Selene has to explore the necessity of her own virginity and isolation. She has to examine how much of her behavior is a choice and how much is simply an acceptance of the role that a male-dominated society has thrust upon her. Acknowledging that those questions exist is, to me, a quintessentially feminist endeavor.

Nearly every chapter heading in the book is another one of Artemis's wonderful collection of epithets. As a writer, what sort of classical epithets would you like to see applied to you?

Great question! My authorial epithets might include "She Who Brings Gods to the People" or the "Blender of Many Genres." But the honest answer, considering how much time I've spent sitting in front of a computer lately, might be the "Less-Than-Swiftly-Bounding One."

What's next for Selene and Theo?

I'm in the process of writing the second book in the Olympus Bound series right now. It takes place a few months later, at Christmas—Selene's least favorite time of the year. We start to get a sense of how the gods—these vestiges of ancient paganism—handle today's modern religions. At the same time, the realities of her relationship with Theo sink in, and Selene, as you can imagine, is *not* an easy woman to date. Even as they work together to combat a new enemy that threatens the future of all the immortals, Selene and Theo must to decide what sort of future they have together. Meanwhile, there are mysteries to solve, secrets to uncover, and plenty of new gods to meet.

**if you enjoyed
THE IMMORTALS**

look out for

WAKE OF
VULTURES

by

Lila Bowen

1

Nettie Lonesome had two things in the world that were worth
a sweet goddamn: her old boots and her one-eyed mule, Blue.
Neither item actually belonged to her. But then again, nothing did.
Not even the whisper-thin blanket she lay under, pretending to
be asleep and wishing the black mare would get out of the water
trough before things went south.

The last fourteen years of Nettie's life had passed in a shriveled
corner of Durango territory under the leaking roof of this wind-
chapped lean-to with Pap and Mam, not quite a slave and nowhere

close to something like a daughter. Their faces, white and wobbling as new butter under a smear of prairie dirt, held no kindness. The boots and the mule had belonged to Pap, right up until the day he'd exhausted their use, a sentiment he threatened to apply to her every time she was just a little too slow with the porridge.

"Nettie! Girl, you take care of that wild filly, or I'll put one in her goddamn skull!"

Pap got in a lather when he'd been drinking, which was pretty much always. At least this time his anger was aimed at a critter instead of Nettie. When the witch-hearted black filly had first shown up on the farm, Pap had laid claim and pronounced her a fine chunk of flesh and a sign of the Creator's good graces. If Nettie broke her and sold her for a decent price, she'd be closer to paying back Pap for taking her in as a baby when nobody else had wanted her but the hungry, circling vultures. The value Pap placed on feeding and housing a half-Injun, half-black orphan girl always seemed to go up instead of down, no matter that Nettie did most of the work around the homestead these days. Maybe that was why she'd not been taught her sums: Then she'd know her own damn worth, to the penny.

But the dainty black mare outside wouldn't be roped, much less saddled and gentled, and Nettie had failed to sell her to the cowpokes at the Double TK Ranch next door. Her idol, Monty, was a top hand and always had a kind word. But even he had put a boot on Pap's poorly kept fence, laughed through his mustache, and hollered that a horse that couldn't be caught couldn't be sold. No matter how many times Pap drove the filly away with poorly thrown bottles, stones, and bullets, the critter crept back under cover of night to ruin the water by dancing a jig in the trough, which meant another blistering trip to the creek with a leaky bucket for Nettie.

Splash, splash. Whinny.

Could a horse laugh? Nettie figured this one could.

Pap, however, was a humorless bastard who didn't get a joke that didn't involve bruises.

"Unless you wanna go live in the flats, eatin' bugs, you'd best get on, girl."

Nettie rolled off her worn-out straw tick, hoping there weren't any scorpions or centipedes on the dusty dirt floor. By the moon's scant light she shook out Pap's old boots and shoved her bare feet into into the cracked leather.

Splash, splash.

The shotgun cocked loud enough to be heard across the border, and Nettie dove into Mam's old wool cloak and ran toward the stockyard with her long, thick braids slapping against her back. Mam said nothing, just rocked in her chair by the window, a bottle cradled in her arm like a baby's corpse. Grabbing the rawhide whip from its nail by the warped door, Nettie hurried past Pap on the porch and stumbled across the yard, around two mostly roofless barns, and toward the wet black shape taunting her in the moonlight against a backdrop of stars.

"Get on, mare. Go!"

A monster in a flapping jacket with a waving whip would send any horse with sense wheeling in the opposite direction, but this horse had apparently been dancing in the creek on the day sense was handed out. The mare stood in the water trough and stared at Nettie like she was a damn strange bird, her dark eyes blinking with moonlight and her lips pulled back over long, white teeth.

Nettie slowed. She wasn't one to quirt a horse, but if the mare kept causing a ruckus, Pap would shoot her without a second or even a first thought—and he wasn't so deep in his bottle that he was sure to miss. Getting smacked with rawhide had to be better than getting shot in the head, so Nettie doubled up her shouting and prepared herself for the heartache that would accompany the smack of a whip on unmarred hide. She didn't even own the horse, much less the right to beat it. Nettie had grown up trying to be the opposite of Pap, and hurting something that didn't come with claws and a stinger went against her grain.

"Shoo, fool, or I'll have to whip you," she said, creeping closer. The horse didn't budge, and for the millionth time, Nettie swung the whip around the horse's neck like a rope, all gentle-like. But, as ever, the mare tossed her head at exactly the right moment, and the braided leather snickered against the wooden water trough instead.

"Godamighty, why won't you move on? Ain't nobody wants you, if you won't be rode or bred. Dumb mare."

At that, the horse reared up with a wild scream, spraying water as she pawed the air. Before Nettie could leap back to avoid the splatter, the mare had wheeled and galloped into the night. The starlight showed her streaking across the prairie with a speed Nettie herself would've enjoyed, especially if it meant she could turn her back on Pap's dirt-poor farm and no-good cattle company forever. Doubling over to stare at her scuffed boots while she caught her breath, Nettie felt her hope disappear with hoofbeats in the night.

A low and painfully unfamiliar laugh trembled out of the barn's shadow, and Nettie cocked the whip back so that it was ready to strike.

"Who's that? Jed?"

But it wasn't Jed, the mule-kicked, sometimes stable boy, and she already knew it.

"Looks like that black mare's giving you a spot of trouble, darlin'. If you were smart, you'd set fire to her tail."

A figure peeled away from the barn, jerky-thin and slithery in a too-short coat with buttons that glinted like extra stars. The man's hat was pulled low, his brown hair overshaggy and his lily-white hand on his gun in a manner both unfriendly and relaxed that Nettie found insulting.

"You best run off, mister. Pap don't like strangers on his land, especially when he's only a bottle in. If it's horses you want, we ain't got none worth selling. If you want work and you're dumb and blind, best come back in the morning when he's slept off the mezcal."

"I wouldn't work for that good-for-nothing piss-pot even if I needed work."

The stranger switched sides with his toothpick and looked Nettie up and down like a horse he was thinking about stealing. Her fist tightened on the whip handle, her fingers going cold. She wouldn't defend Pap or his land or his sorry excuses for cattle, but she'd defend the only thing other than Blue that mostly belonged to her. Men had been pawing at her for two years now, and nobody'd yet come close to reaching her soft parts, not even Pap.

"Then you'd best move on, mister."

The feller spit his toothpick out on the ground and took a step forward, all quiet-like because he wore no spurs. And that was Nettie's first clue that he wasn't what he seemed.

"Naw, I'll stay. Pretty little thing like you to keep me company."

That was Nettie's second clue. Nobody called her pretty unless they wanted something. She looked around the yard, but all she saw were sand, chaparral, bone-dry cow patties, and the remains of a fence that Pap hadn't seen fit to fix. Mam was surely asleep, and Pap had gone inside, or maybe around back to piss. It was just the stranger and her. And the whip.

"Bullshit," she spit.

"Put down that whip before you hurt yourself, girl."

"Don't reckon I will."

The stranger stroked his pistol and started to circle her. Nettie shook the whip out behind her as she spun in place to face him and hunched over in a crouch. He stopped circling when the barn yawned behind her, barely a shell of a thing but darker than sin in the corners. And then he took a step forward, his silver pistol out and flashing starlight. Against her will, she took a step back. Inch by inch he drove her into the barn with slow, easy steps. Her feet rattled in the big boots, her fingers numb around the whip she had forgotten how to use.

"What is it you think you're gonna do to me, mister?"

It came out breathless, god damn her tongue.

His mouth turned up like a cat in the sun. "Something nice. Something somebody probably done to you already. Your master or pappy, maybe."

She pushed air out through her nose like a bull. "Ain't got a pappy. Or a master."

"Then I guess nobody'll mind, will they?"

That was pretty much it for Nettie Lonesome. She spun on her heel and ran into the barn, right where he'd been pushing her to go. But she didn't flop down on the hay or toss down the mangy blanket that had dried into folds in the broke-down, three-wheeled rig. No, she snatched the sickle from the wall and spun to face him under the hole in the roof. Starlight fell down on her ink-black braids and glinted off the parts of the curved blade that weren't rusted up.

"I reckon I'd mind," she said.

Nettie wasn't a little thing, at least not height-wise, and she'd figured that seeing a pissed-off woman with a weapon in each hand would be enough to drive off the curious feller and send him back to the whores at the Leaping Lizard, where he apparently belonged. But the stranger just laughed and cracked his knuckles like he was glad for a fight and would take his pleasure with his fists instead of his twig.

"You wanna play first? Go on, girl. Have your fun. You think you're facin' down a coydog, but you found a timber wolf."

As he stepped into the barn, the stranger went into shadow for just a second, and that was when Nettie struck. Her whip whistled for his feet and managed to catch one ankle, yanking hard enough to pluck him off his feet and onto the back of his fancy jacket. A puff of dust went up as he thumped on the ground, but he just crossed his ankles and stared at her and laughed. Which pissed her off more. Dropping the whip handle, Nettie took the sickle in both hands and went for the stranger's legs, hoping that a good slash would keep him from chasing her but not get her sent to the hangman's noose. But her blade whistled over a patch of nothing. The man was gone, her whip with him.

Nettie stepped into the doorway to watch him run away, her heart thumping underneath the tight muslin binding she always wore over her chest. She squinted into the long, flat night, one hand on the hinge of what used to be a barn door, back before the church was willing to pay cash money for Pap's old lumber. But the stranger wasn't hightailing it across the prairie. Which meant . . .

"Looking for someone, darlin'?"

She spun, sickle in hand, and sliced into something that felt like a ham with the round part of the blade. Hot blood spattered over her, burning like lye.

"Goddammit, girl! What'd you do that for?"

She ripped the sickle out with a sick splash, but the man wasn't standing in the barn, much less falling to the floor. He was hanging upside-down from a cross-beam, cradling his arm. It made no goddamn sense, and Nettie couldn't stand a thing that made no sense, so she struck again while he was poking around his wound.

This time, she caught him in the neck. This time, he fell.

The stranger landed in the dirt and popped right back up into a crouch. The slice in his neck looked like the first carving in an undercooked roast, but the blood was slurry and smelled like rotten meat. And the stranger was sneering at her.

"Girl, you just made the biggest mistake of your short, useless life."

Then he sprang at her.

There was no way he should've been able to jump at her like that with those wounds, and she brought her hands straight up without thinking. Luckily, her fist still held the sickle, and the stranger took it right in the face, the point of the blade jerking into his eyeball with a moist squish. Nettie turned away and lost most of last night's meager dinner in a noisy splatter against the wall of the barn. When she spun back around, she was surprised to find that the fool hadn't fallen or died or done anything helpful to her cause. Without a word, he calmly pulled the blade out of his eye and wiped a dribble of black glop off his cheek.

His smile was a cold, dark thing that sent Nettie's feet toward Pap and the crooked house and anything but the stranger who wouldn't die, wouldn't scream, and wouldn't leave her alone. She'd never felt safe a day in her life, but now she recognized the chill hand of death, reaching for her. Her feet trembled in the too-big boots as she stumbled backward across the bumpy yard, tripping on stones and bits of trash. Turning her back on the demon man seemed intolerably stupid. She just had to get past the round pen, and then she'd be halfway to the house. Pap wouldn't be worth much by now, but he had a gun by his side. Maybe the stranger would give up if he saw a man instead of just a half-breed girl nobody cared about.

Nettie turned to run and tripped on a fallen chunk of fence, going down hard on hands and skinned knees. When she looked up, she saw butternut-brown pants stippled with blood and no-spur boots tapping.

"Pap!" she shouted. "Pap, help!"

She was gulping in a big breath to holler again when the stranger's boot caught her right under the ribs and knocked it all back out. The force of the kick flipped her over onto her back, and she scrabbled away from the stranger and toward the ramshackle round pen of old, gray branches and junk roped together, just barely enough fence to trick a colt into staying put. They'd slaughtered a pig in here, once, and now Nettie knew how he felt.

As soon as her back fetched up against the pen, the stranger crouched in front of her, one eye closed and weeping black and the other brim-full with evil over the bloody slice in his neck. He looked like a dead man, a corpse groom, and Nettie was pretty sure she was in the hell Mam kept threatening her with.

"Ain't nobody coming. Ain't nobody cares about a girl like you. Ain't nobody gonna need to, not after what you done to me."

The stranger leaned down and made like he was going to kiss her with his mouth wide open, and Nettie did the only thing that came to mind. She grabbed up a stout twig from the wall of the pen and stabbed him in the chest as hard as she damn could.

She expected the stick to break against his shirt like the time she'd seen a buggy bash apart against the general store during a twister. But the twig sunk right in like a hot knife in butter. The stranger shuddered and fell on her, his mouth working as gloppy red-black liquid bubbled out. She didn't trust blood anymore, not after the first splat had burned her, and she wasn't much for being found under a corpse, so Nettie shoved him off hard and shot to her feet, blowing air as hard as a galloping horse.

The stranger was rolling around on the ground, plucking at his chest. Thick clouds blotted out the meager starlight, and she had nothing like the view she'd have tomorrow under the white-hot, unrelenting sun. But even a girl who'd never killed a man before knew when something was wrong. She kicked him over with the toe of her boot, tit for tat, and he was light as a tumbleweed when he landed on his back.

The twig jutted up out of a black splotch in his shirt, and the slice in his neck had curled over like gone meat. His bad eye was a swamp of black, but then, everything was black at midnight. His mouth was open, the lips drawing back over too-white teeth, several of which looked like they'd come out of a panther. He wasn't breathing, and Pap wasn't coming, and Nettie's finger reached out as if it had a mind of its own and flicked one big, shiny, curved tooth.

The goddamn thing fell back into the dead man's gaping throat. Nettie jumped away, skitty as the black filly, and her boot toe brushed the dead man's shoulder, and his entire body collapsed in on itself like a puffball, thousands of sparkly motes piling up in the place he'd occupied and spilling out through his empty clothes. Utterly bewildered, she knelt and brushed the pile with trembling fingers. It was sand. Nothing but sand. A soft wind came up just then and blew some of the stranger away, revealing one of those big, curved teeth where his head had been. It didn't make a goddamn lick of sense, but it could've gone far worse.

Still wary, she stood and shook out his clothes, noting that everything was in better than fine condition, except for his white shirt, which had a twig-sized hole in the breast, surrounded by a smear of black. She knew enough of laundering and sewing to make it nice enough, and the black blood on his pants looked, to her eye, manly and tough. Even the stranger's boots were of better quality than any that had ever set foot on Pap's land, snakeskin with fancy chasing. With her own, too-big boots, she smeared the sand back into the hard, dry ground as if the stranger had never existed. All that was left was the four big panther teeth, and she put those in her pocket and tried to forget about them.

After checking the yard for anything livelier than a scorpion, she rolled up the clothes around the boots and hid them in the old rig in the barn. Knowing Pap would pester her if she left signs of a scuffle, she wiped the black glop off the sickle and hung it up, along with the whip, out of Pap's drunken reach. She didn't need any more whip scars on her back than she already had.

Out by the round pen, the sand that had once been a devil of a stranger had all blown away. There was no sign of what had almost happened, just a few more deadwood twigs pulled from the lopsided fence. On good days, Nettie spent a fair bit of time doing the dangerous work of breaking colts or doctoring cattle in here for Pap, then picking up the twigs that got knocked off and roping them back in with whatever twine she could scavenge from the town. Wood wasn't cheap, and there wasn't much of it. But Nettie's hands were twitchy still, and so she picked up the black-splattered stick and wove it back into the fence, wishing she lived in a world where her life was worth more than a mule, more than boots, more than a stranger's cold smile in the barn. She'd had her first victory, but no one would ever believe her, and if they did, she wouldn't be cheered. She'd be hanged.

That stranger—he had been all kinds of wrong. And the way that he'd wanted to touch her—that felt wrong, too. Nettie couldn't recall being touched in kindness, not in all her years with Pap and Mam. Maybe that was why she understood horses. Mustangs were wild things captured by thoughtless men, roped and branded and beaten until their heads hung low, until it took spurs and whips to move them in rage and fear. But Nettie could feel the wildness inside their hearts, beating under skin that quivered under the flat of her palm. She didn't break a horse, she gentled it. And until someone touched her with that same kindness, she would continue to shy away, to bare her teeth and lower her head.

Someone, surely, had been kind to her once, long ago. She could feel it in her bones. But Pap said she'd been tossed out like trash, left on the prairie to die. Which she almost had, tonight. Again.

Pap and Mam were asleep on the porch, snoring loud as thunder. When Nettie crept past them and into the house, she had four shiny teeth in one fist, a wad of cash from the stranger's pocket, and more questions than there were stars.

2

Nettie barely slept a wink that night. Every time her eyes blinked shut, she imagined the stranger pulling himself together, the sand shifting back into the shape of something like a man and slithering into the house past Pap sleeping on the porch. One eye dripping black, he'd rise up like a rattler, snatch his teeth from inside her boot, poke them back into his gums, and rip her throat out.

After the third time she jolted up with a fright, alone in the dark with a stick-knife in her fist, she figured to hell with it and just got on up. Despite the drenching Durango heat, she'd taken to dressing like a bandito's grandmother with one of Pap's old, faded shirts over her bound chest, baggy pants held up by a rope, and a moth-gnawed serape over that. The less the folks of Gloomy Bluebird could see she was a girl, the less trouble they gave her.

Mam and Pap had taken to sending her on all their errands into town, considering they owed so many debts. Nettie'd learned that if she kept her head down and sucked in her cheeks, folks usually took pity and gave her the tail end of a sack of cornmeal or their most pitiful, nonlaying chicken. At first, she'd been embarrassed. But then she'd overheard two of the old biddy church ladies whispering about how shameful it was for Pap to send his half-breed slave pup around to beg, and she realized that they counted her for less than a dog and Pap only slightly more than that.

Mam and Pap Lonesome were of old East stock, pale as salt fish and just as odorous, with matching hay-colored hair and blue eyes that seemed ever confused thanks to eyelashes and eyebrows as light as dandelion fuzz. The pair were shapeless and old enough to look like someone else's aunt. Nettie couldn't have been more different, with medium brown skin that could've been called liver chestnut, if she'd been a horse worth noticing. Her hair was thick and frizzy, a dead giveaway to anyone trying to puzzle out her breed. Half black and half Injun, or maybe Aztecan; any way you added it up, the end result was somehow less than the individual components. She was built tall and narrow like a half-starved antelope, with eyes as dark and thick as a storm-mad creek and high cheekbones framing a mouth that had little reason to smile. She was ugly, was all they'd told her. But she didn't find them beautiful, so what did it matter? The entire town was an eyesore.

It was widely agreed that Gloomy Bluebird was a stupid name for a town, especially considering Old Ollie Hampstead had shot the only bluebird they had back in 1822, right outside what passed as a general store. The damn thing had been stuffed and posed with little skill and now sat proudly on the storekeeper's counter as a reminder of what looking cheerful and bright would get you in a town as dusty as an old maid's britches. Nettie herself had seen a bluebird when she was just a little thing, hunting lizards out by the creek. When she'd run home to tell Mam, she'd been told to go fetch a switch for lying. Over time, she'd come to believe she must've seen a crow. But crows didn't have red bellies, did they? At least the town lived up to the gloomy part.

The excitement of last night had burned off, and Nettie was feeling downright gloomy herself, like some part of her had blown away with the impossible, sparkling sand. A strange thing had happened, and she had no one to tell, no one she trusted enough to question. Being alone wasn't so bad when nothing ever changed, but now Nettie didn't trust herself, and she was generally the only person she could trust.

Although Pap handled most of her punishment, Mam had once

thrashed her for lying about a bluebird, and then thrashed her again when she'd started her monthlies and ruined an old striped mattress and screamed that she was dying. How was she supposed to know that was what women did? Nettie didn't reckon much about the world, but she knew that what happened last night had changed things as much as her flux blood. The world was suddenly more dangerous, but she had no idea why or how to protect herself from it. Seemed like the best way to keep her skin was to get on with breakfast and not say a danged thing, to hide it like she hid everything else.

When she went to shake her boots for scorpions, it was four pointed teeth that fell out. Considering no crevice of the shack was safe from Mam's quick fingers, Nettie shoved them into the little leather bag she kept tied around her waist with what few precious things she'd found over the years. A glittery white arrowhead, hardly chipped. A shiny gold button with a bugle on it. A wolf claw, or something like it. A penny given to her once in the town when she'd been kicked in the leg by a frachetty horse. She'd kept a piece of dirt-dusted ribbon candy some town brat had dropped in the pouch for two weeks once, allowing herself one suck a day. The four teeth added a weight barely felt, but she stood a mite taller. Whatever that stranger had been, she'd won. And that felt pretty goddamn good.

Mam and Pap weren't up, of course. They gave the sun time to stretch and get cozy before they stopped snoring. It was almost peaceful, setting up the porridge in the pot and watching the skillet shimmer with fatback grease. She always loved snatching warm eggs from under the scrawny, sleepy hens; this brood was the result of Pap's once-a-year victory at the poker table. They'd definitely seen harder times, although Nettie didn't much get to enjoy the bounty herself. If Mam and Pap left any eggs on their plates, that was usually treat enough.

The sun came up so fast that if you weren't watching careful, you'd miss it. For just a second, it was a flat circle, hot-red and bleeding all over the soft, purple clouds. Nettie stared at it as long as she could, not blinking, then leaned over to turn the eggs, and when she looked again, the sun sat high and white, relentlessly beating down on the endless prairie. Sunset, at least, took its time, nice and lazy. She liked the colors of it, and the way that no one could own the sun. It couldn't be compelled, couldn't be roped. You could yell at it all day long, threaten and plead and cuss, and the sun would not budge a goddamn inch. It was what it was, and it took its damn time about it.

But Nettie had fewer choices, so she quickly bolted down her small share of the porridge. Not only because Mam and Pap would give her an earful if they woke up with her in the house, but also because she wanted to mosey over to the Double TK before the surlier of the cowboys were awake and taking out their hangovers on whoever happened by. The ranch next door was far richer than Pap's, considering they had more than a one-eyed mule, two nags for renting, a herd of cattle too thin for the butcher to carve, and one milk cow that barely squirted enough milk for weak porridge. Mam had sent her toddling over to the Double TK for the first time to have a knife sharpened when she was just five years old, and Monty had taken her on like a lost pup. The old cowpoke had told her, years later, that they'd figured her for a boy at first, as she'd been in britches and had a shorn head. But since she'd been mannerly and offered to help the wranglers by sweeping out the pen or tossing rocks at vultures, they'd generally tolerated her presence.

Over the years, she'd learned by watching Monty and had figured out better ways to work a colt than using Pap's whip. She was awful shy of the other cowpokes and never went near the ranch house or Boss Kimble, but Monty said he was right glad for her calm hand with the horses and general quietude. He was still thin and tough as leather, with a luxurious mustache, but she'd noticed that in the last couple of years, Monty had saved the wilder horses for her visits and chosen gentler mounts for himself, and that his mustache had gone to gray.

On her way to the Double TK, she stopped to feed the few critters Pap hadn't used up yet. Blue greeted her with his usual hollering, and she gave him a once-over and a fine scratch and fed him a precious handful of grain, plus a bite she'd held back from the porridge. He pressed his big, ugly mule nose over her shoulder, and she leaned into his skinny chest and breathed in his good horse smell. He didn't know he wasn't a horse, and he didn't know he was ugly. Pap's swayback mare, Fussy, took the grain and turned her tail, just as sour as her owner, and the aged nag they called Dusty refused to get up off the ground. The wild black mare was still gone and the water trough still clean, thank heavens. Nettie had already fed the cow and scattered the morning's corn for the chickens, but the poor things crowded around her with hopeful clucking. It was a sad joke, calling it a ranch.

Before heading off, Nettie snuck into the other barn to see if the stranger's clothes were still there. They were, rolled up tight on the old rig's seat beside his hat, which was rugged and new and featured cunning strings to keep it on a feller's head. For a reason she couldn't explain, she tried it on and found it a good fit. With the wide brim pulled down and her pigtails tucked up underneath, maybe people would notice her even less. If asked, she could just say she'd found the hat floating in the creek. By the time she'd walked past the fence and Pap's ranch was just a shimmer on the horizon, the hat felt like it was part of her body and always had been.

Slipping under the fence to the Double TK, Nettie felt instantly calmer, almost at peace. It was business as usual on Boss Kimble's land, just a passel of grown men doing men's work, and she liked the feeling of being part of the simple but effective machinery.

She headed toward the colt pens, where Monty and Poke sat on the rail as Jar clung to a bronc's back, and poorly at that. Monty shouted easy encouragement while old Poke leaned out and hollered through cupped, stubby hands about how Jar rode like a one-legged frog. Which he did, a little, as the young cowpoke was fine on his feet but all knees and elbows in the saddle. As Nettie got closer, she admired the bronc crow-hopping around the round pen—a big, bone-white stallion. No way a proud, uptight feller like Jar could break a mustang like that, especially not with his saddle cinched so tight. She couldn't help smirking.

"I got a penny says he falls off within a minute," she called, feeling lucky and reckless in her fine new hat.

Monty and Poke turned with good-natured smiles. Poke pulled out his dented watch while Monty fetched up a penny out of his disreputable pants, which looked as though they'd been made out of the curtains in a whore's bedroom, all velvet with gold curlicues.

"I'll take that bet, Nat," Monty hollered.

He never called her Nettie or treated her like a girl, even though he knew well enough what she was. When she'd started her monthlies, Mam had tried to set her up in skirts, but she'd ripped the hated things into strips and used them to bind her growing chest instead. Mam had given up and wished her quietly to Hell, so long as she kept cooking and cleaning and breaking colts. Monty had called her Little Lady once around that time, and she'd whipped out her jackknife, all fierce and cold, and told him that she was no girl, and he'd nodded, all thoughtful, and started calling her Nat instead. It was one of the many reasons she all but worshipped him.

Just now, he was looking at her with his head cocked and a friendly grin. "Nice hat. Who'd you kill for it?"

Goose bumps rose on her arms, and she pulled the hat down

lower. "Nobody you know. Found it in the creek." Hitching up her too-big britches, Nettie climbed to sit by Monty on the top rail of the round pen. She'd always admired the clean, white boards of the Double TK's fencing. Of course, you couldn't stab a stranger in the heart with one of their fence boards, but they sure looked nice.

"How long's he been working that white stallion?"

Monty rubbed the curled end of his gray mustache between two fingers. "Not long. Big fellow came in with the raid last night. Boss wants him broke right fast. Might keep him for himself, if he has a gentle gait. Otherwise, he'll be the nicest fancy in the territory."

Jar flew off said horse in a graceful arc and landed, spread-eagled, in the dust. He rolled to the side right as the big bronc's dish-sized hooves hammered the dirt where the boy's so-called handsome face had been just seconds ago. Before the bronc could stomp again, Jar had skittered back to the edge of the round pen and rolled under the boards to safety. Monty held up a shiny penny and winked at Nettie.

"You beat his time, Nat, and I'll double your winnings. Hell, I'll give you a nickel."

Nettie admired the big bronc trotting around the pen, always keeping a sharp, intelligent eye on the four folks watching him back. Jar climbed up next to Poke and mopped off his face with a hanky that had seen better days.

"Big white bastard. Boss deserves him," Jar said.

Nettie slipped off the fence, wriggled out of her serape, and stood to face the bronc, watching him watch her. Poor feller's saddle was too narrow for his withers, his girth was too tight, and his bridle pulled at his lips, giving him a meaner look than she liked.

"Gimme a rope, Poke."

Poke threw his lasso to her, and she caught it in midair. The bronc stomped a foot, but before he could decide what sort of gangly, dangerous critter she might be, she'd looped him around the neck with a gentle toss. He reared back, first off, but she held tight and gentle, like Monty had taught her. When he stepped back, she went with him. *You can't force a horse, but you can't let him force you, neither*, the old cowpoke always said. As she approached the stallion, calm and murmuring sweet words, she looped the slack from the rope and watched for him to lick a little. The wranglers on the fence whispered, and she heard the clank of coins as they placed their bets.

When she'd got up to the bronc's side, she reached to stroke his neck. His white skin shivered, and dust came away on her fingertips.

"Ho, big feller. We're gonna be friends."

The horse's ears flickered back and his eye stuck to her as she undid the cinch and knocked the saddle off his back, leaving a sweaty stain. The bronc bowed his head and danced in place as he shook and blew air. Nettie smiled and touched him all over. When she got to his face, she went straight for the throat-latch and then slipped the whole bridle off his ears. Once the reins were over his head, the horse stretched out his neck like he'd grown two sizes.

"Thought we taught you how to break a bronc, Nat. Nobody gets paid for settin' 'em free," Jar hollered, but Monty only snickered.

"Somebody else taught me you've got to loosen a creature up to get what you want," she whispered so only the bronc could hear.

A rope halter hung on the other side of the round pen, and she walked the bronc over there with Poke's lasso loose around his neck. He followed, not like he really wanted to, but like he was willing to see what her next idea might be. With fingers gentle as last night's rare breeze, she slipped the halter over the bronc's nose and ears and tossed down Poke's lariat. The horse let her pull his face close, and she blew into his twitching pink nostrils.

Murmuring all along, she walked him a bit, turned him, got him to cross over his back hooves so she had control of his haunches. That was where all the power was—in the rump.

And when the horse had mostly got used to doing what she wanted, she slipped off her boots, grabbed a handful of mane and rein, kicked up off the fence boards, and launched herself onto the white bronc's broad, sweaty back.

Nettie had rarely been so high up, but she only had a second to enjoy the view, as the surprised bronc crow-hopped sideways. Still, it was nothing like the bucking he'd put Jar through, so she just tightened her knees and held on while he tried to puzzle out what was clinging to his back. The cowpokes took up hollering, trying to excite the horse into dumping her, but she clung tight and let the bronc wiggle out his worries. She knew the exact moment the fight drained out of him—when he realized she wasn't trying to fight him at all. She was just trying to go with him. His front hooves hit the ground, and he shook his head and craned his neck around to stare at her.

Patting his thick neck, Nettie murmured, "Good boy."

The horse blew air, and the wranglers on the fence clapped and hollered. She gave the stallion a squeeze and urged him into a walk. He'd be a fine horse with a little care, and not the kind a puffed-up feller like Jar was likely to give him. The bronc still looked like he wanted to take a chunk out of Jar's side as they passed the cowpokes seated on the fence. Poke's wide pumpkin face had cracked into a jack-o'-lantern grin, and Monty held up a nickel, a rare sight for Nettie Lonesome.

"Get him under saddle today, and I'll give you a quarter more."

Nettie just nodded and nudged the bronc into a trot. She'd never imagined such riches as a nickel, much less a whole quarter.

Until she remembered the roll of money she'd taken out of the stranger's sand-dusted pocket last night. The dollars were wound